D1797345

A Red Sister

A Story of Three Days and Three Months

Catherine Louisa Pirkis

MINT EDITIONS

A Red Sister: A Story of Three Days and Three Months was first published in 1891.

This edition published by Mint Editions 2021.

ISBN 978-1-5131-3289-1

Published by Mint Editions®

 MINT
EDITIONS

minteditionbooks.com

Publishing Director: Jennifer Newens
Design & Production: Rachel Lopez Metzger
Project Manager: Micaela Clark
Typesetting: Westchester Publishing Services

To My Friends,

Sir Myles and Lady Fenton,

of ridge green,

I Dedicate this Book,

with sincere regard, and in the hope that the fortunes of
"A Red Sister" may serve to while away a leisure hour.

C. L. Pirkis.

Nutfield, 1891.

Contents

Volume III

VOLUME I

I

"Here we must part, my friends," said the priest, resting his hand on the stile which divided the high road from a footway running across fields. "This must be the 'short cut' of which the inn-keeper spoke. It will be easy enough for me, with only this light bag to carry, to make the rest of my journey on foot."

The speaker was a tall, dark man, between fifty and sixty years of age, with aquiline features, and clear, penetrating grey eyes; the persons whom he addressed were a man and a young girl. The former was standing beside a dog-cart, with his hands still grasping reins and whip; his healthy, bronzed face, and his appearance generally, seemed to denote that he belonged to the small-farmer class. The girl, who was standing beside the priest on the footway, bore a rather more refined appearance. She was small and slight in figure, her face looked worn and anxious, its pallor being thrown into greater relief by the deep crape she wore; her large, grey eyes had a forlorn, far-away look in them; her hair was of a beautiful, though colourless fairness.

"I wish we could be of more service to you, Father Elliot," said the young man; "we owe you a heavy debt of gratitude—"

He broke off abruptly, giving a furtive glance towards the girl.

"Thanks, my good friend," said the Father, cheerily; "I was delighted to be able to break my long journey at your house. I hope times will soon be better for you. There's something egregiously wrong in the state of a country when a farm, worked as yours has been, can't pay its own expenses and yield a comfortable income to two plain-living people like you and your sister."

Then he turned to the girl:

"Where was it you applied for a situation as maid? I don't think you mentioned the name of the people or the house."

"The lady is Lady Joan Gaskell, wife of Mr. John Gaskell, the millionaire coal owner, of Longridge Castle," said the girl.

Here a sudden change of expression swept over the Father's face; his lips parted, as if he were about to speak, but no words escaped them.

"Longridge Castle is just behind that clump of trees," she went on; "but the trees hide it so that you can't see it till you are close up to it."

The Father had by this time recovered himself.

"Ah, well," he said, "if you succeed in obtaining the situation, I shall see you on Sundays at mass, for St. Elizabeth's Church is only a mile and a half distant from the Castle."

He turned as he finished speaking and crossed the stile, then, resting his arms on its topmost rail, bent forward, and for a moment keenly scrutinised the pale, sorrowful face which fronted him.

The young man led his horse and cart forward a little. He knew that the priest's last words were to be spoken now, and they were not words to be thrown on the empty air.

The Father smiled kindly at him.

"Don't lose heart, Ralph," he said. "Be diligent—remember, you can put conscience even into driving a plough—put your best work into everything you do, and, sooner or later, a blessing must follow."

Then he turned to the girl.

"And you, my child, whether your lot be cast in Longridge Castle or elsewhere, be zealous in the performance of your religious duties. Thank heaven that nothing more is required of you than loving trust and childlike obedience, and make no effort to discover that which, providentially no doubt, has been hidden from you."

His last sentence was said with a slow emphasis. The girl sharply turned her face away from him as if she shrank from the scrutiny of his keen though kindly eyes. Her fingers twisting nervously one in the other showed that she was greatly agitated.

"Once more, good-bye, my children both," said the priest, "Dominus vobiscum!"

He stretched his hands towards them as he pronounced his blessing; then turned, and began rapidly to make his way along the footway through the fields.

The brother and sister had bowed their heads reverently.

"Come, Lucy," said the man, turning his horse's head and preparing to set off once more along the dusty high road.

Lucy did not reply. She stood motionless in the blazing sunshine, shading her eyes with her hands, and watching the retreating figure of the priest.

"Come, Lucy," called her brother again, and this time a little impatiently, "we shan't be back any too soon if we set off at once. I've a hundred and one things to see after when I get home."

A bend in the footpath he was following hid the priest from her view, and Lucy, letting her veil fall over her face, rejoined her brother.

Father Elliot steadily pursued his road. The surrounding country was not particularly picturesque. It was flat, as if a gigantic steam-roller had passed over it, and but scantily wooded. The only point of interest in the landscape was the clump of distant elms, behind which Lucy had said stood Longridge Castle.

As the Father drew near to the clump of not very ancient trees, he could catch glimpses of the frontage of the newly-built, many-towered edifice.

"It is fatality," he thought. "Here am I, exiled from London and the work I was doing there, and thrown, as it were, into the arms of these Gaskells once more. My superiors tell me, forsooth, they are sending me out of the way of temptation. 'Through pride,' the Cardinal wrote, 'the angels fell. Your pride in your powers of oratory and the large and intellectual congregations which you draw, is leading you to preach doctrines other than those which have been taught by the Church in all ages. Go now and minister to the poor and ignorant colliers and cottagers, and, by plain teaching—not the preaching of doctrines which spring from the exercise of a subtle intellect—win souls to the Church.' Yes, those were his words. I know them by heart. The exercise of a subtle intellect! Is it that, I wonder, or the exercise of clear vision and common sense which leads a man, after staring for years at the problems of life, to cry out from his pulpit, 'My children, purgatory is present, not to come; this world is not our first start in existence—here we are sent for our sins—'"

Here the Father suddenly paused, passing his hand over his brow. Thoughts such as these required curb and rein.

"Ah, well," those thoughts presently resumed, "submission to my superiors is one of the first of my duties, and I submit. They little know how valueless to me is the praise or blame of the multitude. All things are to me shadows and hollow mockeries of what might have been!" Here his eye for a moment rested on the façade of the Castle as it gleamed white in the afternoon sun, between the shadowy trees. "Thirty years," he went on, bitterly, "and I have not been able to kill the memory of that 'might have been!' Thirty years of battling with the ghosts of that past, and then I am sent as it were to banquet with them—to entertain, and be entertained by them! Joan, Joan, I wonder if your memory is clear and strong as mine is today! I wonder if, when we meet, you will shake hands calmly as with an utter stranger, or if you will start up and cry aloud, as you did on the day I cursed you for breaking faith with me, 'Go away, Vaughan, go away, and never let me in this life look upon your face again'?"

These were the priest's thoughts as he made his way across the fields towards the cottage which represented the Clergy-house of St. Elizabeth's Church. At this point, however, his visions of the past seemed suddenly to goad his footsteps into a speed prohibitive of thought.

A countryman at that moment swinging back the gate of an adjoining field, in order to drive home his cows for milking, stood, open-mouthed, gazing at the tall, dark gentleman approaching at such a rapid pace.

"Be 'ee goan to th' merry-makin'?" he asked in broad Yorkshire dialect, in response to the Father's passing nod and greeting.

"I'm making for St. Elizabeth's Church or rather Father Bradley's house; I dare say you know it," said the Father, resuming his usual calm, frankly-courteous manner, which always seemed to open hearts towards him. "What merry-making is taking place today? Where is it?"

"Wa'ay down yonder," answered the man, jerking his head towards the Castle which had conjured up such a tumult of memories in the Father's mind. "Th' old master's turned ninety today, and there isn't a soul far or near but what's to be the better for his living so nigh upon a hundred; so Muster John—that's his son—says."

"What!" cried the priest; "Is old Mr. Gaskell still alive!"

He paused a moment. "Joan, Joan," his thoughts ran during that pause, "you've had to wait long enough for the good things for which you sold yourself!" Then aloud to the man he said:

"How far do you make it from here to the Castle?"

"A short half-mile as the crow flies. But the merry-makin' is i' the fields you'll come upon just after you've passed the heath; that's about a quarter-mile from here."

And then the man went on to say that the whole country for miles round had turned out to do honour to the nonagenarian's birthday; that the village was deserted; that, after dark, bonfires were to be lighted, and fireworks let off; that there was to be a supper for the collier lads, and a dance for them afterwards; in a word, the birthday celebrations were to outrival those which had taken place seven years ago, when the young master had come of age.

All this Father Elliot listened to attentively, saying never a word until "the young master" was mentioned. Then he put a question as to who this young master was.

CATHERINE LOUISA PIRKIS

"He's Muster Herrick, the son of Muster John, and Lady Joan," the man explained. "Muster John married nigh upon thirty year ago the Lady Joan Herrick—she came of grand people down South, somewhere. She was poor enough she was, and she's nae sich a kindly body as—"

"Good day, my friend," here interrupted the Father, brusquely. "Your cows are straying—see. I'm right for St. Elizabeth's, you said?"

The man went after his cows; the Father went on his way, his brain filled now with so many phantoms of the past that the country through which he passed was a blank to him.

He seemed to see himself once more in the pretty Devonshire village, where his father had been rector as long as he could remember. He could see, also, as vividly as if days, not decades of years, had since passed; his constant playmate and companion by his side, the Lady Joan Herrick, only daughter of the Earl of Southmoor. Now, they were scampering over breezy moors together on their rough-coated little ponies; anon, they would be bending over their books side by side in his father's study; or, he would be angling in the Southmoor trout stream, while she, on the bank, sat listening to his ambitious hopes and projects to win name and fame for himself in the Church by his learning and oratory. He could picture himself, also, a little later on, a young fellow of twenty, starting on his college career, and Lady Joan, a handsome girl of fifteen, bidding him Godspeed. The scene changed, and he seemed to see himself, four years after, returning from college and about to enter the ministry, standing hand-in-hand with Joan, praying her to wait for him till he could make a home and position in life which he might fitly ask her to share, and hearing in reply her vehement promises of unswerving constancy.

Last scene of all, he could picture himself, some three months after this, alone, face to face with Joan, hearing from her own lips the story of her betrothal to John Gaskell, the only son of the millionaire coal-owner. He could hear her calm, passionless voice trying to prove to him how much better it would be for him to begin his career unfettered by a wife, and how unsuited she was for being the wife of a poor man. He could hear, too, his own vehement denunciations of her falseness and worldly wisdom; and then her one bitter cry—startled out of her, as it were, by his angry words—"Go away, Vaughan, go away, and never in this life let me look upon your face again."

Well, they never had looked upon each other's face again. She had left her Devonshire home to take her place among her husband's wealthy, if parvenu, relatives; and he, after drifting aimlessly about the world for years, had joined the Roman Church, and had qualified for the priesthood. And then life, like a great ocean, had rolled in between the two.

Here a sudden break in the path which the Father was following compelled him to give a truce to his memories, and consider which road it behoved him to take.

The country through which he had passed had gradually been growing flatter and less verdant, proclaiming in its general aspect the propinquity of the coal country. He was standing now on the edge of a wide heath—not the wildly-beautiful expanse of purple heather and golden gorse which is frequently associated with the name, but a bleak, stony, treeless waste, with here a stunted juniper bush, there a straggling bramble. On the left it was bounded by a low, scrubby hedge, on the right it stretched away endlessly to where, against a night-sky, the sullen, red flare of furnaces and forge-fires would show. A second thought told him that his way lay in a direct line across the very middle of this waste.

Straight ahead of him Longridge Castle showed plainly enough now, and distinct sounds of cheering and shouting proclaimed that he was nearing the fields where the birthday festivities were taking place.

Half-way across the heath, Father Elliot paused to note a deep pit, possibly a shaft which had been sunk in search of coal, and which was protected only by the slightest and most inadequate of hand-rails. The grass growing up its sides, the tangle of nettles and weeds which covered the mounds of earth thrown up beside it, showed that many a spring had passed since it had been dug. Prompted by a boyish instinct, the Father took up a stone and threw it into the pit. The seconds which elapsed before it sounded the bottom told of the formidable depth of the hole.

"It would be an ugly business to cross this heath on a dark night," thought the Father, as he once more went on his way.

This led him now along a narrow road with high hedges on either side. After five o'clock in the afternoon, towards the end of August, the sun's rays begin to slant, and shadows to lengthen. This road looked cool and shady by comparison with the treeless heath. Through the breaks of the hedge on one side he could catch a glimpse of bright-coloured flags and white tents in a not very distant field. The sounds of a military band greeted his ear, together with a hum and buzz of voices as of many people assembled.

"In the midst of that crowd," he thought, will stand Joan with her young son, her elderly husband, her ancient father-in-law. I wonder if

I suddenly presented myself among them all, would she turn pale and shrink from me as from a ghost at her banquet, or would she come forward and greet me in that stately way of hers I used to know so well? I can't fancy Joan without her stateliness. I could as soon fancy her without her voice! That will ring in my ears when I lie on my death-bed—soft, deep, musical, and slow in speech, the voice of a woman who should have had a heart. Yet Heaven, in place of a heart, planted a stone in her bosom!"

Sounds of footsteps on the other side of the hedge, almost at his elbow, at that moment arrested his attention. Through the intervening greenery, bushy here, scanty there, he could catch a glimpse of the small slight figure of a young girl approaching with rapid steps. She was evidently making for a gate which, about twenty yards further on, led from the field into the road.

The Father reached this gate just at the moment that the girl was passing through it.

Her face attracted him strangely. It was of a type he knew well enough. Scores of times he had seen it, painted by different hands; now as that of baby cherubs on the panels of triptychs; anon as that of ascending and descending angels on some gigantic altar-piece. It was round, child-like, with a tiny cupid's bow for a mouth, and such brilliant gold on the hair, such forget-me-not blue in the eyes, and such rosy tints on cheeks and lips it seemed as if the sun must be shining full upon it, in spite of the protecting shade of a big sun-hat. It seemed a face formed for happiness, innocence, and a perpetual round of childish pleasures and lo! there were traces of tears on either cheek.

The Father was touched. He accosted the young girl.

"I beg your pardon," he said, "I am a stranger here; will you kindly tell me if I am in the right road for St. Elizabeth's Church? I am the newly-appointed priest. I take Father Bradley's place there."

The girl's manner matched her face, it was frank yet shy, as a child's can be at one and the same moment. The sound of tears in her voice jarred upon the Father like a false note in a sweet, gay melody.

"I am going towards St. Elizabeth's now," she answered. "I will show you the way with pleasure."

II

S ounds of hearty and prolonged cheering fell upon Father Elliot's ear, as, under the guidance of his young companion, he made his way along the road towards St. Elizabeth's.

"It's the health-drinking," the girl explained. "They do it heartily. They think there never was such a master as old Mr. Gaskell, although, I suppose, no one there can remember him at his best."

"There never was such a master!" Those words, or their equivalent in broad Yorkshire, went the rounds among the collier lads, as, with throats hoarse from their shouting, they put down their empty tankards.

This health-drinking was the event of the day, and it was drunk, one fashion or another, at the same moment, by every member of the Gaskell family, and every man, woman, and child on the Gaskell estate. Immediately after the ceremony had been gone through, old Mr. Gaskell was to withdraw from the festivities, farther excitement being deemed injurious to him at his advanced age.

In the field where this health-drinking took place, Gaskells of three generations—father, son, and grandson—stood side by side. There, immediately in front of a bright-coloured silk pavilion, which had been specially erected for him in the midst of the meadow, stood the old man, supported on one side by his son John—a fine, soldierly man of fifty-five—on the other, by his grandson, Herrick. A frail, shrunken figure—with pallid, wrinkled face, and scant, silver hair—he showed between these two stalwart men.

Herrick owned to as many inches in height as his father, although to considerably less in width; an agile, muscular young fellow he was, with straight, clean-cut features, an abundance of dark-brown hair and full-pupilled grey eyes. There was no need to proclaim his relationship to the tall, stately lady who stood a little distance apart, on his left hand. The most careless observer would have said, "Mother and son, not a doubt," when once they had seen the two faces in profile.

In voice, in manner, in graceful walk, and easy carriage of the head and shoulders, the likeness between the two was not less remarkable.

"I can't picture Joan without her stateliness," Father Elliot had said to himself, when trying to draw a fancy-portrait of his old love as time had left her after thirty years of wear and tear. He did not stand alone; all who had ever known her could as lief have pictured a star without its light as Lady Joan without that "grand manner" of hers which kept alike friends and foes at a ceremonious distance, and which, if she had been dressed in homespun, and had been compelled to feed off wooden platters, would still have proclaimed her every inch the aristocrat.

In Herrick this stateliness had been somewhat modified by education and circumstances, but still it was there. Though he worked as hard as his father in the management of the colliery, and of the estate generally, there was not a collier lad or farm labourer on the land who would have approached him in the easy, off-handed manner in which they approached his father, sturdy democrats though they were to their very marrow.

With physique and manner, however, the likeness to his mother came to an end. A veritable Southmoor he might be in appearance, but in heart he was a Gaskell. His interests and hopes in life were identical with those of his father and grandfather; and he cared as little as they for the accidents of birth and rank.

Now as Lady Joan watched his face kindling into sympathy with the bright, ruddy faces around him, and heard his clear voice joining in what seemed to her coarse and vulgar cheering, she said to herself bitterly:

"He has some of the best blood of England in his veins, and he is at one with such a crowd as that."

The cheering had scarcely died away, and the hum and buzz of broad north-country dialect re-commenced, when Herrick, turning to Lady Joan, hurriedly asked:

"Mother, where is Lois? Is she tired? Has she gone indoors to rest?"

Lady Joan's brows contracted into a frown.

"Lois!" she repeated, coldly.

"Yes. Lois White, the young lady I introduced to you and left in your charge while I acted as umpire in the next field."

"I beg your pardon. The introduction was so hurried I did not catch the young lady's name. She left some little time ago. She said she must get back to her pupils. She is nursery governess somewhere in the neighbourhood is she not?"

The young man did not notice her concluding sentences.

"Left," he repeated, blankly. "You let her go without telling me! I drove her here; of course I intended driving her back to Summerhill. I don't understand it," and he walked hurriedly away in the direction of the stables as he finished speaking, leaving his mother to conjecture that he meant there and then either to drive or ride after the young lady in question.

Before, however, he could carry out his intention, a note, brought over by one of the smart young pages at Summerhill, was put into his hand.

It ran as follows:

"I have gone home with a bad headache. Come and see me tomorrow morning."

"L. W."

III

L ady Joan stood watching the retreating figure of her son, the frown on her brow deepening. Her husband's voice, loud, ringing, cheery, suddenly interrupted the train of her angry thoughts. He was returning thanks for old Mr. Gaskell.

"My father wishes me to thank you, my friends," he said, "for the hearty manner in which you have drunk his health. He bids me say that such a day as this is worth living ninety years to see, and to the last hour of his life it will live in his memory. One with you in heart he has ever been, and one with you in heart he hopes to be to the end; he can never forget that where the Castle now stands there once stood a little farm-house in which he was born and reared. Finally, he bids me say: 'God bless every one of you, and give you, one and all, lives as happy and prosperous as his has been.'"

Prolonged and hearty cheering followed the close of the speech. As it died away John Gaskell whispered a word to his father; an order was then given, and a bijou pony chaise was brought round. A little, grey, apple-faced man came forward fussily. He was old Dr. Scott, the village practitioner, to whom the Gaskells paid a good yearly income for his daily attendance on the nonagenarian. He on one side, John Gaskell on the other, assisted the old gentleman into the pony carriage which stood waiting to take him back to the house.

Lady Joan's lip curled slightly.

"It would have been far less trouble to have taken him up in their arms and have lifted him in," she said to herself. "To think that the opinions and whims of a man in this stage of incapacity should be law in a household, and that men like John and Herrick should bend to it! It is simply incomprehensible!"

A message brought to her by a servant a minute later accentuated the bitterness of the thought.

"Mr. Gaskell wishes to know, my lady," said the man, "if you have given directions for the presentation picture to be at once hung in the drawing-room, so that the subscribers may have the pleasure of seeing it on the walls before they leave."

This "presentation picture" was a large painting of the identical farm-house to which John Gaskell had just alluded, and which had stood on the site of the present castle before the lucky finding of coal on the land had brought gold to the family coffers, and had turned a pretty pastoral district into a grimy, manufacturing one.

The painting had been made, on a considerably enlarged scale, from a small water-colour sketch of the old house, taken before it was pulled down, and had been presented as a birthday offering to old Mr. Gaskell by the colliery workmen.

The look on Lady Joan's face as the servant delivered his message might have been understood to say:

"I heartily wish the picture were behind the fire."

She did not, however, give expression to the thought. To "kick against pricks," to her way of thinking, was objectionable, less for the pain it might bring than for the loss of dignity it involved. So she replied merely:

"If it is to be placed there, no doubt your master has already given the necessary orders." And mentally she added: "Henceforth the drawing-room will become unpleasant to me by reason of the plebeian reminiscences that picture will perpetuate."

It was not that Lady Joan could, by any chance, ever have been guilty of the essentially plebeian offence of endeavouring to disguise the mushroom-like origin of the Gaskell family. On the contrary, she was in the daily habit of laying stress upon it in her correspondence with her own well-born relatives. All she asked was, that in her own home, in the rooms in which she was compelled to pass her daily life, the fact should not be perpetually flourished before her eyes as a thing wherein to glory.

That very evening there was to be a dinner-party at the Castle. Certain guests would be there whom naught but the patrician presence of Lady Joan could have tempted within the newly-built walls. The enormous painting, hung in a conspicuous position, would set flowing a stream of talk as to the luck and money-making qualifications of the Gaskell family, a stream whose tide she knew well enough neither Herrick nor her husband would make the slightest effort to turn.

This dinner had already been a sufficient cause of annoyance to her, in that it had been fixed at a ridiculously early hour, in order that old Mr. Gaskell, who dared not attempt to sit down to table, might see and shake hands with certain of the guests before he retired to his room for the night. It was hard to have its annoyances doubled and trebled in this fashion.

Annoyances such as these were of almost daily occurrence in the Castle, and Lady Joan knew that so long as old Mr. Gaskell had breath in his body there was no likelihood of their coming to an end.

In heart, she bitterly rebelled against the supremacy to which John and Herrick so willingly bent their necks.

"If I had known," she would sometimes say to herself, "that for close upon thirty years I should be condemned to play a strictly subordinate part in the Gaskell household, that my opinions on important matters would be persistently ignored, and that this old man would live on to keep alive in the country the recollection of the newness of the gold which built the Castle and supplied its luxuries, I might have thought twice before I married John Gaskell."

But, though thoughts such as these ran as a steady under-current to the surface of her life, her manner towards the old man expressed nothing but a stately, calm indifference.

That stately calm of manner, however, had gone nearer to a collapse on the day of the birthday festivities than it ever had before. Perhaps Herrick's eccentric conduct, in forcing upon her notice a young lady whose existence she had hitherto steadily ignored, might have been held responsible for the fact.

Lady Joan's maid, as she assisted her mistress to undress that night, thought she had never before seen her look so like the harassed, hampered mistress of a large household, fretted by many cares and responsibilities, so unlike the stately lady who kept all trivial and uninteresting matters—and people—at a ceremonious distance.

The girl thought she might never get a better opportunity for preferring a request she had just then very much at heart, and seized it accordingly.

She had, however, to repeat her request once and again, before its full import reached Lady Joan's preoccupied mind.

"Oh, you would like me to see the young person who wishes to come as maid!" at length said "my lady," indifferently. "It seems to me you are in a great hurry to leave."

The girl blushed, and began hesitatingly to explain:

"I told you, my lady, that Robert wanted to get married at once, now that he has been promised one of the new cottages, and—"

Lady Joan cut short the plebeian details.

"Is this young person who wishes to come, I forget her name, likely to suit me? You know my requirements."

"Oh yes, my lady. Lucy Harwood is her name. She is highly recommended, and she is neat, and pale, and thin, and quiet-looking, and doesn't speak broad Yorkshire; she comes from Devonshire."

The girl had hurried through her speech, anxious to get to her final words, which she knew would considerably enhance the possible attractions of the new maid in Lady Joan's eyes.

"From Devonshire!" Lady Joan repeated. "What part of Devonshire?"

"Her father, my lady, at one time lived within a few miles of Southmoor. He is dead now; and her brother, who has a farm near Wrexford, can't make it pay, so she is obliged to go out and get her own living. Will you see her, my lady?"

"Harwood," repeated Lady Joan, slowly, "and her father lived within a few miles of Southmoor. I can't recall the name. Yes, I will see her tomorrow morning directly after breakfast."

And then she dismissed the whole matter from her thoughts; for, to her way of thinking, a maid was not a creature like herself, who could love or hate, rejoice or be sad, but just a detail of daily life, needful, but uninteresting, like the clocks which wanted winding up, or the fires which needed replenishing.

IV

On the morning after the birthday festivities Lady Joan sat at her writing-table in her boudoir with a very sore heart.

For one thing, her husband, instead of riding over to Wrexford, the centre of the colliery district, according to his wont immediately after breakfast, had remained closeted with his father for nearly two hours. That two hours' talk with the old man Lady Joan knew from experience meant mischief; in other words the concoction and development of some scheme of an essentially plebeian nature.

For another, Herrick had not presented himself at the breakfast-table; and instead, had left a message with the butler that he had gone over to Summerhill to breakfast. That meant that he had no intention of paying the slightest regard to his mother's wishes in his choice of a wife.

Hitherto, Herrick had shown himself singularly unsusceptible to feminine attractions, and, on this slender foundation, Lady Joan had built a castle sky-high. Her brother, the present Earl of Southmoor, had but one child—a daughter—who shortly would leave her school, at Brussels, and make her début in society. To this young lady, in default of heirs male, Southmoor, with its dilapidated mansion and acres run to waste, would descend. Now, what in life could be more suitable than that Herrick should marry this cousin of his, and, with the wealth that must eventually come to him, restore and beautify the old place, and settle down there among his mother's people?

And this cherished plan of hers, which had been growing and gathering strength as the years went by and Herrick remained fancy free, was to be all in a moment swept away by a girl who had come—Heaven only knew whence—to officiate in the family of a wealthy iron-master in the neighbourhood as nursery governess!

The room in which Lady Joan was seated was perhaps the only one in the Castle that showed no touch of the Gaskell hand in its furnishing and arrangement. It was redolent of another atmosphere. She had selected it on account of a view it commanded, beyond the newly-planted trees in the park, of a little glade—a tangle of bracken and bramble backed by a copse of hazel and wild plum—which vividly recalled to her the wild Devon scenery surrounding Southmoor. She had crowded into the room abundant reminiscences of her old home.

Over the carved oak mantelpiece hung the portrait of her dear old grandfather, the tenth Earl of Southmoor. Side by side, on the opposite wall, hung the likenesses of Lady Joan's father and mother, both of whom had died in her early childhood. Around the room hung other family portraits, copied from those in the great gallery at South-moor, by Lady Joan's own hand.

It would, however, have been rash to conclude from these evidences of her skill that Lady Joan was a devotee of any one branch of art. That davenport pushed close to the grand piano, held the score of an unfinished opera. The writing-table at which she sat contained the beginnings, or endings, or middles of at least a dozen essays on subjects which, from time to time, had engaged her attention. The bookcases in various corners of the room, proclaimed what those subjects were. They covered a wide range: political economy, social science, modern religious thought, were all abundantly represented in those well-filled shelves.

A casual observer entering the room and glancing round, might have expatiated upon the high intellectual gifts and varied artistic tastes of its occupier. A deeper thinker, possibly, would have surveyed it from another point of view, and found in it evidences of a mind restless and ill-at-ease; of a life which had, somehow, missed its mark.

It was further characteristic of Lady Joan that, although the writing-table at which she sat contained, in an inner drawer, many prized relics of the dear Devon days—so many, in fact, that they seemed to make an atmosphere all their own in the room, and she never sat down to that table without being conscious in a subtle sort of way of what it held— yet among them all was there not a single memento of Vaughan Elliot and his early lovemaking.

"You must make your choice, Joan, and make it finally, with no whining after-regrets," her grandfather, the old Earl, had said to her when John Gaskell had made his offer of marriage. "If you want to marry Elliot, marry him and be a country parson's wife. You know what that means—there are many typical examples in the neighbourhood. If you marry John Gaskell, you will have all the luxuries in life you desire, and, when the old man is dead, your influence with your husband no doubt will be paramount. You can make him shake off his plebeian associations, and live where and how you please. There is no third choice for you. I am too poor to give you a season in town, and as you know, when I die, everything here must go to your brother."

So Lady Joan had made her choice, and had been as resolute as her grandfather had wished her to be in excluding all "whining after-regrets" from the scheme of her life.

After that passionate final interview with Vaughan Elliot, in which he had seen fit to conduct himself for all the world like a man with a heart in his body, she had said to herself: "This man must go utterly out of my life now—as utterly as I, no doubt, shall go out of his." For thirty years she had held to her resolve, and though John Gaskell, no doubt, might have had abundant reason to complain of his wife's coldness and want of sympathy, never for an instant had she given him cause for jealous distrust.

Yet, although Vaughan Elliot and his passionate love had ceased even in memory to be more to her than last year's blighted crop of summer roses, Fate, throwing her shuttle hither and thither, had cast the threads of his life athwart the warp of hers. Here, to her very doors, the man had come, silently as any Nemesis "shod in wool"; and by-and-by, so Fate had decreed, he was to knock and ask for admission.

V

L ady Joan found her correspondence that morning uphill work. While her pen "presented compliments" to Lady This or Mrs. That, and accepted or refused this or that invitation to dinner or "at home," her thoughts rang painful changes on Herrick and his ill-advised love-making. It was something of a relief when her maid came, with many humble apologies, to ask if "my lady" would be pleased to see Lucy Harwood, the would-be new maid, who waited below.

The engagement of her maid was always a matter of first importance with Lady Joan, and one that she delegated to no one else. Her standard, as regarded the maid's acquirements, was a high one, and involved not only thorough knowledge of her duties, but exceptional refinement of manner and appearance.

When Lucy Harwood was shown into the room, Lady Joan's eye, as it lifted, saw that her standard in these latter respects was reached. Before, however, she had talked with the girl five minutes, other things, beside her pleasing appearance and gentle voice had impressed her—the hurried, nervous manner, the deep sadness of tone, and the wandering, far-away look in the eyes of the young woman.

The nervousness of manner Lady Joan thought natural enough. No doubt it was an ordeal for a girl in her station to be suddenly shown into the presence of a great lady; the sadness also, she thought, might be accounted for by the black dress the girl wore; but that far-away, wandering look in the eye, puzzled her. Only once before in her life did she remember to have seen such a look, and that was in the eyes of a girl charged before her husband, in his official capacity as a local magistrate with attempting suicide. She closely questioned Lucy as to her bringing up and present surroundings.

The girl's replies were simple and straightforward enough. Her father, she said, had lived as butler at a rectory within a few miles of Southmoor—Elliot was the name of the Rector.

Lady Joan slightly smiled.

"I knew him quite well," she said, easily, as if the name conjured up no bitter reminiscences. "And your mother is dead?" she added, glancing at the girl's deep black.

The girl's lip quivered; she did not reply.

Lady Joan, desirous to avoid a display of emotion, resumed her questioning at another point.

"You were born and educated at Southmoor, I suppose?" she asked.

"I was born at Southmoor, my lady," answered Lucy, "but was sent away when I was very young to live with an aunt in London, and only occasionally went home. When I was about fifteen, my father broke up his home in Southmoor and took a farm, the one my brother has now near Wrexford. When my aunt died I came home to Wrexford; then my father died—"

"Yes, I know," interrupted Lady Joan, for the story had but a scanty interest for her when it drifted into the details of the girl's private affairs.

Then she concluded arrangements. Lucy might come for a week on trial, be initiated into her duties by the present maid, and if she gave entire satisfaction, Lady Joan would engage her permanently. If she liked, now that she was at the Castle, she might remain, and one of the grooms would drive over to the farm and fetch what she might require for a week's stay.

This offer Lucy gratefully accepted. As she left the room John Gaskell's firm, brisk footsteps were heard in approach.

"I'm late," he said, as he came in. "Joan, did you wonder what had become of me? I fear I can't get back from Wrexford now much before dinner."

As a rule, John or Herrick, or sometimes both, were in the habit of rising from the breakfast-table and setting off straight for Wrexford, where every matter, small or great, which concerned the working of the colliery received their individual attention. Millionaires they might be—these Gaskells of three generations—but that, to their way of thinking, was no reason why they should neglect the mill which ground out the gold, so long as their names continued to be connected with it.

Lady Joan looked up from the writing-table, where she was rearranging her correspondence.

"Not till dinner!" she repeated, a little absently, meanwhile trying to get her thoughts together, and decide whether she should at once consult her husband respecting Herrick's foolish love-making, or whether she should defer so doing till his return in the evening, when business matters would be off his mind, and he would be able to give her a more undivided attention.

"I'm afraid not," her husband continued. "My father and I had so many things to talk about, that I hardly knew where to break off. By the way, Joan, he's not looking at all as I should like him to look. I'm afraid yesterday was a little too much for him."

He paused, waiting for a reply from his wife.

Although John Gaskell and his wife were both past middle life, they still made a handsome couple. Tall as she was, he stood at least half a head taller; and though his features might lack the aristocratic curves and lines which hers owned—notably those of the upper lip and nostril—there was yet in his face a frankness of expression, a straightforward look from his blue eyes right at the person he chanced to address, which abundantly compensated for the deficiency.

His manner of addressing his wife was perhaps a trifle more ceremonious than is that of most men after a married life of close upon thirty years. John Gaskell, however, before he had been wedded a year, had discovered upon what footing he and his wife must live, if "peace were to dwell within their walls," and, like the sensible north-countryman that he was, had looked the fact in the face, and had shaped his course accordingly.

"I think it was a little too much for every one," said Lady Joan, coldly, for the keeping of this ninetieth birthday with such effusion had seemed to her a ridiculous business throughout.

"Well, it was too much for him, at any rate," interrupted John, knowing that he and his wife looked at this matter from different points of view, "and I shall be glad if you'll go in once or twice while I'm away and see how he is getting on. Where's Herrick? I've not seen him this morning."

"Ah, I wanted to speak to you about Herrick," said Lady Joan, feeling how impossible it was to neglect this opportunity for mentioning the subject which had caused her such disquietude.

But her husband interrupted her again, feeling that a lengthy discussion threatened now.

"When I come back, Joan, will do for that. After dinner I will tell you exactly what I think about Herrick and his love-making. Just at this moment I've a good many things in my head—small matters, perhaps— matters of detail, most of them, but till they're got rid of, my mind is not free to attend to other things. Now, good-bye till dinner-time." He turned towards the door as he finished speaking, then paused a moment, with his hand on the handle. "Oh, by the way, Joan, I may as well give you a hint as to the matter my father and I were discussing this morning; we've rather a big scheme on hand just now. My father has always insisted that the coal-seam dips under there"—here he pointed to the little glade crowned by the hazel copse—"and he wants to buy up that slice of land, and a little bit that skirts the heath, and sink a shaft. It'll bring the colliery business rather close to our doors; but, of course, the inconvenience to us will be slight compared with the money it will bring into the district; it'll be the making of Longridge."

Lady Joan drew a long breath. So, then, the little hazel copse, which recalled the wild Devon scenery, was to be uprooted, a coal-shaft sunk, and the whole nasty, grimy colliery business was to be brought to their very doors! And this at the suggestion of the feeble old man who couldn't walk across the room without help! Was the greed of these Gaskells for money-making never to be satisfied?

She drew her lips tightly together, but never a word escaped them.

John Gaskell's mind, however, was so full of other things that he did not see the look which clouded her face. His eyes were fixed, like hers, on the glade and hazel copse, and in fancy he saw the wood cleared away, the shaft sunk, truck lines laid down; in a word, the whole country around for miles astir and at work.

He noted her silence, however, and said to himself:

"As usual, she sees things from another point of view, and is too honest—or too proud—to affect a sympathy she does not feel."

Aloud he said:

"Good-bye again, Joan. Don't forget to look after my father and attend to all his wishes while I'm away."

This was how John Gaskell left his home on that bright August morning. Stalwart, cheery, his heart full of kindly thought for his wife and aged father; his brain teeming with visions of the increased prosperity which would flow into the district so soon as his "big scheme" began to work.

VI

"At last I get you to myself," said Herrick, drawing a long breath. "Now tell me, Lois, what on earth made you run away, as you did yesterday, without saying a word to me?"

Lois, hanging her head like a naughty child expecting a good scolding, answered confusedly:

"I was frightened, and so I ran away—I didn't think about what I was doing—I ran away just because I was frightened."

It was no wonder that Herrick should say "At last!" Although he had arrived at Summerhill before breakfast, in that most irregular household, had come to an end, yet it was not until after luncheon that he could get five minutes' quiet talk with Lois.

Lois White not only officiated as nursery-governess to Mrs. Leyton's seven small children, but acted generally as that lazy little woman's factotum and representative on every possible occasion. This was no sinecure in a household where, though wealth abounded, order was at a discount. Summer-hill was now full of guests, and Lois was everywhere in request. Herrick, naturally enough, chafed under a condition of things he intended to bring to an end as speedily as possible; but, for the time being, he was obliged to submit to seeing Lois at the beck and call of every one except himself.

Mrs. Leyton, so far as it was in her to look with favour on anything disconnected with herself and her own immediate pleasures, was disposed to view with a friendly eye Herrick's love-making to her pretty governess. She had bitterly resented Lady Joan's slight in not calling at Summerhill when Josiah Leyton, buying an old house that chanced to be in the market and lavishing his gold upon it, had made a bid for county society. To put no bar to Herrick's intercourse with Lois seemed to her an easy way of paying off this debt. "For if," as she confided to her maid, with whom she was on very familiar terms, "anything should come of it, that proud woman will be taken down a peg."

Herrick's passion for Lois had been of remarkably rapid growth. The first time he had seen her in church, his eye, wandering from his mother's statuesque and inscrutable features, had been struck by the girl's mobile and childlike beauty.

He had made vigorous efforts to induce Lady Joan to show some sort of civility to the new arrivals; but, failing lamentably, had taken matters into his own hands, and had got himself invited to certain social gatherings, at which he knew they would be present. Being a young man of strong will and very decided opinions, he, naturally enough, preferred the society of women in whom these characteristics were kept well in abeyance. Also, naturally enough, since he stood something over six feet in height, and in face was dark and pallid, he had a strong predilection for the society of the petite and the blonde. Lois White fulfilled all his requirements in these respects, and his love-making to the little governess had been ardent and persistent accordingly. Neighbours, after a time, had begun to talk; and their talk had even reached Lady Joan's ears. She, however, had at first thought it wiser to disregard these rumours, and had not even deemed it necessary to mention them to her husband, saying to herself, that this must be a flirtation—nothing more—on Herrick's part, and that, if no stress were laid upon it, it must die a natural death.

Later on, however, her opinion had had to be modified, for Herrick, in her presence, had made one or two remarks which could not be altogether ignored; such as: "I think it is nearly time I settled down as a married man;" or, "Father, you were younger than I am, when you married, weren't you?"

Lady Joan's fears, however, had not risen to danger point until the morning of the birthday festivities, when Herrick, as he rose from the breakfast-table, had said:

"Mother, this afternoon, I am going to introduce to you a young lady with whom I hope you'll fall in love on the spot. I sha'n't say any more till you've seen her."

Lois had, with difficulty, been induced to allow Herrick to drive her over to the Castle. "I want them to see your beautiful face, my darling, and to hear your sweet voice; and then, one and all, they'll say, 'Herrick, you're a lucky fellow, get married at once,'" he had to say over and over again, before she had yielded.

On arriving at the Castle, he had taken her straight to the pavilion, beneath which sat old Mr. Gaskell, and had introduced her to him as his "darling little wife that was to be." Whereupon, the old man had taken both Lois's hands in his, and had bidden "God bless her," in his kindliest tone. Then Herrick had intended introducing her to his mother; but, before he could find Lady Joan, he had come upon his father in the thickest of the crowd, endeavouring to adjudicate upon the rival claims of two competitors in a "consolation race."

"Here, Herrick, come and help as umpire," he had cried, catching sight of his son. "You're wanted here, there, everywhere."

Upon this, Herrick had gone through a hurried introduction of Lois to his father, from whom, amid so many distractions, little more than a nod and a smile could be expected. Then, promising to return speedily, he had, very much against her will, taken Lois into the adjoining meadow, where Lady Joan was distributing sundry gifts to the old people, and, introducing her with special emphasis, had left her in his mother's charge, while he returned to the village athletes. Lady Joan had at once developed so arctic a manner that poor little Lois could almost have fancied herself in latitude eighty degrees north, in spite of the blazing sun which poured down on them.

"I was frightened, and I ran away," was all the account she could give to Herrick of what followed, as side by side they strolled under the big branching oaks and beeches with which the park at Summerhill abounded.

The explanation was not to Herrick's mind entirely satisfactory. For a minute there fell a silence between the two. Then he said:

"Lois, will you tell me, word for word, what my mother said that scared you so?"

"Said! Oh, she said nothing at all!" answered Lois, readily enough.

"Nothing! And yet you were scared!"

"Oh, yes; her silence was so dreadful, I felt it—felt in a moment that she didn't like me. Oh, and now I think of it, she did say something. I made a remark about it being so fortunate that the day was fine for the sports, and she said: 'I beg your pardon!'"

Herrick's grave look gave place to one of amusement.

"And that scared you!" he cried. Then he added, not knowing what a prophetic undertone rang in his light words: "Is that the way in which you mean to get through life, Lois, fleeing like a little bird to covert at the first alarm? It is lucky for you you'll have me to look after you, or I don't know what would happen."

How like a child in disgrace she looked as she walked on beside him in silence, her head drooping so low that her big sun-hat hid her face from him! She was dressed in a simple white frock tied with broad sash ribbons. In her hand, the one that Herrick left free—she carried a child's spade and a large bunch of wild flowers. These she had been laden with as she came out of the house by little four-year-old Daisy Leyton, with the injunction that "Loydie"—as she most disrespectfully styled her governess—would remember to make the Adonis garden under the big beech-tree as she had promised to do more than a week ago.

Right into the heart of a "regal red poppy" there fell a big, round tear.

Herrick's arm was round her in a moment, and her big sun-hat, pressed against his shoulder, suffered in shape accordingly.

"My darling, what is it?" he cried. "What have I said—what have I done? Tell me."

When Lois found her voice, her words came all in a rush:

"Oh, Herrick! I see it all now—I did not understand it at first when—when—you spoke to me. But yesterday, as I stood beside your mother, I seemed to feel what she thought, and to see things with her eyes—and that was why I wanted you to come today—that I might tell you—"

But she was not allowed to finish her sentence, for Herrick's lips kissed her to silence, and the sun-hat suffered in shape again.

"I beg your pardon, Lois," he said, presently, as she straightened her hat, "but I knew you were going to talk nonsense, and took measures accordingly. My poor child! You are trembling from head to foot. Come and sit down under this beech, and if you don't mind we'll just quietly talk this matter out together."

Under the spreading shade of this beech there were one or two wicker seats. Lois declined the one which Herrick placed for her, and kneeling down on the turf, began to make Daisy's Adonis garden. It was an easy way of keeping her face turned from Herrick, for she was still bent on saying the words he had so summarily cut short, and it seemed to her easier to say them with her face thus hidden from him.

He flung himself on the ground beside her, handing her the flowers as she planted them.

A pretty scene it made—these lovers planting their Adonis garden—in the wide expanse of russet-green sward, broken only by the black blots of shadows cast by the oaks and beeches. The stillness around them was that of early autumn, when Nature—always a strict economist of her wondrous forces—bids bird-notes to cease, while she flings her glorious reds and yellows athwart creation.

"In spring I called upon you to open your ears," she seems to say; "now I say open your eyes, stand still, and admire!"

Herrick broke the stillness.

"You said just now, Lois," he began, gently, as he handed her a purple foxglove, "that, when you stood beside my mother, all in a moment you seemed to see things with her eyes, and to feel as she felt. Will you mind, now that you are beside me, seeing things with my eyes, and feeling as I feel? I assure you it will be much more satisfactory to me if you will."

Lois's face turned brightly towards him; she was half-smiling now, though her eyes still glistened with tears.

"Your mother is older than you—" she began.

"Naturally," interrupted Herrick.

"And, of course, knows better than you do what is likely to make your happiness," she said. But she said it in a wavering tone, as if she were quite willing to be convinced to the contrary.

"Pardon me, I can't admit that. My mother has no more conception of what would constitute my happiness, than she has of what would make the happiness of any one of the collier lads over at Wrexford. However, if you are going in for the wisdom which age brings with it, I'll tell you what my father said yesterday when I wished him good-night. 'Herrick,' he said, 'I like the look of that little girl you brought over today. You must let us see more of her.'"

"Did he say that?" broke in Lois, impetuously.

"Ay. And he's five or six years older than my mother; so of course, in your eyes, he knows better than she. And there's the dear old grandfather, he's forty years older than my mother—think of that—and he said: 'Thank Heaven I've seen your wife before I go, Herrick. Now I know your happiness is secure—,'" he broke off, exclaiming: "What, darling, tears again! Why, you're watering your flowers!"

In very truth the girl's tears were falling like a summer rain among the already drooping blossoms.

But still, like a child who won't forego repeating some speech which it has mastered with difficulty, Lois set herself to say the words which Herrick was so loth to hear.

"What I wanted to tell you, Herrick, was that—if—if, on thinking things over, you thought that—that you'd been hasty in—in asking me to marry you—"

Again she was not allowed to finish her sentence. She was planting a thick border of heather round her minature garden. Herrick laid both his hands on hers, stopped her work, interrupted her speech.

"My darling," he said, and his voice now quivered a little, "I know exactly what you are wishing to say, and I beg of you beforehand not to say it. Remember, I'm not a feather-headed boy who tumbles into

CATHERINE LOUISA PIRKIS

love one day and out of it the next. I knew perfectly well what I was doing when I asked you to marry me, and I say to you now what I said to you then, that if only you love me, not father, not mother, nothing in all creation, nothing in this world, or in any other, shall ever come between us."

For a moment after he finished speaking the great stillness around them once more made itself felt. Then suddenly, sharply, breaking in upon it, came the sound of a tolling bell.

It seemed to come inopportunely. They started and looked at each other.

"Oh, I know," cried Lois, presently, "it's St. Elizabeth's bell. I met the new priest yesterday, and he told me he was going to start afternoon and other services, and I should hear the bell going at all sorts of hours. I had a long talk with him. I fancy you would like him, he seems such a nice man."

"Does he?" answered Herrick, indifferently, not knowing what a factor in his life's history that priest was to be.

Although there was but little of the poet in Herrick's composition, assuredly he rode forth that afternoon through Summerhill Park gates into a very ideal world.

> No common object but his eye
> At once involved with alien glow
> His own soul's iris-bow.

In other words, Lois's simple, unselfish love for him, which her hesitating attempts at self-sacrifice had revealed, had awakened so deep a joy in his heart that for the moment the commonplace stretch of country he traversed was transformed into paradise. Surely never before did afternoon sun spread abroad so golden a glamour; never before had the rough Yorkshire air seemed so laden with the sweetness of the hedgerows! The very echoes which his horse's leisurely hoofs woke in the dusty road appeared to have a music all their own in them, and to rise and fall to Lois's tender, halting phrases.

The echoes of another horse's hoofs clattering along the road at a tremendous pace was only too soon to take the music out of these.

Herrick speedily recognised the approaching rider as his own groom. As the man drew nearer he saw that he held a telegram in his hand.

"For you, sir," said the man, drawing rein. "My lady has opened it and told me take it to Summerhill."

Herrick ran his eye over the messsage. It was from his father at Wrexford, and ran thus:

"Serious explosion of fire-damp. Come over at once."

Herrick turned his horse's head at once towards the Wrexford Road.

"Tell Lady Joan I'm off at once," he said. A second thought followed, a kindly one for the old grandfather, and he added: "Say also that I think it would be better not to mention this explosion in my grandfather's hearing; it would distress him terribly."

Old Mr. Gaskell, however, had unfortunately heard the sad news even before Herrick. The telegram containing it had, in Herrick's absence, been taken to Lady Joan as she sat in the old gentleman's room, and her exclamation of surprise, as she had read it, had apprised him of the fact.

CATHERINE LOUISA PIRKIS

Lady Joan, as soon as her husband had set off to Wrexford, had said to herself that, since it was expected of her, she had better at once pay her visit to her father-in-law's rooms and get it over as quickly as possible. It had been her habit all through her married life thus to do "what was expected of her," knowing well enough that if she once let herself break into rebellion, even in trifles, against the iron rule of these Gaskells, there was no knowing where that rebellion would end.

One thing, however, seemed to conspire with another to prevent the proposed visit to the old gentleman's quarters, and possibly the night might have found it unpaid if she had not received a somewhat urgent message from Parsons—old Mr. Gaskell's attendant—saying that he wished to see her at once. Parsons was a privileged person in the house, and had permission at any hour of the day or night to communicate with any member of the family on matters connected with the old gentleman's comforts.

Parsons's message was a written one, and to it she had added a word on her own account to the effect that Mr. Gaskell seemed very weak that morning, and unable to rally from the fatigue of the day before.

Lady Joan with a sigh put on one side an essay she was writing with deep interest on "The Beautiful, as opposed to the Terrible, in Art," and bent her steps to her father-in-law's quarters.

These had been assigned to him on the sunniest side of the Castle, and consisted of a suite of seven rooms leading one into the other, and in addition communicating by a second door with a long, narrow corridor which ran off the big inner hall of the house. These seven rooms had been most elaborately and luxuriously furnished, and Lady Joan never passed through them without thinking what an absurd amount of time and thought and money had been lavished in their fittings and decorations. A bedroom, a dressing-room, a sitting-room, were of course necessities to the old man; but here in addition was a billiard-room in case he might want to watch a game of billiards, a library, a smoking-room, and a room set apart as a sort of museum for patents connected with the working of coal-mines. This last was a room in which the old gentleman specially delighted. As a rule it was his sitting-room; and here he generally received his guests and visitors. Nothing gave him greater pleasure than to spend an hour or so in describing to an attentive ear how this or that lamp, hanging in one of the glass cases which surrounded the room, worked, or in exhibiting the various specimens of local coal which, carefully labelled were ranged upon shelves.

Lady Joan, as she passed through these handsome rooms, and let her eye wander around on their artistic accessories—pictures, statuary, embroideries—could not help contrasting them a little bitterly with the room in which her own grandfather had died, and which, although it rejoiced in relics and heirlooms of priceless worth from an antiquarian point of view, owned a carpet literally threadbare, and curtains burnt to their woof with the sunshine of over a hundred years.

Parsons came forward to meet her in the old gentleman's sitting-room.

"He is in an easy-chair in his dressing-room, my lady," she said. "He seems very weak today, and says he will get into bed soon."

The easy chair had, by the old gentleman's orders, been wheeled into a sunny bow-window; and, although his eyes were watering with the blinding light, he persisted in remaining there, saying that the sunshine put warmth into his bones, and was more than food or medicine to him.

The sunshine lighted up pitilessly his wrinkled face, half-shut sunken eyes, and thin hands, as they rested one on either arm of the chair.

When he opened his eyes, however, a change so great, as almost to amount to a transformation, took place. The eyes were dark blue like his son John's, and so clear and luminous, so keen and searching, that one look from them was enough to establish the fact that though ninety years of wear and tear had reduced his muscles to the weakness of a child's his brain and his will remained strong as ever.

And sometimes another look, a look neither keen nor searching, would come into those clear blue eyes; a look of sudden thoughtfulness, so deep as to amount to sadness, and which, let her fight against the idea as she might, never failed to bring back to Lady Joan's mind her dear old grandfather's eyes when, as he lay on his death-bed, he had turned his face towards her and had said, "If life were to come over again, Joan—" and then his eyelids had drooped, and the sentence had remained unfinished.

Worn and aged though the old man looked in the bright sunshine, his voice was cheery and firm as ever, when, after acknowledging Lady Joan's greeting, he said:

"Joan, I want you to send over to Summer-hill the first thing after breakfast tomorrow to fetch that pretty little girl who is to be Herrick's wife. I want her to come and talk to me."

Lady Joan started back aghast. Without word of warning, that would enable her to determine her course, to be met by such a request as this! For a moment she did not speak.

The old man did not seem to notice her surprise, and went on calmly and authoritatively as before.

"I don't want her to come today, because I'm not feeling quite myself this afternoon; but tomorrow, immediately after breakfast, send the dog-cart round and fetch her."

Lady Joan began to recover herself.

"Would it not be as well to wait a day or two?" she began, slowly.

It was at this moment that Parsons came forward, bringing the telegram for Herrick.

Lady Joan, not a little glad of the diversion, opened it at once. As her eye mastered its contents, she uttered an exclamation of surprise.

"What is it?" said the old man, sharply, turning towards her.

Then Lady Joan had to tell him the sad news. He sank back in his chair, covering his eyes with one hand.

"Poor lads! poor lads!" he moaned.

Presently he withdrew his hand from his face, and letting his eyes for a moment rest full on Lady Joan's, said:

"Joan, if I had my time to come over again, I don't think I should thank Heaven for the finding of coal on my land."

Lady Joan turned sharply away. At the moment she almost hated the old man for the rush of painful memories those words and the look combined had brought to her.

VIII

L ady Joan did not take the colliery disaster so much to heart as did old Mr. Gaskell. The mines at Wrexford were dangerous ones, and during her married life had been the scene of more than one dire calamity. No doubt it would give her husband a good deal of worry, and some positive hard work, since he took such an exaggerated view of his duties as master and employer. He, doubtless, would spend days at the mouth of the pit; would take a personal interest alike in the victims and their desolate families. For weeks to come, most likely, the only talk between him and Herrick, whenever they sat down to table together, would be of new methods of precaution to be taken in working the mines, varied, perhaps, by consultations as to how Widow This and her sons, or Widow That and her daughters, could be best provided for in life.

Personally, however, Lady Joan felt herself chiefly touched by the tiresomeness of the whole thing, a tiresomeness that was doubly accentuated by the fact that it had happened just at a moment when she wished to claim her husband's undivided attention to a matter of first importance—Herrick's ill-advised choice of a wife.

To tell the truth, when she thought over old Mr. Gaskell's request that Lois White should be sent for to the Castle on the following day, the thought of the twenty or thirty poor colliers scorched or suffocated out of their lives, speedily faded from her mind.

The longer she dwelt on the old gentleman's request, the more irritated and bewildered she grew. If she refused to comply with it she had but little doubt that he would himself ring his bell, transmit his orders to the stable, and despatch a message to Summerhill, and she would be placed in the undignified position of being compelled to stand by and witness the doing of a thing towards which she had assumed an openly hostile attitude.

This request of his was, indeed, a danger signal not to be disregarded, for it meant without doubt, that in her opposition to Herrick's folly, she would have to contend not only with Herrick, but also with Herrick's father and grandfather.

She sat far into the night thinking over these things, trying to face her difficulties, trying to answer the by no means easy question: what must be her first step in the very unequal battle she intended to fight? A game was often lost, she told herself, by a first false move. Now, would it be a false move, before doing anything else, to appeal to Herrick to show consideration to his mother's wishes in his choice of a wife?

A moment's thought answered this question with a very emphatic affirmative. Years ago, when Herrick was quite a boy, it had been borne into Lady Joan's mind in all sorts of trivial ways, that he had taken her measure, so to speak, by precisely the same standard by which his father and grandfather had judged her, and that her wishes and opinions carried with him as much or as little weight as they carried with them.

In this dilemma a bright thought came to her. Why not make her appeal in the first instance to the young girl who was supposed to be in love with Herrick, and professed, no doubt, to have his best interests at heart. A talk of five minutes with her on the morrow, before she could be shown in to old Mr. Gaskell, might convince her what those interests really were, and bring that love of hers to the test. Of Lois White Lady Joan knew so little that she could not even conjecture what might be the immediate results to such an appeal; but it was manifestly the thing that stood first in order to be done, whatever else might have to be done afterwards.

The night was creeping away while Lady Joan was thus facing her anxieties and arranging her plans; two o'clock was chimed by the clock over her mantelpiece. The night was intensely hot; evidently a storm was threatening. Lady Joan, with her brain still teeming with thought, felt that sleep for another hour or two would be an impossibility. She recollected a book which she had been reading on the previous day—a collection of Elizabethan lyrics, one of which had seemed to set itself to music as she had read it. She thought she would fetch the book, which she had left in one of the drawing-rooms, and jot down the melody which had run in her head before she forgot it. It would clear her brain from painful thought, and perhaps enable her to get a little sound sleep before day dawned; so she lighted a small lamp, and went her way through the dark, silent house to the rooms below.

That faint stream of light which her lamp threw, now high, now low, lighted up a lavishness of wealth, a sumptuousness of beauty wherever it fell. Those pictures which hung upon the staircase walls she herself knew the value of, for her opinion had been asked in their choice and purchase. That little niche on the landing—place held an all—but priceless statuette, and there below in the hall stood a cabinet containing china, for which a Royal Duke had bid in vain at Christie's against the millionaire coal-owner; now the stream of light fell upon a dainty Venetian glass tazza which had been pinched and moulded into its beautiful form by fingers which loved their art; and anon it glinted upon—ah! what was that? Here Lady Joan with a shudder turned her head sharply away. She knew well enough that that photographic album whose mediæval silver cover caught and threw back the lamp-light, contained portraits of the older members of the Gaskell family in various stages of what she was pleased to call vulgarity—John's mother in a dress fearfully and wonderfully made; John's uncle in a coat of equally marvellous cut. What an odd medley of luxury and art, of vulgarity and refinement, the roof of the Castle covered, she thought, as she entered the drawing-room, and, holding high her lamp, looked around her for her volume of poems.

Something else instead of the little book greeted her eye as she stood thus—"the counterfeit presentment" of her own tall stately figure in a pier-glass let into the opposite wall.

For the moment she started, and drew back. The mirror reached from floor to ceiling, and with the lamp held high as she was holding it, reflected not only every detail of her dress and figure, but also, with a cruel exactitude, every line, every feature of her dark, austere face, rendered possibly a shade more dark and austere than usual by the unpleasant train of thought in which she had been indulging.

This sudden apparition of herself struck a jarring note, and set her measuring not only the years that had passed, but the years that were to come.

Slowly, step by step, she drew nearer to the mirror and steadily looked herself full in the face.

Lady Joan's passage across the plain of Mars, as the ancients loved to call the middle period of life, had been easy and luxurious as wealth could make it; yet, assuredly, no hard-working bread-winner or brain-worker, could have owned to harder lines than those which marred the beautiful outline of her mouth and cut deeply across her low white brow. Making due allowance for her hair, which still retained its girlish hue, that rigid face of hers expressed, uncompromisingly, every one of her fifty years.

"Yes," she said, aloud, "that elderly woman is me—me—Joan Herrick that was, who thought she had so many young years at command that she could easily give a half-dozen or so to be spent amid plebeian surroundings for the sake of the decades of happiness that would follow.

And, instead of a half-dozen years, you poor woman, you have had to give your decades, and the promised happiness has not arrived yet! Now, should a happier order of things come about tomorrow, who will give you back any one of those thirty years of yours spent in bondage?"

Lady Joan turned sharply away from the mirror. "Make the most of the time that is left to you, Joan," that sombre, austere face seemed to say to her as a last word. "Soon the dark days will be on you, in which you will care little enough for anything, good or bad, that life can bring."

A slight sound of movement in the hall outside at this moment caught her ear, and brought her bitter thoughts to a halt.

What could it have been? A sound of rustling; a light footfall was it?

She went hastily out into the hall. Though an ill-made dress would set her shuddering, and a bit of crude colouring make her cover her eyes with her hand, yet she would have gone out into her own hall, at any hour of the day or night, and faced a dozen armed burglars or any other danger that might be there, for physical fear was unknown to her.

No sight so terrible, however, as armed burglar met her view as she peered hither and thither in the darkness; nothing more alarming than a slender, white-robed figure coming slowly, step by step, down the big staircase.

At first, Lady Joan did not recognise the face of this white-robed figure. As it approached, however, and the light from her lamp fell full upon it, she recognised the features of the girl, Lucy Harwood, whom she had in the morning engaged as her maid. She was dressed in her white night-gown; this, together with her slow, dreamy movements, proclaimed the fact that she was walking in her sleep.

Lady Joan advanced towards her as she touched the lowest stair. Slowly and dreamily the girl came along the hall, feeling the wall with one hand as a blind person might, and the other outstretched in vacancy. Her face was slightly upturned, her eyes wide open and stonily fixed. There was a look of pain upon her face which seemed to suggest that the errand on which she was bent was a sad one.

"Where? Where? Where in the world?" Lady Joan heard her say slowly and sadly as she came along.

Without thinking much of what she was doing, Lady Joan laid her hand on the shoulder of the girl, who started violently and awoke. Then she burst into a flood of tears, and clasping her hands together, cried:

"Oh, where am I? What have I done?"

Lady Joan's quiet manner somewhat reassured her.

"You had better take my lamp and go back to your room," she said; "and tomorrow I should like you to see a doctor. No," she added, as the girl began to protest, "I can find my way upstairs easily enough in the dark; but you, as a stranger, would lose yourself in this big house without a light."

And as Lucy departed, looking white and frightened, Lady Joan found herself wondering, with a degree of interest that surprised herself, what was the mystery this apparently commonplace life held.

IX

Lady Joan's rest was a short one that night, and her appetite for breakfast the following morning was taken away by a message from her father-in-law, which greeted her as she sat down to table, to the effect that he hoped the dog-cart had already been despatched to Summerhill to fetch Miss White.

The old gentleman had the—to Lady Joan's way of thinking—reprehensible habit, not only of expressing in decisive fashion any wishes that might occur to him over night, but of sending down the first thing the next morning to ascertain if those wishes had been carried out.

Annoyance was to follow annoyance that morning. The first post brought with it a very big annoyance indeed, in the shape of a letter from the Lady Honoria Herrick.

It was dated from Southmoor, and ran as follows:

DEAREST AUNT,

You will be surprised to hear we are all at home again. Father and mother returned last week from Belle-Plage, and I have been sent for from Brussels, because I'm told I'm finished, whatever that means. I have wonderful news to tell you—father says he hasn't the heart to write it, so I must—Southmoor is to be sold! Father says the place is going to utter ruin, and there is not the slightest likelihood of his ever being able to keep it up. So I have had to sign a lot of papers, and the thing will soon be an accomplished fact. Between ourselves—I'm awfully glad. I hate the place; it's so mouldy and dilapidated, and there's such a horrible odour of ancestors hanging about it one feels as if one were living in a vault. I will write again soon and tell you all our plans so soon as we have any. At present, things are very unsettled. Mother is about as usual: that is to say, the weather doesn't suit her, and she is living on crumbs of chicken and egg-spoonfuls of jelly. Give my love to my uncle and cousin. Your loving niece,
HONOR

Southmoor was to be sold! That was the only idea Lady Joan brought away from her niece's letter. Southmoor, the home of her childhood; the house where generations of Herricks had been born and had died was to come into the market to fall to the lot, perhaps, of some millionaire tradesman of democratic ideas and plebeian tastes; or, worse fate still, perhaps, be seized upon by some speculative building society, and the old park, with its stately trees, be parcelled into lots, upon which, in due course, red-brick middle-class villas would spring into existence.

Lady Joan had not visited the place much of late years. Her brother, the present Earl of Southmoor, married to an invalid, though high-born lady, and, haunted by the family spectre of poverty, had spent the past fifteen years of his life wandering about the Continent in search of health for his wife and cheap education for his only child. In tastes, he was Lady Joan's counterpart; in intellect, considerably her inferior. His pride had had to be largely deferred to in all Lady Joan's efforts to be of service to him. It went without saying that he and the Gaskells had nothing in common; and though Lady Joan would gladly have adopted her niece and brought her up as her own daughter, the Earl preferred for the Lady Honoria an atmosphere of aristocratic poverty to the plebeian luxury of Longridge Castle.

If the young lady herself had been consulted on the matter, she would undoubtedly have made a different choice, for, the truth must be told, Lady Honoria was that anomaly in nature, a child as unlike its race as if it had been born in another planet. The one or two glimpses she had had of Longridge Castle in her childhood, even now contrasted pleasantly in her mind with the life she had since been compelled to lead in cheap continental hotels, or in later years in a cheap school at Brussels.

Lady Joan in making plans for Herrick's future, had freely admitted the fact that her niece was not everything that an aristocratic damsel should be. She comforted herself, however, with the thought of Honoria's youth, and the possibility that her faults of character, though glaring, were purely superficial. Married to Herrick, settled down at Southmoor, under her own immediate eye, what might not be hoped for in the way of reformation for so young a girl!

She did not care to dwell upon the girl's undisguised satisfaction at the thought of the sale of the old home. The bitter fact alone riveted her attention.

"It shall not be," she exclaimed aloud, as she folded the letter, and laid it on one side. "If I have to go down on my knees to my husband to make him buy the place, it shall not come into the market!"

A second thought followed—that of the feeble old grandfather, who, once before when the purchase of Southmoor had been hinted at by Lady Joan, had exclaimed: "Don't touch it, John, it would be a non-paying investment."

Surely never did messenger bring more ill-timed tidings than the servant who at this moment entered and announced that Miss White had arrived.

Lois White, in her schoolroom at Summerhill, surrounded by her small pupils, had been not a little surprised at the message brought to her that morning "with Lady Joan's compliments."

"Wishes to see me?" she repeated, blankly, as she fetched her hat and gloves, and despatched a message to Mrs. Leyton, asking to be released from schoolroom duties that morning.

Her heart beat fast as she thought of a second ordeal, even more terrible than the one which, two days back, she had gone through under the ægis of Herrick's presence. Now, neither Herrick nor his father would, she knew, be at Longridge to receive her, and alone she would have to face Herrick's mother in her rigid stateliness. Her fears increased upon her as she sat waiting for Lady Joan in one of the big drawing-rooms.

"Oh, if Herrick had but been born to poverty instead of to wealth such as this!" was her thought, as her eye took stock of the beauty and luxuriousness of her surroundings.

Another thought trod on the heels of this one:

"What silly presumption for me to think for a moment that Herrick's mother, with her aristocratic blood, in addition to her wealth, would ever receive poor, little me as a fit wife for her son."

Lady Joan's manner when, after about a quarter of an hour, she entered the room, was not reassuring:

"I hope my sending for you in school-hours has not inconvenienced you," she said, after a formal bow, and a touch with the tips of her fingers. "Mr. Gaskell, however, was anxious to see you, and one feels compelled to defer to the wishes of one at his great age."

Lois murmured a string of polite commonplaces in reply, and Lady Joan resumed:

"I am glad on my own account, as well as on Mr. Gaskell's, that you were able to come, for there is something I particularly wish to say to you—something, in fact, that must be said; could not be written."

The methodical manner in which she spoke showed that she had not kept Lois waiting fifteen minutes for nothing.

Lois flushed crimson. She felt that the thunder-cloud she had dreaded was about to break now.

Lady Joan went on:

"But before I speak what necessity has laid upon me to speak, may I ask one question—a very important one—do you really consider yourself to be engaged to be married to my son?"

The words were spoken now. Lois started, her lips opened; but never a word escaped them. Did she consider herself to be engaged to be married? No, not in the sense in which most young girls consider themselves to be engaged to be married after the momentous question has been asked and answered. That Herrick looked upon marriage as the inevitable ending to his courtship there was not a doubt. Lois, however, before the day on which Herrick had slipped a diamond and ruby ring on her finger had come to an end, had said to herself: "There is such a thing as loving and letting go. If I thought my love for Herrick might be detrimental to him in the days to come, I would take myself out of his life at once and for ever."

Lady Joan, waiting for her answer and looking down into that frank, childlike face, read it as easily as she would have read an open book.

Lois had put on a small round hat that morning, and neither drooping brim nor veil hid the pained, bewildered look which said, as plainly as words could: "I am brought face to face with a matter beyond my capabilities. Where shall I look for help and guidance?"

Lady Joan—with a slight feeling of wonder over the girl's simplicity—said to herself that her course lay plain before her now. An appeal to the girl, founded on her love for Herrick, a few words of advice, some golden guineas, and the thing was done.

"A pretty enough child," she thought; "the very wife for a struggling artist—she would save him a small fortune in models. But a wife for Herrick! No!"

Aloud she said:

"I am sorry if my question has given you pain. Pardon my abruptness in asking it. Let me put it in another form. Do you love my son?"

Lois knew well enough how to answer that question.

"Love him!" she cried passionately, clasping her hands together, "oh, I would lay down my life, gladly, at any time, to save him a moment's pain."

"Then of course," said Lady Joan, coldly, and with great decision, "you have given careful thought to the question whether his marriage with you would be likely to conduce to his real happiness in life?"

"Careful thought!" cried Lois, impetuously. "I have thought of nothing else from morning till night since the day he—he asked me—to be his wife; but how can I—how is it possible for me to decide what will or what will not make his happiness?"

"No self-seeking there, no ambitious views for herself, so I may as well speak out plainly," thought Lady Joan. So she said, with great deliberation:

"And I, too, as Herrick's mother, have thought of nothing else from morning till night since I knew that marriage was in his thoughts; but I have had no difficulty in forming a decisive opinion on the matter. Shall I tell you what it is?"

Lois turned her face eagerly towards her.

"It is this," said Lady Joan, coldly, bluntly, cruelly. "That a marriage between you and him would be about the most disastrous thing that could happen to him; for the twofold reason that it would sow dissension between him and his relatives, and prevent him making a marriage suitable to his station in life."

A sharp cry, such as a child cut with a knife might utter, broke from Lois's lips. She grew pale; her hands clasped together convulsively.

"Help me, help me!" she cried piteously. "What am I to do?"

"If you are asking the question, really wishing for an answer, I will tell you," said Lady Joan, calmly and coldly as before. "Go away at once. Leave Longridge at once and for ever. Don't go into hysterics over it and talk about a breaking heart and such like—ah, pardon me—nonsense; but write, after you have left here, a plain, common-sense letter to my son, telling him that, having well thought over the matter, you have come to the conclusion that unequal marriages are good for neither party concerned, and that consequently of yourself, of your own free will—kindly lay stress on that—you have taken steps to end the engagement."

"Go! where shall I go!" said Lois, plaintively. I haven't a friend in the world, except Mrs. Leyton."

Lady Joan looked at her incredulously.

"Not a friend!" she repeated. "Where were you living before you came to Summerhill?"

"I was brought up at a big orphanage. My father was a naval officer, he and my mother both died when I was a child. I went straight from the orphanage to Summerhill when I was old enough to teach."

"And had you no relatives save father and mother?" asked Lady Joan. "Pardon my questions; but I am trying to see my way to helping you in the future, in any manner you may like to choose."

"My father had a cousin I used to see at one time; but he went to America long ago. I have not heard from him for years."

"I dare say you could find out his present address in some way. It seems to me that America would be a very desirable destination for you, all things considered. It would involve complete change of scene and surroundings—a very great consideration—and—"

But Lady Joan's sentence was not to be finished; for at this moment Dr. Scott's voice, in loud tones, was heard immediately outside the door.

"Never mind about announcing me," he was saying, no doubt to a servant. "I must see her without a moment's delay."

Then he pushed open the door and entered without ceremony.

"Lady Joan," he said abruptly, "I have just received a telegram from your son containing sad news. There is no time to tell you as you ought to be told, for the telegram has unfortunately been delayed in transmission, and the news will announce itself unless I make haste. So far as I understand the message, there has been a second terrible explosion at the Wrexford mines, and your husband—there, I see you understand me—no, not killed; severely injured. They are bringing him now. The ambulance is almost at the door. More than this I do not know."

X

Herrick's account of the terrible occurrence, given in short, disjointed, sentences, was easy enough to understand. His father had not been indulging in any Quixotic deeds of heroism, but had simply been doing his duty at the pit's mouth, and in the mines, as he had ever done in similar circumstances, organising search-parties, and seeing that the men already rescued were properly attended to. A second explosion had not been anticipated, and he, and his father also, had several times descended the shaft in the miner's cage. Help had been greatly needed in all quarters, and he himself had helped to bear away the last ambulance of rescued men in default of sufficient bearers.

Meantime his father, in company with the chief engineer, had descended the shaft in order to ascertain if a certain improved system of ventilation which had been submitted to him were practicable. When the cage was within twenty feet of the bottom, the second explosion had occurred; his father and the engineer had both been violently precipitated from the cage, the engineer had been killed on the spot, and his father had sustained—so far as could be ascertained—terrible bruises to his limbs, and serious injuries to the spine.

"Terrible bruises to his limbs, and serious injuries to the spine!" The verdict of the doctors, after a more prolonged examination had been made, was simply the translation into technical language of Herrick's words.

They expressed their gravest fears as to his chances of ultimate recovery.

Old Dr. Scott went a step farther than the Wrexford Doctors who had accompanied the ambulance home, and confided his opinion to the nurse whose services had been hastily called into requisition, that "twenty-four hours must see the end of it."

In order to avoid additional jolting, John Gaskell had been carried on the mattress on which he had lain in the ambulance, into a room on the ground-floor—one of old Mr. Gaskell's luxuriously-furnished suite of apartments. Here they had hastily placed a bedstead, and here, within two rooms from where his aged father was lying, it was fated that John Gaskell's last hours should be spent.

Lady Joan had borne the shock of the ill tidings better than Herrick could have anticipated. At first, possibly, she had scarcely realised the full import of Dr. Scott's words; but when, about five minutes after, the slow ambulance-bearers had brought in the once-stalwart John, one single glance at his white, drawn face, must have told her the whole terrible truth.

"Come in here, mother," Herrick said, drawing her back into her boudoir, which opened off the Hall. "There are several doctors—you will be in the way just now. I shall remain beside my father."

Then he looked up and saw Lois standing, looking pale and scared, at the farther end of the room. He did not at the moment realise the strangeness of the fact of her presence in the house—only hailed it with delight. In the terrible sorrow which had come upon them, who so likely to be helpful and sympathetic as the sweet girl so soon to be one of the family?

"You will look after my mother, Lois," was all he said, as he hastily withdrew.

Lois's heart sank; her instincts warned her that she would be the last person in the world to whom Herrick's mother would turn for consolation.

She made one step from out her corner.

"Shall I go—shall I stay—can I be of any use?" she asked, timidly.

Even with the shadow of a great sorrow falling upon her, Lady Joan's brain was quite clear to decide whether the girl whom she had judged to be no fit wife for Herrick was to be admitted to that position of friendliness in the house which alone justifies the acceptance of service in a time of need.

"You could not by any possibility be of any—the slightest—use in the circumstances," she answered coldly. "I would suggest that you return at once to Summerhill and think well over the conversation we have had this morning. When you have thoroughly considered the matter, I feel sure—"

But at this moment the door opened, and Herrick entered the room as hastily as he had quitted it.

"Mother," he said "my father has for a moment recovered consciousness, and has spoken your name. I think he wishes you to sit beside him."

XI

My father has spoken your name!" To John Gaskell, with the first faint gleam of consciousness, came the thought of his wife. Nearly thirty years of wedded life forges something of a bond between a man and woman. The mere fact that two people have thus long walked side by side through life is in itself a guarantee that a bond of companionship has been formed. More than this there may be, but this at least there must be. At times, one of the two may have wished to turn to the left when the other would fain go to the right, and each may occasionally have given a sigh for more congenial companionship. In spite of this, however, the sense of comradeship remains unbroken, and when at last death, with sharp touch, smites the hands of the two asunder, the loss is measured by what might have been rather than by what actually has been.

Thus, at least, it was with John Gaskell now as he lay upon his death-bed.

He had not been married a month before his shrewd common-sense had laid bare to him the fact that Lady Joan had married him for his wealth, not for himself. Characteristically, he had surveyed the "situation," and had done his best to save his life, as well as his wife's, from shipwreck.

"There never again can be any talk of love between us," he had said to himself, "but we can at least remember that we are an educated lady and gentleman bound to live together for life, and treat each other with proper respect and consideration."

Lady Joan he was inclined to pity rather than to blame. He laid the blame of their ill-advised marriage entirely on the shoulders of the courtly and impecunious old Earl, her grandfather.

Of Vaughan Elliot he knew nothing, or, possibly his estimate of Lady Joan's conduct might have suffered some modification. His acquaintance with the Southmoor family was but slight: a tramp on the Devon moors after snipe in company with Joan's brother, a subsequent introduction to the fascinating sister, a stay of three days at Southmoor, and the thing was done.

John Gaskell was very young at the time. His gold had not opened all doors to him; and the flattering attentions showered upon him by the ancient aristocrat, for the moment had dazzled and blinded him.

Later on, when disillusion came, he was not the one to sound the town-crier's bell and cry: "Oyez, oyez, oyez. I've been tricked into a marriage for the sake of my gold. Come and pity me every one who passes by."

The utmost that outsiders could note was, that after his marriage, John became devoted to his business in a manner not to be expected of so wealthy a man. Also, that Lady Joan's opinions or advice were never on any occasion sought for by him, though he would spend hours closeted with his old father, discussing all matters, great or small, that concerned the welfare of his household or that of his workpeople. All, however, who knew John Gaskell intimately, were forced to admit that he treated his wife from year's end to year's end with the most unvarying politeness, lavished his gold upon her, saw that every one of her whims and wishes was gratified so soon as formed, although possibly he did not seem to trouble himself much as to what went on in her heart.

Lady Joan, on her part, had seemed to acquiesce in a condition of things she was powerless to alter. To tell the truth, it very well suited her cold and unsympathetic temperament that no exhibitions of ardent feeling should be required of her. To do her justice, she was incapable of the small hypocrisies by which so many women make their household wheels to work smoothly. No flimsy self-deception hid from her eyes the fact that she was as much a stranger and an alien in her own home as if she had been born in another clime, and had been taught to speak a tongue different from that which her husband, her son, and her father-in-law spoke.

Even now as she entered the darkened room and took her seat at the head of the bed, whereon her husband lay stricken to his death, there were no tears on her face, and not for a moment did she say in her heart, as so many wives in similar circumstances would have said:

"Life ends for me today, though I may breathe and eat and drink for another fifty years to come."

Her husband made no sign, by so much as a quiver of the eyelid, that he was conscious of her presence. After one brief gleam of consciousness he had relapsed into insensibility; his heavy stertorous breathing proclaiming the fact.

"It is partly the effect of the opiate we have been compelled to administer," said the old doctor, coming forward. "You need not remain, unless you choose, Lady Joan. Your husband will not be conscious of your presence."

Lady Joan, however, chose to remain. She leaned back in her chair with her hand pressed over her eyes, her face by only one degree less white and rigid than that of the suffering man beside whom she sat.

"Poor soul!" thought the doctor, pityingly, "she is thinking of what lies before her in the future."

Yes, that was exactly what Lady Joan was doing, although not quite in the fashion which the doctor imagined. She was thinking what a miserable position hers would be, by-and-by, when John was gone and Herrick and the old man reigned paramount at the Castle.

She knew exactly the financial position of the Gaskells, one towards each other, for John had never been reticent on the matter. "I am my father's administrator, head-steward, general manager, what you will," he had been wont to say, when his friends had made complimentary allusions to his wealth or position, as the largest landowner in the county. It was true that yearly, as a matter of convenience, a large sum of money was placed to John's banking account, so that cheques might be drawn and payments made by him; but this in no wise affected the fact that Longridge and the mines at Wrexford, and all other land and investments—great and small—belonged in their entirety to old Mr. Gaskell, and only at his death could become John's.

Now, if the old man had died, as he might reasonably have been expected to do, some twenty years back, Lady Joan's thoughts ran, all this wealth and property would have been John's. He, no doubt, would have made liberal provision for her by will, and—

Ah! here a sudden recollection flashing across her mind put all other thoughts to flight. John had once, long ago, made a will; so long ago, indeed, that until that moment she had forgotten all about it. Some twenty years back, John had been called upon to undertake a tour of inspection among certain South American mines, in which he possessed an interest. The will which he then made, on the eve of his departure, had been framed to meet two contingencies—old Mr. Gaskell's death during his absence, and his own subsequent death through misadventure. Both these events were within the range of the possibilities; for the old gentleman had passed his threescore and ten years, and John was about to run the gauntlet of all sorts of dangers amid mines and machinery.

The will though elaborated by the lawyers into folios and sheets, was, in itself, a very simple document, and merely gave all the property— "real, landed, or personal"—of which John might die possessed to Lady

Joan for life, with reversion to Herrick on her death. Old friends of John Gaskell's were appointed trustees to this will, and, until Lady Joan's death, Herrick could only draw a certain fixed income from the estate. At this time Lady Joan's health was very fragile, and there seemed to be little likelihood of her living to see Herrick grown to manhood.

"Read it, Joan, and let me see that you understand it," her husband had said to her with a look, half-pitying, half-contemptuous, in his eyes, which she had found even more easy to read than the sheets of parchment which he handed to her.

"Here, you poor woman, who have sold yourself for wealth and luxury," that look seemed to say, "I have taken care that Fate shall not cheat you of your dues."

"Remember, Joan," he had said, as he folded the will and placed it in an envelope addressed to his solicitors, "this is only so much waste paper, unless my father dies before me."

No other will, to Lady Joan's certain knowledge, had since been made by him; for, until the death of his father, no necessity for so doing could arise. No doubt, if the thought of this will had ever come into John's mind, it must simply have figured to him, as he had before phrased it, as "so much waste paper."

"So much waste paper," thought Lady Joan bitterly, the echo of her husband's words, spoken twenty years back, ringing sharply in her ears now. "My thirty years of bondage served to no purpose! Southmoor to be sold, and the will that would enable me to buy Southmoor twice over with ease, so much waste paper! And all because an old man's useless life has been unnaturally prolonged! If the two must die, it is a thousand pities that the old man should not go first!"

XII

"I t will be better for me to creep quietly away now," said Lois, speaking hurriedly, as the door closed on Lady Joan, and she found herself alone with Herrick. "I can be of no use to any one. I should only feel myself in the way."

Herrick's face showed simple blank astonishment.

"In the way!" he repeated. "Going! You mean to leave us in the very midst of our sorrow."

He felt as one might feel who, overtaken by a flood, and planting his feet on what he thinks a rock, suddenly feels it crumbling into sand beneath them.

Lois tried to explain.

"I would give worlds—worlds if I could be of use—of comfort to—to you all; but—but—" she faltered, and broke off abruptly.

With a heart filled as hers was at the moment with conflicting emotions, it was difficult to let forth even one little scrap of feeling without suffering all to escape.

Herrick stood for a moment, steadily looking at her, trying to gather the real meaning of her words from her flushing tearful face. There could be but one, it seemed to him.

"I don't think you quite understand, dear," he said, sadly, "the greatness of the sorrow of that is coming upon us. It has not been made clear to you that by this time tomorrow death will have entered our house."

That must be what it was; she did not realise the blackness of the overhanging cloud. It was not only that she was little more than a child in years, she had been so secluded from the world, knew so little of the deeper joys or sorrows of life, that she was even below her years in development.

Her mouth quivered, great tears rolled down her cheeks.

"Oh, Herrick," she cried, clasping her hands, and looking up in his face, "if only I could bear it for you!"

Herrick's calmness began to give way.

"No one could do that. No one knows what my father has been to me all my life through," he said, unsteadily. And then he sank into the chair which she had just quitted, hiding his face in both hands.

Lois could see the tears trickling through his fingers. She bent over him, putting her arm round his neck; words failed her.

"Oh, Herrick, my poor boy, my poor boy!" was all she could find to say.

The difference in their years seemed to vanish. She felt mother-like over him, strong and protective, ready to fight sorrow—death itself, with her little hands, should either dare to approach him.

For a few minutes Herrick wrestled silently with his grief, and Lois stood bending over him, caressing his dark-brown hair, and finding no better words of comfort than:

"My poor, poor boy! If only I could bear it for you!"

Deep down in her heart was another and bitterer cry.

"Can I go away and leave him to bear his sorrow alone? Can there be another in the whole world who could comfort him as I would?"

It was altogether a new experience to see Herrick thus overcome with grief. As a rule, his young vigour and masterfulness were the things that first and foremost made themselves felt when he entered a room. Face to face with him and his masterfulness it had been comparatively easy for her to persuade herself that he could get on very well through life without the aid of such a poor, little, insignificant creature as herself. But now, with him brought thus low, her heart had but one cry in it: "I love him so, I cannot, cannot give him up."

The room was so still that the loud ticking of a clock on a pedestal in a corner seemed to speak as with a warning voice: "I am telling, one by one, the seconds of that life which so soon will have run itself out." Herrick could fancy it cried aloud to him. He withdrew his hands from his face. It looked haggard and aged by a dozen years.

"Forgive me, Lois," he said, brokenly. "I ought not to give way like this—so much devolves upon me."

Even as he spoke his words were to be verified, for a servant entered, bringing him a message. The manager from the Wrexford mines was wishing to see Mr. Herrick; he apologised very much for intruding at such a time; but tomorrow would be pay-day for the miners, and it would cause great inconvenience to the men if they were not paid. Did Mr. Herrick know if the cheque which was handed over regularly every month had been signed, so that he could draw upon it?

With the message the servant delivered a note from Parsons, asking if Mr. Herrick would, as soon as possible, pay a visit to his grandfather. The terrible news had not as yet been told him, and his enquiries as to what had detained Mr. Gaskell so long at Wrexford were incessant.

Herrick stood for a moment in thought over this note. "Yes, he must be told," he said presently, with a sigh. The message from the

Wrexford manager, coming simultaneously with the note from Parsons, brought before his mind the fact that business relations might render it imperative that the painful tidings should be broken to the old man.

"But Dr. Scott must be present," he decided. Then he turned to Lois:

"Wait here, Lois. I shall like you to come in to my grandfather presently. You may be able to say some word of comfort to him. I will come for you in a few minutes."

Lois, in silence, shrank back into her corner once more. With Herrick gone, the room seemed to resume its distinctive character as Lady Joan's boudoir. She felt strangely out of place amidst these ancestral surroundings.

The aristocratic portraits on the walls seemed with their thin lips, to repeat Lady Joan's cold, cruel words: "I consider that a marriage between you and my son would be about the most disastrous thing that could happen to him;" while all the four corners of the room, with their luxurious fittings and works of art, seemed to cry out at her in chorus: "It would sow dissension between him and his relatives; it would prevent him making a marriage suitable to his station in life."

Even the loud-voiced marqueterie clock on its high pedestal, which had seemed to bring a message to Herrick, had one for her now, and ticked away to a refrain—what was it, the ending of a poem, or of an old song she had heard somewhere?—"I love thee so, dear, that I only can leave thee."

XIII

Herrick performed his dreary task as gently as possible.

At first old Mr. Gaskell did not seem to catch the full import of Herrick's silence in response to his eager question: "But tell me, his injuries are not serious?"

Then, as the truth flashed into his mind, he fell back in his easy-chair moaning pitifully:

"My boy John, my stalwart laddie to go first after all!"

Dr. Scott came forward with a cordial draught, but the old man waved him on one side, saying that he was tired, and would go to bed.

"Let me get to sleep, let me get to sleep," he said; "it's all I want."

"Come now, Lois," said Herrick, about ten minutes after, beckoning Lois to follow him to his grandfather's room.

It seemed to the young man that everyone, aged or youthful, could not fail to respond to sweet Lois's gentle sympathy.

Lois followed him readily enough; where-ever he led it was easy enough for her to follow; but alas for her, if he were not there to lead, and her fears or her love chose to show the way!

When they entered his room, the old man was lying back on his pillows with closed eyes; his thin fingers beat restlessly on the coverlet; while ever and anon a feeble moan, as from one in pain, escaped his lips.

Herrick noted sadly that a change had passed over the aged, shrunken face, even during the brief space of time that he had been out of the room.

"Grandfather," he said, gently, "I have brought Lois to see you. Don't you remember—I introduced her to you on—on your birthday?"

It needed an effort of memory on the young man's part to fix the date of that birthday. It seemed to him that a lifetime, not barely two days, had elapsed since, light-hearted and full of hope, he had brought Lois to his grandfather's side to receive and to offer congratulations.

The old man slowly opened his eyes; there was a dreamy, far-away look in them.

"Take off your hat, dear," whispered Herrick, "and let my grandfather see your face."

Lois did so; then, as if moved by a sudden impulse, she laid her soft cheek, all wet with tears, upon the old man's thin hand.

"God bless you, my child!" he murmured softly.

CATHERINE LOUISA PIRKIS

There came a sudden look of deep tenderness into his eyes; it as suddenly faded, swept away by one of keen annoyance—one might almost say of anger—which overspread his countenance.

Old Mr. Gaskell's bedroom led into his dressing-room, this again opened into the room to which his son had been hastily carried.

Suddenly and softly the door of this dressing-room had been opened, and Lady Joan had looked in.

Lois's instincts must have been strangely at one with those of the old man beside whom she sat, for though her back was towards this door, and the handle had been turned without a sound, she felt Lady Joan's presence on the threshold, and in a flash of thought she attributed old Mr. Gaskell's sudden change of expression to its right cause.

Silently, as she had come, Lady Joan closed the door and departed, saying never a word.

Herrick, not possessing Lois's quickness of perception, heard and saw nothing.

"Does Lady Joan want you—me—anything, do you think?" Lois asked him in a low tone.

"Perhaps my father may have recovered consciousness, and wishes to see me," answered Herrick, eagerly, a wild hope springing up in his heart that, after all, this much of mercy might be granted him, and he might, once again, hear his father's loved voice.

He beckoned to Parsons to place a chair for Lois beside the grandfather's bed, and hastened to his father's room by way of the corridor.

His hope was but short-lived. A glance at John Gaskell's face—on which one moment of agony had set its seal—convinced him that his heavy insensibility remained unbroken.

Dr. Scott was in the room.

"It is partly the result of the opiate," he said, "which we have been compelled to administer." Then looking hurriedly round to see that they were alone, he added: "Get your mother out of the room into the fresh air for a few minutes. Her strength is being severely taxed. She has been wandering restlessly from room to room for the past quarter of an hour."

While he was speaking, Lady Joan reentered. Her step was slow and uncertain. To Herrick's fancy, she seemed strangely preoccupied. He could almost have imagined her to be some soulless piece of machinery wound up to go through certain performances for a given time, so automatic and unnatural her movements seemed.

"Mother," he said, drawing her away from the sick-bed to a window recess, "I'll stay here while you get a little fresh air. Your strength won't stand this for long together."

She scarcely seemed to hear him; but, looking beyond him, addressed Dr. Scott:

"Have you seen old Mr. Gaskell, lately—since he heard the bad news, I mean?" she asked. "Has it had a bad effect upon him, do you think?"

"I was present when your son broke the news to him," answered the doctor. "I can scarcely say yet what effect it may have had. I am going into see him again shortly."

"Go now, if you please; I am anxious to know," she said in low tones.

"Mother," said Herrick, "I wish Lois to stay in the house now she is here. Will you send a message to Summerhill, or shall I?"

"I wish Lois!"

Lady Joan repeated the words. It seemed to her that the young man had spoken them with a good deal of authority, as if he were already preparing to take up his position as master of the house.

"Yes," said Herrick with great decision, "I wish Lois to stay in the house. Her presence here is a comfort to me and to my grandfather; I hope it will be also to you. Shall I send a man over to tell Mrs. Leyton not to expect her back today?"

Lady Joan did not reply for a moment, and Herrick had to repeat the question.

"Shall I send to Summerhill, or will you?"

"You will do as you please," presently she answered, coldly and formally. "The house is large. If she remains here, pray keep her away from these rooms."

Then she turned away from him and went into the adjoining room—the one intervening between the two sick-rooms—and stood waiting there for Dr. Scott's reappearance.

Herrick took her place beside his father's bed. "She is unlike herself today, and no wonder," he thought. "She shall not be distressed by word or deed of mine. By-and-by I can fight Lois's battles easily enough. My poor father, my poor father, he is the only one to think of now!" and the young man laid his head on the pillow on which lay John Gaskell's white face in its whiter bandages, and sent up a heart-broken prayer to Heaven that those dear, blue eyes now so closely sealed might, if only for a moment, open once again and rest on his face with a gleam of recognition in them.

CATHERINE LOUISA PIRKIS

Presently, the voices of Lady Joan and the doctor in the adjoining room fell upon his ear.

"You think a change has set in?" Lady Joan was saying.

"I do," was the doctor's reply, in sad tones. "A very marked change for the worse. His pulse is by many degrees feebler; his temperature is lower."

"Is there any immediate danger?" asked Lady Joan.

The doctor paused before replying. Then he said, slowly:

"It is a difficult question to answer. I have seen him very low before, and he has rallied. A great deal depends upon the amount of nourishment he can be induced to take. At his great age, one cannot expect much warning of the approaching end. I know you like me to be frank with you, Lady Joan; my own impression is that his last hour will be sudden and painless."

Lady Joan's voice was unlike her own as she asked the next question:

"Will he go before my husband, do you think?"

"Heaven only knows," replied the doctor, solemnly. "Send for another doctor, and have a second opinion, Lady Joan." He broke off for a moment, and then added, sadly: "I may be wrong; but it seems to me, as I go from one sick-room to the other, that it is a race between the two, with death for the goal. Heaven only knows who'll reach it first!"

XIV

T he twenty-four hours that were, as the doctor had phrased it, "to see the end of it," were swiftly and surely ebbing themselves out; the hot morning wore away into a hotter afternoon; the storm seemed to draw near and nearer, but still it did not break.

No appreciable change took place in John Gaskell's condition; the narcotics acted powerfully upon him, and he appeared slowly and imperceptibly to be passing over the border which divides sleep from coma.

Old Mr. Gaskell also remained in much the same condition. He had ceased to moan over his "stalwart laddie," and now lay still and quiet, with his hand clasping Lois's, like some tired child being soothed to sleep.

Lois's presence at his bedside was so evidently a comfort to him, that Herrick, in spite of his mother's request that the young girl should be kept away from that suite of rooms, did not like to disturb her.

It was a difficult subject to mention to Lady Joan, without a display of feeling which would be most unseemly in the circumstances. So he let matters take their course, hoping and believing that when his mother saw how manifestly Lois had won his grandfather's favour, her request would not be repeated.

His presence for the nonce was not needed in either sick-room. All sorts of tiresome business details claimed his attention that afternoon; the state of confusion into which the colliery at Wrexford had been thrown by the explosion, called for the presence of one of the proprietors on the spot. As this, however, in the present sad condition of things was an impossibility, Herrick did what he could by means of telegrams, and all through the early afternoon the wires between Longridge and Wrexford were working incessantly.

It was not until close upon five o'clock that he found himself free to return to the dying beds of his father and grandfather. When he entered his grandfather's room the old man appeared to be dozing. The look on Lois's face—always so easy to read—puzzled him. She looked startled and pained at one and the same moment, as if something had occurred which had frightened and troubled her.

"You have been sitting here too long, darling," he said, in a low voice; "come for a few minutes out on the terrace."

Then he whispered a word to Parsons, that if his grandfather aroused, and enquired for Miss White, she was to send for her immediately.

The terrace was easily reached by any one of the long French windows of the grandfather's suite of rooms. The sun was on the other side of the Castle now, and the slanting shadows gave refuge from the intense heat.

"What is it, Lois—what has troubled you?" was, naturally enough, Herrick's first question, when they found themselves alone in the open air.

Lois seemed greatly disturbed.

"Oh, Herrick," she said, in low, vehement tones, "I feel—I know—I ought not to speak as I am going to speak—but tell me, has your grandfather any reason to dislike Lady Joan?"

Herrick's face changed.

"There has never, to my knowledge," he answered, "been any open quarrel between them, although, I am sure, you will easily understand that two people so opposite in character could never be expected to get on particularly well together. But why do you ask, dear? What has happened to put such a thought into your head?"

"Nothing much has happened. I dare say I'm wrong to lay stress on such a simple thing; but twice, while I have been sitting beside Mr. Gaskell, Lady Joan has opened the door leading from the dressing-room, and looked in."

"Well?"

"And each time I knew that she was there without turning my head, by the look which passed over Mr. Gaskell's face and the way in which he clutched—yes, clutched my hand."

Herrick did not speak for a moment. Lois went on:

"He looked—I scarcely know how to explain—like someone who was having a bad dream. He only opened his eyes for half a moment the first time; the second time he did not open his eyes at all, only seemed to feel that she was there looking at him; and he held my hand so tightly and muttered something. I could scarcely hear what it was; but I think it was, 'Don't leave me, my child.'"

"Did my mother say anything?"

"Not a word; but oh, Herrick, when I turned and looked at her she looked so dark and so—so unlike herself, that I could have fancied that another soul had taken possession of her body."

Herrick could see a reason, of which Lois knew nothing, for what she called a "dark" look on his mother's face. To his mind, it was evident that Lady Joan had looked into the room to see if her wishes had been attended to, and Lois had been requested to withdraw. Finding the contrary to be the case, her feeling of annoyance had no doubt showed in the expression of her countenance. The look on his grandfather's face, as described by Lois, was to him inexplicable. Surely she must have allowed her imagination to run away with her.

He felt perplexed. It seemed to him that the slightest wish of the old man, now lying at the gates of death, should be complied with. Yet his mother, with this terrible sorrow hanging over her, must have due consideration shown to her. It was hard to know what to do for the best. The next moment his course was to be decided for him.

"My lady wishes to speak to you, sir. She is in the library," said a servant at that moment approaching.

"Wait here for me, Lois; the fresh air will do you good," said Herrick, as he prepared to comply with his mother's summons. "Don't be afraid, dear; I shan't betray your confidences."

The library was on the ground floor. Herrick found Lady Joan standing just within the room, with, what he was willing to admit, was a very "dark" look, indeed, on her face.

"Is this a time to think of marrying and giving in marriage?" she asked, sternly, before he had time to open his lips. "Have you done well, do you think, in forcing upon me, at such a time as this, the presence of a young woman who is distasteful to me?"

Herrick felt his temper aroused.

"Forcing upon you! Distasteful to you! I do not understand!" he cried, hotly. Then his better angel conquered; he bit his lip and restrained himself. "This is not a time for bickering and contention, at any rate," he said; "that at least can wait. Lois I found in the house when I returned home—I supposed she was brought here by your wish, or my grandfather's. Whether this was, or was not, the case, one thing is clear, my grandfather likes to have her beside him, and I am sure you will so far respect his wishes as to allow her to remain in his room."

Lady Joan laid her hand upon his arm. "Listen, Herrick, I have only five minutes to spare from your father's dying bed, and I have something to say to you which must—must be attended to. I suppose this young lady, of whom we have already spoken, is to remain here for the night?"

"Assuredly," answered Herrick; "I have sent a message to Summerhill to that effect."

"Very well. You have acted in the way in which, I suppose, you think you have a right to act; now I intend to act in the way in which I have an undoubted right to act. The sick-rooms are under my

CATHERINE LOUISA PIRKIS

supervision—both of them, in all their arrangements, and I positively forbid the entry of—of that young woman into any one of that suite of rooms. I have already given Parsons orders to that effect."

As she finished speaking she left the room, and Herrick, exasperated though he might be at her sentence, yet felt that in the circumstances there could be no appeal from it.

XV

The sun went down a great ball of lurid fire behind the young trees in the park. As its flames died out of the stormily purple west, rugged masses of cloud spread themselves athwart the night sky. No refreshing coolness came with the darkness. Every window in the Castle stood open; but air there was none, outside the house nor within.

"Don't trouble about me, Herrick," said Lois, as for a moment the two stood together in the hall before separating for the night; I am not in the least tired. Ah, if you would only let me sit up! If I go to bed I shall not be able to sleep."

Herrick had decided that the unseemliness of a discussion between him and his mother at such a time was a sufficient reason for yielding to her wish that Lois should be kept out of his grandfather's room. Furthermore, he had decided that, all things considered, it would be better for Lois to return to Summerhill on the following morning. Later on he would know well enough how to make good her position in the house as that of his future wife, and every living soul, mother included, should be taught to respect it. But for the present he resolved that not so much as a jarring look between his mother and himself should ruffle the serene atmosphere that ought to surround a dying-bed.

He had spent the twilight hours now in one sick-room, now in another, and anon in brief five minutes in the library dictating telegrams to the manager of the Wrexford mines. Now, as eleven o'clock chimed, the Castle was beginning to settle down into quiet, and he had crept away to say a farewell word to Lois, and and to bid her go to rest for the night. He felt sorely at a loss how to refuse her request without betraying his mother's ill-will towards her.

"If you sat up, darling, you could be of no possible use," was all he could find to say.

Lois did not speak for a moment. She was standing immediately beneath one of the swinging bronze lamps which lighted the hall the soft yellow light falling full upon the upturned, dimpled face, the straying gold of her hair, the tremulous mouth. The simple, infantine face might have been that of a child praying to have the moon given it for a toy, rather than that of one making a request whose granting or refusal might carry life or death with it.

She clasped her hands together imploringly.

CATHERINE LOUISA PIRKIS

"Oh Herrick, Herrick," she cried, "why won't you let me go near him? I beg, I entreat you, let me see him once again!"

Tears ran down her cheeks; her voice gave way with her last word.

Herrick was greatly distressed.

"If I could I would, darling, you may be sure; but for some reason or other my mother—" Here he checked himself sharply, then added: "You shall see him the first thing in the morning before you go back to Summerhill, I promise you that. Dr. Scott told me only a minute ago that he had slightly rallied, and he thought that he might have a fairly good night."

Lois guessed at the words he had so sharply held back.

"Tell me Herrick," she said, in a low voice, "why does Lady Joan wish to keep me away from him? He seemed so happy to have me beside him. He held my hand so tightly! I can hear his poor weak voice now, saying: 'Do not leave me, my child.'"

Here, again, tears choked her words.

Herrick's calmness nearly gave way.

"Do not add to my anxieties tonight, Lois," he said. "Believe me, I feel already as if my brains were leaving me. Will you take my word for it that my grandfather is much better left alone with his usual attendant for the night? Dr. Scott has said, more than once, that the slightest divergence of routine might be bad for him. I beg of you, go upstairs to rest now; tomorrow, before you go back to Summerhill—"

Lois suddenly laid her hand on his arm.

"Herrick," she pleaded, "if you will not let me go inside his room tonight, will you let me sit outside his door in the corridor? I will be so quiet, I will scarcely breathe. Lady Joan shall not know I am there—Oh, do, do let me!"

She clasped her hands over his arm, her tears falling in a shower now.

Herrick grew more and more distressed and perplexed.

"Give me a reason, Lois, for such a strange request," he said.

But he might as well have asked Lois to fetch him down one of the stars at once. Her eyes drooped.

"I wish I could," she said, falteringly. "I can't tell you why, but I feel as if I were called upon to—take care of him tonight—"

"Oh, Lois, do you not think that my mother and Parsons and I are enough to take care of my dear old grandfather till morning? I shall sit in the dressing-room—that is, you know, the room between my father's and grandfather's rooms—and shall be going from one room to the other all night. If anything should happen, if my grandfather should express any wish to see you, I promise you faithfully you shall be sent for at once."

But Lois was not to be satisfied even with this promise. Her entreaties grew more and more vehement. Might she sit in the hall, if not in the corridor? Might she come down once in the middle of the night for a report as to how things were going on?

Herrick had to feign a sternness he did not feel to silence her. If she could have given him the shadow of a reason for her request, he would have attached more importance to it. As it was, the thought in his mind was that she was overdone, hysterical, and was attaching a significance to trifles which did not of rights belong to them.

"Sleep will be the best thing for you tonight, dear; by-and-by you shall help me bear the brunt of everything," he said with a decision that ended the matter. "You have had a terribly fatiguing day—the intense heat, the thunder in the air is telling on you. Don't you know you told me you could feel a storm coming a week before it broke?"

"Thunder in the air! is it that I feel?" said Lois vaguely, dreamily. But she made no farther opposition to Herrick's wishes. In good truth, accustomed as she had ever been to yield submission to the will of others, it had cost her not a little to assert her own wishes in the way she had already done.

There followed "one long, strong kiss" between the lovers, a kiss that could not have had more of truth and passion in it if they could have turned over a page of Time's volume and read what lay before them in the future.

Then Lois went her way up the broad oak staircase to the room which had been assigned to her on the upper floor; and Herrick went back to the sick-rooms.

His last word to her was a repetition of his promise, that before she went back to Summer-hill the next morning she should see and say good-bye to his grandfather.

He stood at the foot of the staircase watching the dainty little figure, with its flushed, tearful face and straying golden hair, till it disappeared at the turn of the stairs; taking it as much for granted that he and she would meet on the morrow as he did that the sun would rise and the shadows flee away.

XVI

S he looks as if another soul had taken possession of her body."

Lois's word flashed into Herrick's mind as he entered the corridor leading to his grandfather's quarters, and found Lady Joan standing on the threshold of his father's room, with a look on her face he had never seen there before.

In view of the coming night-watch, she had exchanged her tight-fitting dress for some long, dark, clinging robe; round her head and shoulders she had wrapped a grey shawl of light texture; from beneath this her eyes looked out at him, large and glittering, with a strange light in them. A prophetess of old time, a daughter of Jerusalem sitting beside the waters of Babylon, and gathering herself together to pronounce a curse upon the race which had conquered and enslaved her Fatherland, might have had much such a look shining out of her eyes and settling in rigid lines about her mouth.

"I have been waiting—waiting here to speak to you, Herrick," she said, and her voice sounded to him hard and unnatural, "to make arrangements for the night. The quieter these rooms are kept during the night hours, the better for the invalids. Dr. Scott I have already dismissed—"

"Dr. Scott dismissed!" interrupted Herrick, astonished beyond measure. "Why, he is the one we may need most of all!"

"You need not doubt my capacity for managing the routine of a sick-room. Dr. Scott himself told me that there was scarcely a likelihood of any change taking place in your father's condition before the morning; so I suggested to him that he should take his rest during the early part of the night, and I have promised to have him called at daybreak. I have had a mattress placed for him in one of the sitting-rooms—the first at the farther end of the corridor, so that in case of need he can be easily aroused."

"It seems to me," said Herrick, steadily eyeing his mother, "that if rest is to be thought of tonight for any one, it should be for you—"

"My place is here," interrupted Lady Joan, with great decision; "no one can fill it, no one shall fill it."

She added the last words excitedly, and Herrick, knowing at what terrible tension his mother's nerves must be held at that moment, forebore to press the point farther.

"Of course, you will have Parsons and Jervis"—the newly-engaged nurse—"in attendance," he said. "And I will remain in the dressing-room, and will be in and out both rooms all night. But still—"

"I beg you will do nothing of the sort," interrupted Lady Joan—Herrick would have thought angrily, if anger at such a time had seemed to him possible—"you would be greatly in the way in the dressing-room; it is required by the nurses for all sorts of purposes. These rooms must be kept in perfect quiet. It would be far wiser if you followed Dr. Scott's example, and went to rest during the early part of the night."

"I—rest! with my father lying at death's door!" was all that Herrick said in reply, but the tone in which he spoke showed that he had not by a long way attained the perfect control over his feelings which his mother exhibited.

"Why not?" she asked. "Two such sickrooms as these cannot possibly require the attendance of more than three women. The nursing duties are next to nothing!"

It was only too true—the nursing duties were "next to nothing." The administration of an opiate, the renewal of bandages steeped in aconite, was all that could be required of nurse or doctor in John Gaskell's sickroom.

In old Mr. Gaskell's room the duties required of the nurse were scarcely heavier. Nourishment or a stimulant of some sort had to be administered hourly to the feeble and tractable invalid, but beyond this nothing could be done.

Herrick laid his hand on his mother's arm.

"Mother say no more," he said gently, but with a decision as great as her own. "No living soul could keep me away from my father tonight, so pray give up the attempt. I will fall in with any routine you may think best for the night-watch; but here I am, and here I shall remain until—"

Again he broke off.

It was unintentional that he spoke as if his mother had, with deliberate purpose, done her utmost to keep him from his father's bedside.

Lady Joan looked at him for a moment.

"The Gaskell strong will again," was the thought in her heart. Aloud she said:

"If your mind is made up, I waste time in endeavouring to alter it. As I have already told you, I wish both sick-rooms kept in perfect quiet; divergence of routine in your grandfather's room, Dr. Scott tells me, will have a bad effect on him, and it will be best for him to be left till morning entirely to the care of Parsons, who knows his requirements. In this room as I have already told you, your presence can scarcely be needed. If you choose to sit up, therefore, I should prefer your remaining in the room opening off this on the other side—the billiard room, that is."

This then was the arrangement of the suite of seven rooms on that memorable night. Dr. Scott, with his mattress, occupied the first of the suite—the one at the extreme end of the corridor. Herrick, in compliance with Lady Joan's wish, took possession of the second—his grandfather's billiard-room. John Gaskell, attended by his wife and Jervis the nurse, lay in the third. The fourth room, old Mr. Gaskell's dressing room, which intervened between the two sick-rooms, was left empty for the use of the nurses, also in compliance with Lady Joan's wish. In the fifth room lay old Mr. Gaskell. Two sitting-rooms followed in succession, both untenanted. Each of these rooms, in addition to the doors by which they communicated with each other, owned to a third door opening direct into the corridor. This corridor communicated at one end with the big inner hall of the house, and at the other led by a staircase to the upper floor.

XVII

Herrick placed a chair for himself just within the billiard-room, leaving the door ajar, so that the slightest sound in the sick-room could be heard by him.

He leaned back in his chair, a prey to the sad thoughts which his familiar surroundings summoned forth with relentless hand. What pleasant games of billiards he and his father had enjoyed at that table in the after dinner hour, while the old grandfather looking on, gave canny counsel, now to one side, now to the other. Great Heavens! how long ago it seemed now! He could have fancied that years, not days, had elapsed since he last heard the old man say in his thin, quavering voice, "Play with caution, laddie, one chance missed gives two to your adversary"; or listened to his father's hearty tones saying, "Bravo, Herrick, I never made a better break than that at my best."

A passionate longing rose up in his heart, there and then to look once more on those loved faces; to touch once again those kindly hands, while yet the warmth of life remained to them. He repressed it with the thought of his mother's evident wish that he should keep away from the sick-rooms during the night. It was a strange wish on her part no doubt; but still, as it was her wish, he felt bound to respect it. As before in the day, so now he resolved that his mother should not be called upon through him to bear any—the slightest—additional heart-ache to those she now suffered. "After all," his thoughts ran, "for all practical purposes he was as near his father one side of the door as the other." It might be that the solution to his mother's apparently inexplicable conduct lay in the fact that a sudden mood of jealous love had taken possession of her; and she wished no living soul to share with her the last watch beside her dying husband. Second thoughts however refused to be satisfied with so simple an explanation. As long as he could remember his father and mother had always seemed on a fairly amicable and friendly footing towards each other; but of love of the sort that breeds jealousy, there had not been a jot.

With his mother thus in the foreground of his thoughts, other things in her conduct that day struck as it were uncomfortable key-notes. It was strange that Lois's child-like instincts had appeared to meet the old grandfather's at this point, and that both should shrink from Lady Joan as if—well as if she were unfit for the onerous duties which had thus suddenly devolved upon her.

"Well, what wonder!" he thought, "if she were unfit for such duties. What wonder if she had strangely altered during the past twenty-four hours; he himself had felt older by at least a dozen years, and her frame, her brain were not to be compared with his in youth and strength—ah!"

Herrick's thoughts here broke off abruptly as a sudden ugly suspicion crossed his mind. What if the true solution of the mystery was to be found in the fact that her brain had not been strong enough to bear the terrible strain put upon it that day, and that her reason even now tottered in the balance!

Ugly as the suspicion was, Herrick forced himself to look it in the face.

And the longer he looked at it the more likely it seemed to grow. It gave a show of reason alike to Lois's and the old grandfather's nameless terrors. They had noted a change in Lady Joan which his pre-occupied mind had debarred him from perceiving, and had shrunk from her in a manner unintelligible to themselves.

Herrick, still leaning back in his chair, covered his eyes with one hand; this, not to shut out the terrible embodiment which his fears had thus suddenly assumed, but the better to answer the practical question: "What could he do for the best? How was he to meet this unexpected emergency?"

One thing speedily made itself plain to him: his mother must be watched as much for her own sake as for the sake of those helpless ones left in her charge.

"I must keep eyes and ears on the alert tonight," he said to himself. "And remember that I am keeping watch not over two, but over three."

It was an appalling thought; his brain seemed to grow dizzy beneath it. A clock in a corner of the room chimed the hour—one o'clock. From different quarters of the Castle the same hour was repeated, and then, to Herrick's fancy, a great stillness seemed to fall upon the house, a stillness which, combined with the sultriness of the air, seemed to proclaim that the storm must be almost upon them. Not a leaf stirred in the outside darkness, nor so much as a buzzing fly or gnat whirred in the hot air. Herrick, with his hand still covering his eyes, felt oppressed and stifled by the intense silence which, like some heavy pall, seemed to overhang the house. The heat was almost beyond endurance. Was it possible, he wondered, that every one of the windows was open? He thought he would softly make the round of that suite of rooms, and see if a little more air was not to be had.

Before, however, he could put his resolve into execution, tired nature asserted itself—as well it might, after the heavy strain it had that day been called upon to endure—his head sank back upon the cushions of his high-backed chair, his arm dropped limply to his side, and he fell into a heavy, though uneasy slumber.

XVIII

Lois, on the upper floor, tossing restlessly on her bed, felt, like Herrick, oppressed by the great and sudden stillness which had seemed to fall upon the house.

"It is the coming of the Angel of Death," she said to herself. "All creation sinks into silence before him. Perhaps even now he stands upon the doorstep." And acting as she ever did upon impulses for which she could offer no reason, she sprang from her bed, flung wide her casement, and peered into the outer darkness as if she expected her eyes there and then to be greeted by some strange and awful sight.

Lady Joan, keeping her drear night-watch in the room below, was likewise conscious of the sudden lull which seemed to have fallen upon creation, and which seemed something other than the herald of an approaching storm. As she sat there, a mute watcher beside the dying man, with eyes fixed, strange to say, not upon his pain-stricken features, but upon a small table at the foot of the bed, the thoughts of her heart seemed in that intense stillness to speak as with living voice to her:

"Southmoor to be sold! Only that feeble useless life in the other room between you and wealth that would buy Southmoor thrice over! Thirty years of bondage for nothing! And there in that little bottle on that table is aconite enough to end that feeble life a dozen times over."

This was about the pith of those thoughts which, with ceaseless iteration, had rung in her ears, and which now seemed to be, as it were, proclaiming themselves from a housetop.

That hard-featured Yorkshire woman with a handkerchief tied over her head, who sat like a wooden piece of furniture in a farther corner, must surely hear them, and would presently start up and put that bottle under lock and key. John, too, as he lay so white and still, possibly caught the gist of them in some troubled dream; and that was why ever and anon his breathing grew so painful and laboured. Herrick, even, in the other room, must be conscious of what was making such a racket in her brain, and would presently rush in and call her a—ah!

Lady Joan, with a start, put her hands over her ears. Would to Heaven the storm would break, the thunder crash over the house, and put to flight this awful stillness! It seemed to her as if all creation had suddenly ceased its own work on purpose to spy in upon her at hers.

This was a terror for which she had not bargained when she had made out her programme for the night.

She rose unsteadily to her feet. She felt she must break the spell of that terrible stillness, or else succumb to it utterly. A word with Herrick in the next room might put all her weird fancies to flight. Why was he, too, so still and silent in there? How was it that never a sound of movement came from the other side of the door?

As she pushed open that door her question was answered. There sat Herrick, leaning back in his chair, locked in sleep. He looked pale and worn; his brow was knotted into a deep frown. Most mothers, looking down thus on a sleeping son, would have yearned to kiss the sad young face.

"My boy! my boy! Would to Heaven I alone could bear this sorrow!" would have been the cry of most mothers' hearts. Not so Lady Joan. Her thoughts flowed in another current. She took his measure, so to speak, and appraised him as calmly as if he were an utter stranger. How like to her own people he looked, with his handsome, clean-cut features, and dark-brown wavy hair! Why, there were at least a dozen Herricks to be found in the picture gallery at Southmoor; some in Elizabethan, some in Cavalier, and others in Jacobean dress. What in life could be more suitable than that he should marry a daughter of her house and settle down at Southmoor as a representative of the race? What in life would have been more likely to come about if he could have been earlier separated from the baleful *bourgeois* influence of the old grandfather who, even in his dying hour, was bent on encouraging the young man's infatuated passion for a girl of no birth and breeding?

Here a sudden change of expression swept over Lady Joan's face; for the light of the one lamp which hung above Herrick's head was caught and refracted by a half hoop of diamonds and rubies on his finger exactly similar to one she had noted upon Lois White's hand as it had rested in old Mr. Gaskell's clasp.

Her lips tightened.

What would be the end of all this, if she were to remain quiescent and inactive in this crisis of his life and her own? Now, supposing she were to go to him—not today nor tomorrow, but at some future time—and say: "Herrick, Southmoor is to be sold." Would he at once exclaim; "Mother, let us give up this odiously new place and detestable plebeian trade, buy the old acres, and settle down in your own county among your own people!" No, a thousand times no! Would he not be much

CATHERINE LOUISA PIRKIS

more likely to say, as his father and grandfather had before him; "it would be Quixotic to invest money in such a non-paying concern."

Lady Joan turned sharply away. Instead, however, of going back direct to her husband's room, she went out by another door, and along the corridor towards old Mr. Gashell's room.

And if one passing along that corridor had chanced to meet her in her clinging grey draperies, he would not have needed to say; "Who is this approaching with weird white face and gleaming eyes?" but would rather have exclaimed; "Where is her knife hidden? Why, here is Atropos herself!"

Whether embodied or otherwise, Fate assuredly must have been abroad in the Castle that night. For there was Lois overhead flinging wide her casement and peering out into the dark, silent world for some invisible nameless terror; there had been Herrick saying to himself over and over again: "I must keep watch tonight not over two, but over three;" and yet Lady Joan, with steady, silent footsteps, went her way without let or hindrance to old Mr. Gaskell's room.

Parsons lifted her head as Lady Joan entered and rubbed her eyes, for the old body had been indulging in a quiet nap in her easy-chair between the intervals of her attendance upon her patient.

She made a little stumble and a rush towards the table on which stood cups and glasses containing beef-tea, eggs and milk, or other nutritive food.

Lady Joan laid her hand upon her arm.

"Wait a moment, don't disturb him. I want you to go downstairs for me—give him that when you come back. What is it?"

"Beef-tea, my lady! Downstairs, my lady? It won't keep me away from the sick-room long, will it, my lady? For Dr. Scott he did say to me the last thing, my lady, 'Parsons,' he said, 'everything depends on you tonight—give the food and medicine regularly, and—'"

"It won't keep you five minutes out of the sick-room; and I will stay here till you return. There is a storm coming, as perhaps you know."

"Yes, my lady."

"Very well. Mr. Herrick's dog, Argus, has no doubt as usual been left by him in the outer hall; the dog has a terror of thunderstorms, and with the first peal will begin to howl so terribly we shall hear him here. I want you to take him down to the servants' hall at the other side of the house, and shut him in for the remainder of the night. Stay a moment! Jervis can go with you if you are afraid to go about the house alone in the middle of the night. I would ask Mr. Herrick to do this, but he has fallen asleep in the other room, and I do not like to disturb him."

As Parsons and the other nurse departed in company, Lady Joan, softly looking in upon Herrick, saw that he still soundly slept.

After this her movements became hurried and nervous; one look she gave to her still unconscious husband. Was it her fancy, or was his breathing growing fainter and less regular than it had been before? She took possession of the small phial of aconite which stood on the bedside table, and made her way once more to old Mr. Gaskell's room; this time passing, not by way of the corridor, but through the intermediate room. Time was precious; three minutes it would take those two women to reach the outer hall, ten minutes must be allowed to their slow middle-aged movements for reaching the servants' hall on the other side of the house, fastening in the dog, and returning to their post. But no more; it would be rash to allow even a half minute more than this.

She approached the bedside of the old man slowly, stealthily. Mute, motionless, helpless he lay; his faint, hurried breathing much the same as that of a tired child sinking to sleep after a day of play which has over-taxed his strength. His head and shoulders were propped high on his pillows, his face showed grey and sunken against the white linen; his silvery hair, pushed back from his brow, left every wrinkle bare to view. The contour of his head was noble and impressive, and was thrown into bold relief by the purple satin curtains which canopied the bed, and the purple satin quilt which covered it. Lady Joan could easily have persuaded herself that she was looking down on some dead king lying in state; so regal and motionless the old man looked amid his costly surroundings.

She took the cup of beef-tea which Parsons had placed ready for her patient, and with the phial of aconite in her other hand, went into the room which intervened between the rooms of the two invalids.

This intermediate room was lighted only by a single lamp, turned low. Lady Joan with her cup and phial, stood beneath it. Her hand was perfectly steady now; every nerve in it seemed made of steel.

Yet that terrible stillness around, here, there, everywhere! Not so much as a ticking clock within, nor "lisp of leaves" without to drown the clamour of her own thoughts, which once more seemed to cry aloud to her.

"Now or never, Joan," those thoughts seemed to say now. "Wait till the morning, and your chance is gone! Strike for your freedom, Joan;

shake off your manacles! Why should you serve thirty years in bondage for nothing?"

One, two, three drops of the poison fell into the cup.

Hush! What was that? For a moment her hand paused, and her heart seemed to stand still. She looked hastily round. Ah! it was only the big yellow rose in a jar on a side-table falling to pieces. But her nerves had been shaken; her hand trembled; and now the poison drops fell uncounted into the cup.

Hush! Another sound. The door opening, was it? Once more Lady Joan looked round with terror in her eyes. Assuredly the door of the room—the door that opened into the corridor—had been softly opened, and softly, hurriedly closed again.

She set down her phial and cup, and went out hastily into the corridor. It could not be the nurses returned already, she thought, as she strained her eyes right and left along the long, dark passage. In view of possible emergency, this passage had been left dimly lighted at one end, the end at which she stood. Amid the deepening shadows at the farther end she thought she saw a fluttering white skirt disappearing round the bend of the staircase.

Lady Joan's thoughts flew to Lucy Harwood and her somnambulistic tendencies. No doubt tonight, as on the previous night, the girl had come down the staircase and gone along the corridor, feeling her way, and looking for the person or thing whereon her mind was set. Most likely the touch on the cold door-handle had thrilled and awakened her, and she had hastily fled, fearing to encounter Lady Joan's anger.

"She must be taken in hand tomorrow," said Lady Joan, setting her lips tightly together. "In the dim light, and in her half-sleeping state, she can have seen nothing definite."

Moments were getting precious now. Lady Joan swiftly and softly went back to her phial and cup of beef-tea; the one she replaced on the bedside table, the other she carried straight to old Mr. Gaskell's room. She paused for an instant in the doorway to ascertain if his slumber were still unbroken. Then, swiftly and softly still, she approached his bedside. With one hand she covered her eyes, with the other she set down the cup of beef-tea on the small table.

One wistful, pathetic look from those blue eyes, which recalled at times so vividly the look in another pair of dying eyes, and she felt that her dread purpose might remain unfulfilled.

XIX

Two o'clock struck in succession softly and sonorously, or briskly and blithely, from a variety of clocks in different parts of the Castle.

Herrick, with a start, awoke and jumped from his chair. All his fears, anxieties, and forebodings came back upon him in a rush. He had been sleeping for an hour! What might not have happened in that hour! He went at once and hastily into the adjoining room.

The nurse came forward to meet him.

"I was about to call you, sir," she said. "I fear Lady Joan's strength is giving way; and I fear, too, a change has taken place in your father."

"Go, call Dr. Scott immediately," was Herrick's reply; and then he went to his father's side and took his hand in his.

Yes, the pulse beat more feebly now; a slight change, a more rigid look, had come into the grey, drawn face. His breathing, however, was as before—hard and laboured.

Lady Joan, at the foot of the bed, seemed clinging, as if for support, to the brass rail.

Herrick poured out a glass of wine and took it to her.

"Drink this, mother, or your strength will altogether give way," he said.

Her face appeared to him strangely flushed; her eyes shone with an unnatural light. She drank the wine—eagerly, it seemed to him—and as she gave him back the glass he could see that she was trembling from head to foot, and that the support of the foot-rail of the bed was a necessity to her.

At that moment his attention was diverted from Lady Joan by a sudden, uneasy movement of his father's arm which lay upon the coverlet. His hard, laboured breathing, also, suddenly ceased; his eyes opened wide, and fixed, with an odd, startled look in them, on the door which led through the ante-room to old Mr. Gaskell's room. Slowly, slowly, his eyes, still with the odd, startled look in them, moved, as if following the motion of someone walking from that door towards the other end of the room.

Lady Joan, standing still at the foot of the bed, seized Herrick's arm in a state of nervous terror.

Clear, slow, and stern, at that moment came John Gaskell's voice from the bed.

"Stand back Joan," he said, "and let my father pass."

At the same instant the door of old Mr. Gaskell's room opened, and Parsons, looking white and flurried, came in.

"Oh, my lady," she whispered, in a quaking voice, "Mr. Gaskell has just breathed his last. I went to his side a moment ago, and saw that he was sinking rapidly. I had not time to call you or Mr. Herrick before he was gone."

Lady Joan made a strange acknowledgment of the sad tidings. She still trembled from head to foot; her hands, clay cold, still clutched at Herrick's arm; but she contrived to control her voice sufficiently to say:

"Let there be no mistake, Parsons. At once write down the exact hour and minute at which Mr. Gaskell died."

XX

The storm which had so long threatened broke before day dawned; thunder, lightning, hail, and rain came in one terrific outburst. The sky had the whole of the grandeur and beauty of the storm to itself; for in this low-lying country there were no sharp-peaked mountains to rip open the packed clouds and make them discharge their cargoes of fire, nor amphitheatre of hills to throw back an echo to the loud-voiced thunder.

The racket of the storm set the household at the Castle stirring at an early hour. The first crash of thunder sent Lois down on her knees praying for all poor souls in danger or distress; and there she remained, with hands covering her face, until the last peal had growled itself out in the far distance where daylight was faintly breaking.

There were two sleepers in the Castle that night, however, for whom it mattered little whether the thunder growled high or growled low— John Gaskell and his aged father.

After those brief, stern words addressed to his wife, John Gaskell never spoke again, and within two hours from the time at which his father had died he breathed his last.

Lois, coming downstairs, dressed ready to set off for Summerhill, had the sad news told her by Lucy Harwood, who chanced to be crossing the corridor at the moment.

A door on her right hand suddenly opening, led her to hope that her eager longing to clasp Herrick's hand, to look up in Herrick's face with eyes that spoke their sympathy, was to be gratified. She turned hastily round, and her heart fell, for not Herrick, but Lady Joan stood before her.

No pale, heavy-eyed watcher this, such as one might expect to see issue forth from a chamber of death, but a woman with bright, tearless eyes, hard-set mouth, and two brilliant spots of red on either cheek.

She closed the door behind her with a steady hand. The room she had just quitted was old Mr. Gaskell's room; she had nerved herself to pass through it on her way to the corridor, without so much as turning her head away from the white-swathed form lying still and silent beneath the purple-curtained bed.

Thirty years ago Lady Joan, as she had heard the door close behind Vaughan Elliot, had said to herself, "That man must go at once and for ever out of my life." Now as she closed this door behind her, the same

CATHERINE LOUISA PIRKIS

words were in her heart. "What is past is past," she said to herself. "This man must go as utterly out of my life as that other did."

But the remorselessness of the tearing, ravening beast of prey is not attained by the human animal without cost. Lois, as she looked at the hectic spots on either cheek, and noted the feverish, dancing eyes, said to herself:

"She will break down before night. Ah, if only I could be a help and comfort to Herrick's mother!"

Lady Joan's first words were addressed to Lucy, not Lois.

"You are up singularly early—how is this?" was all that she said; but the voice which spoke the words had a ring of iron in it.

Both the girls shrank from her instinctively. Lucy looked confused and frightened.

Lady Joan repeated her question, fixing what seemed to Lois a hard, scrutinising look upon the girl's face.

"I had bad dreams, my lady—I could not sleep," answered Lucy, "and so I thought it better to get up, and come down."

"Quite so. I shall have something to say to you presently about those bad dreams of yours. Go into my boudoir, I will speak to you there."

Lucy hurriedly departed. Then Lady Joan addressed Lois: "I see you are ready to go. I will give orders for one of the grooms to drive you to Summerhill. No doubt you have well thought over the conversation I had with you yesterday, and have come to the conclusion that the course I advised was the right one."

"Come to the conclusion!" She might as well have asked a rain-cloud, with a hurricane blowing, if it had come to a conclusion whether it would travel east or west, as ask this poor child with her heart counselling one thing, and her conscience another if she had come to any conclusion on the matter.

Words did not come easily to her, so Lady Joan resumed:

"In the course of the day I will send you a cheque that will amply provide for your travelling and other expenses. America I think you said was likely to be your destination. Of course you will lose no time in leaving Summerhill, and I would farther suggest that your letter to my son, breaking off your engagement—that is if one has ever existed—should not be written until after your departure."

Lois looked all around her helplessly. Where was Herrick? How was it that Lady Joan dared speak in this way, as if Herrick were miles away, instead of under the same roof, and perhaps not twenty yards distant?

But Lady Joan knew well enough where Herrick was—kneeling in a stupor of grief beside his dead father, with his warm young hand clasping the clay-cold one, as he had clasped it in the moment of death.

Again she waited for Lois to speak; but as never a word escaped the girl's lips, she went on once more:

"Any details on this matter which may embarrass or trouble you, I shall be very pleased to arrange for you; but I would suggest that all our communications should be by letter—to any letters you may send me I will promptly reply."

Lois gave another hurried look around her. With all those doors in sight, was there no hope of any one of them opening, and Herrick coming forth?

Her eyes drooped beneath Lady Joan's fixed gaze, and she said, timidly, "Before I go this morning, may I say good-bye to old Mr. Gaskell? Herrick promised me last night that I should do so."

A peculiar expression passed over Lady Joan's face. "He was too free with his promises," she said, coldly. "'Old Mr. Gaskell' is dead."

"Dead!" repeated Lois, blankly. Her eyes grew round and startled. She staggered against the wall of the corridor as if her limbs had suddenly failed her and she needed support.

Lady Joan frowned.

"There is nothing surprising in the fact, I suppose. Will you be good enough to tell me what there is in it to affect you so strangely?"

But Lois only grew white and whiter, and kept repeating, with her large startled eyes fixed on Lady Joan's face:

"Dead! dead!"

Lady Joan lost patience.

"My words are easy enough to understand, I imagine. At any rate, I have neither time nor inclination to repeat them. I will wish you good morning. I suppose you are leaving at once?"

Lois clasped her hands together impetuously.

"And you are Herrick's mother!" she cried in a low, passionate voice. "Go! Yes—I will go! I will never look upon your face again in this world if I can help it!"

Then, with an effort, she seemed to gather her strength together, and, with feet that stumbled as she went, she crossed the corridor and went towards the hall-door.

It had already opened that morning to admit and despatch messengers in spite of the storm and the early hour, so its heavy bolts were drawn back, and she could let herself out without difficulty.

Lady Joan for a moment stood watching her.

"An ill-trained, hysterical young woman," she said to herself. "Madly in love with Herrick, not a doubt! Well, so much the better in one way; it gives me a sort of guarantee that she will not mar his future for him!"

And without so much as a thought of what Lois might suffer in the effort "not to mar Herrick's future for him," Lady Joan went on her way to her boudoir, there to question Lucy as to her "bad dreams."

Outside the deluge of rain had ceased, and only a heavy drizzling mist fought with and quenched the brilliance of the early dawn.

It was about half-past five when Lois passed through the park-gates and gained the high road, which ran a very river of mud. Her feet were wet through before she had gone a quarter of a mile towards Summerhill. She shivered from head to foot, yet her cheeks burned and her eyes glowed and danced as if from fever. Her steps grew swift and swifter, as if a matter of life or death hung upon her speed. Her breath came in quick gasps; the drizzling, heavy mist seemed to choke her; all sorts of strange noises were humming and buzzing in her ear, yet on and on she went with ever-increasing speed till she gained the cross-roads which lay between the Catholic church of St. Elizabeth and the private road leading to Summerhill.

Then, from sheer want of breath, the girl was compelled to pause. So far along her road she had met no one, not even a farm-labourer or gipsy tramp. Now, as she leaned for a moment against a wet, mossy fence, and tried to think where she was going, what she meant to do, she could distinctly hear the sound of approaching footsteps.

Something else, besides approaching footsteps, made itself heard above the rush and murmur of strange sounds in her ear—the tolling of St. Elizabeth's bell.

She started, and for a moment felt puzzled and bewildered. Then, as her thoughts began to clear themselves, she recollected what Father Elliot had said to her about the early and other services which he intended holding daily. And, lifting her eyes, she saw the Father himself approaching by a lane which led from his cottage straight to his church. He saw and recognised her immediately.

"Good morning! You are an early riser!" he said, as he crossed the road towards her. Then as her tearful, scared face caught his eye, he added, in a changed tone: "My child, what is it? What has happened? Tell me."

Lois clung to his arm.

"Help me! help me!" she cried, piteously. "I want a hiding-place!"

XXI

At whatever cost secured, Lady Joan's calmness, as she cross-questioned Lucy as to her "bad dreams," presented a marked contrast to the manner of the girl, who was flurried and nervous to a degree, and seemed utterly incapable of giving a clear account of her broken rest of over-night.

"I have no recollection whatever what my dreams were, my lady," she reiterated. "Indeed, indeed, they have quite gone out of my mind."

"Do you ever have any recollection of your bad dreams when the morning comes?" asked Lady Joan, bending a curious look on her.

"Oh, yes, my lady, when I wake up and find myself in a strange place."

"Then you are in the habit of walking in your sleep?"

The girl grew confused. She had evidently been surprised into making this admission.

"Not in the habit. Oh no, my lady. I have done so once or twice in my life," she said, after a moment's pause.

"When did you last walk in your sleep—I mean before you came here?" pursued Lady Joan.

"About a year ago, my lady."

"Well, and you woke up and found yourself—where?"

"In the churchyard, my lady," said the girl, and her eyelids drooped; her colour changed again.

"In the churchyard! Then, of course, you recollected the dream which had sent you there?"

The girl hung her head lower still. She was evidently too frightened of Lady Joan to refuse to reply, and too truthful to prevaricate. So she answered, falteringly: "I dreamt I was looking for—for someone's name on a gravestone, and I suppose in my sleep I got up, put on my hat and cloak, and walked to the churchyard—it was the touch of the cold gravestones which woke me."

She nearly broke down as she finished speaking. Lady Joan, however, went on mercilessly as before.

"And I suppose, when I met you two nights ago in the hall walking and talking in your sleep, you had been dreaming of the same person, and had come down from your room in search of him or her?"

"Ye-es, my lady."

"Now be so good as to fix your mind steadily for a moment on the thoughts which filled your brain when you went to bed last night, and see if you cannot recall some vestige of those bad dreams which made you get up so unconscionably early this morning?"

But the question was a useless one. Lucy's only rejoinder to it was a repetition of her assertion that here her memory failed her altogether.

So Lady Joan resumed her cross-examination at another point.

"Have you ever," she said, still steadily eyeing the girl, "walked in your sleep, and—having no recollection of so doing—been told of it afterwards by someone who had seen you?"

"Yes, my lady," answered Lucy hesitatingly. "If I wake up in my bed in the morning I have no recollection of what I have done in the night—I mean, I cannot tell whether I have really done a thing or have only dreamt it"

"Ah-h." And here Lady Joan drew a long breath, and thought awhile. After all, the danger might be less than she had imagined it to be. Lucy had perhaps opened and shut the dressing-room door in her sleep, and in her sleep had returned to her room and got into bed. It might be this, or it might be that the girl was so accustomed to prevaricate and tell falsehoods as to her somnambulistic propensities—about which she appeared to be very sensitive—that she was able to give an air of veracity to her narrative which a less-practised story-teller would have found an impossibility. In any case, it would be as well to keep an eye on the girl for the present, and in a variety of ways at different intervals to test the truth of her narrative.

So, after a few moments of thought, she said in a less stern voice than that in which she had pursued her interrogations:

"You may go now. Later on I will speak to you again. I think, as I told you before, that you should have medical advice. And I will like to see your—your—I forget, father or brother, was it?"

"Brother, my lady."

"Your brother, and speak to him on the matter. Write to him in the course of the day, and tell him I wish him to come here to see me."

"As the girl withdrew, Herrick's voice was heard outside the door, asking her:

"Is Lady Joan here?"

The question gave Lady Joan time to withdraw her thoughts from Lucy to the matter on which, without a doubt, Herrick had come to interrogate her.

Most mothers and sons meeting thus within a few hours of the death of husband and father, would have been in each other's arms in a moment, and tears and kisses would have done duty for any amount of spoken sympathy.

Not so this mother and son. Their common sorrow had been no "cord of love" to draw them nearer to each other, but rather a measure that enabled them to gauge the distance they stood apart. When, at the moment of his father's death, Herrick's voice had rung forth its one passionate cry of rebellion against the iron law which made death, not life, the ruler of the Universe, Lady Joan had stood by saying never a word; and when he had knelt in a stupor of grief, clasping his dead father's hand, she had quietly left the room, bent on her own business and on dismissing from the house the girl he loved.

The young man looked white, dazed, forlorn as he entered the room. He bent one long, scrutinising look on his mother. The terrible suspicion of her wavering reason which he had found himself compelled to entertain overnight had not yet faded from his mind, and he was in hopes that the morning light might put it to flight.

Lady Joan's flushed face and brilliant eyes were scarcely reassuring.

"I thought you had gone to your room to lie down, mother," he said, still prepared to show her any amount of kindness, though tenderness in the circumstances could scarcely be expected of him.

Then he put the question she was prepared for.

"Have you seen Lois this morning? Or is she not stirring yet?"

"Pardon me, Lady Joan. One moment!" said Dr. Scott, coming into the room in a great hurry, "will you kindly tell me what has become of the aconite and other liniments which were in use in the sick-room overnight? The nurses seem to know nothing about them."

"I have locked up all the medicines and liniments in my medicine-cupboard," said Lady Joan, calmly; "I do not like such deadly poisons lying about."

"Ah, quite so! Then it is all right," said the doctor, as he withdrew.

Then Lady Joan turned to Herrick:

"I saw her about half-an-hour ago," she replied, "just as she was leaving."

"Leaving!" exclaimed Herrick, incredulously; "she surely cannot have gone without a word to me!"

"She seemed in a hurry to get home. She came down with her hat on. I told her I would give orders for someone to drive her home; but she evidently preferred walking."

With an exclamation of annoyance, Herrick turned and left the room. The thing seemed to him easy enough to understand. Lois, in compliance with his wish that she should return to Summerhill that day, had come down stairs prepared to depart; and, on the look out for him, had been met by Lady Joan. Some cold and formal speech had scared the timid girl, and she had fled precipitately. Lady Joan's stately "I beg your pardon," had sufficed to put her to flight on a former occasion; most likely some equally trivial speech, spoken with equally frigid emphasis, had done the deed now. What a nervous, impulsive child she was! How marvellous it seemed that his mother's heart had not opened towards her, and her strong nature yearned to protect her, as most strong natures yearn to protect the fragile and weak!

Sick at heart, and sick at brain, and though the muscles of his hand almost refused to guide his pen, he nevertheless sat down at once and despatched a few loving lines to Lois—a tender chiding for her hurried flight, a hint of his own weariness and sadness and a promise that, when his week of dreary duties had come to an end, he would at once repair to Summerhill, for he had many things to talk over with her.

The "many things" to Herrick's mind represented Lois's resignation of her post in Mrs. Leyton's household, and the selection of a suitable home for her, in the house of some intimate friends of his own, until the wedding-day could be definitely fixed.

He did not expect a reply to this letter; for as yet he and Lois had not fallen into the habit—so dear to lovers—of making trifles an excuse for correspondence.

Before nightfall his vexation at Lois's abrupt departure had to give way to other and more pressing claims upon his time and thought; for Lady Joan had broken down utterly, and the arrangement of all matters, small and great, devolved upon him. Lady Joan was found by her maid lying upon her bed in a high state of fever, and half unconscious. Before evening delirium set in. Upon which, Parsons, the faithful old creature that she was, at once took possession of the sickroom, carefully keeping every one, except Dr. Scott, on the other side of the door.

"Poor soul, poor soul," said the doctor next morning to the old nurse. "It's only what one might expect. I suppose, last night, Parsons, she raved incessantly about her dead husband?"

"My lady's ravings," answered the discreet Parsons, "were mostly incoherent; and when she did say a word I could understand, it was not worth remembering."

And the shrewd look which she gave the doctor as she said this, might have been understood to mean:

"I know my place, Dr. Scott, and I know yours; and I don't intend to make my lady the talk of the town in order to gratify your curiosity."

END OF VOLUME I

VOLUME II

I

For nearly a week Lady Joan lay on her bed in a state of semi-consciousness. During that week the little village churchyard, which had already received the poor maimed and scorched collier lads, once more swung back its lych-gate to give its six feet or so of quiet earth to John Gaskell and his father.

And the country-side mourned for the two, just as they had mourned for the collier lads who were their own kith and kin.

Not a man, woman, or child far or near but what, one way or another, paid their tribute of affection and respect. Crowds lined the road along which the funeral cortège passed, and church and churchyard were filled with mourners of every degree.

Herrick's gaze wandered in vain down the aisle for Lois's sweet face in her accustomed place in church. One look from her tender, tearful eyes he felt would say more to him than the volumes of letters of condolence of which he had been the recipient during the week, and which had seemed to go over his heart like an iron harrow as he had read them.

A flash of painful thought brought before him Lois's dependent position in a not too orderly household, a position which compelled her to make her inclinations bow to her duties. Following the thought came the sudden, angry impulse, to end as quickly as possible so intolerable a condition of things.

And then he pulled himself together sharply, rebuking himself for thoughts which, in the circumstances, seemed a treachery to the newly-dead.

This, in some sort had been Herrick's frame of mind during the past week—a week in which the most trivial and the most momentous details of life and death had jostled and elbowed each other with hideous and jarring familiarity. Lady Joan's illness had doubled and trebled his anxieties and responsibilities. The colliery disaster and its consequences in ordinary circumstances would have claimed every minute of his time from morning till night. Now, in addition, all sorts of duties, trivial and tiresome, ponderous and sad, pressed upon him hour by hour.

One duty most unwelcome to him at the moment was that of playing host to his uncle and cousin, who arrived from Southmoor two days after his father's death.

Lord Southmoor was not a little discontented at the necessity which had driven him from his ancestral, if dilapidated, home into the mushroom grandeur of Longridge Castle.

"You can absolutely smell the wealth," he said, turning to his daughter, as he entered the wide hall, and threw a contemptuous glance around at its sumptuous furnishing.

"Yes, I can," she answered, with a little laugh, "as the fox did the grapes—covetously."

"She enters the house of death with a jest," thought Herrick, as he advanced to meet her, reading her manner easily enough, though he was out of ear-shot of her words.

He was not prepared to give these relatives of his a very warm welcome; he needed no telling of the light in which the Earl regarded his father and grandfather. He had not seen any of his mother's people since his early college days, and the impression they had left upon his mind then was renewed now.

"He is an effeminate counterpart of my mother," was his terse summing-up of the Earl—using the adjective advisedly.

And "she is the most self-assertive young woman I have ever met," was his equally terse summing-up of his cousin; which speech on Herrick's lips meant a great deal, for, of all objectional types of womanhood, the self-assertive was to him the most objectionable.

There was no gainsaying the fact, however. The Lady Honor's appearance alone justified the epithet.

To begin with, her hair was the brightest red in tint—one seemed to see it before anything else as she entered a room. It was not the "rich ripe red" which artists love to paint, and poets to sing, but of that very violent hue commonly dubbed "carrots." Her eyes were red-brown, round and prominent, with a fixed look in them; her mouth was large, showing large white teeth; her nose was short, her cheek-bones high. In figure she was plump, and fairly tall, with large hands and feet. Her voice matched her appearance—it was loud and ringing—and her manner was frank and a trifle domineering.

During the first day of her arrival, it seemed to Herrick that it was with great difficulty she subdued herself to a frame of mind suitable to a house of mourning and woe. Yet she did her best to be sympathetic.

"Poor Aunt Jo! No wonder she's cut up!" she said, more than once, when she was told of Lady Joan's illness.

Herrick stared at her.

"Aunt Jo!" "Cut up!"

Was it possible that the girl could be speaking of his mother, lying unconscious on her bed upstairs with her life well nigh beaten out of her with sorrow!

He made no reply, but mentally thanked Heaven that his Lois was not like this abrupt, loud-voiced damsel. He furthermore resolved that cousin though she might be, he would see as little as possible of her during her stay in the house—a task of no difficulty this with the thousand and one matters that claimed his attention from morning till night.

Even on the solemn day of the double funeral, five minutes of quiet and seclusion seemed to be begrudged him.

Weary and dispirited, he had gone to his "den" seeking a respite from sad thoughts by penning a few lines to Lois. But his pen could not put into words how he hungered and thirsted for his darling, or with what passionate desire he longed to feel once more the touch of her soft hand on his hair, and to hear her sweet voice saying: "My poor, poor boy! If only I could bear this for you!" So he wisely determined that his words should be few; just as many, in fact, as would tell her that he would be with her on the morrow immediately after breakfast, and bid her, at all cost secure an uninterrupted half-hour for their talk.

But his words, few as they were, were not to be written in peace. The inevitable rap-rap—which betokened business—came to his door. Into the mists vanished sweet Lois's dimpled face, and in its stead there stood confronting him the round head and clean-shaven chin of Mr. McGowan, the representative of the firm which, for over fifty years, had conducted the legal business of the Gaskell family.

With a profusion of apologies Mr. McGowan introduced the purport of his visit: when would Mr. Gaskell be able to give him a morning for the discussion of the arrangement of important business details respecting the valuation of the estate?

"Valuation!" Herrick repeated the words blankly. "I'm afraid I'm all at sea."

"I suppose there is no will," said the lawyer, beginning to fear that young Mr. Gaskell was not half so good a man of business as his father had been before him.

"Will! No, there could be no sense in making one so long as my grandfather lived."

"It's most unfortunate that things should have happened as they have. The absence of a will so greatly complicates matters," said the lawyer.

Herrick drew a long breath.

"Forgive me; I'm beginning to understand. My head is not quite clear for this matter just now. Whenever it has come into my mind I have always taken it for granted that things would go on the same as before."

He sighed wearily. An endless vista of intricate law business seemed to open before his mind's eye now.

"If Mr. Gaskell could have foreseen such an emergency as this, no doubt he would have made preparation for it. It might be as well to ask Lady Joan if she knows of any document—will it could hardly be called—of her husband's drawing up," said the lawyer.

"My mother insists on getting up, if only for a few hours, tomorrow; but I shall scarcely like, yet awhile, to trouble her on this matter," said Herrick. "Any such document would, I should say, as a matter of course, have been deposited with you."

"I have been close upon twenty years in the firm now," said Mr. McGowan, "and assuredly it has not been deposited with us in my time: but search shall be made in the Gaskell safe in my strong-room. The papers have been accumulating there rapidly of late years."

And with this testimony to the increased and increasing wealth of the Gaskell family, the lawyer departed, leaving Herrick free to conjure up the image of sweet Lois once more.

II

If, as the poet bids us to do, we counted time "by heart-throbs," some of us would out-live Methuselah in less than a fortnight. Lady Joan stood once more at her boudoir window, asking herself vaguely, dreamily, if creation could be only older by seven days since she had last looked out on that little glade, with its copse of hazel and wild plum. Was it only seven days since she sank back on her pillows, with all sorts of hideous voices ringing in her ears, and all sorts of unknown terrors knocking at her heart? Yet so it was. Seven days had been time and enough to spare to drag this woman through a burning fiery furnace of delirious terror; time enough and to spare to confront her with actual facts, and possible consequences, beside which the fiery furnace of her delirium seemed like a heavenly vision; time enough and to spare for her to learn the terrible lesson that what was past was past, and no power, human or divine, could undo it; time enough to set the iron of those three little words, "no going back," eating into her very soul.

Yet from her own lips no human being would ever hear the story of those seven days. Those about her no doubt would sooner or later remark that "my lady had sadly changed since her illness." Parsons, by-and-by when she goes for a week's holiday to her married nephew, will, in the sanctity of the little parlour behind the grocer's shop, let fall mysterious hints as to the strange language "my lady" used when her fever was at its height. "She cursed her soul, did my lady," the old body will say, "she declared herself shut out of Heaven, poor dear; but it's my belief that one half of it was the chloroform the doctors are so fond of giving nowadays." But on Lady Joan's own lips would be set a seal of silence, never to be broken in this world.

Herrick, during that seven days' illness had on the whole seen but little of his mother. For some unaccountable reason his presence in her room had seemed to disturb her, so he had wisely curtailed his visits to her as much as possible.

On the first day of her sitting up, when he went in to wish her "good morning," he started back aghast at the change which a few days had wrought in her.

"This was not my mother a week ago," he thought, with a twinge of pain; "a week ago her hair was as brown as mine, now it is as white as snow! A week ago she—ah! What is it? Wherein is the change?" He abruptly cut short his wonderings, saying to himself that it was the white hair surmounted by the conventional widow's cap, which made her look so unlike herself; for in his heart lurked a coward dread of raising once more the spectre of that hideous suspicion of her wavering reason, which he had done his best to put to rest.

Herrick and his mother were not given to much outward demonstration of affection; but he kissed her this morning with a warmth unusual with him, and said how glad he was to find her better. Then he delivered a message—considerably curtailed from its original prosy stiffness—from Lord Southmoor much to the same effect; and a second greeting from Lady Honor—this, a not too literal translation from its original, free-and-easy heartiness.

Lastly, he had something to say on his own account: he was going over to Summerhill that morning, and he asked if she had any message to give him for Lois. This was the manner in which, after due consideration, he chose to convey to her the intimation that Lois's position as his future wife must henceforward be formally acknowledged.

Lady Joan frowned; her manner grew frigid. Her reply was two words:

"None whatever."

Then she turned her face away from him, and steadily looked out upon the September landscape.

The long drought and subsequent heavy rains had brought autumn upon them early. Damp, rotting leaves lay in bushels under the park trees; the flowers in the parterre, immediately below the windows, looked beaten and draggled. Overhead there was no glorious burning expanse of blue, but an even spread of silver-grey, here and there browned to a tarnished silver by struggling sunshine.

"To everything there is a season," thought Lady Joan. "Now the time to die is coming. This is as it should be. If leaves hang too long upon a tree, driving rain or hurrying winds sweep them away; otherwise what would become of the spring greenery?"

Herrick stood for a moment looking at her a little sorrowfully, a little wistfully. His heart yearned to comfort her in her sorrow. Why would she not let him? Why would she insist on building up this wall of ice between them? Why did she not turn her head, and modify, if not retract, her heartless words?

But her eyes, still steadily fixed on the misty park, with its rotting leaves, seemed to betoken that she had almost forgotten his presence.

CATHERINE LOUISA PIRKIS

"Just as it should be," her thoughts ran.

"In Nature there is the autumn mist and hurrying wind, which put an end to the things whose course is run; among men there are the strong souls who stand out here and there in a generation and say 'this or that life is useless, and must be blotted out.'"

But Herrick had grown tired of waiting.

"No message did you say, mother?" he asked, a little impatiently.

"None whatever."

He would not invite the ungracious words to be said a third time, so he hastily left the room.

Half-way downstairs, a rush of skirts, a scamper, and a stumble told him that his cousin was behind him, and was coming downstairs, as he had heard her more than once before, a succession of small jumps.

"Herrick! Herrick!" she shouted. "Stop a minute. How is Aunt Jo? And what are you going to do with yourself this morning?"

Aunt Jo again! It seemed as apt a designation for Lady Joan as Betsy might have been for Lady Macbeth!

Herrick drew back into a recess, to allow his cousin to pass down the stairs before him.

"My mother is better, thank you. I hope in a day or two she will be quite herself again, and able to entertain you."

Lady Honor swooped down the stairs in front of him. On the bottom step she caught her foot, and fell forward headlong on top of Herrick's big mastiff, who couched there, waiting to accompany his master on the ride which he scented in the air.

There ensued profuse apologies to the mastiff, diversified by frank little speeches addressed to Herrick.

"Did she hurt its little paw then!"—the "little paw" was about the size of a lioness's—"she's in a bad frame of mind, Argus—been kept indoors for days, and doesn't know what to do with herself." Then to Herrick: "Someone must take charge of me today, or something dreadful will happen." Then to Argus: "He'd ask me to go out riding with him if he only knew how I long for a scamper." Then to Herrick: "I won't answer for the consequences if I'm again left to my own devices till dinner-time."

Her frank, easy manner almost—not quite—precluded the idea that flirtation was intended. Although Lady Joan had never in so many words expressed her wishes concerning her niece to Herrick, the idea, so to speak, had been "in the air," and he had caught scent of it. Honor, it was just possible, might be of one mind with Lady Joan on this matter. It was not a thought he liked to entertain; but there it was, and he could not help it.

So he said, a little formally, perhaps:

"I'm very sorry, Honor, that I can't ask you to accompany me this morning; some other time I shall be delighted."

"And I'm verry sory, too," said Honor, in the same frank tone as before; "because, as I told you, mischief will come of it if I'm shut in here the whole morning with myself to entertain myself. I shall have to look up Aunt Jo—"

"No, no," interrupted Herrick, "don't do that! I mean my mother is not well enough yet to—to—"

"To stand my noise and chatter, I suppose you mean, only you're too polite to say so. Well, then, since I may not do that, will you be good enough to tell me what I may do by way of diversion while you're enjoying your canter this morning?"

Herrick's face showed his annoyance. Diversion! If she wanted diversion why had she come to a house of mourners? Music, of course, was out of the question, or he would have referred her to the music-room with its variety of instruments. Riding, unless some sober-minded person could be found to ride alongside of her, he did not care to suggest, as well for her own sake as for that of the animal she might ride.

"What is your father going to do this morning? He might perhaps like to ride or drive. You have only to give your orders, you know," he said, after a moment's pause.

"That's a delightful phrase! It suggests Aladdin and the genius of the lamp at once! But of course you said it ironically! My father, at the present moment, thinks he is reading in the library. That is to say, he has chosen—no, the butler and two footmen have chosen for him— he has had all three in attendance on him ever since breakfast. Well, these three individuals have selected for him the most comfortable chair in the library, and one of the three has cut all the papers for him, another has placed a table for him, a third has fetched him half-a-dozen books; and at the present moment his legs are crossed, he is leaning back in his chair with a newspaper on his knee, and his eyes half-shut. In that beatific attitude he has requested me to allow him to remain undisturbed."

After this fine flow of words, delivered in as short a space of time as possible, Honor drew a long breath.

CATHERINE LOUISA PIRKIS

Herrick, in spite of himself, felt amused. No, she could not be a flirt! But still, he thanked Heaven that Lois was as unlike her as one woman could well be to another.

"Well," resumed Honor, waiting for him to speak, "what are you going to give me to do? I warn you if you leave me to my own devices, the family name will suffer at my hands. I shall either spend the morning in the stables with the dear horses, or I shall go down into the kitchen and help the scullery-maid, or I shall flirt with one of the footmen—"

"Good Heavens!" interrupted Herrick, more than half in earnest. "You ought to be locked in your own room, and be only allowed out on parole! Have you no letters to write? I thought girls always had any number of 'special correspondents' to whom they indited volumes every morning?"

Honor's cheeks suddenly grew as nearly as possible the colour of her hair. For some unexplained reason she appeared to be unwilling to continue the conversation.

"An idea has suddenly come to me! Adieu! I see you are in a hurry to be off," she said, hurriedly, then kissed her fingers to him, and was gone.

III

The poet who wrote that "Coming events cast their shadows before," gets a flat denial given him at every turn of life's path. This was how Herrick rode forth to Summerhill that morning: depressed, it is true, by mournful memories, solemn with the sense of the responsibilities suddenly laid upon his shoulders, yet withal daring to be joyful in spirit whenever his thoughts turned to Lois and her great love for him.

And this was how he rode back to the Castle, after a brief ten minutes' interview with Mrs. Leyton: sadness and seriousness gone together with his joyfulness, his brain one whirling chaos of anger and gloomy forebodings, the future as much a blank to him as for the nonce the past had become.

His interview with Mrs. Leyton had been as stormy as it had been brief. He had had to wait close upon half an hour before the lady made her appearance, and then she had received him in her robe-de-chambre in her boudoir.

He had lost no time in preliminaries. "The butler tells me Miss White is not here! How is this, Mrs. Leyton? Please explain," he had said as he shook hands.

Whereupon, the little lady had drawn herself up haughtily, and had said: "It is to me, not you, I think that explanations are due."

"I don't understand! Am I dreaming?" Herrick had exclaimed. "Miss White returned here from the Castle, did she not, early on Friday morning last week?"

"Yes," Mrs. Leyton had replied, "and early on Friday morning last week, Miss White thought fit to pack her box, desire one of my grooms to take it to the Wrexford station, and depart, leaving with one of my maids the exceedingly polite message, that 'circumstances compelled her immediate departure,' nothing more."

"Why in Heaven's name, Mrs. Leyton, did you not send round to me?" Herrick had exclaimed, hotly.

"Why in Heaven's name should I have taken the trouble to do such a thing?" the lady had replied, tartly. "I concluded that it was at your instigation that the young lady was behaving in such an extraordinary fashion. You had spoken to me about your wish for her to stay with certain friends of yours till your marriage. I took it for granted that neither you nor she considered farther explanation to me necessary.

I said to my husband, 'This is the polite fashion in which things are generally done at Longridge Castle.'"

The slightly sarcastic tone in which the last words had been spoken, had showed that Mrs. Leyton had neither forgotten nor forgiven the one or two snubs which Lady Joan had dealt her.

Herrick had grown more and more bewildered and distracted. He put a hundred wild and disconnected questions to Mrs. Leyton, which her first words had already sufficiently answered. Had she enquired at Wrexford station, as to Miss White's destination, had she cross-questioned her groom, the maidservants, also, rigorously?

To all which Mrs. Leyton had replied, sarcastically still, that in the circumstances she had not thought it necessary to do so, but that if he had any wish to cross-question either the men-servants, or the maids, he was at perfect liberty to do so. And furthermore, in order to avoid embarrassment of any sort to questioned or questioner, she had forthwith wished him "good morning," and had left the room.

As a parting word, the lady had expressed her conviction that to her way of thinking Mr. Gaskell need be under no apprehensions respecting Miss White's safety or comfort. She herself had paid her her half-yearly salary only the week before, and there was every likelihood, she opined, that the young lady had, for the present, at any rate, taken refuge in the big orphanage, whence she had recently emerged—St. Margaret's—in the environs of Croydon.

The opportunity of bringing Lady Joan's pride into the dust gone, the lady showed an evident disposition to wash her hands of the Gaskell family, whence so many affronts to her social standing had emanated.

Herrick's cross-questioning of Mrs. Leyton's servants threw little or no further light on the matter. None of the maids had seen Miss White on the morning in question, except the nurse; she stated that at about six o'clock, or half-past, Miss White had come into the nursery with her hat and veil on, and had kissed the children as they lay asleep in their beds. Her impression was, that Miss White was returning to the Castle to stay, and this impression was confirmed by the sound of tears in the young lady's voice, which in the circumstances seemed natural enough.

The groom had even less to tell. He merely stated that Miss White had come to him and asked him at once to take her box to Wrexford station in the luggage-cart, and he had done so. On arriving at the station he had deposited the box in the cloak-room according to his orders, but the young lady was nowhere to be seen. This was all that Herrick could elicit from the servants.

On leaving the house, however, just as he was bringing his horse to a trot through the Park, the sound of hurried footsteps and his name called made him draw rein and look round.

A young girl, the under nurse as he supposed, came up breathlessly with a letter in her hand. "For you, sir," she said, "Miss White left it in my hands when she went away. 'I can trust you, Rhoda,' she said, 'it is to be given into Mr. Gaskell's own hand—no one else's—when he comes to the house, but not before.'"

Herrick snatched the letter from the girl, in his eagerness forgetting the fee with which she no doubt expected to be recompensed.

The note, written in a hasty, scrambling hand, was very brief, and ran thus:

> Only a few lines to say good-bye to you. I have felt from the very first that our engagement was a mistake; I am thoroughly convinced now that a marriage between us could bring no happiness. Do not be uneasy as to my future; I am going at once to friends who will protect and advise me. I beg, I implore you make no effort to follow me and find out my hiding place. Let me, I entreat you, at once and for ever pass out of your life. Believe me, it will be as much for my good as for yours that I should do so. God bless you.
>
> Lois

The letter needed no second reading; its straightforward plainness made it easy enough to understand. The fears and misgivings which he had argued away—scolded away—kissed away—had once more taken possession of her; and, yielding completely to them, she had taken sudden flight. But whither. Who were these friends of whom she spoke so confidently? He knew, or he thought he knew, every friend she had ever had. They could be counted on the fingers of one hand—a girl at the big orphanage, a young teacher there who had been kind to her, a cousin of her father's in America, who at one time used to send her Christmas-boxes, and all were told. Who then were these newly-found friends in whom she placed such implicit confidence?

A great wave of jealousy for a moment swept over him that his Lois should flee for refuge to other guardianship than his; it faded, giving

CATHERINE LOUISA PIRKIS

place to a darker thought, an ugly suspicion lest this sudden impulsive flight might have been suggested by an older and warier brain than hers. His mother from the first had opposed his choice of a wife; what if she had found opportunity to work on the girl's unselfish misgivings, and had not only suggested this sudden flight of hers, but had supplied her with means to make it, and had found for her a hiding-place at the end of it!

He touched his horse with his whip. Well, thank Heaven that doubt at least could be decided at once by a question and answer. All his pity, all his respect for his mother for one brief moment seemed engulfed and gone. "She has had her own choice, she has made her own life, why in Heaven's name does she seek to mar mine for me?" was his thought as he sped swiftly along under the Summerhill beeches, which dropped now and again a rough little coffin of a nut into his horse's glossy mane, now and again a damp, blurred leaf.

Only once did he turn his head on his way through the Park. That was to give a rueful glance to the spot where, with light heart and lighter words, he had helped Lois to make her miniature Adonis garden. A few limp, battered flower-stalks, a handful of mud-spattered petals, was all that was left of it now.

IV

"Mother, do you know anything of this?" asked Herrick, standing, white and wrathful before Lady Joan, with Lois's scrap of a letter in his hand.

Lady Joan had quitted her chair beside the window, and was seated now at her writing-table addressing an envelope. Before she looked up in response to Herrick's question, she carefully reversed her envelope on her blotting-pad.

Lady Joan's troubles were to come now all together it seemed. Not a quarter of an hour ago a momentous piece of intelligence had been communicated to her, and here was Herrick confronting her with such a question as this!

The momentous piece of news had been told her by Parsons in response to her order for Lucy Harwood's immediate attendance, and was to the effect that, nearly a week ago, Lucy had been fetched away by her brother, who evidently considered that she had received her dismissal. Upon hearing this, Lady Joan had at once taken pen in hand, and had written a note to Lucy's brother, requesting him to come and see her immediately.

It was the envelope of this letter that she was addressing when Herrick entered the room.

He had to repeat his question.

Then Lady Joan looked up, and said slowly, as if doing her best to gather together her forces to meet a new difficulty or danger:

"What is 'this'? I do not understand? What is it I am supposed to know?"

For answer, Herrick spread Lois's letter before her, and bade her read it.

Though he stood there closely watching her face as she did so, never so much as a change of colour showed her surprise and sense of relief that the young girl had so literally fulfilled the few short and somewhat indefinite instructions that she had given her.

She took long to read the few simple lines. He grew impatient.

"Have I to thank you for this?" he asked, hotly, forgetting all his former kindly thought for her, forgetting everything, in fact, in his eager haste to get to the bottom of the mystery.

Lady Joan looked up at him. A slight flush passed over her pale face.

"Directly, no," she answered, with great deliberation; "indirectly, perhaps, yes. I have made no secret to her, to you, to anyone of my disapproval of your choice of a wife."

He made a gesture of impatience.

"You can throw no light whatever on this hurried, ill-advised step of hers?" he asked in a restrained voice, desirous to bring her back to the main point.

"None whatever."

Still he was not satisfied.

"It was not in the first instance suggested to her by you?" he questioned, recollecting the two opportunities that Lady Joan had had of private conversation with Lois.

Now, surely it could not have been from any refinement of the moral sense that Lady Joan hesitated to speak the glib lie that would have set this matter at rest, but rather through the habit of obedience to the maxim, "noblesse oblige," which figured to her in guise of moral code.

She rose with great dignity from her chair and stood facing him, with her head thrown back, her nostrils dilating.

"Am I to sit here and be cross-questioned by you as if I were a school-girl coining fibs to meet an emergency?" she asked haughtily. "I have told you already that, if you please, you may connect me indirectly with this young lady's extraordinary conduct. I shall reply to no more questions on the matter."

It was possible that if Lady Joan's mind had not already been greatly disturbed by what to her was a matter of greater moment, she would have adopted a more conciliatory attitude. As it was, in default of settled plan, she merely followed the dictates of inclination and instinct.

Herrick was cut off from the possibility of a reply by the door suddenly opening, and Lady Honor entering the room.

She had in her hand a plate with a magnificent bunch of grapes upon it. She had not, since her arrival at the Castle seen or spoken with Lady Joan, and assuredly could scarcely have selected a more inopportune moment for paying her first visit to her aunt's room; she looked from Herrick to Lady Joan, from Lady Joan to Herrick.

"They told me you had come down," she said, addressing her aunt. "And though Herrick told me not to go near you today, I didn't see why I should not. I've been through the grape-houses and picked out the finest bunch I could find for you. Now, you'll devour every one of them, won't you, Aunt Jo—an?"

The last syllable of Lady Joan's name was evidently added as an after-thought. The young lady made this speech somewhat in the manner in which she generally chose to come downstairs—in successive jumps.

Before she was half-way through it, Herrick, with an exclamation of annoyance at the interruption, left the room.

Yet if he had stayed for an hour questioning and cross-questioning his mother, he said to himself after a moment's thought, he did not see what he could have gained by it. Lady Joan's manner carried conviction to his mind that she was utterly in ignorance of Lois's movements, and as unprepared as he was for her sudden flight. One thing seemed clear to him; he must go at once, without a moment's delay, to the big orphanage in the vicinity of Croydon, where, as Mrs. Leyton had suggested, tidings of Lois, if not she herself, might be found.

It was easy for him to say "without a moment's delay," it was not so easy for him to put his intention into execution.

First, there came a telegram from Mr. McGowan, asking when he could see him on an urgent and important matter.

Herrick's reply to this was the somewhat vague one: "When I return from London."

Following this, came a request from Mr. Champneys, the manager of the Wrexford mines, that he might see Mr. Gaskell on matters of business. Now an interview with Mr. Champneys "on matters of business" meant at least an hour's work, at most an afternoon's.

Herrick thought awhile, then he looked at his watch. With the utmost despatch there was no saving a train from Wrexford for London before five in the afternoon. So then, with a terrible misgiving as to what might be the consequences of this enforced delay, the young man beat down his burning impatience to be off—going—doing something somewhere—and forced himself to sit still for an hour and a half without a break, listening to the driest business details, and giving in return the most methodical of instructions.

As he crossed the hall on his way out of the house a sheet of paper lying on the floor caught his eye; it had evidently fluttered from a small portfolio which lay on a table, and which he recognised as his cousin's.

Mechanically he picked up the paper, intending to replace it; as he did so the pencil sketch on it caught his eye. It was done with a bold, free touch, and represented the interior of a boudoir—his mother's, was it? Yes; there was the old Earl's portrait over the mantelpiece, and the two full-length figures which faced each other, one either side of the

CATHERINE LOUISA PIRKIS

table, were—good Heavens! who were they? That young man with his head thrown back and his fingers clenched into the palm of his hand was evidently meant for him, but it had his mother's face, crowned with its widow's cap, given to it! And that tall, stately lady, with her head thrown back and hand outstretched, was endowed with his own moustached visage, and hair cut "à la militaire." The words beneath the sketch, in Honor's big writing, "Which is which?" made it plain that the young lady possessed the gifts, doubly dangerous when conjoined, of caricaturist and satirist.

Herrick laid down the sketch, ashamed of himself for the feeling of annoyance which so trivial a matter had raised in his mind.

Had he been forced to speak out all his thoughts, he would have confessed that the real sting of the thing lay, not alone in the fact that a moment so tragic to him had been made material for a jest, but also in the vividness of the likeness between his mother and himself, which, with an artist's eye, the girl had seized and emphasized.

Why or wherefore, however, this should be a cause of annoyance to him, he might have found it hard to say.

V

H errick was away two days in London; he might just as well have stayed at home for all the news of Lois that he brought back with him. The principal of the big orphanage at which the young girl had been educated heard with amazement of her disappearance. She immediately cross-questioned the teachers and pupils of the establishment, with whom Lois was in the habit of corresponding, but with no result. Herrick was sent on a wild-goose chase to the other side of London, by one of the teachers, to the house of an ex-pupil with whom she thought Lois was on intimate terms. Thence he was sent down into Hertfordshire by the ex-pupil to another ex-pupil, married and settled down as a vicar's wife. But always with the same result. One and all averred that Lois's letters had been infrequent of late, and were absolutely destitute of details respecting herself and her doings. The only scrap of information likely to be of the smallest use which Herrick brought back with him, was the name of the distant cousin, who had from time to time sent Lois a present of a five-pound note as a Christmas-box. But even this sadly lacked individuality. "John White" is not a very distinctive appellation. The address matched the name in vagueness, and ran simply thus:

> "TACOMA,
> U.S.A."

These three words and three initials were all that Herrick had to show for his two days of harass and hard work.

A cablegram to so indefinite a personality as John White of Tacoma was not to be thought of—there might be a score of John Whites in Tacoma, for aught Herrick knew to the contrary. Only one thing remained now to be done, he said to himself, as with a white face with an ugly frown on it he locked himself in his "den," and pushed helter-skelter the accumulated letters of two days into a drawer, and that was to set off for America at once; find out John White, of Tacoma; and see if he had received any information of Lois's intention of making her home with him! "Stand on one side now, mother, home, friends, responsibilities great and small, till I get my darling back again," was the thought of his heart.

During the two days of Herrick's absence Lady Joan had shaken off her convalescence, and had gone about the house as of old. Yet not altogether as of old; her duties, which formerly she had discharged in light, indifferent fashion, were now emphasized and made much of. Indeed, to speak exactly, occupation of some sort or another appeared to be a necessity to her, and she seemed now to shun leisure as at one time she had seemed to court it.

Even Lord Southmoor, feeble of observation though he was, had his attention attracted by what he considered a remarkable trait in her character.

"It makes my head whirl to look at you, Joan; you seem to be always seeing people or writing letters," he said in a tone of feeble remonstrance, as if he feared that the family dignity was about to suffer injury at her hands.

Lord Southmoor as a rule was not apt or aphoristic in his remarks. In conversation he generally sat staring hard and frowning heavily, as if all absorbed in listening. And then he would open his lips and make a commonplace remark, or ask a question altogether wide of the subject in hand.

His remonstrance to his sister had been called forth by the fact that on the second day of Herrick's absence from home, Lady Joan had been closeted the whole morning with an entire stranger; leaving the Earl and his daughter to entertain each other.

That stranger was Ralph Harwood, who responded with as much despatch as possible to Lady Joan's summons.

Ralph had not so refined an appearance as his sister. Lady Joan quickly enough took his measure as that of a young farmer of the old school; that is to say, a man lifted above the farm-labourer class by a better education, but willing at any moment to let himself down to the level of the farm-labourer, and do farm-labourer's work, if by so doing his land would be better tilled, and his livestock better cared for.

In type he was florid and Saxon, tall and sturdy, with hair of a darker tint than Lucy's, and eyes that had an anxious, worried look in them. He looked miserable and ill at ease as Lady Joan laid stress upon what she called his extraordinary conduct in taking his sister away in so hurried a fashion. "Where is she now," she asked; "what is she doing? She can come back to me here if she is so disposed."

"Not possible, my lady," answered Ralph; "she has been ill in bed ever since she has been at home. It's my belief—" Here he broke off abruptly, then added, a little bitterly: "What with one thing, what with another, I scarcely know which way to turn."

Lady Joan looked at him steadily for a moment. No, it was not the beggar's whine for charity, but the real outcry of a harassed man.

She tried to lead him on to speak of his own and Lucy's early days. She began by recounting the story of the two occasions on which the girl had walked in her sleep while at Longridge.

"The first occasion she seemed to remember perfectly, and could give a clear account of," the lady went on to say, "but the second appeared to have entirely faded from her memory."

"It has been so before, my lady," said Ralph; "more than once she has got out of bed and walked about the house, and I have guided her back to her room and helped her into bed, and when the morning has come she has known nothing of what she has done. It is a terrible affliction, this habit of hers."

"In what way terrible?" asked Lady Joan, eyeing the man keenly.

A shade of embarrassment passed over his face, his manner grew less frank. "Well, my lady, she will not be able to get her own living for one thing. No lady would engage her as maid if she knew she had this habit."

"No," said Lady Joan, "that goes without saying. No lady would engage a girl with such an undesirable habit; but I should have thought good medical advice might do something for it, that is unless," here she bent a scrutinising glance on Ralph, "it runs in the family."

He flushed crimson, but said never a word. His embarrassed silence seemed to admit the fact.

"Pardon my enquiries," pursued Lady Joan, in a kindly, condescending manner, which she rarely adopted, but which, when assumed, never failed to make an impression on her listener. "Believe me, I am most desirous to be of service to you and to your sister, in whom already I feel deeply interested."

Then, little by little, in response to delicately-put questions and kindly expressions of sympathy, Ralph told the sorrowful story of his early years, and of his father's married life.

It was, in fact, the untold half of the tale which Lucy had already related in outline to Lady Joan.

The wife whom John Harwood, whilom butler to the Vicar of Southmoor, had married, had, after the birth of her second child, Lucy, developed symptoms of insanity. On more than one occasion she had attempted suicide, and after ineffectual endeavours to keep her safe

CATHERINE LOUISA PIRKIS

at home, her husband had been compelled to place her in the county lunatic asylum. Here she had remained for over fifteen years, at the end of which period she had been discharged as cured. The greater part of the time spent by her in the asylum was of necessity a blank to her, and she had returned home expecting to find her children much as she had left them. Her husband, who from time to time had visited her during her confinement in the asylum, she had recognised; but her children she had denounced as aliens and impostors, who had taken the place of the small boy and girl she had kissed and said good-bye to long ago. It had been thought advisable from the first to keep from Lucy the knowledge of her mother's insanity, lest it might have a bad effect upon her. She was a delicate child; in physique the living picture of her mother, and in temperament her very double. The child came back from an aunt in London who had brought her up, prepared to lavish her love upon a mother who, in her fancy, figured as her ideal of everything a mother should be. The mother not only failed utterly to recognise her daughter, but in the dead of the night was detected in an attempt on the girl's life. This attempt was concealed from Lucy, who was immediately sent back to her aunt. Other symptoms of lunacy soon showed in the poor woman, and she was sent for a time to the house of a doctor in the neighbourhood, a connection of her husband's through marriage. Shortly afterwards this doctor had removed to Ireland, taking his patient with him. From time to time there had come reports of her improved state of health, and then had come the news that she had eluded his vigilance and escaped from his care. From that day forward she had never been heard of.

Her one desire and aim from morning till night had been to re-discover the tiny daughter she remembered so perfectly, and whose likeness she wore night and day in a locket round her neck. It was thought possible that she had started on this quest, and either had been overtaken by some accident, or else had committed suicide. Mr. Harwood's enquiries on the matter, Ralph admitted, had been neither searching nor prolonged, and nothing had since transpired to confirm either surmise.

The death of Lucy's aunt at this juncture had rendered it necessary for Mr. Harwood to provide another home for his daughter. Beset by the dread lest his wife might find her way back to her home and make another attempt on Lucy's life, and possibly also anxious to escape from a place of sad memories, he had sold his farm in Devon, and had purchased one near Wrexford. Then pecuniary difficulties had begun. The Devon farm had been sold at a loss; the Wrexford farm had too high a price paid for it. The worthy farmer found himself crippled at every turn by want of capital. His spirits sank, his health gave way, and he died, leaving to his son an unprofitable investment, and the care of his fragile sister. Ralph had no easy life before him; do what he would, the farm did not pay its expenses; and Lucy's daily increasing likeness to her mother caused him daily increasing anxiety. The girl had been told that her mother was dead; this, the conversation of some farm-labourers overheard by her proved to be false; and henceforward every statement made to her on the matter she disbelieved. She drifted into a morbid condition of mind, and little by little developed the symptoms which her mother had developed before insanity had set in. One idea took possession of her brain—to find the ideal mother of her childhood's love. She settled to no occupation, she wandered listlessly about the country all day, slept badly at nights, and eat next to nothing. In this extremity Ralph bethought him of his father's early friends, and wrote an imploring letter to Mr. Vaughan Elliot.

Lady Joan raised her eyebrows.

"Mr. Vaughan Elliot!" she repeated. The name, unheard for so many years, fell strangely on her ear in this connection.

"Yes, my lady, Father Elliot that is," said Ralph. "He had just been appointed, so I had heard, to St. Elizabeth's Church, at Long-ridge—"

"St. Elizabeth's! Here within two miles of the Castle!" interrupted Lady Joan, her surprise increasing on her.

"Yes, my lady."

"Go on with your story," said the lady. But though she said, "Go on," it was easy to see that her thoughts had been set wandering.

Ralph went on.

"I wrote to him, begging him, on his way to his church, to spend a few days at our farm. He was kind enough to do so, and in three days he did Lucy more good than anybody else had ever done in as many years. He made her promise to give up her wanderings about the country in search of she knew not what, and advised that she should at once take a situation where constant occupation would be given her—" He broke off for a moment, and then added, bitterly: "And this is how it has all ended!"

Lady Joan had listened with a keener ear to Ralph's story than she had to the other half of it as told her by Lucy.

It seemed to her that a very straightforward course lay before her now.

"It is a sad tale," she said. "It has greatly interested me. I think, however, you ought not to lose heart, as you have done, on your sister's account. She is very young, and, as I said before, medical treatment ought to do something for her. Now, what do you say to sending her for a time to stay at a doctor's house—to a doctor, of course, who understands such cases—say, to the man to whom your father confided your mother?"

Once get the girl treated as the semi-lunatic she undoubtedly was, and who would believe any wild story she might tell as to what had gone on in a certain sick-room on a certain night?

Ralph shook his head.

"I haven't the money, my lady—" he began.

"Leave that to me. What is the name of this doctor? Where is he living now?"

"His name is Gallagher, and he lives at Ballinacrae near Cork, my lady. Just now, however, he is in Liverpool, trying to arrange a troublesome lawsuit with which he is threatened."

"Ah; no doubt he would be glad to increase his income by a lucrative patient. Is he competent, do you think, to treat such cases as your mother's and sister's?"

Ralph did not seem to notice the way in which she bracketed Lucy with her mother. He answered readily enough:

"Oh, thoroughly competent, my lady. He was at one time head-keeper in one of the big county asylums. Then he married my father's cousin, who was an attendant there, and took it into his head he knew so much about lunatics that it would pay him to enter the profession, and set up as a doctor to the insane. That was in our prosperous days, and my father, off and on, helped him a good deal with his college expenses."

"I should like to see this man," said Lady Joan, "and talk to him about your sister."

Ralph had an objection to raise which she did not expect.

"Before anything is done, my lady, I must see Father Elliot and consult him on the matter. I can do nothing without his consent."

Lady Joan frowned. Father Elliot again! Thirty years ago she had said to herself: "This man shall go at once and for ever out of my life." And lo, here was he confronting her at a crisis!

"I think," she said, with not a little asperity, "you are unwise not to avail yourself at once of my offer. It is the advice of a doctor, not that of a priest, which you are needing for your sister."

Whatever Ralph might desire for his sister, assuredly advice from a priest was not what Lady Joan desired for her. Priests had the uncomfortable habit of counselling confession, and so of getting at a variety of matters which did not concern them.

"Give me a little time to think it over, my lady," said Ralph humbly. "I am going straight to the Father's from here; and, if you will allow me, I will call in again on my way back in the afternoon."

With so much of concession Lady Joan was obliged to be content, and to allow the man to depart.

VI

On the Castle terrace, the sun-dial, gorgeous in new bronze and sparkling granite, lengthened its shadow over the flying hours. Half-past four struck, and Lady Joan went indoors to afternoon-tea in the library. Lord Southmoor was there awaiting her. He was standing in one of the long narrow windows of the room, holding one of her delicate Sèvres tea-cups to the light.

To every man, say the artists, comes in the course of his life an inspired moment, when, if his portrait be taken, the man is seen at his best.

To see Lord Southmoor with a Greuze before him on an easel, or with a dainty bit of china in his hand, was, so to speak, to catch him at high-water mark, and to get a glimpse of that special commodity which, in his organism, did duty for a soul. A something of intelligence would come into his eye, a something of animation into his speech, and it was possible to conceive what Lord Southmoor might have been under happier conditions, that is to say, if life could have been made "all Greuze and Dresden china" for him.

"If only I had been moulded in a pottery, and fired in an oven, I should have been appreciated," Lady Honor was in the habit of saying. "I should have been fondled, and admired, put upon a pedestal, and under a glass shade. Thank you! I prefer my ugliness and my freedom."

He passed his finger caressingly over the teacup, as Lady Joan entered the room. "After all, there's nothing like Sèvres for tea-cups," he said musingly; "the very touch of the glaze to the lips is a pleasure."

Lady Joan's reply was not to be spoken, for at that moment the door was opened, and Lady Honor, followed by Argus, came in at a rush. She had evidently just returned from a ramble with the dog, who, during his master's absence, had transferred his allegiance to her; her hands were full of field-flowers, and a big trail of bryony decorated the mastiff's collar.

"Tea for one, bread and butter for two," she said, giving the order as if she were entering a pastry-cook's shop. Then the straw hat, which she was swinging vigorously, on one finger, came into contact with a photograph frame that stood on a small table, and the thing came down with a crash.

Honor stooped to pick it up. The action seemed to displease Lady Joan more than the accident had done.

"William will do that," she said icily. Then her eyes rested with manifest disapproval on her niece's ungloved hands.

Honor felt the look. "I only took them off after I had passed the lodge, Aunt Joan. See, here they are, safe in my pocket." She pulled forth a big leather-like pair of gloves from the pocket of her coat, and held them up to view.

Lady Joan surveyed them with a critical eye. "I shall be glad, Honor, if you will allow my milliner to supply you with gloves for the future," she said. "I have never seen gloves of that description on a lady's hand."

"I gave three francs for them only the day before I left Brussels," exclaimed the girl indignantly. Then she took her tea and a plate of bread and butter into a window recess at the farther end of the room, whistling to Argus to follow.

"She has not been a widow a fortnight, and she can think of the cut of my gloves!" said the girl to herself. "Why, if I had a husband, and he were to die, all I should pray for would be sticks enough to make a suttee fire, so that I might go up to Heaven after him as soon as possible."

From the far end of the room, fragments of the talk between her father and aunt came to her.

"I can tell, by the way his lips move, what he is saying," she thought. "He's apologising for my shortcomings. 'It's the school at Brussels, that's what it is!' Yes, there's a big 'B' coming out of his mouth. Just as if I had chosen my own school, and sent myself there! Oh, good gracious! What are they saying now!"

"I shall be delighted," the Earl was saying, "to leave Honor in your care for as long as you like to keep her—your society will be of inestimable advantage to her. I must return in a day or so. Lily tells me her present quarters don't suit her, and I expect we shall have to get back to Cannes before the cold weather sets in."

Lady Southmoor, it may be mentioned, in passing, generally found that her "quarters didn't suit her" after about three weeks' stay in them. The pleasant little flutter caused by a removal to a fresh hotel, the inspection of new menus, and the attendance of another doctor, was the nearest approach to a diversion that she admitted into the role of interesting invalid, which she filled so well.

"I'm to be left behind, am I! To be pruned, and trimmed, and tortured into a second Aunt Jo? Too late in the day, good people. Now, ten years back, before my hair was quite so pronounced in colour, Aunt Jo, you might have done something with me; but not now. What, all your bread and butter gone, Argie dear? Never mind, we'll go in for the

CATHERINE LOUISA PIRKIS

cake, now. Ah! who's this? Aunt Joan, here's such a nice-looking man coming up to the house—carries himself like a soldier. No; I think he looks more like a gardener in his Sunday clothes."

The library was at the side of the house, and, facing the window at which Honor sat was a small pine-wood. Possibly, by the time three more generations of Gaskells had been reared and had passed away, that plantation might be worth looking at. At present it was just a bit of scrubby woodland, through which a bridle-path led into the high road. From out this woodland Ralph Harwood had just emerged.

"Yes, a gardener in his Sunday clothes," Honor went on, taking up an opera-glass, and steadily scrutinizing the man; "and, now I look at him again, I fancy I should very much prefer him in his shirt-sleeves with a spade in his hand."

"Are you addressing your conversation to me, Honor?" interrupted her father, in mild, lazy tones. "Your aunt left the room directly you announced the approaching stranger. Dear me! She seems to have a great deal on her hands just now."

Those were the very words on Lady Joan's lips at that moment, as she leaned forward on her writing-table, addressing Ralph, who was seated facing her on the other side.

"I have a great deal on my hands just now," she was saying, "and I shall be glad to arrange this matter with as little delay as possible. What does your priest—Father Elliot—say to my offer?"

"He says, my lady, that he must think it over; Lucy's future cannot be decided for her at a moment's notice."

Lady Joan's face changed.

"Surely," she exclaimed, "you could not have made it plain to him that my offer meant the providing for life for your sister, who is so incapable of providing for herself?"

"I did, my lady, and he seemed surprised—startled I might say— when I told him who you were, and what an interest you had taken in her; but still he said he must have time to think the matter over."

Lady Joan's face grew darker still.

"Am I to understand," she asked coldly, "that you mean this priest's advice to stand in the way of your sister's undoubted advantage? I told you before it is a doctor's advice, not a priest's, she is needing. Why do you not, now that the doctor who attended your mother is so near at hand, write to him to come and see your sister? His professional opinion might carry weight with your priest."

"Oh, my lady, I'm expecting him to come every day. I owe him a good deal of money; he'll be sure to come over and see me," answered Ralph, a little recklessly, and not a little bitterly.

"Very well then, when he comes to see you, you must let him see your sister also; and then I should like you to come here again and tell me exactly what his opinion is. I suppose you clearly understand that I am willing to pay all his fees, and whatever he chooses to charge for receiving her into his house as a patient?"

"Oh, yes, my lady; and I shan't know how to be grateful enough to you, if the Father will let me accept your offer," protested Ralph, repeating words that grated on Lady Joan's ear in a manner impossible for him to understand.

"Will you write down the name and address of this doctor," said Lady Joan, handing a pen to him, "in case I may wish to communicate with him at any future time?"

Ralph rose from his chair and took the pen, placing his hat, which, until then, he had held in his hand, on the floor, beside the writing-table.

"Gallagher!" repeated Lady Joan, "an Irishman, of course?"

"No, my lady," said Ralph, as his pen slowly travelled across the paper, "his father was Irish, but he was born and brought up at Liverpool."

Lady Joan did not hear the reply; her eye, unconsciously following the man's movements, had discovered a letter lying in the crown of his hat, which he had placed almost at her feet. This letter was addressed in handwriting which sent a thrill through her. Thirty years since she had last set eyes on that bold, clear hand! Then it had conveyed to her, in glowing language, burning, passionate messages of love; now, it merely addressed an envelope to:

MISS WHITE,
Convent of our Lady of Mercy,
Mount Clear,
near Liverpool.

For a moment she sat staring blankly at it. Here was blind chance absolutely playing into her hands and making her game easy to her!

Ralph laid down the pen. She pointed to the letter.

"You know the young lady to whom that letter is addressed?" she asked.

An expression of annoyance passed over Ralph's face.

"Not at all, my lady. It was a letter given me to post in Wrexford by Father Elliot—I am sorry you have seen the address, I hope your ladyship will not mention it to any one. The Father gave me strict orders not to let the letter pass out of my hands, and on no account to post it in Longridge."

Father Elliot again! And with two of the most important threads of her life in his hand now!

"The address shall not pass my lips, I assure you," she said, with a double meaning, lost on Ralph.

For a moment there fell a silence between them, a silence which Ralph made busy with the thought of how strange it was that Lucy's two days' residence at the Castle should have aroused in this lady's mind so strong an interest in her.

Lady Joan's next words set his wonder travelling in another direction.

"Now I want to speak to you about the young lady to whom Father Elliot's letter is addressed. I know her slightly, and requested her to write to me when she left Longridge. She has not, however, done so. Tell me, do you know what sort of a place this convent at Mount Clear is?"

Ralph shook his head.

"I know nothing of the place, my lady. I could easily make enquiries about it through Father Elliot."

"No, don't do that. I was only thinking—" She broke off abruptly. She had a delicate matter to handle now, and one that must not be approached in too straightforward a fashion. She leaned back in her chair for a moment, then resumed: "I was only thinking that, as this young lady is very young, and very friendless, her inclinations might incline towards a religious life, and as I consider she has a strong vocation for it, I should be very pleased to assist her views."

This was her manner of expressing the thought that it would be a most desirable thing if this foolish and hysterical young person could be induced to expend her folly and hysterics in a religious channel; she was evidently designed by Nature to fill the rôle of the emotional religious recluse.

Ralph's face expressed simple, stolid astonishment. He was not quite sure that he grasped the lady's meaning; but if he had, what an amazing benevolence she was showing towards two friendless young girls!

"I don't know anything about her views, my lady," he answered, slowly. "In fact I know nothing at all about her, except that the Father gave me this letter to post, and was very anxious that no one should see it."

"Let no one see it! Tell the Father that it was quite by accident that I saw it. No doubt he has some wise reason for wishing to keep the address secret. At the same time, I want to know a little about this young lady's doings; in fact, I have a special reason for wishing to keep my eye on her for some little time to come."

"Ye—es, my lady," said Ralph, slowly, his curiosity in the matter' beginning to subside.

After all, it was no business of his what the lady's motive for wishing "to keep her eye" on this young person was.

"She is very poor," Lady Joan went on, presently, "and it occurs to me that I may possibly be of service to her. There are certain convents, I think, which expect a sum of money down before they admit a novice. Now, if this should be the case here, I should like you to make Father Elliot understand that I am anxious to assist in removing what might be a difficulty to a girl in Miss White's position in life."

"Yes, I will do so, my lady," said Ralph, rising to take his leave.

As he did so, a sudden rush of probabilities and possibilities came into Lady Joan's mind. First and foremost, there was Vaughan Elliot to be thought of. A bait to which, perhaps, ninety-nine priests out of a hundred might rise, would not tempt him—unless he had strangely altered since "the days of long ago." She must be cautious.

"Stay a moment," she said, arresting Ralph's departure. "Does Father Elliot, do you know, advocate conventual life for women?"

"Not in all cases, my lady. He says a nun is born, not made."

"Quite so; I agree with him. Then before you even mention my offer to him, will you kindly find out if he considers this young lady born to the vocation; do you think you can do this for me?"

"I will try, my lady," answered Ralph, hesitatingly. "The Father doesn't make much of a confidant of me; but still I'll do my best."

Lady Joan bethought her of the readiest way to ensure his "doing his best!" She took out her purse, and without preamble, handed him a bank-note. "I've already taken up a great deal of your time, which, no doubt, is of value to you, and if you act as my agent in this matter, I shall probably encroach still farther on it," she said.

"But, my lady, I've not earned so large an amount," said Ralph, gazing in amazement at the twenty-pound note, which suggested such an easy way of solving one or two of his pecuniary difficulties.

"Never mind about that," said Lady Joan, pleasantly; "your sister, if she is ill, must be wanting all sorts of things, which, perhaps, you are not able to get for her—"

"That's true," sighed Ralph.

"And remember, I shall want to see you again in a day or two—that will mean more outlay of your valuable time."

Ralph began a profusion of thanks. Lady Joan interrupted them.

"Now this is the sum total of what I want done," she said. "With regard to your sister, I shall be glad if Dr. Gallagher will write to me his professional opinion of her mental and physical condition, and I shall be glad if you, on your part, will do all you can to induce Father Elliot to give his consent to her remaining for a time, at least, under Dr. Gallagher's care."

"Yes, my lady, I understand."

"With regard to Miss White, I shall be glad to know what her plans are for the future. She may wish to emigrate; she may wish to do a great many things for which her resources are insufficient. Make Father Elliot understand, please, that I wish to help forward her plans for her future, whatever they may be—whatever they may be—do you see?"

Once more Ralph protested his willingness to do the lady's bidding to the utmost of his ability. Then he took his departure, his mind holding but one thought now: gratitude for the lady's great benevolence, which could not have come at a more opportune moment.

A great golden moon was throwing gaunt shadows across the greensward as he crossed the Park on his way back. At the lodge gate he paused, to hold it open for a white, weary-faced young man, who came riding slowly along.

"That must be young Mr. Gaskell," he thought, as he touched his hat respectfully.

If Herrick could have known of the letter which lay hidden in that hat, he would scarcely have ridden past as he did, with a slight nod and indifferent "Good-night."

VII

I t seemed as if all heaven and all earth had conspired together to retard Herrick's departure for America; as if every one and everything about him said with one voice: "See now, isn't one wild-goose chase enough? Why attempt another?"

He had no sooner got into the house, pulled off his boots in his "den," and sent a message to his mother that he would not sit down to dinner that night, than there was put into his hand a telegram from Mr. McGowan, reiterating the question he had before asked: "When can I see you on important business?"

Herrick's reply to this: "On my return from America"—as vague and somewhat more startling than the one he had before dispatched—had the effect of bringing Mr. McGowan to the Castle before breakfast was ended on the following morning.

He entered the room with a flushed face and an air of subdued excitement, which made itself felt.

"Get him out of the room as quickly as possible, Herrick," whispered Honor, "his complexion and my hair combined would send someone crying out for the fire-engines."

Herrick complied with her request, though from a different motive.

"Champneys is waiting for me. I can only give you half an hour," he said to the lawyer, rising from the table and leading the way to the library.

But less than half that time was enough and to spare to convey the startling news that a will made by John Gaskell, nearly thirty years ago, had been discovered in one of the strong boxes which contained the Gaskell family documents.

"The man who drew it up is dead," said Mr. McGowan; "my father, who knew about it, is dead; the clerk, to whose charge it most probably was committed, has long since retired from the business. No doubt"—here the lawyer threw an anxious glance at Herrick—"if Mr. Gaskell ever gave it a thought he intended, when necessity arose, to render it null and void by making another will."

"Why so?" asked Herrick, a slight annoyance showing in his tone. "Any will made by my father, depend upon it, had careful thought given to it, and was not likely to be revoked afterwards."

For all response to Herrick's "Why so?" the lawyer drew the will from its envelope and read aloud to him the document which gave the whole of the vast Gaskell wealth to Lady Joan for her life, and to Herrick a certain fixed yearly income, which, side by side with this vast wealth, seemed microscopic.

Herrick listened to the last word, saying nothing. Not a muscle of his face moved. He grew a little white, that was all.

The lawyer looked up, waiting for him to speak.

"Of course," he resumed, as Herrick still sat silent, "if old Mr. Gaskell had outlived your father this will would have been worthless. My partner and I conjecture that it was made to meet certain contingencies which might—but were not likely to—arise, and that, possibly, afterwards, it was treated as so much waste paper. A court of Equity might—"

"Stop," said Herrick, speaking now for the first time; "let it be clearly understood that, so far as I am concerned, no litigation will arise on this matter."

His voice was perfectly steady; his manner showed little or no disquietude.

"From my knowledge of your father's character, I feel confident that, as time went on, he must have intended adding a codicil, at the very least, to this will. It is monstrous to think of all this wealth—these responsibilities I mean—being left upon a woman's shoulders," said Mr. McGowan, who had more than once been snubbed by Lady Joan, and with whom, consequently, she was no favourite.

"I see nothing monstrous in it," said Herrick, curtly, not choosing to have either father or mother discussed by the lawyer; "so far as I see, this will leaves me in very much the same position as I was in before my father died. I suppose all active responsibility in the management of the estate will devolve upon me; only, instead of having to account to my father or grandfather, as heretofore, for my management of affairs, I shall have to be accountable to the trustees. Who did you say they were?"

"One of them is dead. The other is a Mr. John Rothsay, an old friend of your father's, a man now over seventy years of age. He will have to appoint a new trustee."

Herrick looked at his watch and rose from his chair.

"I can't give you another minute," he said. "I have to give Champneys a long morning. I have so much to arrange with him during my absence."

"Sir!" interrupted the lawyer, anxiously, "must that journey to America take place?"

"Must!" said Herrick with a grave decision; "ten thousand times over it must."

"It's a thousand pities! all sorts of legal formalities must be gone through, and the appointment of a new trustee is an important matter—"

"It's no use, McGowan. The matter on which I am bent overweighs this and everything else in importance. Nay, it is of so much moment that this"—here he swept the will on one side with his hand—"counts, with me, as nothing beside it. It will be better for you to see my mother at once and acquaint her with the state of affairs. When I return I may be able to give you all my attention."

"When you return! Can you name a date, sir?"

"Impossible! I go first to Tacoma, thence I may return, or may go on—well, Heaven only knows where."

This unsatisfactory statement the lawyer was compelled to take as an answer, and he reluctantly departed to seek an interview with Lady Joan.

Herrick's long morning with the manager of the Wrexford mines proved to be a very long morning indeed, for it covered the luncheon hour—represented to the two by sandwiches and sherry in the library—and extended right on to the hour of afternoon tea.

It had been a "glorious, golden autumn day"—a day one gets sometimes after a spell of bad weather; and Herrick, looking out from the library window, saw that his mother and Lady Honor had had tea brought to them under the shadow of the young pine plantation which faced that side of the house. He had not, as yet, spoken to Lady Joan of his intended journey across the Atlantic, and it seemed to him that here, with his cousin present, was an opportunity for so doing. Before a third person, there would be less likelihood of angry speech on her part, angry retaliation on his.

Lady Honor appeared to have spent her afternoon in sketching: her easel and painting materials stood beside her. As he approached she suddenly put down her cup and saucer and took her sketch-book on her knee.

The action irritated him more than he cared to avow.

"What ridiculous posture is she putting me in now, I wonder," he thought. And as he drew nearer, in spite of himself, his eyes wandered beyond the miniature tea-table to her sketch-book.

Argus, couchant, sat about a yard or so distant, and Argus, couchant, covered half the page of the young lady's sketch-book, complete in outline, but with face lacking.

The girl seemed to feel Herrick's gaze.

"I have just discovered an extraordinary likeness between Argus and a friend of mine. I shall add the face later on," she said.

"I have had no time to speak to you yet"—said Herrick, addressing Lady Joan a little formally, and in a tone that showed he was resolute to bring an ugly subject into full view—"of the result of my journey to London. I am sorry to say it has been altogether fruitless."

"Indeed," nothing more, was her reply.

Herrick bit his lip and resumed:

"I followed every clue that could possibly be had; but I could get no definite tidings of Lois and her movements."

He waited for his mother to speak. She said nothing. So he turned to Honor, and said:

"Lois White is the young lady to whom I am engaged to be married."

"Indeed!" said Honor, and—was it possible?—in that one word she reproduced Lady Joan's voice and intonation to the life.

Herrick tried to speak unconcernedly:

"The only thing in the shape of a clue given to me was the address of a cousin of Lois's father, now in America. As the address is not very definite—distinctive, perhaps I should say—it would be useless to send a telegram to him. So I am starting for the place myself, tomorrow."

Now Lady Joan showed unmistakable interest.

"You—to America—tomorrow!" she exclaimed.

"Of course. There is nothing else to be done. Do you suppose I should stay here quietly and allow my future wife to drift away from me without an effort? You don't know me if you think that!"

"Capital!" said Lady Honor under her breath.

Lady Joan looked round at her in amazement.

"I was referring to Argie's portrait," said the girl, holding up the faceless sketch to view.

Lady Joan turned to Herrick:

"Of course you will do as you think best. Mr. McGowan just now, when he brought your father's will to me, told me you were going away for a time; but I had no idea that America was to be your destination," she said in her ordinary tone of voice.

"Your father's will!" Herrick stared at her with wonder. She spoke as calmly as if she were talking of the will of a man who had lived and died a century back. And he could recall much such a golden, hazy afternoon as this, not a fortnight ago, when his father had stood about a yard distant from the spot where they now stood, and, pointing upwards to the pines, had said: "They'll be grand trees, Joan, when Herrick's children have stepped into our shoes."

Lady Joan did not seem to notice the cloud on his face.

"Mr. McGowan had a good deal to say to me," she went on in the same level tone as before; then she paused a moment before adding: "but I don't see that anything in the will he read to me will materially alter my position or yours."

This was said in a kindly, conciliatory tone. Why not? She had power in her hands now, and could afford to be conciliatory. Besides, it was a course which promised, so far as Herrick was concerned, better results than a declaration of open war.

Herrick's face showed unmistakable anger. His voice vibrated as he answered:

"It's a matter to which I am simply incapable of given my attention at the present moment. Beside Lois and her strange unaccountable flight, I can think of nothing, not even my father's will."

The last words were added with sarcastic bitterness.

There fell an uncomfortable pause. Did his ears deceive him, or, did Lady Honor give a low, long whistle?

Lady Joan turned sharply towards her.

"I was calling Argus," said the girl, coolly. Then she pushed on one side her half-finished sketch, and, as if seized by a new idea, commenced another.

Lady Joan slightly shivered, and rose from her chair.

"It gets chilly when the sun has gone. Don't stay here too long, Honor," she said, drawing her shawl around her.

The golden haze of evening sunshine, filtering through the young pine boughs, fell on a face so pale and wan that Herrick felt himself conscious-stricken for his momentary blaze of anger.

"It would be like her to speak coldly and feel deeply," he thought. "Who am I to say that she is not as broken-hearted as I am?"

Aloud, he said, with real concern in his voice:

"Mother, you are not feeling so well today, I'm certain. Pray do not overtax your strength."

"I am not likely to do that," was her reply, spoken with a double meaning lost on him.

Was it likely that anything the commonplace days might bring would be too much for strength which had stood the wear and tear of nights beyond the experience of all save the souls shut out of heaven?

CATHERINE LOUISA PIRKIS

Honor's society had but little attraction for Herrick, so he turned to follow his mother back to the house.

"Would you like a shawl sent out to you?" he said, by way of a farewell politeness to his cousin.

Lady Honor's acknowledgment of the politeness was a curious one. Just six blunt, straightforward words that admitted of no double interpretation:

"Herrick, what a fool you are!"

"I beg your pardon!" was his astonished exclamation.

"Oh, don't make me say it over again! To think of you starting off to America when—"

Here she suddenly broke off and sketched away faster than ever.

"Pray say right out all you have to say, Honor. Don't let a sense of politeness stop you," he said a little sarcastically.

"No; that isn't likely. Now will you mind telling me how you think Œdipus solved the riddle of the Sphinx? How have all the Œdipuses who ever lived solved their riddles? How was the law of gravitation discovered; the mariners' compass; the steam-engine; the uses of electricity?"

Herrick stared at her. Was she a lunatic, or was it possible his ears were playing tricks with him?

Aloud he said:

"Am I supposed to answer all those questions? It's like a page out of the 'Child's Guide.' 'Who first carried an umbrella? Who drank the first cup of tea in England?' will follow next, I suppose. Really, Honor, you've been to school since I have, and ought to know these things better than I can tell you."

Honor rose from her chair and gathered together her painting materials.

"I know one thing better than you can tell me at any rate," she said bluntly, as before; "and that is, that no riddles, from that of the Sphinx downwards, would ever have been solved if people had run away from them instead of looking them full in the face. I've been sitting alone all this afternoon with Aunt Jo, and off and on I've had a good deal of her society the last two days; and I've come to the conclusion—"

Again she broke off.

"Pray, as I said before, don't let a sense of politeness deter you from finishing your sentence," said Herrick half-banteringly, but in his heart more eager to hear the conclusion she had arrived at than he cared to avow.

"As I said before, I'm not likely to; but it'll come better a little later on, perhaps. Meantime, I'll give you this for a keepsake, to take to America with you, if you like."

She handed to him a leaf hastily torn from her sketch-book; and with a smile so frank and genial that it almost made her look handsome, she disappeared into the house.

Herrick stood still for a moment, looking down in amazement at the hastily-executed drawing. It was a rough, bold sketch, made with about a dozen strokes of a full brush. A dash of ochre represented a stretch of sandy desert, out of which a full brush of sepia had made to rise the gigantic form of the mysterious Sphinx. The face of the Sphinx had been added in lead-pencil, and—there could be no doubt about it— it owned to the aquiline features and austere expression of Lady Joan.

VIII

Although Herrick did not find time to sit down to dinner that night; although he emphatically declined Lord Southmoor's leisurely challenge to an after-dinner game of écarté; though he swept half his correspondence unanswered into his portmanteau, and knew that the other half would keep him up till the small hours of the morning, yet there was one thing which he resolved should not be pushed into a corner, not even by his hot haste to catch the out-going Atlantic steamer—that was his first visit to his father's grave.

His father's grave! He seated himself at his writing-table in the quiet little room where he and his father had got through so much real hard work together, and for a moment leaned back in his chair, pen in hand, trying to realise that those three little words had not been spoken by him under the influence of a dream, trying to realise that, in very truth, they covered an episode which would leave its scar upon him for life.

His father lying in the churchyard! It would have been far easier to believe that he had only that minute left the room, that he had but now laid down his pen as he so often had, saying: "Well, good-night, Herrick, you are thirty years younger than I am, and can stand late hours a trifle better." Why, not a fortnight ago, as they had discussed together certain matters connected with a "lock-out" in the adjoining county, he had done so. There, on the writing-table, which immediately faced the one at which he sat, was the very pen he had seen in his father's hand, and there, too, was the piece of blotting-paper, with the impress of the firm, well-remembered writing still upon it. If the door had at that moment opened, and John Gaskell had entered, and had once more seated himself in his old place, it would have seemed the most natural thing in the world—far more natural than the thought which the young man was trying so hard to make real to himself, that on the morrow, before he started for Liverpool, whence he would embark for New York, he must go forth and visit "his father's grave."

Herrick once more took up his pen, and made one vigorous effort to fling himself, heart and soul, into the paper which lay spread before him on the table—a contract which a big firm of engineers had wished to conclude with the proprietors of the Wrexford mines, and over which he had promised Champneys "to run his eye."

No use! His father's very shadow seemed to fall across the blue paper with its many items written in clerk's school-boy hand. "Item No. 1.

Now what would my father have said to this?" was the thought with which he began to read that foolscap sheet, and the thought with which he laid it down. Great Heavens!—here he pushed back his chair, and began to walk impetuously up and down the room—how was he to get through his work, how, indeed, was he to get through his life without that "final word" which his father had been in the habit of speaking on every matter, great and small?

It was long past midnight, so long, indeed, that from afar there came a faint, sleepy sound of cock-crowing, and he knew that if he threw back the venetian shutters of the room, the grey of dawn would do battle with the yellow light of his lamp.

"This time tomorrow I shall have sailed," he thought, wearily trying to fence with that other haunting thought of a dead face—a dead voice. "Now what, I wonder, will come of this journey of mine? Shall I find my darling safe and sound at the other end of it? Ah"—there it was back again—"what would my father have said of my hurried departure, and my chances of success?"

And because the thought would not be shaken off—trampled under foot—quenched, Herrick set himself steadily to face it.

Now could he fancy his father standing before him, grave and thoughtful, and saying, "Herrick, is it right, do you think, for you to cast all responsibility to the four winds, and to leave your mother at a crisis in her life, to do battle with sorrows, and unknown anxieties, while you give chase to a poor little butterfly of a girl, who ought to have stood by your side and been comfort and strength to you?"

Could he not rather hear him in a kindlier tone, and with a softer look, saying:

"God bless you, my boy, and give you success; be true and strong, and then the weak ones will learn truth and strength from you!"

But, oddly enough, there seemed to mingle with these words the tones of another voice, a trifle loud, a trifle dominant, and as unlike John Gaskell's as voice could well be, saying:

"Herrick, what a fool you are!"

Here was a harsh and jarring note to mingle with those softer and sadder memories!

"A fool, am I!" he said, to himself, with more irritation than he could account for. "Is it because I am true to the woman I love, and won't acknowledge her right to throw me over, that this girl calls me a fool? Or is it—no, that can't be possible—because the young lady thinks that

CATHERINE LOUISA PIRKIS

I'm not setting to work in the right fashion to get my darling back, that she impugns my wisdom? Yet, what in Heaven's name am I to do, where am I to go, if not to the only relative Lois has in the world? She tells me in her scrap of a note that she will be among friends who will protect her in the future. I know all the friends she has in England, poor child, and I have been to every one of them; now where else am I to go, what on earth am I to do, if not set off to this cousin of hers?"

Again and again he racked his brain to think if any other course lay open to him, any course that approved itself to common sense and reason. But rack, and strain, and weary his brain as he might, none other could he see.

His lamp began to burn low, the dun-grey of early dawn began to flow in coldly, slowly through cracks and crevices in the shutters. It found its way over his portmanteau, lying packed and strapped on the floor, to the débris beside his writing-table—fragments of letters and envelopes—which told the tale of his hard work at that desk.

Among those fragments, his cousin's rough sketch of the Sphinx, torn in half, caught his eye.

He pushed it irritably on one side with his foot.

"It's not worth thinking about," he said, aloud. "A girl of eighteen! what can she know of men and women, of the world and its ways, that she presumes to lay down the law as to what is or is not folly?"

Yet, fight against the idea as he might, he was constrained to admit that no better illustration of his mother in her present mood could be found than that of the enigmatical, impenetrable Sphinx of classic story. Yes, enigmatical was, indeed, the only word that could be applied to her conduct at the present moment. Together with the most violent demonstrations of grief—of delirious abandonment to grief—she had exhibited the extreme of coldness and self-restraint. And Honor had noted this, evidently, with eye as keen as his own. Now what if in addition to these clashing moods Honor had seen and had taken note of other things, equally matters of fact, which he had not seen or noted, and hence had made her blunt animadversion upon his folly?

When Herrick had reached this point in his thinking, his irritation against Honor had somehow subsided. In its stead there had come to him a feeling of bewilderment, a distrustfulness of his own senses such as a man might feel who, having been gazing fixedly at what he considers a red rose, is suddenly convinced of his colour-blindness by one telling him that the flower he is staring at is as yellow as a buttercup.

He passed his hand wearily over his forehead; his eyes ached, his head ached.

"I must get a couple of hours' sleep," he thought. "My head isn't clear enough to think out these things. Physically, as well as mentally, I'm not quite up to the mark just at present."

But harassing thoughts are not to be scared away by the sight of a pillow, like sparrows from the wheat by an old coat and hat. His dreams from beginning to end of the two hours to which he restricted his rest were a painful réchauffé of the day's anxieties, ending with a vision of Honor, standing in front of him with Medusa's head in her hand, and saying: "Since you choose to shut your eyes and your ears, now for ever lose the use of both."

IX

The thought with which Herrick lay down to rest—of his own folly in not being able to see what he ought to see, or to hear what he ought to hear—rose up with him and went with him through the fields and lanes that, with many a wind and curve, led to Longridge village churchyard.

His road lay in an opposite direction to the bleak heath and the outskirts of the coal country. Round the village church lingered all that was left of rural pastoral life in the district. The School Board—by the strenuous efforts of the vicar—had, as yet, been kept at bay, and the children on their way to the parish schools dropped little curtseys or pulled at curly locks as Herrick went along the village street. He beckoned to one of the curly-headed urchins to hold his horse for him while he went into the grave-yard. The church lay a little way back from the village street, and was reached by a long, narrow avenue of low-growing, solemn yews. Beneath these the autumnal mist still lingered, as if kept from rising by the heavy boughs. But beyond, on the farther side of the church, the morning sun shone resplendent from out a sky—blue, as if dyed with cobalt—on graves of all sorts and conditions of men: on low, sunken mounds, with never so much as a wooden cross to proclaim the names of their occupants; on lofty granite obelisks, like the one of which Herrick was in quest; and here and there on mossy lichen-eaten stones with scarce a trace of inscription left to them.

As Herrick quitted the avenue for this sunnier portion of "God's acre," he was not a little startled by the appearance of his dog Argus, who came suddenly bounding from behind a tall tombstone, and with loud bark and exceedingly wet paws, gave him an enthusiastic greeting.

Looking in the direction whence the dog had come, his eyes were met by a greater surprise still. In a spare plot of ground, immediately facing the granite obelisk which marked the last resting-place of the Gaskells, stood an old thorn-tree, ablaze now with its own scarlet berries, and the wild luxuriance of bryony which twisted itself round about the split trunk and peeped in and out among the branches. Beneath this old tree sat a lady, in deep black, with a sketch-book upon her knee. A second glance told him that this lady was his cousin, Honor.

A sudden flush of annoyance passed over him. He had come for a quiet ten minutes to a spot to him more hallowed than any other on earth, and here was this girl, who had called him a fool to his face, with whom in fact he had nothing in common, on the holy ground before him!

With her pencil in hand, too—the pencil which had already satirised his mother and himself! What preposterous caricature had she on hand now that she must needs come to this solemn place for inspiration? Was nothing sacred in her eyes, not even the last resting-place of her own kith and kin? Was it possible that she was making a sketch of that granite obelisk in order to introduce it effectively as a background in some ridiculous character-sketch! He checked the thought with difficulty as Lady Honor, having had his arrival announced to her by Argus, came forward to meet him with outstretched hand.

She did not pick her way over the still dewy grass—straight over everything she went. Possibly, however, this mattered little, for no doubt her skirts were already bedraggled and her boots soddened by her walk down the deeply-rutted lanes—a walk most likely accomplished in similar free and easy fashion.

"I did not know you were coming here this morning," she said, with the fixed, straight look in her eyes habitual to her, "or else I would have stayed away."

Herrick was more than half inclined to repeat her remark verbatim for an answer. He restrained himself, however, saying only:

"It is the only opportunity I shall have before I go. I sail this evening, you know."

"Yes, I know," answered Honor, hastily, and in a tone which, to his fancy, painfully recalled the one in which she had passed judgment on his lack of wisdom. "But it did not occur to me that you would be here so early this morning, and, as I particularly wanted to make a sketch to send to a friend of mine, I came."

There was no possibility of ignoring what that sketch was. Her sketch-book, held open to dry the fresh colours, displayed to view the gaunt granite obelisk and massive iron railings which marked John Gaskell's grave.

"That friend of yours ought to be a very near and dear one to have such a sketch as that sent to him—or her," said Herrick, gravely.

"That friend of mine is a very near and dear one," said Honor, in precisely Herrick's tone of voice—if it had cost her her life this girl must indulge her habit of mimicry—"and I have sent already to that friend of mine," she resumed, "a sketch of Longridge Castle—"

"And its inhabitants?"

"Why, of course! What's the good of a shell without its kernel? Now I want to send him the sketch of Uncle John's grave."

Could it be that her voice faltered over the last three words? thought Herrick, his heart for a moment softening towards his cousin.

As they had talked they had walked towards the tall obelisk, and now stood beside it on the lately-removed and replaced turf, over which, here and there, the gravel still lay in brown patches.

On the big block of granite, from which the obelisk sprang, lay a thickly-twisted wreath of wild honeysuckle and ivy. The dew still lingering here and there on the luscious flowers showed them to have been freshly gathered.

Herrick looked from the wreath to Honor, from Honor to the wreath.

She turned her head away. There could be but little doubt whose hand had laid that wreath there.

His first thought was one of surprise; his second was an ungracious one. What right had she thus to associate herself with him and his mother in love and grief for the dead? Relative, though she might be, she knew nothing of his father or grandfather, save their names; and these, no doubt, had often in her hearing been associated sneeringly with plebeian wealth and mushroom grandeur.

"It was very good of you, but—" he began, coldly.

She turned her face quickly towards him. There was a shining light like that of tears in her eyes.

"But what right had I to lay it there?" she said, finishing his sentence for him.

Herrick was silent.

"What right, indeed!" she said, speaking very fast and with an undernote of pathos which he had never heard in her voice before. "What right has such ugly duckling as I to show affection for any living soul! What presumption on my part to imagine that any one, living or dead, would be the better for my giving them a thought!"

Herrick was amazed at the depth of feeling she threw into her words. The occasion did not seem to warrant it.

"No girl with a father and mother living should speak in that fashion," he said quietly.

Lady Honor turned and faced him.

"A father and mother!" she cried impetuously. "Shall I tell you what my father and mother think of me for having dared to come into the world a girl, and a girl, too, with an ugly face and a clumsy figure? Shall I tell you that my first recollection of my mother is her giving an order to my nurse to keep me out of her room as much as possible? My face was a shock to her nerves, and my voice gave her a headache, she said. And 'To think that you should be a Southmoor and the last of the name,' were the words with which my father packed me off to school at Brussels, and received me back with, when I came home the other day."

Herrick was touched. He took her hand.

"You would never have heard such words as those from him," he said, pointing downwards to the newly-turned sod with its browned grass and trampled daisies.

"I know it," said Honor, releasing her hand quickly, as if such forms of sympathy were unknown to her. "When I looked at his big picture hanging in the hall, and saw his kind eyes and beautiful mouth, I said to myself: 'If I could only have known you, how I should have loved you,' and then I felt as if I must—must do something for him; lay a wreath upon his grave; say a prayer for him." She broke off for a moment, then added: "Ah! that's why I envy the Catholics so! They can pray for their dear, dead friends as well as for their living ones."

It was all said in the girl's usual frank, impetuous, rush-ahead fashion.

Herrick stood silent, self-convicted of stupidity for not having guessed at a condition of things which seemed to him now perfectly intelligible.

She misinterpreted his silence.

"But there, I'll take the wreath away," she went on impetuously. "Why should I force my way into your holy ground?"

She bent over the railings. Herrick laid his hand upon hers.

"Pray, let it be, Honor," he said in a low, disturbed tone. "I am very grateful to you for your kind thought of my father."

Then there fell a silence between them; a silence during which Herrick's compassion for his cousin in her loveless young life grew apace. He longed to offer her sympathy, but did not know how to begin. His thoughts flew to Lois.

"How I wish you and Lois could have met!" he said, "you'd have been bound to like each other, and—"

"I'm not so sure," interrupted Honor, quickly; "I don't take to everybody I meet."

Herrick froze a little.

"Everybody? No! But if you have an eye for beauty, and truth, and goodness—"

"I'm not so sure that I have," again interrupted Honor. "I have an eye for ugliness, and meanness, and wickedness—"

"And folly," finished Herrick, meaningly.

"And folly? Yes; when it's thrust under my very eyelids!" she answered, quite unabashed; although, the moment after she added, apologetically, "you see I've had so few opportunities of making acquaintance with what is 'beautiful, and true, and good.' As a rule, I'm more accustomed to the ugly and mean, and, therefore, recognise it more quickly."

"I think you do yourself an injustice," said Herrick, gravely. "Have you not, only a moment ago, confessed that when you looked up at my father's portrait, before anything else, you saw the kindness in his eyes—"

"I beg your pardon," interrupted Honor, "I did not say 'before anything else.' When I first looked up at Uncle John's portrait, before anything else, I saw that the artist had given him a streaky complexion. It was after that I found out that he had kind eyes and a beautiful mouth."

Herrick turned sharply away. Was nothing too sacred for ridicule in this girl's eyes? He pulled out his watch. She did not heed the action, but went on frankly, carelessly:

"And the first time I saw you—before even I saw that you were the image of Aunt Jo, I saw that you were a slovenly writer, for you had ink under your finger-nails. Now, if I were to see your Lois, before I saw her beauty and goodness, I should find out her weak point, for of course she has a weak point?"

"Yes;" said Herrick sadly, "she has a weak point, and it has cost me dear: she can't stand her ground and face an enemy. If she is scared, she takes refuge in flight."

"Poor child! I would love to take care of her," said Honor, for all the world as if she were in the forties, instead of little more than a child herself. Then, after a moment's pause she said, as if struck by a sudden idea: "Herrick, I would give anything to frighten Aunt Jo nearly out of her life."

Herrick started. The idea, thus abruptly expressed, assuredly sounded oddly in its present connection. It struck a curious vein of thought. Here had Honor been little more than a week in the house, and in that short space of time had evidently made observations enough to fill a note-book. The lookers-on, sometimes, see more of a game than the players.

He hazarded a question:

"Do you mind telling me, Honor, if you have any special reason for saying this?"

"Not in the least," she answered. "Aunt Jo seems to me to be one of those persons who are sent into the world for the whole and sole purpose of frightening the timid and weak—a sort of embodied nightmare. One look at her would be enough to set old people or children shuddering."

Lady Honor did not know what a painful memory of an old man's death-bed her words conjured up to Herrick's mind. Nevertheless, he felt called upon to enter his protest against her sharp criticism.

"Kindly remember that you are talking of my mother," he said, a little stiffly.

He laid his hand on her arm, and led her away from the grave as he spoke. To his fancy the very turf, with its trampled daisies, seemed to cry out to him:

"Would you two dare to talk thus if he who lies beneath your feet stood there by your side?"

Honor assuredly did not share his sensitiveness.

"Why, what difference can that possibly make?" she said bluntly. "You may call my father or mother embodied nightmares, or embodied anything else you please, and I shan't find fault with you. But, honestly, Herrick, I came to your house prepared to love—yes, to love Aunt Jo—you know, I have had very few people to love in my lifetime. And when I saw Uncle John's picture, I said to myself, 'No one could live thirty years with that man and not be the better for it.' And I tried to get into her room while she was so ill, but they wouldn't let me. Then you know how I bounced in on her with a bunch of grapes—oh, I had taken such trouble in choosing that bunch! And what do you think she said to me after you had dashed out of the room as you did in a temper? Not 'Honor, you are a darling;' or 'How I shall enjoy them;' but, 'Honor, I shall be glad if you will allow my maid to do your hair for you while you remain here; it does not look as it ought to look!' That was how my grapes and the offer of my affection were received!"

They had turned down the yew avenue as they had talked, and now stood at the churchyard gate.

The lad came forward with Herrick's horse. He twisted the reins round his arm, and side by side the cousins walked through the quiet village street, with Argus at their heels.

Herrick's thoughts were very busy. Lady Honor, throwing a straight look at him with her bright, prominent eyes, said, a little suddenly, a little brusquely:

"Poor Herrick! From the bottom of my heart I pity you."

Herrick started; her outspoken sympathy struck a harsh note of contrast with a gentle voice which had whispered in his ear: "My poor, poor boy! If only I could bear this sorrow for you," while a soft hand had tenderly caressed his hair. Yet, such as it was, it was not sympathy to be rejected.

"Thank you, Honor," he said presently. "You don't see me at my best just now, I'll admit. Yesterday you called me a fool, and, honestly, trouble has come upon me so thick and fast lately, that I feel as if my brains were leaving me!"

"Oh, I didn't mean I thought sorrow had turned your brain, I meant I thought you were a fool for the way you set to work to meet it."

"I shall be grateful to you if you will tell me a better way of meeting my troubles," he answered, sadly. "If you refer specially to my trip to America in search of Lois, will you kindly tell me what better course you see open to me?"

"Staying at home," said Honor promptly. "Look here, Herrick, Aunt Jo told me a little about you and Lois. That is to say, she said you had formed an undesirable attachment for a girl beneath you in station"—here Herrick made an impatient movement with his hand—"but that, left to itself, she had no doubt that the attachment would die a natural death." Here Herrick uttered an angry exclamation.

Lady Honor went on:

"Of course, when Aunt Jo spoke of an 'undesirable attachment,' I fell in love with the girl on the spot; and I thought, 'I wonder what you have done to scare that undesirable girl away from the place.' I looked straight at her—so—"here Honor faced Herrick with so fixed a stare in her prominent eyes that it seemed as if they must possess the crab-like power of protruding themselves—"and Aunt Jo's eyes drooped immediately. I've done it once or twice since, and her eyes invariably droop when I stare hard at her. Now, Herrick, if Œdipus—"

"Oh, for Heaven's sake let Œdipus alone!" exclaimed Herrick.

"I can't; it's a case in point. Now, it seems to me, if Œdipus had done as you are doing—started off on a voyage to the other side of the globe, the riddle of the Sphinx would have remained unsolved to the present day; but no doubt he stared and stared at the monster until its ugly face was stamped on his mind, and—"

"You needn't go on any further, I see what you mean," interrupted Herrick, a little sharply, for the simile pained him; "but I assure you you are mistaken if you think my mother has had anything to do with Lois's sudden flight. I have her express assurance on the matter. I know her to be as incapable of subterfuge and petty lying as—well—as you are. No, nothing else in life suggests itself but this journey to America, and go I must."

"Go, then," said Honor, "and I will stay here at Longridge, and stare at the Sphinx for you. I rather like the idea, it turns the tables on father and Aunt Jo. They've concocted a little plan to keep me here for my benefit—I'll fall in with it for theirs."

After this, the talk between the cousins grew easy and confidential. During their walk back to the Castle, there did not fall a single five minutes of silence between them. Herrick, in glowing language, told the story of his wooing and winning of Lois White, and Honor reciprocated with the tale of her loveless nursery days, and the miserable school life at Brussels which had followed.

"The pupils, one and all, were ill-fed, ill-taught, and brow-beat," was her terse summing-up of a condition of things which she had depicted vigorously in detail. "They were poor, and had no one to speak up for them. I was treated somewhat better than the rest, because I had a handle to my name, and, if I had chosen, could have visited at the Embassy. The teachers were mean, under-bred, detestable—with one exception."

Herrick turned sharply and faced her. "Name him," he said, brusquely, and bluntly, as she herself would have spoken.

"M. Henri Van Zandt, the drawing master," she said, boldly, defiantly; but, for all that, with a sudden flame in her cheeks, which made them approach in colour to her hair.

"Is that the friend for whom you made your sketch this morning?"

"Yes."

"And those you have previously made of the Castle and its inhabitants?"

"Yes."

"Take care, Honor, I may think it necessary to ask my mother to give an eye to your correspondence."

Honor clapped her hands. "Oh, the very thing!" she cried, "it would be heavenly to feel that one was defying every relative one has in the world! I've told father and mother, over and over again, that on the very day I'm one-and-twenty, I'm going over to Brussels to marry M. Van Zandt, and we have had no end of storms over it; but, fancy the exquisite pleasure of holding up a letter to Aunt Jo, and saying, 'Aunt Jo, I'm going into the village to post this letter to my dear old drawing master, and by-and-by I'm going to marry him, and together we shall set up a shop on the Montagne de la Cour, for the sale of lead-pencils and artist's colours.'"

　　　　　　　　　　　　CATHERINE LOUISA PIRKIS

"Honor!"

"Oh, don't draw a long face! It's my very life to be always 'in the opposition.' I'm a born Nihilist, Democrat, Socialist, whatever you like to call it. Directly a thing is forbidden to me by 'the powers that be,' I find it's the only thing in life worth doing."

Herrick interrupted the girl's light talk with a serious question:

"Tell me what sort of a man is this M. Van Zandt, for whom you are ready to defy every relative you have in the world."

Lady Honor's answer was characteristic.

"When I first saw him I saw only that he was old—over forty, that is—and ugly; oh, as ugly as I am, and very badly dressed. After I had tumbled into the water one day, and he had jumped in and saved me, I found out that he had beautiful eyes, and that he was as chivalrous as a knight-errant, and that nothing in the world could suit him so well as his own shabby coats and hats. After this we naturally got on amazingly well together," she broke off for a moment, then added, "but before this I had won his heart. Shall I tell you how?"

"I am deeply interested, I shall like amazingly to know," answered Herrick.

"Well, it was in class, and the Gorgon-eyes of the teachers were upon us, and we were all silent as mutes. The water-colour class were drawing from a study after Cuyp, a level Dutch meadow with sheep and goats browsing. I was always quicker than the other girls at drawing, and before they were half-way through, my sketch was finished, all except the faces of my animals, which I left vacant. M. Van Zandt passed once and looked over my shoulder. 'Pourquoi donc, mademoiselle?' he said, pointing to the eyeless, noseless creatures. He didn't say 'Pourquoi donc?' next time he passed, for every one of those creatures had had a face given to it in lead pencil. All the poor little persecuted teachers and pupils in the school figured as sheep, all the mean, tell-taling, underbred pupils and teachers came out as goats. He put the sketch into his pocket at once, and told me that it was worth living his twenty years of cheap teaching over again to see Mademoiselle Dutertre—the head of the school—with a beard and curly horns."

They had now reached the hall-door of the Castle, and Lady Honor, with a look on her face which seemed to say that she considered the last word on M. Van Zandt's perfections had been spoken, disappeared into the house.

X

So Herrick sailed away in search of his lost darling, leaving affairs, great and small, at Longridge, to settle themselves. It would have been as profitless a task to have stood on the sea-shore and told the tide not to follow as the moon led, as to have attempted to persuade this young lover to stay quietly at home and wait the course of events.

"A fool I may be. I dare say I am," he said to himself over and over again as he paced the deck of the Atlantic steamer, whose speed was all too slow for his hot haste; "but if I don't follow this clue, slight though it may be, what in Heaven's name am I to do? What other course lies open to me?"

It took him three weeks to reach his destination in that out-of-the-way corner of Washington territory, which, not three years back, had been a rank forest, and which now was the site of a busy and well-populated town.

During those three weeks, events followed in a rapid succession at Longridge. The first event of importance was the appointment of a trustee to John Gaskell's will in the place of the one who had died.

It seemed to Mr. McGowan that Lady Joan showed an altogether unaccountable anxiety to get this matter settled.

"It had far better stand over till Mr. Gaskell's return," he remonstrated. "He ought to have a word to say on the matter."

But no. Lady Joan would listen to no remonstrance.

"My son may be away for six months or more, for all I know to the contrary," she said in that frigid manner of hers, which always made Mr. McGowan feel as if cold water were being poured down his spine; "and, as Lord Southmoor must return to Devon in a week, at the farthest, I think the sooner all legal formalities are got through the better."

The lawyer pricked his ears and took fright at the mention of Lord Southmoor's name.

"If I may offer a suggestion, Lady Joan," he said, speaking out boldly, "Mr. Gaskell is the right and only person who should be nominated co-trustee with Mr. Rothsay."

Lady Joan slightly bowed in acknowledgment of the suggestion; then added, in frigid manner as before, "I shall have the greatest objection to any one, save Lord Southmoor, acting in that capacity."

To this she adhered, and the upshot of it all was, that before Herrick had time to reply to Mr. McGowan's cablegram, acquainting him with

CATHERINE LOUISA PIRKIS

the state of affairs, Lord Southmoor—idea-less and incapable—was bracketed with Mr. Rothsay, eighty years of age and incapable, as trustee to the vast wealth that John Gaskell had left behind.

There could be but little doubt that Lady Joan had her team well in hand now, and could drive it any way she listed.

With the sense of power, however, there seemed to come to her but little of serenity or satisfaction. A spirit of restlessness appeared to have taken possession of her. She rose early, went to bed late, ate little, and from morning till night incessant occupation of some sort seemed to be a necessity to her.

Lady Honor's keen eyes noted all this, together with her aunt's changing personal appearance. "There'll soon not be enough of her left to throw a shadow, Argus," said the girl, as she fondled the mastiff's big, tawny head and fed him with lumps of sugar with which, surreptitiously, she had stuffed her pockets.

Off and on, Argus was the recipient of a good many of Lady Honor's confidences just then. Life at Longridge, with Lady Joan at one end of the dinner-table and Lord Southmoor at the other, was not a very cheerful affair. Argus seemed to the girl the only bit of honest, cheery, young life about the house, and morning, noon, and night found the two in each other's company. He accompanied her in her walks or rides, and her easel was never seen on terrace or shady walk without Argus's big, brawny form stretched beside it. He was called upon for sympathy on all sorts of matters which might be reasonably supposed to be outside the range of canine taste. For instance, the sketch of his own thick-limbed self, of which Herrick had caught a glimpse, minus a face, was put literally under his nose, and he was called upon to admire himself, endowed with large, kindly human eyes, very bushy eye-brows, and moustachioed lip.

"It's the image of him, Argie, and it's going off to him today with a few others," said the girl as she slipped it into an envelope addressed to:

M. Henri van Zandt,
25, Rue Hainault,
Bruxelles.

This despatch evidently was precious in her eyes, for she did not trust it to the Castle letter-bag, but rode herself with it to the village post-office.

By the same post she despatched a less bulky packet to Herrick, to the address at New York to which he had requested his correspondence to be sent. It was a very informal missive. There was never much beating about the bush in Lady Honor's letters; and in this one, as usual, she dashed into the very middle of her subject without any preamble.

"Father," she wrote, "has suddenly developed an increase of starchiness which is very funny. He is stinging-nettles, chevaux-de-frise, stilts, and high-heels boiled down into essence. I suppose it is because he has been made trustee, or something or other, to Uncle John's will, that his dignity has grown so rapidly. He has tried to sit upon me a good deal lately; but, of course, I never fail to turn the tables, and sit upon him. There's one comfort: he'll soon be out of the house now, for mammy, down in Devon, is crying out for change of quarters. The Sphinx remains impenetrable, as usual, and, although I have kept my eyes fixed on her, as yet I am a long way off from reading her riddle. We spend long mornings together—they could be measured by the mile. She has recommended to me all sorts of improving books. I take them up, lean back in my chair, hold the book in front of me, and—study her. She writes a great deal. I'm sure she is composing an essay; and I think its subject is Catherine the Second of Russia, for a bulky volume—the life of that beauty—is always beside her on her writing-table; and whenever she has a spare moment I see it in her hand. Now that's a curious subject to take up, isn't it? Here is something else I can't understand. All the law business that has been done during your absence has been got through at express speed, as if business were hateful to her. Mr. McGowan, for some reason or other, does not appear to be a favourite, and he seems no sooner in the house than he's out of it again. Yet there comes a person to the house—a person, by the way, who has been more than once before—and he is closeted with Aunt Jo for the whole afternoon in the library. I met him coming to the house as I was going down to my favourite seat in the pine wood, early in the afternoon, and when I returned, somewhere about five, I could see him as I passed the library windows seated there still. He's not a bad-looking man. I've dubbed him Adam from the nice, frank, open-air look he has about him. I should think he would look positively handsome divested of his churchgoing coat, with his shirt-sleeves tucked up, digging up potatoes."

Here there followed a sketch of Ralph Harwood, in shirt sleeves, in the act of potato-digging—a sketch that so cleverly caught his likeness that Herrick could not fail to recognise the man who had on one occasion held open the park gate for him.

CATHERINE LOUISA PIRKIS

"This suits me best," was written as legend beneath the sketch.

The picture absorbed the remainder of her sheet, and crowded into one corner her signature, preceded by the letters Y. A. C., which, in a bracket, she informed Herrick meant "Your affectionate Cousin."

It may be conjectured, however, that could Lady Honor have made a third at the interview which had taken place between Ralph and Lady Joan, she would have modified her opinion respecting the "fine, frank, open-air look" which, in the first instance, had won her admiration. As he sat facing Lady Joan, watching her changes of expression, while she read a letter which he had just put into her hand, his brow was knotted into a deep frown, his face looked white and anxious, his fingers played nervously with the brim of his hat which he held between his knees.

His changed manner even attracted the attention of Lady Joan, who, naturally enough, attributed it to the serious condition of his sister's health as stated by Dr. Gallagher in the letter she held in her hand.

"I confess I do not understand some of the technical expressions this doctor employs," she said as she laid the letter down; "but it is quite clear to me that he considers your sister's mental condition far from satisfactory."

"Yes, my lady."

"And he lays great stress upon the unfortunate fact of her mother's insanity. 'The disease known as melancholia,' he says, 'is so frequently hereditary.'"

Here she keenly scrutinised Ralph's face.

"Yes, my lady," he answered once more, fidgeting a little under her steady gaze.

"Well, I can only say I am very glad your priest has given his consent to the only sensible course that could be taken in the matter, and that your sister's health will be at once and thoroughly attended to. Two hundred a year I think you said was Dr. Gallagher's charge for receiving her as a patient?"

"Yes, my lady."

"As you will have many preliminary expenses, I will pay you the first quarter in advance: fifty pounds that will be. Please remember, however, that I only charge myself with your sister's maintenance so long as she remains under the care of this doctor."

The cheque for fifty pounds was made out and handed to Ralph; but, somehow, he did not appear half so effusively grateful as he had been on a former occasion for a lesser sum.

"Now, with regard to Miss White," pursued Lady Joan as Ralph folded the cheque and put it into his purse, "her wishes incline to a religious life?"

"So Father Elliot says, my lady. I've not seen her; I know nothing about her," said Ralph, bringing out his words with a jerky rapidity.

"Since that is the case, I will put my offer of the other day into a more definite form. I believe it is usual when a young lady enters a convent for her friends to pay down a certain sum into the convent treasury. I am willing, in this matter, to fulfil the obligations of Miss White's friends. If your priest or the mother-superior of the convent she wishes to enter will fix the required sum I will pay it: one half on the day she begins her novitiate, the other half on the day she makes her full profession."

Ralph made no reply to this, so Lady Joan put a direct question to him:

"Will you kindly convey this offer of mine to your priest?"

"Yes, my lady."

"Of course I will like you to send me fullest particulars of the convent the young lady enters, and when and where the novitiate will begin," resumed the lady; "but I think that can very well be done by letter."

"Yes, my lady."

"Finally—and on this matter I wish you to be very exact—you must make your priest to understand clearly that he can have no direct intercourse with me. All communications to me must be made through you. I have my reasons for wishing this; but I think it is not necessary to state them to you."

"Not necessary!" it would have been well-nigh impossible for her to have stated in so many words her fixed resolve that no ghosts of early days should be resuscitated now to haunt her path and enfeeble her purpose.

Once more there came no response from Ralph, so once more she put a direct question:

"Do you understand me?"

To which Ralph replied, a little brusquely, perhaps:

"I do, my lady."

"One thing more, and then I think our interview is ended. It concerns your sister. When she has been some little time—say a month—under Dr. Gallagher's care, I wish to see him and have a viva voce report of her condition. I have his address, and will write and tell him when it will be convenient for me to receive him. That is all there is to say, I think."

XI

Although Herrick had again and again admitted to himself the possibility that Honor's indictment of folly might be a true one, yet, as he made the last stage of his journey—that by rail from New York to Tacoma City—his hopes revived, and all sorts of bright anticipations filled his mind.

He wondered over the first words of the greeting that would pass between him and his darling; what she would be doing in her cousin's home; how she would be looking when he caught his first glimpse of her. Would she be dressed in one of her usual simple white frocks, with a dainty little posy in her waist-belt; and would he see on her finger— and this thought sent a hot flush of blood to his brow—the ruby ring over whose making he had spent so much time and thought in order that it might be the counterpart of his own?

He lived on the memory of happy meetings and greetings in days gone by, much more than he did on his bread and butter just then; or, in other words, on the hurried meals which the breaks in his railway travelling allowed him. Over and over again he lived through the last hour they had stood face to face together, when, with clasped hands and tears running down her cheeks, she had besought him for permission to watch beside his aged grandfather. Over and over again he lived through "that tick of his lifetime's one moment of bliss," when he had held her in his arms under the beeches at Summerhill, and had vowed that "nothing in this world nor in any other should come between them." Once more the silent, stately avenue, the sea of green-sward with its black blots of shadows, rose up before him, and the sudden sharply-tolling bell sounded in his ears together with Lois's sweet tremulous words of love and trust.

Beautiful delusive visions all of them! Tacoma city, with its hum of traffic and bustle of money-making, made them all to vanish like ghosts at cock-crowing, and brought him face to face with a long list of "John Whites," which seemed altogether out of proportion to its population.

It took some little time to hunt down the owners of this far from distinctive patronymic, interview them, and convince himself that they were none of them the "John White" of his hopes.

The proverbial search for a needle in a bundle of hay would have been easy work beside this, which might have been compared rather to a search for a needle in a packet of needles, every one as like another as a needle could well be.

Mr. McGowan's cablegram, conveying the intimation of Lord Southmoor's appointment as co-trustee to John Gaskell's will, found him in the thick of his dreary task. "John White, of 1059, Yakima Avenue. Thomas White, horse dealer, 1090, Market Broadway. He'd be no use. Ah yes, though, he might have a father who might be a John White. I must look him up," he was saying to himself, when the message was brought to him.

He read it a little indifferently. "What on earth is there in that to make a hue and cry over!" he thought. "McGowan must be going off his head to make such a fuss about nothing. It can't matter two straws whether my uncle or someone else is trustee. He's not a man to trouble himself as to how things go on, and of course, virtually, all responsibility will rest on my shoulders. By and-by, when things are a little more settled"— that meant, when Lois was found and carried back to Longridge as his wife—"I shall have a good deal to think of; but now—!"

Here he crumpled the cablegram in his hand, tossed it into the fire, and went back to the question whether Thomas White of Market Broadway might have a father who might be the John White of whom he was in search.

Lady Honor's letter, which, in due course, followed the cablegram, perhaps had a little more attention accorded to it for the reason that it was a source of greater annoyance to him—ruffled his temper—made him feel somewhat as if he had been thrashed with stinging-nettles. When he had given Honor permission to write to him and tell him anything that might transpire concerning Lois, he had not dreamed that she would in this way set up a deliberate system of espionage on his mother. The whole letter, from beginning to end, so to speak, set his teeth on edge with its rough handling of people and things which young girls are supposed to hold in some little reverence. How could it concern Honor, he asked himself angrily, whether his mother studied the life of Catherine of Russia or of anybody else? What had it to do with her or with him that she received the visits of a man, say, of the small farmer class?

The whole tone of the letter seemed to him not only an insult to himself, but, in some sort, an insult to the memory of his father, who, to the last hour of his life, had never failed to treat Lady Joan with the utmost of respect.

CATHERINE LOUISA PIRKIS

His mother had expressly denied all knowledge of Lois and her movements. To suppose her capable of a series of small deceptions on a matter which had had the most honest and open opposition at her hands, would be to create an entirely new conception of her character. It was far easier for him to let go the favourable estimate he had begun to form of Honor, and to credit her with a malice which, under the mask of a love of fun, ran riot at will. So Lady Honor's letter followed Mr. McGowan's telegram into the fire.

Her next letter shared a similar fate. It was, she said, "only a line to say she had nothing to say," that is, nothing of importance to report, except that the man whom she had before described as Adam had been again to the house. There was a postscript to this letter, saying that Catherine of Russia had been banished, and her place had been taken by ponderous volumes on ethics by Mill and Bentham. Also, that "Aunt Jo" had given up going to church.

A second postscript followed this. It was to the effect that, as "the Sphinx" was a ponderous and clumsy appellation to write frequently, she would, for the future, substitute the initials "E.N.," which, if Herrick would carry back his thoughts to the day on which he had first shown any amiable feeling towards her, and recall the conversation they had had together in the churchyard, he might understand to mean "embodied nightmare."

This letter did not bring back on its writer a sharp reprimand, for the whole and sole reason that it reached Herrick at a moment when he had a more difficult question to decide than any over which hitherto he had racked his brain. Scouring the environs of Tacoma in search of his "John Whites," he had lighted on the traces of a man who, there was little doubt, was the one he sought. He had searched out this man's antecedents, and had found that he had come from England about ten years back, that he had spoken from time to time of a cousin of his who was an officer in the navy, and of this cousin's only daughter who was being educated in an orphanage. This man's name was John and his wife's name was Lois, after whom, Herrick conjectured, there could be little doubt that his Lois had been christened.

By profession, this John White was a civil engineer, he had pursued his calling in Tacoma and its environs until about six months back, when professional duties had taken him to California, where he was at the present moment. There could be no difficulty in finding him out there; he was a rising and a thriving man, and the laying out of a new railway in the gold country had been committed to his supervision.

The question which Herrick sought to answer now was, should he at this point give up the hope of finding Lois in America, or should he push on to California to her cousin's house?

Was it probable that Lois had known of her cousin's change of locality, and had, in the first instance, made California her destination? or, if not this, had she on arriving at Tacoma, learnt the news for the first time, and thence continued her journey to California?

Either supposition held its full measure of pain for him. It nearly drove him frantic to think of this child—she was little more—setting off without guardian or guide on this second long journey. It was bad enough to picture her crossing the Atlantic alone; but that was safety itself compared with the perils her infantine face and sweet, timid ways would seem to invite in a journey of this sort across country.

His hopes sank very low; he began almost to feel that, after all, Honor was right, and his journey to the West had been but a fool's errand.

Yet if Lois had not taken refuge here with her only relatives, where in Heaven's name had she gone? And if he decided at this point to give up the pursuit of those relatives, what else in Heaven's name was he to do?

It was a difficult question to answer. It took him hours of weary thought before he even approached a decision. He almost regretted that he had not in the first instance called professional skill to his aid. Yet he acknowledged to himself this was scarcely a thing which, in the circumstances, he had had a right to do. If a girl throws her lover over, and bids him respect her hiding-place, he has scarcely the right to hunt her down as if she were a criminal.

These, and a thousand other thoughts crowding into his mind, made his decision yet more difficult to arrive at.

It was arrived at at last, however, by help of a night without sleep, a day without food.

To follow this American clue to its end was the one and only thing he could see before him now. This done, other things might suggest themselves; but this thing left undone, he could see nothing before him but a blank wall.

So he turned his back on Tacoma city, and set off for the Far West, with his heart more like a lump of lead than the living, beating thing it was supposed to be.

XII

Winter set in early that year. Before the roaring east winds had finished sweeping avenue and byways of their autumn wreckage, the ice season was upon them: great jewels of icicles hung from slanting roofs and corniced windows, and frost spangles were flung galore over field and forest.

Lady Joan seemed to feel the cold this winter as she had never done before. She took no out-door exercise; was never seen without some woollen wrap over her shoulders; and shut herself up as much as possible in her boudoir, which she averred was the only warm room in the house.

Lady Honor, on the contrary, rejoiced in the keen, bracing air and iron-bound earth, which rang out a defiance to every step she put upon it, as young things in full health are apt to rejoice in all that sets the blood dancing. Her one lament was that there was no one to skate with, no one to slide with, no one to toboggan with. In fact, just then there appeared to be no one to do anything at all with. The society which the neighbourhood offered had never had much attraction for Lady Joan; and her acquaintance with her neighbours had consequently been kept upon a strictly formal footing. A call at informal hours, a chance guest at breakfast or luncheon were things unknown at the Castle; and, of necessity, entertainments of every sort were for the present tabooed to Lady Joan and her niece.

Lord Southmoor had returned to Devon, and was supposed to be preparing to take flight with his "Lily" to the South. A good deal of correspondence, however, appeared to be going on just then between him and Lady Joan, for every other day seemed to bring a letter with the Southmoor post-mark on it.

Lady Honor wondered over this as well as over one or two other matters. She had plenty of time for wondering. Deprived by the frost of her morning's wild gallop across country, in company with Argus, having no taste for music, and ignoring utterly the existence of such tools as needles and thimbles, she had a great many spare moments on her hands. These she devoted in their entirety to minute observation of the details of the life being lived out beside her own.

"She doesn't know she's under a microscope, eh Argie, does she?" she whispered, as she fed the mastiff with the best of everything she could lay hands upon. "Time will show; but if I don't read the riddle of the Sphinx, there's no one else will, take my word for it, Argie!"

In those early winter days, when Lady Joan was thrown so much upon her niece for society, slowly, but inevitably, it was borne in upon her mind that this girl, upon whom she had counted as a passive, if not active, coadjutor in her plans, was a failure and a disappointment. "Give it a chance and blood must show," she had said to herself over and over again, as she had tried to balance Lady Honor's numerous disadvantages of education against her name and her race. But assuredly "blood" was having every chance now under her own austere and stately rule, and yet Honor remained the untrained, defiant, care-for-nothing damsel she had been from her cradle.

Nothing daunted her, nothing troubled her. The sternest of looks or of reprimands left as little mark upon her as rain upon a rivulet. Lady Joan, who had known so well how to freeze the boldest into silence with an "I beg your pardon," found herself more than once cowed and discomfited by one of Honor's steady, fixed looks from her bright, prominent eyes.

In spite of all this, however, Lady Joan found it impossible in a moment to give up the plans it had taken her so many years to mature. Let Honor be loud-voiced, disappointing, disconcerting as she might, she ranked infinitely higher in her estimation than the little nursery governess, with her face of child-angel and voice soft and musical as a woodland echo.

She lost no opportunity of rousing interest in Honor's mind in Herrick and his doings, and of setting before the girl, in a right light, this foolish trip of his across the Atlantic, and the foolish fancy which had occasioned it.

"I've had a line from Herrick—simply a line," she said, looking up from her correspondence at her niece, who sat facing her in a rocking-chair with a book in her hand.

"Indeed!" said Lady Honor, sharply, "he might have had the grace to write to me."

She felt a little piqued that the long letters she had taken such trouble to write had not had so much as an acknowledgment.

Lady Joan, not understanding, rejoiced in the thought that the cousins had reached a stage of friendliness in which correspondence might be expected of each other.

"He is in a disturbed state of mind, just now," she said, apologetically; "by-and-by, no doubt, he will settle down into his old self and do all that is expected of him. If you'll believe it, he is off to California now on his wild-goose chase!"

Lady Honor gave a great start. She fell back on her old form of expression. "Oh, what a fool he is!" she exclaimed, brusquely, as before.

Lady Joan slightly frowned. The form of expression was not to her liking—the sentiment was.

"He has been befooled, I'll admit," she said, after a moment's pause; "but I've no doubt that by-and-by he'll return in a saner state of mind. It is better for him to have a lost journey than a ruined life."

"Aunt Joan," said Honor, suddenly fixing her round, prominent eyes full upon her aunt, "what makes you think that it will be a lost journey? Why shouldn't he find Lois White in her cousin's house in America?"

There could be no doubt about it, the question embarrassed Lady Joan. Her eyes drooped, her face clouded.

"It is a matter of common-sense," she said, after a moment's pause, "that an all but penniless girl is scarcely likely to undertake such a long and expensive journey at a moment's notice."

Then she took up her pen and began to write rapidly across one of the quarto sheets which lay before her.

Lady Honor, still eyeing her keenly, saw that her hand trembled slightly. "She knows where the girl is if any one in creation does," she said to herself, as she pushed back her rocking-chair and walked lazily to the window, triumphant in the thought that she had given Aunt Jo a shock to her nerves, and resolute to repeat the operation on the first opportunity.

Acres of frosty grass, bare, brown-limbed trees—showing black against a leaden sky—met her eye. The only sign of life in the sunless, wintry landscape was the appearance of two men coming up the long avenue which led to the house.

One of the two she immediately recognised as a former visitor of Lady Joan's. His companion appeared to be a man about a dozen or so years older. His figure was narrow and sinuous, his face dark-skinned and lean.

"Here is Adam," she thought to herself. "I wonder if he's bringing the serpent with him." Aloud, she said: "Delightful! Aunt Joan, here are visitors. Oh, what a heavenly break in the day's monotony!"

Lady Joan frowned, but said nothing. Her pen steadily travelled over her quarto sheet. "Standards of Morality Compared and Differentiated," stood as the title of that sheet. Below, she had started her essay with the words: "What is the criterion of a moral act?"

The answer to this question held a deeper interest for her than the coming of chance guests to the house, to bore her with their commonplaces of sympathy or gossip.

Honor's steady, fixed eyes seemed to read her thoughts easily enough.

"Houses—castles especially—should be made with drawbridges, shouldn't they, Aunt Joan? Cards to be left on the other side of the moat," she said, with the slightest possible touch of sarcasm in her tone.

"Dr. Gallagher and Mr. Harwood wish to see you, my lady," said a servant entering the room at that moment.

The expression on Lady Joan's face changed. She, however, carefully crossed her final "t" before she said, composedly:

"Honor, will you kindly take your book into another room? These persons have come to see me on business."

Lady Honor immediately vanished. She did not take her book with her, however, and, instead of retiring to the library or drawing-room, went straight to her own room, where she made an excuse for the attendance of the young girl who had been assigned to her as maid.

She thought she would like to know a little about this Dr. Gallagher and Mr. Harwood.

Amid a variety of directions as to dresses, ribbons, and hats, she put a few questions to the girl which elicited from her, in reply, the story of Lucy Harwood's short stay in the house, and of her sleep-walking propensities. A story which, with slight variations of detail, was now current in the household.

Lady Honor's curiosity was excited.

"Did any one see her walking about in her night-gown beside Lady Joan?" she asked. "I should love to see someone walking in their sleep in the dead of night."

Most ladies' maids, thus catechised, would forthwith have begun to build a fabric of fiction on the foundation of fact. This one, lacking imagination, was truthful.

"I don't know, my lady. I've heard say that she walked into old Mr. Gaskell's sickroom in the dead of night; but I don't know if it was true. Mrs. Parsons, the old gentleman's attendant, or Mrs. Jervis, the sick nurse, could have told you; but they're neither of them here now."

"What has become of them?"

"Oh, my lady has been so kind to them. Mrs. Jervis had a son out in Australia, and wanted to go out to him; so my lady paid her passage out for her. And Mrs. Parsons had a nephew who wanted to open a big

CATHERINE LOUISA PIRKIS

shop in the grocery line in Chester, and my lady has set him up there, and Mrs. Parsons lives with him. My lady has been goodness itself to every one who showed old Mr. Gaskell any kindness or attention."

Lady Honor felt puzzled. Her aunt's conduct seemed to her more enigmatical than ever. "Goodness itself to every one who was kind to the old gentleman," she thought. "Yet father has more than once said that she had wished him out of the world for years! It is all a mystery together!"

XIII

The short winter's day began to wane. Lady Honor bethought her of a certain letter which she had written, with all but frozen fingers that morning, before the fire in her room had been lighted, and which now reposed in her locked-up desk awaiting postage.

The two hours which intervened between afternoon tea and dressing for dinner were the hours she generally held sacred to the posting of these precious missives. Those two hours were more absolutely her own than any other in the day; for Lady Joan, as a rule, retired to her room after the tea-drinking was over, and Honor was left free for the two miles walk which landed her in the village post-office.

Lady Joan had specially requested her niece never to be seen outside the lodge gates unattended by her maid; and Lady Honor had forthwith made the discovery that long country walks were only delightful when undertaken with Argus for sole attendant.

Lady Joan hitherto had forborne to question Honor respecting those walks. She was ignorant of the steady correspondence which her niece carried on with her Belgian lover. M. van Zandt's existence had only been made known to her by the casual remark of Lord Southmoor's—that "A presumptuous jackanapes of a drawing-master had presumed to make love to Honor; but, of course, it was all at an end now." Lady Honor's long, lonely walks to her mind simply represented a breach of the conventional; and, for the present, she shrank from a contention on the matter—a contention which, no doubt, Honor would have welcomed with keen delight.

"So far, Argus, I have paraded my muddy boots before her to no purpose; but, sooner or later, the storm must burst, and we shall have the opportunity of saying no end of sweet things to each other," said the girl, as she and Argus, side by side, scampered down the lanes which lay rutted and frozen between high hedges sparsely powdered with light snow.

Argus had sadly plebeian tastes, and owned to a good many canine friends among the village-bred lurchers and collies, and when, after posting her letter, Lady Honor started on her return journey, he was nowhere to be seen. She whistled and whistled in vain for him; then lost her temper over his bad manners, and informed the rutted ground and snow-powdered hedges that she would teach him a lesson and leave him to his fate.

The sun had gone down—a white-faced, miserable apology for the great golden globe of summer days—twilight was yielding rapidly to the denser shades of night when she reached the miniature pine wood which made the short cut from the high road to the Castle. The moon had not yet risen; never so much as one tiny silver star pierced the blackish-grey of the sky. The pines swayed a little in a gentle passing wind and waved their funereal plumes hither and thither as Lady Honor clambered over the rustic gate: to her way of thinking a far nicer way of entering the little wood than by lifting the latch and walking in. The bridle-path, cleanly swept by the gardeners every morning, showed whitely between two rows of trimly-cut Euonymus bushes grown to nearly a foot above her head.

It did not for a moment occur to the girl that it might have been wiser to have taken the longer road through the park to the Castle until the sound of footsteps and voices approaching attracted her attention.

"Gipsies, tramps, poachers. All three, perhaps," she said to herself. "Now, are they following the path, or are they careering here, there, everywhere under the pines?"

The steady, rapid pace at which the footsteps were approaching answered her question. In the tangle of undergrowth which lay right and left of the cleanly-swept path, that regular ringing tread would have been an impossibility.

Full of the idea of tramps or vagabonds, Lady Honor took advantage of a break in the hedge, and slipped out of the path into the tangle beneath the pines.

She congratulated herself that her dress was a black one. "If only my hair matched it!" she sighed. "It will shine out like fireflies in the dark. I rather wish Argus were here, he'd help me to save my watch and rings."

But the next moment found her thanking Heaven that Argus was not there to betray her with his loud challenging "who goes there?" bark, for strange words fell upon her ear—words so strange, indeed, that she held in her breath and shrank behind the biggest pine-trunk she could find, in order that not one of them should be lost to her.

"What on earth are you in the dumps about, man?" said an oleaginous voice, which Lady Honor felt sure must belong to the dark-skinned man whom, in a moment of inspiration, she had dubbed "the serpent," and who had been announced to Lady Joan as Dr. Gallagher. "This is a capital world to live in if only one knows how to manage one's affairs. Cheer up! cheer up! Everything is going splendidly!"

"Splendidly, do you call it?" replied the other, whom it was easy to identify as Ralph Harwood. "Villainously would be a better word. I've never before played cat's paw to man or woman, and I wish to Heaven I had let myself go into the workhouse rather than—"

"Oh, if you're going to be religious and invoke Heaven," interrupted the other, the oil in his voice giving place to a pronounced sneer, "go down on your knees and thank Heaven for the golden chance that has come in your way. Why, my friend, the lady is as free with her fifty-pound notes as other people are with their fives!"

"I wish to goodness they had never come in my way," said Ralph, gloomily. "Why couldn't she get someone else to do her bidding? Why does she persist in throwing her gold at me in the way she does?"

The men were now abreast of Lady Honor in her hiding-place. A sudden determination came to her. These men had been closeted with Lady Joan for hours, and were no doubt in her confidence. Here, perhaps, was a golden chance of getting a clue to the secret for which Herrick was hunting the other hemisphere. Softly she crept out of her hiding-place, and as the men passed along, step by step, her tread followed theirs.

Only the thick Euonymus hedge divided her from them; their words fell clear and distinct upon her ear.

"I take it," said Gallagher, "that the lady hasn't always had the chance of flinging gold about in this fashion, and that's perhaps why she's a little free with it now. She's a splendid woman—a most interesting case I should have called her if I had come upon her, in the old days, in one of the asylums—a little difficult to understand at first, perhaps; but a keen pair of eyes like mine will read her through and through before they've done with her."

"If your eyes are so keen, I wish to goodness you'd tell me what makes her take so violent an interest in me and mine. It is out of all reason to volunteer as she does to provide for my sister for life."

"Gently, my friend, you go too fast. She will provide for her only so long as she is treated as a semi-lunatic; in other words, she makes it to your interest and mine to stamp her as such."

"Of course, so far as Miss White is concerned," went on Ralph, "it is easy enough to understand why she should wish to hide her in a convent. I've heard lately that it was the talk of the place that young Mr. Gaskell wanted to marry her."

Lady Honor's heart was beating wildly now. Here was a revelation! She began impetuously to thank Heaven that the plot was laid bare to her before it was too late to frustrate it.

"Let me see," said the other, after a moment's pause, "when did the novitiate begin—on the twentieth of last month was it?"

Lady Honor's heart stood still. She ceased to thank Heaven. The novitiate begun! Alas, alas! for Herrick's hopes. Lady Joan might almost cry victory now.

"On the twentieth of last month, yes," answered Ralph, "and a strict novitiate it is, too. In all respects similar to the life of the fully professed nun—perpetual enclosure, no communication whatever with the outer world. Not even deeds of charity are allowed; it is all contemplation and prayer. Great Heavens. How can the women endure it! I'd sooner lie down in my grave at once than become a Red Sister."

"Oh, well, that's their look-out, isn't it? She went in willingly enough, didn't she?"

"Willingly! She was only too thankful to be admitted. The Father would never have allowed her to be driven in."

"What's her name in religion, by the way? It's just as well I should know," asked Gallagher.

"Sister Héloïse. Not that it matters much to anybody what her name is! In these strict orders the novice is as dead to the world as the nun."

This was not to be all that Honor was to hear that night. This wily, dark-skinned Gallagher, whose every sentence she felt ought to end in a hiss, was to be the first to put into plain words the thought which had been lying in her heart for weeks past.

"I say, Ralph," he said, in a knowing tone, "it strikes me this Lady Joan has something on her mind; her manner gives one that impression. On her conscience, I should say, if I had not long ago come to the conclusion that conscience was nothing more than prejudices for or against certain social conventions, transmitted in a straight line from father to son."

"I don't know about what she has on her conscience, I know she has put something on mine—"

"Tush, man, don't whine!" interrupted Gallagher, the oiliness in his voice having given place now to a more natural, if rougher, intonation. "This woman is to me a most interesting psychological study. Depend upon it, before I've done with her, I shall read her as easily—well, as I've read the score or so of patients who have passed through my hands."

They had now reached a point in the bridle-path where the pines were less closely planted, and where the Euonymus hedge was considerably lower. Lady Honor dared not venture farther, the risk of detection was too great. So the men walked on ahead, free from her espionage. Though she strained her ears to the utmost, only a half-sentence of Gallagher's reached them. It was:

"For one thing, whether by fair means or foul, young Mr. Gaskell must be kept out of the way. If he comes upon the scene he'll be sure to spoil sport."

And a minute after, together with the creak of the little rustic gate which led into the high road, she could hear Ralph saying, in hard, bitter tones:

"Yes, I suppose you're right; there's no going back for me now."

XIV

The sound of the men's footsteps on the frosty road died away in the distance, and the silence of the winter twilight fell upon the pine-wood once more.

Lady Honor pushed back her hat from her hot brows; her thoughts for the moment all one wild turmoil.

She almost felt that she had heard too much. When she had vowed, in characteristic language, to solve the riddle of the Sphinx, she had not expected to light upon such a solution as this.

Lois, no doubt through Lady Joan's instrumentality, in a convent; Herrick, "whether by fair means or foul," to be kept out of the way until certain things, no doubt in train now, should be accomplished. These things held the foreground of her thoughts. Side by side with these, it seemed to her of little consequence that Lucy Harwood, of whom she knew next to nothing, should be placed as a semi-lunatic under a doctor's care, or that Lady Joan should be suspected of having something on her conscience—it had not as yet dawned upon her what a fearful "something" that might be.

Her first impulse was to hasten home, confront Lady Joan with the facts of which she had become possessed, speak her mind freely on the matter, and demand the name of the convent where Lois was located, in order to send it to Herrick.

Second thoughts checked the indignant impulse, and counselled prudence. This was no light skirmish of her own in which she was engaged, a skirmish such as those she had fought, over and over again, with her Belgian school-mistress on behalf of some oppressed governess-pupil; but a battle, the issue of which involved a man's life-long happiness. One false step, a note of alarm sounded in Lady Joan's ear, and she felt that she might as well lay down her weapons and strike her flag at once.

For the first time in her life she began to feel a distrust of her own powers, and her need of a counsellor. Yet, where was she to turn for one? It was self-evident that it was of first importance to get Herrick informed of the condition of things. Next in order came the imperative necessity for discovering the convent where Lois was hidden, so that Herrick, on his return, might lose no time in bringing pressure to bear to induce her to renounce the religious life. "A novice is not a nun," said the girl to herself, trying to rekindle hope in her heart, "and there may yet be a chance for Herrick's future."

It was easy enough for her to say "that it was of first importance to get Herrick informed of the condition of things"; but how was this to be done, if Lady Joan were as determined as Gallagher was to keep him away from Longridge, and chose to withold his address? He had been on the point of starting for California when he had last written, so Lady Joan had said that morning; it stood to reason, therefore, that letters sent to the old address at New York might lie for weeks unclaimed.

Once more she anathematised his rampant folly, not only in fleeing from the spot where his presence was most needed, but also in placing such implicit trust in his mother that he made her his sole correspondent, and the depositary of his confidences.

Her thoughts naturally enough flew to M. Van Zandt as a likely person through whom to make enquiries as to the convents in England belonging to the Red Sisters, and thus, perhaps, get a clue to Lois's hiding-place. She knew something about these Red Sisters; they had several convents in Belgium, and it occurred to her that if not in England, Lois might have perhaps been sent to one of these for her novitiate. The Sisterhood, she had heard, was one of the strictest of the contemplative orders. "Redemptoristines, or Nuns of the Most Holy Reedemer," was their proper designation; but the red tunic which the Sisters habitually wore had won for them colloquially the term Gallagher had used. Their vows included one of perpetual enclosure, and the nuns, she knew well enough, were as much cut off from the world as if the grave had received them.

While these thoughts in swift succession had been passing through her brain, she had remained standing among the shadows of the gloomy pines. Now the rapidly-increasing darkness began to warn her that she must hasten home if she did not wish a bevy of servants with lanterns sent out in search of her.

She shuddered as she thought of what she was returning to; daily intercourse and companionship with Lady Joan in the future seemed to her intolerable, for ever so short a period.

"How can I eat with her, breathe the same air, look her in the face, even, without telling her that I know of her wickedness, and am doing my best to thwart it?" she thought, as her feet carried her as swiftly as possible over the frozen tangle of the pine wood.

In her present frame of mind she felt that it would be impossible for her to sit down to dinner with Lady Joan that night. She would, she thought, make some excuse, shut herself up in her room for the remainder of the evening, write her letters respectively to Herrick and M. Van Zandt, and carefully consider what, in Herrick's interests—in the interests of truth and righteousness, she might say—it behoved her to do.

It was characteristic of her fearless, careless temperament, that she did not give a thought to the possibility of Lady Joan having discovered her absence from the house, and the sharp reprimand which might even now be awaiting her return.

She made no attempt to enter by any but the big front entrance, where, necessarily, she had to ring for admission. The Castle was shuttered and lighted from top to bottom.

As she entered, the butler greeted her solemnly, with the intimation that the dressing bell had sounded twenty minutes ago; and half-way across the hall a footman came forward to say that "my lady" wished to speak with her in the library.

Lady Honor at once turned her steps thither. Only yesterday, if she had received such an intimation as this, she would have clapped her hands and cried, "Glorious! Now for a pitched battle!" Today, however, she was in a frame of mind to which pitched battles seemed tiresome things. Side by side with the story of Herrick's luckless love-making, everything else in life seemed for the moment to be of "colossal insignificance."

Coming in fresh from the keen, frosty air, the temperature of the library seemed to Lady Honor stifling—suited rather to the exigencies of orchids than those of human beings. Nevertheless, there sat Lady Joan as usual cowering over the fire, her feet absolutely resting on the brass "dogs" which supported the big logs.

The lights of the room were turned very low, but the leaping, crackling flames of the logs threw a bright glow on Lady Joan's pale face and stately figure. She was already dressed for dinner, her black ostrich fan lay beside her on a chair.

"How is this, Honor?" she said, in a stern voice, and fixing a severe look on the girl's hat and coat. "You surely do not need to be told that I disapprove of young girls taking lonely walks at this hour! Please explain."

Lady Honor laughed lightly.

"There isn't much to explain, Aunt Joan. I had letters—no, one letter—that I particularly wished to post myself, so I went to the village post-office to do so. Argus, who was with me, went off, paying calls on his acquaintance. I hunted after him, and consequently came in later than usual."

It cost the girl something to take the matter thus lightly. She was in a solemn frame of mind, and if she had not put steady restraint on herself, must have turned questioner, and faced her aunt with a few pointed questions which Lady Joan might have found difficult to answer.

"Later than usual!" repeated Lady Joan, in amazement; "Are you in the habit of taking your letters—no, I beg your pardon, one letter—to the post-office in this extraordinary fashion?"

"Do you call it extraordinary?" again laughed Honor. "I see nothing extraordinary in being specially careful over letters to a special correspondent."

"She will make me fight," thought the girl, "so the sooner we get it over and be done with it the better."

"A special correspondent!" repeated Lady Joan, arching her brows. "Will you be good enough to inform me who he or she may be?"

"Oh, certainly, with a great deal of pleasure. He is M. Van Zandt, my late drawing master, the gentleman to whom I am engaged to be married."

"You—engaged to be married to a drawing master!"

Lady Honor ought to have felt herself annihilated by the voice and manner in which these words were said. No shade of embarrassment, however, showed on her frank, careless face. She only said with a slight touch of irritability:

"Oh, Aunt Joan, don't repeat every word I say in that fashion. It was stupid of father not to have told you all about it when he was here, it would have saved me such a lot of trouble."

Lady Joan drew a long breath. "I can scarcely credit my hearing, that is why I require your words to be said twice over. Now I think over it, I remember your father said something about some impertinent advances—"

"Stop!" said Honor, going close to her aunt, and taking off her hat that she might feel the steady fixed stare of her bright eyes, "no one in my hearing shall speak disrespectfully of M. Van Zandt. He did me an honour—it was no impertinence when he made me an offer of marriage."

The girl's spirit was thoroughly aroused now. It was with difficulty that she prevented herself adding, as a sequel to her defence of her lover, "You! you! who have been, and are doing on the sly, all sorts of wicked things; how dare you throw scorn on a man like M. Van Zandt?"

Lady Joan's eyes for a momemt drooped under Honor's bright ones. Then she rose, with great dignity, from her chair.

"I will not permit you to discuss this matter with me, Honor, in this or any other fashion," she said, with slow emphasis. "But I warn you, I shall take what steps I deem right and necessary to protect a headstrong girl from her own folly. Meantime I must insist that so long as you remain under my roof you make no more extraordinary excursions into the village at extraordinary hours, not even to post letters to M. Van Zandt, your late drawing master."

It was impossible for Lady Honor to ignore the sarcastic emphasis with which the final words were spoken.

She made a little curtsey by way of acknowledgment for them, then turned towards the door.

"Thank you, Aunt Joan," she said, lightly, as before. "I'm glad to be dismissed. And please don't expect me down to dinner tonight. I'm rather tired, and I have a good deal to think of, and another letter to write to M. Van Zandt. Oh, and one to Herrick also, if you'll be good enough to give me his address."

As she said this, her bright, round eyes fixed themselves full upon Lady Joan's white lids once more.

Again those white lids drooped, and there fell a moment of silence. Then Lady Joan recovered herself, and Honor had the answer she might have expected. It was:

"Bring your letter to me when it is written, and I will enclose it in mine. I have not Herrick's letter at hand at the moment."

"Thank you, it doesn't matter," answered Honor, curtly, as she left the room, regretting now that she had drawn her aunt's attention to her wish to correspond with Herrick, since it might possibly strike a note of warning.

Her correspondence that night kept her pen in her hand till past midnight. In spite of her late hours, however, a letter to M. Van Zandt was dropped by her own hand into the village post-office before breakfast the next morning.

Her letter to Herrick could not be so easily disposed of. How was she to get at his address, she wondered, for she knew it would be useless to approach her aunt again on the matter. The possibility that he might have written to Mr. Champneys, or the lawyer, Mr. McGowan, suggested itself, and she forthwith resolved at once to make inquiries of both these gentlemen.

"I dare say it will set them both wondering what's up between Aunt Jo and me, that I can't go direct to her for my information," she thought; "but that won't matter much, so long as I can get tidings to Herrick of his poor little sweetheart."

XV

Nearly a week of warfare between aunt and niece followed. Lady Honor, when she found that she was, as she would have phrased it, "in for it," carried on the skirmishing with unflagging energy.

Her mental attitude towards her aunt, during the early part of that week at any rate, was one of anger more than slightly tinged with contempt. Later on, perhaps, when the secret of a dark night's work would be brought to light, horror and pity might take the place of that anger and contempt; but for the present her feeling was simply one of scornful anger at being brought to book for an infringement of the conventional by one who, there could be little doubt, was trampling under foot the first principles of truth and honour.

On the day after Lady Honor's late afternoon ramble, Lady Joan greeted her with the information that she had written to Lord Southmoor, telling him of what she was pleased to call Honor's discreditable correspondence. Also to M. Van Zandt, asking him to inform her of the exact position in which he considered he stood towards her niece; and at the same telling him that a matrimonial engagement between him and Lady Honor could in no circumstances receive the sanction of her family.

"I have deemed it my duty to do this, Honor," she said, in conclusion; "for during your father's absence from England I stand in his place towards you."

"With a difference," replied Honor, promptly, "for my father, so far as I am concerned, has never deemed anything his duty. But write away, Aunt Joan—a dozen letters if you like—to M. Van Zandt; they won't have much effect after the one I sent him yesterday."

The next battle was fought two days later, when M. Van Zandt's letter in reply to Lady Joan's was received.

"I will read it to you, Honor, if you like," said Lady Joan, coldly, formally. "He writes like a gentleman—"

"Why, of course, how could he write in any other fashion? That is equivalent to saying he has written with his fingers, not with his toes," interrupted Honor; "and as for reading it to me, there is not the slightest necessity to do so, I could tell you word for word what he has said."

Lady Joan arched her eyebrows. "I cannot credit such a thing," she replied, formally, as before.

"I will prove it to you," said Lady Honor, defiantly. "He begins with saying that you have written to him under a misapprehension; that no engagement whatever exists between us, for I am too young to be allowed to have an opinion on so momentous a matter. Is it not so?"

Lady Joan slightly bowed in affirmation.

"He goes on to say," Honor continued, "that had his landscape-painting been successful, and brought in the gold, he would not have looked upon a marriage with an English Earl's daughter in the light of a *mésalliance*, for he comes of a long line of nobles—has, in fact, some of the best blood of old Flanders in his veins, although the terrible wars in the Low Countries have utterly deprived his family of their fortune and position. Is it not so?"

Again Lady Joan bowed assent, and turned over the last page of M. Van Zandt's letter, as if to check by it Lady Honor's farther statements.

"Of course I know what he has written," laughed the girl, noting the action. "He has said all this nonsense to me over and over again. And now I suppose he ends as he began, by saying, that these things being so, he will not allow me to consider myself affianced to him, although once, in a moment of excitement, he suffered himself to speak words of love to me."

Lady Joan closed M. Van Zandt's letter.

"Honor, will you be good enough to tell me what was that moment of excitement?" she asked, in a tone that seemed to imply she dreaded lest some indignity had been done to the family name.

"Oh, certainly. It was nothing much. I fell into the canal just outside our school one day; I should have been drowned—not that that would have mattered much to anybody—if M. Van Zandt, who was just coming out of the house, hadn't jumped in and dragged me out. When I came to I was very grateful; and from that day forward we've been engaged."

"An engagement contracted under such conditions—" began Lady Joan.

Lady Honor sharply interrupted her.

"Oh, Aunt Joan, we'll continue the discussion tomorrow, if you don't mind. I must save this post to Henri, and scold him well for the ridiculous letter he has sent you."

And forthwith she had flown to her room, and there and then had dashed off a most characteristic epistle to M. Van Zandt. The first page consisted of a series of bluntly put questions, thus:

Did he wish to make her tell falsehoods by the square yard? Had he forgotten the times without number that she had assured him of her unalterable intention of spending the day after her twenty-first birthday in his mother's house? Did he absolutely intend to ignore the wish she had so often expressed of writing her name and title in full over a small shop on the Montagne de la Cour, devoted to the sale of lead-pencils and artists' colours? If, however, the truth was that he wished to wash his hands of her because she was so ugly and so poor, why not say so at once to her, and be done with it, instead of writing high-flown epistles to her relatives?

On the next page she dropped the interrogative form for the imperative, and desired him to give up his romantic notions, and listen to the dictates of his common-sense.

The third page was less closely written, containing merely the simple words:

"Without you, my Henri, I haven't a friend in the world."

Over leaf there followed a postscript, begging him to let her have the result of his enquiries respecting the convents of the Red Sisters as speedily as possible, and entreating him to suggest any ways and means for discovering where Sister Héloise was located that might occur to him.

While Lady Honor awaited a reply to this, she received letters respectively from Mr. McGowan and Mr. Champneys, in answer to her request for Herrick's address.

The gist of both letters was pretty much the same. The lawyer's letter was couched in a slightly injured, indignant tone. He knew nothing of Mr. Gaskell's movements, he said, for he had not once written to him, although he, Mr. McGowan, had over and over again written to his New York address, directing his attention to important matters of business.

The reply from Mr. Champneys was to the effect that no necessity for communicating with Mr. Gaskell had arisen since he had left Longridge, all business details having been thoroughly arranged by him before starting; and that if he—Mr. Champneys—had wished to refer any matter to Mr. Gaskell, he would have sent to the Castle for his address, taking it for granted that Lady Joan would be kept informed by him of his movements.

Lady Honor's hopes fell as she read these letters. The fact of Mr. McGowan's letters remaining unacknowledged seemed to imply that letters addressed to Herrick at New York were not forwarded to him. Her course did not seem plain to her now. She looked angrily at the Castle letter-box, which she felt sure would sooner or later become the depository of letters to Herrick from his mother, and all sorts of wild schemes for rifling it filled her brain. In her present frame of mind she felt herself equal to the doing of deeds she would have scorned at another time. It was an altogether new experience for her to find herself in a dilemma in which her usual weapons of courage and straightforwardness availed her nothing.

Towards the end of that week the warfare between aunt and niece began to slacken. Lady Joan was the first to show signs of flagging. Lady Honor, on the principle that a battle once begun should be fought out to its bitter end, made one or two vigorous efforts to arouse her aunt's evidently waning courage by pointed allusions to the wars which had, in times past, devastated the Netherlands, and to the terrible manner in which certain noble families had suffered through them.

Lady Joan did not take up the gauntlet. She had suddenly grown distrait, self-absorbed, pre-occupied. To Honor's fancy, she looked like one trying to think out a matter beyond her capabilities, or endeavouring to carry on two trains of thought at the same moment. Whether rightly or wrongly, Lady Honor attributed her aunt's suddenly changed manner to a second visit from the man whom she had dubbed "the serpent." She looked impatiently at the closed library door, behind which sat Lady Joan and "the serpent" in close confabulation.

"If those panels could speak, a fine tale of wickedness I should hear," she said to herself, racking her brain to think of a hiding-place in the room, where in the interests of truth and justice, she could secrete herself, and so, perhaps, get hold of a thread that might help her to unravel the tangle of evildoing by which she felt herself to be surrounded.

The very air, to her fancy, seemed charged with wickedness of some mysterious kind. Daily life at the Castle might be flowing on as smoothly as ever; there, nevertheless, seemed to her, an under-current to it—an under-current of something strange, unknown, inexplicable—close to her eyes, yet she could not see it, close to her hand, and yet for the life of her she could not grasp it.

End of Volume II

CATHERINE LOUISA PIRKIS

VOLUME III

I

If Lady Honor could have had her wish, and have found a hiding-place for herself in the library during Lady Joan's interview with Dr. Gallagher, the first name she would have heard on Gallagher's lips would, contrary to her expectations, have been, not Herrick's, not Lois's, but her own. "This young lady must have our first attention, my lady," she would have heard the man saying in his usual oily tone; "if we don't mind what we're about, we shall have Mr. Gaskell back at Longridge before we know where we are."

"We," "our." For all the world as if they were two men rowing in one boat, or two soldiers defending one citadel, or two sailors trying to bring a leaky vessel into port.

A few months back Lady Joan, with a word or look would have frozen into silence and respect any man who had dared thus to bracket his interests with hers. Now, instead of rebuff, he received simply the question:

"What do you advise?"

A big blazing fire crackled up the library chimney. Lady Joan had drawn her chair as close to it as it could well go. Sideways to her, and facing the light, sat Gallagher, leaning forward, with his arms resting on a small table, and his eyes from beneath his bushy brows closely scrutinising her face.

Seen thus in the full light of the wintry sunshine, the man assuredly was not "good to look at." Lady Honor, in the brief glimpse which she had had of him, had seen only that he was lean and sinuous in figure; dark-skinned and dark-haired. If she could have had a full view of him now, as he faced the light, she would have further noted that he had sunken, restless eyes, set very close together, bushy eyebrows, a flat forehead, and face literally scored with oblique wrinkles.

"My advice is very simple," he said mellifluously still, in reply; "the young lady has asked for her cousin's address, and is, no doubt, bent on keeping him in touch with events here. Very well, then; supply her with an address to which she may post her letters. Those letters will be a splendid outlet for her energy, of which you say she has enough and to spare, and will do harm to nobody."

"Supply her with an address!" repeated Lady Joan, blankly. "I do not understand you."

Gallagher gave a short, low laugh—a laugh which, strange to say, set not one of those oblique wrinkles of his moving, nor as much as raised a sparkle in his eye.

"Ah, my lady, you haven't knocked about the world and had the experience of life that I have, or you would catch my meaning more quickly." Here he felt in his waistcoat-pocket, and drew thence a card.

"On this card," he continued, "is the address of an old friend of mine at Cleeve's Hill, Luton West, California. Now, my lady, if you'll be good enough to transfer this address to the back of an envelope with Mr. Gaskell's name upon it—in which you have already placed a blank sheet of paper—and seal, and leave it lying about as if ready for the post, I'll wager ten to one that the Lady Honor lights upon it, and forthwith pours out her confidences to her cousin in a letter similarly addressed. I will, on my part, take the precaution of writing to my old friend, asking him to return all letters addressed to Mr. Gaskell to me. Now do you understand me, my lady?"

Lady Joan took the card which he held towards her, glanced at it, tossed it contemptuously on a side table.

"I am not in the habit of descending to artifices of this sort," she said, with a flash of her old haughty manner.

Gallagher eyed her keenly for a moment, beneath his bent, bushy eyebrows. He did not press the matter farther, however; but changed the subject suddenly—one might almost say with a jerk.

"I heard from my wife at Ballinacrae last night," he said; "that was my real reason for coming over to the Castle this morning."

Lady Joan was all attention at once.

"And the girl—Lucy Harwood—how is she?" she asked, turning towards him.

He shrugged his shoulders. "Her health is exactly what one would expect in the child of such a mother—capricious; one day she is out walking, the next she is in bed."

Lady Joan seemed to keep her self-control with difficulty. "Tell me exactly what her mental condition is. I am deeply interested in the girl," she said, with an ill-disguised eagerness.

"No doubt," he answered. Did Lady Joan's ears deceive her, or was there the suspicion of a sneer in his voice? "Well, my lady, at the present moment she is as sane as you and I are; but let her live on for another ten years or so, and she will be as mad as ever her mother was—I'll stake my professional reputation on it!"

Lady Joan put her hand to her brow as if smitten by a sudden pain there.

Gallagher, still steadily eyeing her, made a remark which seemed apropos of nothing at all. It was:

"The study of temperament and character is to me the most delightful of studies."

Lady Joan made no acknowledgment of the remark, did not so much as withdraw her hand from her eyes.

Gallagher went on:

"The temperaments of these two women, Lucy and her mother, were not, however, sufficiently complex to interest me keenly. They belong to a type with which our asylums abound, and which is the product of the union of the lymphatic with the melancholic temperament. Ah! Asylums are the places for the study of character. Temperament has to be thought of there before anything else, and studied under the most difficult conditions, if a cure is to be attempted. No doctor who understands his business, would administer drugs, except for the alleviation of transitory symptoms."

Lady Joan withdrew her hand from her eyes. The expression on her face seemed to say: "I do not follow you; I haven't the remotest idea of your meaning; but I know it is of first importance that I should hear you out."

Gallagher resumed:

"It was hard work at times; but the skill I acquired in the discernment of character and the discovery of motives under the most complex conditions, amply repaid me. After a time I attained a wonderful facility in following the intricacies of ill-balanced brains, and assigning a purpose to apparently purposeless actions. "My lady," here he leaned forward, speaking with arrestive emphasis, "the skill I gained in the asylums I brought out of them with me; and now I defy—yes, defy—a living soul to draw my attention to an apparently motiveless action, or course of action, for which I could not in due course lay bare to view the prompting motive."

Lady Joan gave a great start. This, then was the point to which the man had been leading her.

He gave her no time for reply, but went back suddenly to his former topic of conversation.

"All this is a digression, however, from the point we were discussing, the desirability of supplying the Lady Honor with an address to which she may send her—no doubt—effusive epistles. My lady, our course at the present moment requires to be shaped at once with courage and judgment; there must be no weak hand to guide the helm. So far things have gone well. One girl is in a convent, she is safe enough; the other girl is under my care, she is, if possible, safer still," here he gave another slight, unmirthful laugh; "but a good deal yet remains to be done which Mr. Gaskell's return might seriously interfere with. The purchase of Southmoor, for instance, is not yet complete.

Lady Joan turned and faced him with arched eyebrows.

"Who told you," she exclaimed, "that I contemplated purchasing Southmoor?"

"My lady, it so happens that I have some troublesome law business of my own on hand just now, and as Mr. McGowan is an excellent lawyer, I have commissioned him to carry it through for me. I ventured to give your ladyship's name for a reference as to my respectability." Here Lady Joan gave a great indignant start. Her lips parted, but not a word escaped them. "It was quite casually," he went on, "through a junior clerk in the office, that I became aware that Southmoor was in the market, and that your ladyship was an intending purchaser."

The emphasis which the man laid upon the words "quite casually," suggested immediately to Lady Joan's mind the thought that his information had been obtained by artfully contrived circuitous means. Possibly, in like manner, he had made it his business to obtain farther information respecting her private affairs.

His next remark seemed to give substance to the suspicion.

"A great deal of nonsense is current as to the secrecy which lawyers maintain concerning their clients' affairs. I suppose it is the locked up tin boxes with which they stuff their offices that have set the idea afloat. They are as great a sham as the flung-back iron gates which some asylums affect in order to give the impression that the patients can walk out whenever they feel inclined."

Lady Joan made an uneasy movement with her hand. It was an uncomfortable thought that this man, with his keen eye for character and avowed skill in the discovery of motive, should have perhaps wormed himself into the confidence of a junior clerk of the firm that had drawn up the will of thirty years back, which had left her sole mistress of her husband's wealth. She could feel the man's deep-seated eyes fixed full on her very eye-balls. She leaned back in her chair, saying nothing, taxing her strength to keep the turmoil in her brain from showing in her face.

He resumed:

"But all this is wide of the mark. What I most wished to impress upon your ladyship was the desirability that Mr. Gaskell's return to Longridge should not be hastened. Let the purchase of Southmoor be complete, and that farm out in Australia be bought for Ralph Harwood, and Mr. Gaskell may come back as soon as he pleases and overhaul the banker's book to his heart's content."

Lady Joan felt it was incumbent on her to speak.

"The price required for that farm seems to me altogether exorbitant," she said. "The money produced by the sale of the Wrexford farm should go towards it."

"My lady," said Gallagher, for a moment dropping his mellifluous tone for a business-like one, "every penny that Wrexford farm fetches in the market must go into my pocket. Ralph owes me the worth of that farm over and over again; and before he sets sail for Australia I shall expect him somehow to raise the money and pay off the thousands he has drained me of during the past few years."

Lady Joan rose to the bait at once.

"I will charge myself with those thousands," she said. "I do not wish the man's journey to Australia to be delayed."

Gallagher's accents grew mellifluous again.

"Thanks, my lady, I will, with your permission, draw up an estimate of the sums I have supplied him with from time to time. I agree with you that the sooner Ralph is shipped off the better. He is a weak, shifty sort of fellow, and completely under the thumb of his father-confessor." He broke off for a moment. Then added, in a deprecating tone: "Ah, those priests, with their fingers in every pie! Don't be afraid, my lady, they're not likely, any one of them, to enter my house at Ballinacrae. I've given strict orders to my wife not to let one of them have access to Lucy."

Lady Joan grew deadly pale; her eyes drooped. She did not dare to put the question which would have come naturally enough to the lips of most people thus addressed:

"How can it possibly matter to me how many father-confessors go near this girl?"

Gallagher, leaning forward still, with his arms resting on the small table, and with eyes never once lifted from her face, went on:

"I said to my wife, 'If one of those long-coated gentlemen get at the girl and put thoughts into her head about the duty of observing the Church's ordinance of confession, how shall I be able to ask of my lady the very handsome sum she is paying me for her care and maintenance?'"

Lady Joan seemed suddenly to feel the heat of the fire. She pushed her chair sharply back from the fireplace. Yet if any one had touched her hand he would have found it cold as the snow which lay so thickly outside on the garden paths.

"Now this Father Elliot," he went on, "who has so much influence over the girl, is a most dangerous man in this respect. You'll be glad to hear, my lady—"

Lady Joan, suddenly and impetuously, rose to her feet.

"One thing—one thing," she said, speaking vehemently, imperiously—"one thing, at least, I will insist on! Whatever else is done or left undone, this man—this priest shall not enter my house. I will not see him—speak to him; I will not have him brought here. Thirty years ago I said that he should go at once and for ever out of my life—he shall not be brought back into it now."

She spoke excitedly. She had evidently forgotten that she was addressing a man to whom her life of "thirty years ago" was a blank page.

He gave her one long, steady, searching look.

"Ah," he thought, "they were lovers long ago, not a doubt. This puts the matter into a nutshell, and explains why the priest was, as Ralph said, so strangely affected when he heard the lady's name."

Aloud he said, not attempting to rise, as she had risen:

"Don't be uneasy, my lady; you're not likely to be troubled with him. I was about to tell you that he left Longridge more than a week ago to join a society for African missions. They have what they call an Apostolic College at Cork. Harwood says the Father has volunteered for the mission to Dahomey, from which delightful bourne I should say it is extremely probable that at his age he will never return. It yearly engulfs any number of religious enthusiasts."

Lady Joan drew a long breath, and sank back in her chair.

"I can talk with you no longer today," she said, in a voice that sounded strained and feeble. "If you have anything of importance to say to me, come again in a day or two. But, but—"

She broke off abruptly, not daring to finish her sentence, with the words:

"But, for Heaven's sake, don't come here with no other purpose than to play with me as a cat plays with a mouse."

Gallagher rose from his chair, and bowed.

"There is one thing of first importance," he said, "to which I shall be compelled to ask for your ladyship's attention—the list of the moneys I have from time to time lent Harwood. I shall be able to make it out in a few days, and will then bring it to you."

He made one step towards the door, then came back for a last word. It was:

"I would strongly urge your ladyship to consider my suggestion as to the desirability of supplying the Lady Honor with an address to which to send her letters." Then he bowed again and was gone.

Lady Joan rose tumultuously to her feet as the door closed behind him. She pressed her icy hands to her burning temples.

"Is it worth it? Is it worth it?" she cried, passionately. "What have I done that I must be hunted, badgered, tortured, by such a creature as this?"

Conscience, with a voice like a herald's trumpet, shouted into her ear what she had done.

She covered her ears with both hands, as if to shut out a living voice.

"The end justified the means—it is a thing that, one way or another, has been done times without number all the world over. The strong souls, the souls who rule the world, who legislate for the good of the race, would call it a brave deed, and hail me as a benefactor. How dare—"

But here she sank back into her chair again, a sudden dizziness and faintness overcoming her, and for the moment all was oblivion to her.

Until now Lady Joan had been the high-bred lady, giving her orders to an obedient, obsequious agent. Henceforward she was to be a tool—nothing more, in the hands of a double-dyed villain.

II

From this point Fate had things all her own way, and events followed thick and fast. Lady Joan condescended to the artifice from which at first she had so indignantly recoiled, and laid a trap for Lady Honor which, for low cunning, could not have been surpassed by an Old Bailey criminal.

Blind as any mole, Lady Honor walked into the trap. On the day after Gallagher's visit she had occasion to go into the library to fetch an envelope from a stationery cabinet, and lo, beside it on the writing-table was a letter addressed to Herrick, in Lady Joan's writing.

"Oh, my good luck!" cried the girl, hastily seizing a pencil and copying the address.

And, before the day was over, with her own hand she had posted to that address the bulky packet over which she had spent her midnight hours.

She congratulated herself not a little on her own prudence and sagacity in thus waiting for chance to favour her, instead of giving way to impatience, and despatching her letter to Herrick's former address in New York, where, for aught she knew to the contrary, it might have lain for weeks unclaimed.

Those self-congratulations would have suffered considerable modification if she could have known that, in little over a fortnight, her recklessly-worded letter would find its way back to England, and straight into the hands of the man whom she had therein described under a variety of contemptuous epithets—"the serpent" being about the mildest of them.

Before the week ended, in the hope of still farther expediting matters, she despatched a telegram after her letter. She rode over to Wrexford to send it, preferring not to set going the tongues of the village gossips over affairs at the Castle.

Her message was a brief one, "Come back at once," was all she said in it, hoping that Herrick would read between the lines, and gather the urgency of the occasion from the mere fact of her sending a message at all.

The next event of importance reached Lady Honor's ears in roundabout fashion, through a letter from her father, and was nothing less than the purchase—all but completed—of Southmoor by Lady Joan.

The Earl stated the fact in the baldest manner possible, in about twenty words, saying nothing of the battle royal which had been fought between Lady Joan and Mr. McGowan over the matter.

Mr. McGowan had contested every inch of the ground, with a persistence worthy of the trust which the Gaskell family had reposed in him through so many years. In the first instance he had protested against the consent of Lord Southmoor's co-trustee, Mr. Rothsay, being so much as applied for until Herrick had been consulted as to the propriety of withdrawing the required thousands from their present investments. His protest fell flat, Lady Joan having taken time by the forelock, and successfully impressed old Mr. Rothsay with her views before she had made them known to the lawyer.

Mr. McGowan's next step was to write an urgent letter to Herrick, stating facts to him in strong language. He applied to Lady Joan for an address to which to send his letter. Her reply to his application was to the effect, that, beyond the fact that her son was in California, she knew nothing whatever of his movements.

Then the lawyer, in his fidelity to the Gaskell interests, did a very foolish thing—refused to have anything to do with a transaction which his judgment utterly condemned. Upon this Lady Joan at once commissioned Lord Southmoor's legal advisers to act as her representatives in the purchase of the property, and the whole thing was hurried through in a manner that showed that the interests of the seller, rather than those of the buyer, had been consulted throughout.

Of all this, however, Lord Southmoor said nothing in his letter to his daughter.

"Your aunt," he wrote, "has begged, as a special favour, to be allowed to purchase the home of her childhood, and the purchase is now all but complete. It cost me not a little to yield to her wish; but I could not find it in my heart to refuse her permission to do what has undoubtedly given her great pleasure." This was said by way of salve to his own personal dignity. "It will, however, be impossible for me to take up the position of tenant where once I was sole master and owner, so I shall continue as heretofore my life of pilgrim and sojourner. However, I hope that you, my child, unburdened by your father's sensitiveness, will live out your young life on the old acres, and will offer no opposition to your aunt's plan for your future, a plan that will, I firmly believe, conduce as much to Herrick's happiness as to yours."

Lady Honor's quick eye pierced what she was pleased to call "the wretched humbug of the whole thing" in a moment. She took a pen and dashed off there and then, a brief, characteristic letter.

"DEAR FATHER," she wrote, "I'm sorry Aunt Jo has wasted her money over Southmoor. It's a wretched old place, and only fit for bats and owls to live in. I don't wonder you prefer the 'dolce far niente' of continental life to the dreary responsibilities of a tumble-down estate. I don't want Aunt Jo to bother about my future—I've already arranged it for myself. Neither my young nor my middle-aged life will be lived out on the old acres, but I hope and trust in a sweet little shop—on the Montagne de la Cour, in Brussels—devoted to the sale of 'lead pencils and artists' colours,' and with the name of Van Zandt written in big letters over the doorway. Give my love to my mother.

"Always your affectionate daughter.

HONOR

Angry and indignant at this persistent ignoring of the matrimonial arrangements which she had made for herself, and with the spirit of defiance strong upon her, she resolved that she would read her letter aloud to "Aunt Jo" before she consigned it to the letterbox.

So, letter in hand, she dashed into Lady Joan's boudoir.

"I've heard from father; shall I read to you my reply?" she asked, in her usual loud, brusque tones, as she entered.

Lady Joan was seated at her writing-table, her pen in one hand, the other supporting he head as it bent over her quarto sheet. Her pen must have been a busy one, for sheets of barely dried manuscript, torn in half, filled her wastepaper basket. In spite of its hard work, however, the essay on "Standards of Morality" had not advanced by a single line, for there, heading a blank page, stood the question with which it had started, "What is the Criterion of a Moral Act?" unanswered still.

As her niece entered, she withdrew the hand which supported her head, and turned so white and forlorn a face towards the girl that her defiant, angry mood at once gave place to one of pity for one who, whatever her sins might be, was evidently suffering some acute mental distress.

Lady Honor flung her letter on the floor, and knelt down beside her aunt, taking one of her hands in hers.

"Oh, Aunt Jo, what is it?" she cried, "Tell me, tell me! Let me help you if I can."

Lady Joan released her hand from Honor's clasp.

"Who said that I wanted help?" she asked, coldly, proudly. "I do not understand you."

Lady Honor was not to be so easily rebuffed.

"No one has said it, but any one who has eyes can see it," she answered, boldly.

Lady Joan looked disturbed.

"See what?" she asked, uneasily. "See that I look ill, old, weary? Can you wonder at it after—after—" She broke off abruptly, not daring to speak words into which her conscience read a double meaning.

Lady Honor upturned her face, and fixed her clear, bright eyes full on her aunt's drooping lids.

"Aunt Joan," she cried, impetuously, not weighing her words, but, according to her wont, speaking right out the thoughts of her heart, "it's that man—that wretched creature who keeps coming to the house, who makes you look so ill and worried. He's wickedness incarnate, and he's killing you by inches, one way or another, I'm confident. Have nothing more to do with him; let me see him for you. There isn't a man or woman living who ever frightened me!"

Lady Joan looked at Honor with cold, astonished eyes.

"Frightened!" she repeated. "Who said—who dared say that I was afraid of this man? Honor, I do not understand your meaning. You may, however, rest assured that when I need your help in the management of my affairs, I will ask for it."

She looked at the letter which Honor had flung upon the ground.

"For your father, did you say? No, I do not wish to read it. You had better put it at once into the letter-box; the post will leave in a few minutes."

She took up her pen, and bent over her manuscript once more.

Lady Honor felt herself dismissed.

"What is it? What is it?" she said to herself, as she dropped her letter into the Castle letter-box. "I feel like one groping in the dark for something that lies close at hand."

She felt that some terrible trouble was overhanging the house. Her thoughts flew back to the conversation she had overheard in the pine-wood. Gallagher had hinted at some secret in Lady Joan's life, of which he intended to get possession. What if such a secret did exist, and the man had found means of fulfilling his intention!

The supposition seemed to solve in one breath the mystery of the man's frequent visits to the house, and Lady Joan's harassed, haggard appearance.

For a moment Honor forgot Herrick and Lois and their wrongs in her indignation against the contemptible creature who was most probably trading on a woman's fears. A great feeling of pity swept over her for the one who, sinner though she might be, was evidently already paying a heavy price for whatever of sin she had done.

"Can I do nothing for her—absolutely nothing?" she cried, passionately.

Echo might have answered her question with the repetition of her last word, since to no living soul has ever been accorded the privilege of turning back and re-writing the pages of the past.

CATHERINE LOUISA PIRKIS

III

The following letters were received about this time by M. Van Zandt from Lady Honor Herrick.

Longridge Castle, Friday Morning
(Don't ask me for a date.)

MY HENRI,

Never again send me such a farrago of nonsense as I had the honour of receiving yesterday, or I shall regret ever having taught you English, and so given you the means of expressing yourself in my mother-tongue. I can only repeat I am ugly, I am poor, and I've no more chance of making 'a brilliant marriage,' as you call it, than I have of riding on a broomstick to the moon. If Herrick and I were the only man and woman in the world, we should each die respectively bachelor and spinster. So if you wash your hands of me, I shall just shape my course for myself, and on the very day that I am twenty-one rush over to Brussels and set up the little shop on the Montagne de la Cour entirely on my own account. And come near it if you dare!

"But I can't stop to scold you as you ought to be scolded; I am all eagerness to ask if you have anything to tell me about the Red Sisters in general, or Sister Héloise in particular. Time is precious. I feel Herrick can't begin too soon to use any influence he may have among Catholic ecclesiastics to get Lois out of her prison—I can think of a convent in no other light. I am so thankful that I chanced upon his address as I did, although at the same time it does seem strange that Aunt Jo should leave her letter lying about in this careless way, when she is so cautious in not allowing a soul to get a glimpse of his letters to her. The last letter that came, I suppose touched upon business matters, for she took notes from it, which she sent to Mr. Champneys, the manager of the Wrexford mines. He in return, sent a messenger to ask for Herrick's address, in order to send a reply to him. I was in the room when the message was brought in, and listened eagerly for Aunt Jo's reply.

"It was short and sweet, like a donkey's gallop. She grew crimson as she gave it. 'Tell Mr. Champneys,' she said, 'that Mr. Gaskell was on the wing when he wrote to me, and his last address is useless. If, however, Mr. Champneys will send to me the letter he wishes forwarded, I will enclose it in one of mine so soon as I hear again from Mr. Gaskell.'

"Then she coloured again, and turned her back on me sharply, as if she felt that my eyes were on her. Sometimes I fancy she is doing all sorts of things she is ashamed of—things she would have scorned to do a short time back. She looks so terribly ill, that I can't help pitying her in spite of all her wicked plotting against poor Lois. You can have no idea how tall, and thin, and stately she looks in her long, flowing, black gowns with her white hair mounted high beneath her widow's cap—the very spectre of the handsome, imperious mistress of the Castle, whose portrait hangs beside Uncle John's in the hall. I am more than ever confident that she has something on her mind—something over and above the horribly mean tricks which she has been playing off on Herrick—something, too, that, little by little, seems to be sending her into her grave. I have been trying in all sorts of ways to get her confidence. But no! I might as well try to make the Castle walls speak to me as Aunt Jo when she has a mind to be silent. Sometimes we sit together for hours without opening our lips. She has quite given up talking about taking a house in town and 'presenting me'; she has even, I fancy, given up all hope of making a match between Herrick and me, for she never mentions his name to me now. She seems to me like a person who requires all her strength to bear some secret sorrow or malady, and so has none to spend upon other people and their affairs.

"Every one is noticing how ill she is looking. She eats next to nothing, and looks as if she never slept. Her maid asked me the other day if I did not think she ought to see a doctor, she has fainted once or twice lately, the girl said. I went to Aunt Jo at once, and said right out that I thought she ought to have Dr. Scott in. She was busy reading a lot of papers—I think connected with the purchase of Southmoor—and I had to speak two or three times before I could get her attention. At last she looked up, with a strange expression on her face, and instead of answering my question, said in an odd, strained voice, 'Honor, whatever else is said of me in the days to come, this at least shall be said—that I saved the home of my fathers from the auctioneer's hammer.'

"It is all strange and bewildering together. I am longing for Herrick to return. But even supposing that he should start immediately after he receives my letter, he can't get back much under three weeks or a month from now. Sometimes I tremble to think what may happen here before that month has run out, with Aunt Jo in her present state, and that man Gallagher always about the house. I've a great mind to lie in wait for him some day, and pounce upon him, and ask him what he means by worrying Aunt Jo in this way. I should thoroughly enjoy making that man shake in his shoes. If only Herrick had used his common-sense, and—but there, I can't trust myself to write about his fatuous folly, so I will say good-bye, and ask you to believe that I am,

"'In spite of all creation, and the claims of my relations,'

Your own,
HONOR

"Postscript.—When you next write, kindly make a marked distinction between the use of letter 'v' and letter 'w,' or people will think I taught you English from the scenes between Sam Weller and his father, in the 'Pickwick Papers.' It is all very well for you to say, in your broken English, 'On my vord of honour'; it doesn't look pretty when written."

Longridge Castle, Wednesday

MY HENRI,

A thousand thanks for your letter, and for all you are doing for me. Since you wish it I will promise not to lie in wait for that wretched Gallagher, and speak my mind to him; but I should vastly enjoy doing it all the same. I am so glad you thought of your Aunt Mélanie. I had entirely forgotten that she was a lay-sister of the Sacramentines at Ghent. Of course she will be the very person through whom to make enquiries concerning the Redemptoristine Sisters. She will know father-confessors by the score, and will find out more in a week than we should in a year. But, oh dear! even a week seems long to wait when I think of Herrick eating his heart out in America, and that poor child in her convent cell trying to get a halo for her head instead of a ring for her finger. Don't try to make me lose heart by telling me that, even if you should find out where she is, there'll be little chance ef getting her out of that cell. You don't know Herrick as I do. His will is iron, and his love for this girl strong as death. Now what is there that love and courage combined cannot effect, especially when backed by enormous wealth. Why he'll go straight to the Pope, and promise to endow any number of convents and churches, if only they'll let him have his darling back again!

"Don't call me heroic. Just now I'm not feeling quite so—well, plucky—as I used to feel. Fighting at one time was the very breath of my life, and I was never so happy as when I was in hot water. I'm sure, in spite of the picture-gallery at Southmoor, that some of my old ancestors must have been rowdy republicans! Now, however, things here are so dismal and gloomy, that I will own to feeling just a trifle limp and spiritless. On Sunday morning Aunt Jo looked so wretchedly ill that I told her I should not go to church, but would stay at home and take care of her. Upon that she gave me a strange, fixed look, and said, in a voice that seemed to come from out a sepulchre, it sounded so hollow, 'Go to church, Honor, and pray while you can.'

"Ah, the luncheon-bell. I must leave off. Adieu.

Your own,
HONOR

"Postscript. Your grammar was atrocious in your last letter—prepositions were anyhow. Also, we don't double our negatives in English—I've told you so times without number—and as for trebling them! I have not never seen it not done! There—put that into decent French if you can."

Longridge Castle, Saturday

MY HENRI,

Only a line to say how delighted I am to get Aunt Mélanie's list of the convents of the Redemptoristines in Europe. I had no idea there were half that number. It is strange, however, with so many in France and Belgium, that there should be only one in Great Britain. Yes, there is a place called Helstone Bridge in Ireland, Co. Cork. I've looked it out in the 'Gazetteer'—kindly note that I spell the word 'Bridge,' not 'Breedge,' though I've no doubt Aunt Mélanie so pronounced it to you. I dare say the Convent of Saint Alphonse to which you refer is there, but please find out for certain. The Père Antoine, who is so kindly helping Aunt Mélanie, is a darling and I would like to tell him so. I suppose he'll enquire now where the English nuns are sent for their novitiate. When once we find out that, I take it there won't be much difficulty in discovering where Sister Héloise is. I'm all eagerness for your next letter and the news it may bring; I shall neither eat nor sleep till it comes. Don't be afraid. I get your letters right enough. Uncle John, I hear, used to do the proper thing, and unlock the letter-bag himself, and distribute the letters. Aunt Jo hands over the business to the butler. I stand over the old fogey while he unlocks the bag, seize upon and carry off my letters before he knows where he is.

"In haste to save post,

Your own,
HONOR

Longridge Castle, Monday

MY HENRI,

I'm in a temper. It's downright wicked of you to try and make me lose heart as you do. 'Those who enter it come not out,' you say. Of course not, if they're fully professed nuns. But our sister Héloise is a novice of little over a month's standing. You say the Order is so strict, that nuns or novices may only see their friends once a year; then, if they see they may not speak to them; or, if they wish to speak they must not see them—the nun must be behind a grille. That may be true; but Herrick will have something to say to that grille, I'm confident. And please, please, please don't croak, or I shall lose all patience with you, and Aunt Mélanie, too.

"As I said, I'm in a temper, so think I had better leave of.

Your own,
HONOR

My Henri,

Jubilate! You are a darling, and Aunt Mélanie is another
darling, and Père Antoine is another darling for the help he
has given us. But poor little Sister Héloise! You say she was
ill when she went into the convent, and has been ill ever since
she has been there! Poor child! No wonder! Just think what it
must have cost her to run away from Herrick, loving him as
she did! And I've no doubt, too, that Aunt Jo beforehand had
nearly frightened her into fits. I felt so angry this morning,
after getting your letter, that I could scarcely sit through
luncheon facing her without speaking my mind right out.
I restrained myself, however, for I don't want to sound an
alarm in her ears and set her brain going on some other piece
of wickedness. You say a Father Elliot from Saint Elizabeth's,
Longridge, took Sister Héloise to this convent at Helstone
Bridge. I made enquiries of my maid, and find that there is
a Catholic church about a couple of miles from here; but the
Father Elliot of whom you speak left some little time ago to
join an African mission. I am so sorry, as I would have gone
to him at once and told him the whole sad story—of which
no doubt he was ignorant—and entreated his help. I will
do as you tell me, and make no effort to see poor little Lois
if, as you say, it may cut her off from all possibility of seeing
anyone else till the close of her novitiate. I think your advice
is excellent; and so soon as Herrick arrives, I will tell him
not to waste time quarrelling with Aunt Jo, but to start off at
once for Brussels, to consult with you and Aunt Mélanie and
Père Antoine as to what should be his first step—one first
false step, as you say, may ruin everything. I heartily hope he
is half-way across the Atlantic by now. If only I knew by what
steamer he was coming, I would contrive somehow to meet
him at Liverpool, and send him straight on to you at once.

"Oceans of gratitude to you, to Aunt Mélanie, and to
Père Antoine, without whom we should have found out
nothing. I shall end this letter as I began it, with a cry of
jubilate. And joyful I mean to be in spite of all your croakings
and the churchyardiness of things here. There is no other
word than 'churchyardiness' that would give you any idea of

the dismalness, the silence, the utter absence of 'go' in the house just now. Why, compared with it Southmoor was a downright cheerful place of abode, even with the wind in the east, and mother at a very low ebb. To add to the general dreariness of things, I have somehow managed to catch a very severe cold. And no wonder! the dear bright frost has gone; a wretched thaw has set in; and the rain is coming down in buckets. But, all the same, I mean to be joyful. Everything will come straight, I feel confident. Such a combination of wisdom and courage as you, and I, and Herrick represent, must—shall—will carry all before it. Adieu.

Ever your own,
HONOR

"As I wrote my last word, the sound of wheels made me look up and out of the window, and, lo! there was the crawling old fly from the Wrexford 'Railway Hotel' bringing a visitor up the drive. I strained my neck to see the visitor alight, and who should it be but 'The Serpent,' in a mackintosh and slouch hat. I wonder what wickedness he'll be dinning into Aunt Jo's ears now!"

IV

"Am I supposed to pay this enormous sum? Impossible!" exclaimed Lady Joan, looking up from a long list of figures which lay before her, to Dr. Gallagher, who was seated within confidential, not ceremonious, talking distance of her.

"My lady, it represents the interest as well as the principal of moneys lent to Harwood for a long period of years. And your ladyship volunteered, as you will remember—it was not suggested to you—to discharge his liabilities, in order that his departure from England might not be delayed," said Gallagher, letting his restless eyes as he spoke rove here, there, and everywhere round the room in which they sat.

Lady Joan, this time, had received him in her boudoir, instead of in the library, as heretofore. The man's attention was halved between closely scrutinising the lady and taking stock of her surroundings.

"When I volunteered to do this," said Lady Joan, "I scarcely expected to be confronted with liabilities to this amount. My trustees would want to know a little about the purpose for which so large a sum would be required. I have already, as you know, given to this man two thousand pounds to buy land in Australia. You cannot expect to receive from me one quarter of this amount."

"My lady, I should not expect to receive from you one twentieth part of it if it were not for the great, the amazing benevolence you have already shown to me and my family; for, of course, as you know, Ralph and Lucy are connections of mine by marriage."

Lady Joan's eyes drooped once more over the long list of figures.

Gallagher went on:

"I said to Ralph—'In all my experience I have never met with anything to compare with it. A young girl, of whom my lady knows absolutely nothing, acts as her maid for two days and two nights, and straightway my lady takes her under her wing and provides for her for life.'"

Lady Joan turned a white face towards him.

"The girl interested me, otherwise I should not have done so," she said, in a voice which she seemed to control with difficulty.

"Quite so," my lady. "She is an interesting young woman. Her talk is interesting—sometimes."

"In what way?"

The question seemed to come in a gasp.

Gallagher laughed his low, mirthless laugh.

"Oh, in many ways. She babbles curiously at times. But you know, my lady, we doctors don't attach much importance to the rhodomontade our patients occasionally talk. Ha, ha! No. But I'm wasting your ladyship's time. I'm to understand, I suppose, that you find yourself unable to discharge Ralph's liabilities? So I must endeavour to get the money out of the man himself."

"How do you mean to do that?" queried Lady Joan, her forehead knotting, her lips tightening.

"Oh, well, of course I can't expect payment in full with his finances at their present low ebb; but I dare say we'll come to some sort of an arrangement. I will at any rate lay an embargo on the two thousand pounds your ladyship has given him for the purchase of a farm at the antipodes, and as for him"—here he shrugged his shoulders—"he must just stay at home and till his farm in Wrexford till better times dawn for him."

Lady Joan leaned eagerly forward.

"No, no; his departure must not be delayed," she said. "Let me think—let me think, how I can meet this large demand on my purse."

"Oh, my lady, there is nothing in life easier than for you to meet any demand on your purse. Other people would think themselves amazingly lucky if they could meet their demands with as little difficulty. I could put you into communication with half-a-dozen men who would be only too delighted to supply you with thrice the amount simply on your own personal security."

His eye by this time had catalogued every item of the sumptuous furnishing of the room in which they sat. "Yes," he thought, "I was right. She is a woman who dreads poverty and ugliness just as other people dread hunger or disease. This is her private sitting-room, and simplicity is as far removed from it as it would be in a room designed for the reception of Royalty."

"I must think over your suggestion," Lady Joan began, hesitatingly.

He ignored the remark.

"I agree with your ladyship that it would be injudicious to retard Ralph's departure," he said, meaningly. "Wrexford is uncomfortably near at hand. Mr. Gaskell will be there daily on his return. He and Ralph may chance to meet."

"What do you mean to imply?" asked Lady Joan. But it was easy to see that the calmness with which she asked the question was maintained with difficulty.

"I was only thinking, my lady," he answered in off-hand nonchalant fashion, "of the possibility that Mr. Gaskell might find out through Ralph—who's about as shifting as the sea-sand itself—the interest you took in introducing Miss White to the inside of a convent. It seems to me that one of two things should be done—either Ralph's departure expedited, or Mr. Gaskell's return retarded."

For a moment Lady Joan's old hauteur of manner returned to her.

"You said something of this sort to me before," she said, "and I foolishly carried out your suggestion. Now, if you please, we will confine our attention to matters that more immediately concern you and your relatives."

"Oh, quite so; quite so!" said Gallagher, obsequiously, with a dark flash in his sunken eyes nevertheless. "It can concern no one but your ladyship whether Mr. Gaskell returns tomorrow and begins to overlook banking accounts the next day, or whether he doesn't put in an appearance for twelve months to come. I think the attitude which your ladyship's legal advisers—the respected firm of McGowan—have assumed in this matter perfectly unjustifiable, and, if you will allow me to say so, grossly inconsistent also."

Lady Joan's hauteur of manner had been but a passing flash. It was gone now.

"How do you mean, inconsistent?" she asked, nervously, hurriedly.

"In this way, my lady. They profess a vast concern for young Mr. Gaskell's interest, and on his behalf have objected to the purchase of the Southmoor property. So, at least, I am told by my young friend in their office—the man who is conducting the little legal business of mine which I mentioned the other day."

Lady Joan's face was growing white and whiter. Her lips parted; but not a word escaped them.

Gallagher went on:

"I said to him the other morning when I called, 'The heads of your firm are about the biggest humbugs I ever had dealings with. They profess the utmost zeal on behalf of young Mr. Gaskell's interests; yet they drew up some thirty years back a will which may keep him out of his inheritance for another twenty years to come.'"

His last words were said with a slow emphasis, and with his keen, cruel eyes fixed full on Lady Joan's face.

White and nerveless, she leaned back in her chair, pressing one hand across her eyes.

CATHERINE LOUISA PIRKIS

He went on mercilessly, as before:

"Shall I tell you what his answer was, my lady? 'Oh, that will, over which there's been so much talk, was made to meet certain possible, but most unlikely, contingencies, and would have been only so much waste-paper if old Mr. Gaskell hadn't died before his son.'"

With a stupendous effort, Lady Joan gathered together all her strength and rose from her chair. Better far at once look the worst in the face and be done with it, than be tortured in this way. It was like being killed by inches by a blunt sword, or being roasted to death over a fire of wet wood.

He rose as she did, and for one instant the two looked each other full in the face.

"What do you mean? What do you intend to imply? Explain! Speak out," she said, in stately, imperious fashion; and for that one instant Gallagher's eyes drooped before hers.

Only for one instant, however. The next he had recovered himself, and, with easy sangfroid, answered her questions.

"My lady, I mean nothing. I was merely relating to you the gossip—it was nothing more—of a lawyer's office. Ah, they do talk sometimes, canny though they think themselves. But I am taking up your ladyship's time unnecessarily. I am to understand, I suppose, that you are not willing to discharge Harwood's liabilities, and I must, therefore, look to him for payment?"

Lady Joan's imperiousness was soon spent. She sank back in her chair, nerveless and pallid, as before. It was easy to see that she was paying a heavy price for her moment of defiance.

"No," she said in low tones, "you are to understand nothing of the sort. I must think the matter over. Go now, and I will let you know by letter whether I will avail myself of your offer to raise this money for me. By letter, do you understand? You need not come here again unless I send for you."

Gallagher bowed, shifted his ground, shifted his attitude.

"May I suggest, my lady, that your decision should be made known to me with as little delay as possible? Time is precious now. I think you said you had received a telegram from Mr. Gaskell. May I ask if it was to give you notice of his immediate return?"

He was evidently bent on harping on that one string.

"My son's telegram stated that he would be at New York on the eighteenth of this month, and would leave in the *Europa* for England on the same day," answered Lady Joan, speaking as if every word were wrung from her.

"Ah, just so. Most inconvenient. That will never do," said Gallagher, his mellifluousness now giving place to a more authoritative tone. "My lady, he must have a telegram on the eighteenth—ah, that will be tomorrow—that will set him once more looking for his needle in a bundle of hay. Let him know that his pretty little sweetheart is shut up in a convent—he must know it sooner or later—but send him off for news of her to Canada, or—"

Lady Joan held up her hands to stop him.

"You must go now," she said, faintly. "My head is not clear. I cannot discuss this, or anything else, with you."

"My lady, you should leave the arrangement of these purely minor details to men of business, like myself," he said, authoritatively, as before. "Now, if you'll be good enough to give me Mr. Gaskell's address in New York, on the eighteenth, I will undertake that he shall have a telegram before tomorrow is over that will ensure his absence from England for another six weeks at least. By that time affairs here will have been comfortably arranged."

Lady Joan again held up her hand.

"You must go now," she said, faintly still, but with a decision that made itself felt. "I will write to you tonight, giving you my final answer on these matters. Now, as I told you before, my head is confused—I cannot think."

Gallagher shrugged his shoulders.

"Very well then, my lady," he said. "Your letter must be sent to me by messenger the first thing tomorrow morning, or it will be useless. I shall be where I have been the past few weeks—at the Wrexford 'Railway Hotel.' Now, if you'll allow me, I'll ring for my fly to be brought round." He made a step towards the window. "Ah, a drenching rain—scarcely the weather to turn a dog out in." Then he turned sharply on his heel, and came back to her side once more. "My lady," he said, in tones that contrasted markedly with his former obsequious accents, "allow me to say that, as regards Mr. Gaskell's return, there is only one course open to you—you have absolutely no choice in the matter. He must receive a telegram sending him farther still afield before tomorrow is over. Ah, my fly! I will wish you good day, my lady." This was added as the door opened, and a servant announced that the conveyance which had brought Dr. Gallagher to the Castle was waiting to carry him thence.

Lady Joan made no acknowledgment of the elaborate bow with which his last word was spoken. She was leaning forward wearily now on her writing-table, with one hand supporting her head.

Her eyes lifted as the door closed behind him. Gone? gone, was he at last? Was that absolutely the roll of the wheels that were bearing him away from the house? Was there no fear of his suddenly turning the handle of the door and coming back to renew the slow torment? She drew a long breath; her eyes wandered wearily around. To her fancy the man had left behind him the troubled atmosphere which he had brought into the room. It no longer seemed to her the refuge, the hiding-place, where in quiet she could gather together her strength to meet threatening dangers, but rather the battlefield itself, where the enemy had drawn up his forces, and from which he refused to be dislodged.

Even the portrait of the old earl which faced her as she sat seemed to have changed its expression since she had last looked up at it, and, instead of smiling, seemed to scowl at her. "Joan, Joan," she could fancy those firm-set lips were saying, "have you forgotten the name you were born to, the crest of your ancestors—the arm holding the broken sword and the motto encircling it, 'broken but unsullied?'"

A mist came before her; that terrible dizziness against which she had struggled so hard of late, seemed to be creeping over her again. For a moment her eyes closed. When she opened them and looked up, the scowl seemed to have faded from the old earl's face, a tender, wistful look seemed to have come into his eyes, and his lips seemed forming to the words she remembered so well: "Joan, if I had my time to come over again"—yes, that was what he was saying now—"I don't think I should thank Heaven for the finding of coal on my land."

"Ah!" She gave a sharp cry and sprang to her feet. That was what that other had said, not this dear old man whose death-bed she had hung over and wept over.

The room swam round her, she sank once more into a chair. All sorts of strange noises seemed to sound in her ear, and to mingle oddly with the drenching down-pour of the rain outside. And through it all, above it all, came the harsh, twanging accents of the man who had just left the room, holding, no doubt, the secret of her life in his hand: "There is only one course open to you; you have absolutely no choice in the matter."

Absolutely no choice! Yes, that was how things had arranged themselves; this was the point at which she had arrived now. She had flung herself on the Juggernaut car of crime, and if she let go her hold for an instant she would fall and be crushed by its giant wheels.

Absolutely no choice! That meant that Herrick's inheritance was to be still farther drained to meet the demands of this man, who stood flourishing his whip over her shoulders; that Herrick's brave young spirit was to be still farther tortured by a lying telegram which would keep him at a safe distance till the meshes of this web of wickedness had had their ends trebly knotted and secured.

Only one course open to her! Better take it at once then, and be done with it. So, with trembling fingers, she dipped her pen into the ink and wrote a few brief lines, giving the arch-tempter the permission he had craved to summon his Jew money-lenders and to despatch the telegram—any he pleased—which would set Herrick winnowing the wind and beating the ocean once more.

And because her fingers now absolutely refused their office, in lieu of appending the address at New York that would find Herrick, she pinned his telegram on to the note, below her signature.

CATHERINE LOUISA PIRKIS

V

Lady Honor sealed her letter to M. Van Zandt, and put it carefully on one side for posting on the following morning. Although she suffered no hand other than her own to consign the precious missives to the village letter-box, she had so far yielded to Lady Joan's wishes as to post them in the early morning instead of in the late afternoon.

Somehow, the pleasure of pitched battles with Lady Joan, as the typical representative of the tyrannical guardians of youth, had lost its flavour. There was little glory to be had in a struggle whose result was a foregone conclusion, and where one look at the adversary proclaimed the fact.

"I wish I could hate her and worry her as I did a day or two ago," mused the girl. "But, for the life of me, I can't help pitying her, shut in, perhaps, for a couple of hours with that wretched man. Why, I would infinitely sooner be shut up in a cage with a wild monkey! There would at least be license to claw and bite each other as long as claws and teeth were left to us."

But Lady Honor was out in her reckoning. In less than half of two hours, the wheels which had brought Gallagher to the house were heard bearing him away. She jumped to her feet, and flattened her forehead against the window-pane to assure herself of the fact.

"My best wishes go with you!" she said, apostrophising the back of the lumbering Wrexford "fly." "I heartily hope you'll have lumbago, influenza, sciatica, rheumatism, and every ailment that spiteful, bad weather can inflict." And then a violent fit of sneezing prevented farther malediction, and brought to her mind the unpleasant recollection of what the "spiteful, bad weather" had already inflicted on her. "I dare say I shan't shake it off till I've had a week between the blankets," she thought, between her fits of sneezing. "Personally, I should prefer the blankets to the frigid atmosphere of Aunt Jo's society; but goodness only knows what may happen if I'm off guard for a whole week!"

The thought of Lady Joan's medicine-cabinet, with its rows of neatly-labelled drugs, suddenly came into her mind. A dose of one of those strong tinctures might perhaps keep blankets and gruel at bay.

Straightway down to Lady Joan's sitting-room she flew.

"Aunt Joan," she said, entering the room with a rush and a flutter, "I want some Aconite, or Nux, or Belladonna, or anything you like to give me; I've got the horridest of colds coming on, and I'm shaking and quaking as if I had the palsy."

There came no response from Lady Joan. She was still seated at her writing-table; but was no longer bending over it. She was leaning back in her high arm-chair, with her head thrown back, and her face marble white; her pen had evidently dropped from her hand, for there it lay on the floor beside her chair.

Lady Honor saw at a glance that she had fainted. Something else, also, she saw at a glance—an envelope on the table before her aunt, addressed to Dr. Gallagher, at the "Railway Hotel," Wrexford, and a letter, which ran briefly and brusquely thus:

> I give you permission to raise the required money for me; also to send any telegram you think advisable to my son. Below is his address in New York.
>
> J. G.

But it was the telegram pinned below the note which set Honor's heart beating loud and fast, and made her exclaim in thought, "Heaven is on my side now." It bore yesterday's date, and in as few words as possible, conveyed the intimation that Herrick would be at New York on the 18th instant, that he would start for England in the "Europa," on the same day, and that telegrams addressed to 937, Astor Avenue, would find him up to nine o'clock at night.

"The eighteenth will be tomorrow, no time to be lost," thought the girl, as, repeating the address to herself again and again so as to learn it by heart, she hastily returned to her room.

There she rang for her maid, and desired her to go to Lady Joan and ask for some medicine for the influenza. Then feeling that, in this way, she had provided for proper attention being paid to her aunt without drawing suspicion upon herself, she at once proceeded with swift fingers to exchange her dress for her habit.

Henniker, stable-manager at the Castle, hobnobbing with a crony over his four o'clock tea, was to have a curious experience that afternoon. A sharp rapping at the door of his cottage, which adjoined the stables, made him drop his hot muffin, and the discussion he was having with his friend over the pedigree of a certain brown mare, at one and the same moment.

When he opened the door and saw Lady Honor standing there in the drenching rain, habited, and with her riding-whip in her hand, he could scarcely believe his eyes. It was still harder to give credence to his ears when the young lady informed him that she wanted a horse saddled, and brought round immediately—"Mr. Herrick's horse—the one he used to ride to Wrexford daily—because he'll know the road," she added, "and it will be dark before I get back. Now do make haste, for I'm in a hurry. I'll wait in here beside your fire."

Henniker's face lengthened to a demur.

Lady Honor would not let him speak it.

"Yes, I know it's raining cats and dogs," she said; "and I shall get drenched to the skin—that won't matter. It won't hurt the horse, because I shan't keep him waiting anywhere; and it won't hurt the groom, because I don't mean to have one. Now go at once, and and I'll give you a guinea when I come back if I'm off and away in less than five minutes."

There was no gainsaying Lady Honor when this mood was upon her; and although Henniker shook his head a good deal, and mentally came to the conclusion that things generally at the Castle were "upside down, now that there was no master there," the girl was "off and away" in less than five minutes.

Herrick's hack never made the distance between Longridge and Wrexford at a better pace than he did this winter's afternoon, through the driving rain and settling mist. Till within about a couple of miles of Wrexford, Lady Honor had the road pretty much to her self. Then, as she quitted the muddy lanes, with their ragged hedges, and dripping, skeleton trees, for the high road, the stir of town life made itself felt. She overtook and passed—for it was impossible to keep behind—a market-cart or two, a railway van, and, finally, the lumbering "Railway Hotel" fly which had already visited the Castle that afternoon. It was not until she was well ahead of this last vehicle that it occurred to her who possibly might be its occupant. Even when the thought struck her, she did not scent danger in it, taking it for granted that she must be, so far, at least as personal appearance was concerned, an utter stranger to Dr. Gallagher. If, however, she had chanced to turn her head as her horse cantered along, she might have seen Gallagher stretching out of the window of the fly to interrogate the coachman.

"That is a lady, and she is going at the pace of a stud-groom sent on a message," he had said to himself. "Now I would like amazingly to know who that lady is," and forthwith he had let down the window and had questioned the man.

His reply that it was Lady Honor Herrick was no surprise to Gallagher. His face for a moment wore an ugly look.

"No one in this world, whether sane or lunatic," he cogitated, "ever does anything without a motive. They may not be conscious of their motive at the moment of action, for volition at times will outstrip consciousness; or, as in the case of the insane, the reason may be rooted in unreason, but all the same the reason is there, and a keen eye will find it out, as lamp-light finds out diamonds. Now the motive which sends that young lady riding at that speed through a drenching rain must be a powerful one. It may be that by some means or other she has become possessed of the telegram, or the address on it, which my lady was pleased to refuse to me, and thus has stolen a march upon us. I must see her ladyship the first thing tomorrow, whether she chooses to send for me or not, and will ask her a few questions. There must be no shilly-shallying now."

Then he once more let down the window of the carriage, bidding the coachman put on the speed, and, instead of making for the hotel, to drive direct to the telegraph office.

"To overtake her on that horse would, of course, be an impossibility," he reasoned; "but if I meet her returning in the main road from the office, it won't require a wiseacre to conjecture where she has been."

Meanwhile, Lady Honor, all unconscious that her movements were watched, had made her way to the telegraph-office, and had despatched the two telegrams which she had carefully thought over and written out before she had started.

The first was addressed to M. Van Zandt, and ran thus:

"H. returns in 'Europa,' which sails on the eighteenth from New York. Will you meet him at Queenstown and tell him everything?"

The second telegram was addressed to Herrick, and was as follows:

> Lois is in a convent in Ireland. Let nothing prevent your
> return in the "Europa." Land at Queenstown, where M. Van
> Zandt will meet you, and tell you everything. Distrust any
> other telegram you may receive.
>
> HONOR

She was drenched to the skin, and her limbs were so stiffened that she could scarcely drag one after the other when she alighted at the office to hand in these telegrams.

"Thank Heaven that's done," was her thought as she did so; "for I'm in for the very worst cold I have ever had."

She was stiffer still, however, by a long way, as she rode her horse back into the Castle stables, and threw the reins to Henniker.

Her telegrams had emptied her purse. "I haven't a guinea to give you now," she said, "for I have spent every penny I had in Wrexford; but you shall have it right enough tomorrow."

She did not enjoin secrecy on the man as to her eccentric ride. She felt instinctively that there was little fear of a skirmish with Lady Joan now, and even had the contrary been the case, it would have troubled her very little. The deed was done. She knew now for certain that, before another day was over his head, Herrick would know the truth concerning Lois, and would take matters generally into his strong young hands. Of course she knew that there was a terrible storm brewing now, and that there were one or two who would not come out of it unscathed. Of this, however, at the moment, she scarcely dared to think.

"Things must take their course now," she thought, as she pulled off her soaked habit and rang for her maid, "come what will, I can only say I have done my best."

VI

Lady Honor's words were to be verified. "The very worst cold she had ever had" had certainly fastened upon her.

Her maid, as she entered, was startled—not only by the drenched hat and habit, but by the young lady's feverish appearance, her flushed face, and brilliant eyes.

"Now I want to tumble into bed as quickly as possible," she said, giving a little jump out of the long skirt. "And you can bring me up hot tea, or hot anything you like—Ah, a letter!"

Here she broke off abruptly, as she detected in the girl's hand a letter bearing a Belgian stamp.

The girl had something to say, which for the moment retarded the breaking of the seal of that letter—something which she said she thought "my lady" ought to know. It was to the effect that when she went to Lady Joan to ask her, as "my lady" had bidden her, for some medicine, she had found her in a fainting fit, in her chair. The girl went on to say that she had rung for assistance, and that restoratives had been administered; but that Lady Joan had been a long time in recovering consciousness.

"I looked for you everywhere, my lady, to know if Dr. Scott should be sent for, but I couldn't find you," said the girl, giving a dubious look at the draggled habit.

"No, I had gone for a ride—the lovely weather tempted me," said Honor, indifferently. "Go on. How is Lady Joan now?"

"A little better, my lady; but she says she won't sit down to dinner tonight."

"Oh, well, and I won't either, out of sympathy. Make haste and take my hair down; I feel as if I had rheumatism in every joint; my head and my hands are like fire."

The next moment, however, both head and hands must have been ice-cold, to judge from the death-like pallor which overspread her face, as, with a pained, startled cry she sprang to her feet.

"Where is Lady Joan?" she cried, passionately, and in a loud voice. "This is her doing—her work—only hers!"

She stumbled, rather than walked, towards the door, with her letter in her hand, as if she were bent, there and then, on going to Lady Joan and bidding her to rejoice in her work.

But, with her hand on the handle, she paused.

"No, I dare not," she said, brokenly. "I should speak words that could never be forgotten or forgiven."

She turned to her maid, who stood gazing at her in mute astonishment.

"Take this letter to Lady Joan. Tell her I send it to her; that is all," she said, steadying her voice with an effort.

Then as the girl quitted the room, she flung herself in a passion of weeping on her bed.

"This is the end of it all!" she cried, bitterly.

The letter which had occasioned her passion of grief was from M. Van Zandt, and ran thus:

Bruxelles, le 16th November

My Honor,

I send you news the most sorrowful—Sister Héloise is dead. She has been invalid ever since she is become a Red Sister. She is dead yesterday. They will on Monday bury her in the cemetery of the convent. This is only a little word of writing, because the post goes to set off.

Adieu.
Your devoted
Henri

VII

D ead!" And Lady Joan bowed her head over the letter which lay before her on the table, hiding her face in her hands.

With most women such a posture would have meant floods of tears. Not so with Lady Joan; her eyes were dry, and though her breath came thick and fast, there was never the sound of a sob in it.

It so chanced that when the maid brought to her the letter sent by Lady Honor, she had just taken her nightly sleeping-draught; not wishing it to lose its effect, she had desired the girl to place the letter, with others which the evening post had brought, on her writing-table in her boudoir.

Consequently, it was not until the following morning that Lady Joan had read the tidings of the bright young life quenched in sadness and gloom. For a moment she had felt stunned by the news, and there had seemed to pass before her mental vision a picture of what that young life might have been if Herrick had been allowed to cherish and nurture it with love's nurturing.

The pictnre, however, quickly enough faded before the pressing and momentous anxieties which the letter called forth. What did Honor mean by sending it to her? How was it she knew that Sister Héloise was Lois White, and that she had entered a Redemptoristine Convent? What, also, had M. Van Zandt to do with the matter? In a word, what did he know, what did Honor know? Was this letter to be considered a danger signal? Were Honor and her lover playing the parts of detective and spy, and did they mean to sift, not only this matter thoroughly, but perhaps also other matters which might have attracted their attention?

The instinct of self-preservation—the instinct which she possessed in common with the ravening wolf, the chattering ape, the crawling beetle—was now to swamp every other thought, and to make her in heart cry aloud for a counsellor.

Thus, even so much of saving grace as lies in the agonies of remorse was to be denied her.

"Pray for an angel, listen for his wings," says the Italian proverb. It may hold good of angels of darkness as well as of light. The thought of her need of a counseller had scarcely arisen in her mind before a door opened, and a servant announced that Dr. Gallagher was below and wished to see her.

It must have cost her a stupendous effort to receive the man with the stately coldness with which she greeted him. Stupendous efforts, however, were now of daily—one might almost say of hourly—recurrence with her.

He was puzzled by it; her agitation of overnight had led him to expect a different demeanour.

"Is she changing her tactics? Does she mean to throw me over? Let her try it, that's all!" was his thought. Aloud he said: "I've called respecting that telegram to Mr. Gaskell, my lady. Circumstances render it imperative—"

She interrupted him.

"Do you know anything of this?" she asked, giving him M. Van Zandt's letter to read.

His astonishment was genuine. As he ran his eye over it, it was easy to see that the tidings were news to him.

"Dead!" he exclaimed. "I knew she was ill when she entered the convent; but—" He broke off abruptly, looking uneasily from Lady Joan to the letter, from the letter to Lady Joan. He grew a shade paler, his restless eyes wandered hither and thither round the room, as if expecting some sudden danger at hand. "Who is this M. Van Zandt?" he asked brusquely, his oiliness of voice and manner vanishing.

"That is beside the mark," Lady Joan answered, haughtily, not choosing to be interrogated by him on such purely family matters. "What I wish to know is, have you, or has Harwood had any communication with my niece, and supplied her with any information on this matter?"

"Not I, my lady," answered Gallagher. "What, however, Ralph has done is another thing. I told you from the first that he was not to be trusted. Not a week ago I had the greatest difficulty in life to prevent him from going to Father Elliot and making a clean breast of everything." Here he drew a chair close to Lady Joan's writing-table, and seated himself, facing her. "Yet," he went on, "I'm at a loss to see how he can have had any opportunity for communicating with the Lady Honor. Yesterday, it is true, the young lady passed me at full gallop on the road to Wrexford; but Harwood is not there just now. Two days ago I despatched him to Liverpool to book our passages in an outgoing steamer—Ah!"

He broke off abruptly. His restless eyes, wandering hither and thither, had settled upon Lady Joan's unopened letters of overnight, and had discovered among them a letter addressed in handwriting which it was easy for him to recognise as that of Ralph Harwood.

"My lady," he said, "will you be good enough to open that letter and run your eye over it? It may perhaps give us a clue to the mystery. Things appear to be thickening a trifle."

But although Ralph's lettter could scarcely be said to give a clue to anything, save and except his own motives of action, it nevertheless sounded an echo to the note of warning which M. Van Zandt's letter had already struck.

It bore neither date nor address, and ran simply thus:

My Lady,

I beg herewith to return to you the cheque for two thousand pounds which you were good enough to send to me for the purchase of a farm in New South Wales. The slight services I have rendered your ladyship do not entitle me to such munificent remuneration, and I am not prepared to earn it by any additional service in co-operation with my cousin, Dr. Gallagher. I have been dragged into villainy by him, and intend for the future to wash my hands of him, and, so far as lies in my power, to make restitution to those whom I have injured. The first step in that direction seems to me to be the returning to your ladyship of the enclosed cheque.

I remain,
Your ladyship's obedient servant,
Ralph Harwood

Lady Joan's calmness was gone now; her hand trembled as she handed the letter to Gallagher to read, and the envelope and its enclosed cheque fluttered to the ground.

"What does it mean?" she asked, excitedly. "I do not understand it."

Gallagher picked up the envelope—and the cheque.

"It means danger, my lady," he said, as he glanced hastily through the letter. "Danger to me and danger to you—for I take it we row together in one boat so far as Ralph is concerned."

Lady Joan flushed crimson; but she did not dare to repudiate the man's easy familiarity.

He saw that he had made her shrink and shiver, as if from the touch of a whip, and so he made her feel his power once more.

"My lady, if you'll allow me, we'll look our common danger in the face, and consult how to meet it," he said.

CATHERINE LOUISA PIRKIS

Lady Joan rose from her chair, and began slowly to walk up and down the room. It was impossible for her to keep her calmness with this man's cold, cruel eyes fixed full upon her eye-balls.

Gallagher slightly shifted his chair so as to be able to arrest her movements by a word if so disposed.

"The post-mark of that letter is Cork," he went on, glancing down at the envelope. "The truth is, the man has had his weak nerves shaken by Sister Héloise's death, and instead of taking our passages at Liverpool, and returning as I desired him to Wrexford to finish arranging for the sale of his farm, has crossed over to Cork to make a clean breast of it to his father-confessor. My lady, that priest is our real danger point—that Father Elliot."

Lady Joan's steps were arrested at this word.

Father Elliot again! Was there never to be a bend in her life's path but that the shadow of Vaughan Elliot was to fall athwart it!

"What do you mean?" she asked, unsteadily, "I do not understand. What can Ralph Harwood have to confess to his priest that will in any way concern me?" But, as she asked the question, her eyes drooped before the look which Gallagher flashed out at her from beneath his bent brows, and once more she began to pace the room. With slow, uncertain steps, however, and Gallagher's next words made her sink into the nearest chair, and set the room swimming round her in mist.

"My lady," he said in a low, half whisper, "the only thing in Ralph's confession which might affect you, would be his avowal that he had kept to himself certain facts communicated to him by Lucy, which it was his bounden duty to make known to the nearest magistrate. But, my lady, are you faint—shall I open the windows?"

He poured out a glass of water from a carafe which stood on the table, and brought it to her.

She waved it on one side, made one more stupendous effort, and faced him again. "And you, how would this—this affect you?" she asked, doing her best to meet his cruel eyes as he stood in front of her.

Face to face with him it was impossible to believe that her dread secret was undiscovered.

"My lady, the consequences of such a confession might be the withdrawal of Lucy from my care—that would affect me to the extent of the two hundred pounds per annum which your ladyship is good enough to pay for her maintainance."

"And what do you propose to do?" asked Lady Joan; her voice sounding strange and unnatural.

Gallagher took a chair, and seated himself within a yard of her. There was to be no escape from the torture of his eye it seemed.

"This, my lady," he answered, in the same low half-whisper as before. "I propose concentrating all my attention on one point—Lucy. We must give up all hope of retarding Mr. Gaskell's return; that is a less immediate danger. With regard to your niece, my lady, I can scarcely at present gauge the danger that may lie in that quarter."

"My niece is ill; she has caught a severe cold, which is ending in rheumatic fever. The doctor has been sent for," answered Lady Joan, briefly.

Gallagher rubbed his hands.

"Capital! Capital!" he exclaimed. "Nothing could have happened better! My lady, I mean no unkindness to the Lady Honor, but it might have considerably added to our difficulties if the young lady had full licence whenever she felt disposed to ride to the Wrexford telegraph-office at the pace I saw her riding yesterday."

"To the Wrexford telegraph-office?" repeated Lady Joan. "What could she be doing there?"

"Well, my lady, arguing on my favourite theory that no living creature acts without a motive—no, not even a snail when he lifts or lowers his horns—I came to the conclusion that the young lady had most likely in some way discovered Mr. Gaskell's present address, and was off to send a telegram to him."

Lady Joan passed her hand over her brow.

"It must have been when I fainted yesterday," she murmured, recollecting the open letter and telegram which had lain on her table.

"Ah, no matter," said Gallagher; "the most pressing danger does not lie that way. Lucy is the point on which we must concentrate attention. Now, my lady, what do you say to Lucy and me disappearing together—with my wife, of course, I should add, as a necessary third?"

Lady Joan stared blankly at him.

"Where? Why?" she stammered.

"I'll answer your second question first, my lady. Because whatever Ralph may see fit to state he has been told by Lucy, must be confirmed by Lucy, or, as evidence, it is worthless. Where?—do you ask? Ah, don't you trouble about that; leave that to me. There are plenty of hiding places to be reached, viâ Liverpool. You give me the means, my lady, to make a bold coup, and it'll be done, never fear."

Lady Joan asked no further questions; she understood the man's meaning thoroughly now. She knew him to be a bad man. She knew him to be a bold man, and that coup with him might be another word for murder; yet her next words were merely:

"How much do you expect me to give you now?"

"Let me think," he said, slowly. "It means, so far as I am concerned, a good deal of risk, and a heavy monetary loss. The Wrexford farm won't be sold till next week; and as it would be undesirable to delay our disappearance till then, Ralph's debt to me will not be discharged. Then there's my practice at Ballinacrae—a good, steady, thriving practice, my lady; nice house, garden, poultry, cattle. Yes, all that will have to be thought of. And then there will be Lucy's board and lodging for a good many years to come—to the end of her life, I may say, for I suppose, my lady, you won't care to have me writing for yearly payments—"

"Whatever sum I give you now must be taken as final," said Lady Joan, speaking with a sudden decision; "there must be no subsequent application to me on any pretence whatever."

"Exactly, my lady. Lucy and I are to disappear for good and all; well, what does your ladyship say to ten thousand pounds paid down in a lump, and this little cheque," here he fingered the one which had fallen from Ralph's envelope, "added to it?"

"Twelve thousand pounds!" exclaimed Lady Joan. "Impossible!"

"Oh, don't say that, my lady," he said in a wheedling tone. "Look at the enormous wealth which lies at your banker's, and how glad anybody will be to cash a cheque signed with your ladyship's name. I assure you if it were not that time presses, and there is no possibility of our calling the money-lenders to our aid, I should say what I said yesterday, twenty-five thousand. Think, too, my lady," he went on, after a moment's pause, "of the enormous pleasure to you to know that the estimable Dr. Gallagher and the somnambulistic Lucy will never again in this world cross your threshold, and that let the weak-minded Ralph babble as he may to his father-confessor, no harm can come of it. My lady, the post-mark on this letter," here he extended Ralph's envelope, "cries aloud to you that there's no time to be lost. Father Elliot and Ralph together at Cork! Ballinacrae not thirty miles distant! Why, if I'm not off and away this very minute, I may return to find Lucy carried off to the nearest magistrate by the priest, and Ralph standing at her elbow ready to give confirmatory evidence."

Lady Joan rose wearily from her chair and went to her writing-table. "Only fools fight the inevitable," she said, half to herself, as she drew out her cheque-book, and wrote the order which was to transfer ten thousand pounds from her keeping to that of Gallagher.

He stood at her elbow meanwhile, profuse in his thanks.

"So soon as I leave here, my lady, I start for Holyhead, and directly I arrive there I will send a telegram to my wife, bidding her bring Lucy and join me there. And then off we go, all three of us, and my lady will never again have the pleasure of looking your humble servant full in the face." The marked sneer with which the last words were spoken, showed that the manner in which Lady Joan had writhed under his cruel eye had not been lost on him.

Could, however, Lady Joan have followed the man to Holyhead, and have looked over his shoulder as he dispatched his telegram to his wife, she might have been not a little surprised at its wording:

There was never a word about Lucy in it. "Let the bailiffs into the house," it ran. "Meet me at our old rendezvous at Holyhead."

Which form of speech was Dr. Gallagher's method of conveying to his wife the intimation that the crash had come; that he had thrown up his cards, and would amazingly like to shuffle them and begin all over again in another hemisphere.

VIII

Herrick had had no difficulty in discovering the John White of whom he was in search, at his work of railway-laying in California, and had listened with a heavy heart to his vigorous disclaimer of all knowledge of his young cousin's movements. Then he had hastened to shake off the dust of the Californian city from his feet, and had taken passage in the "Europa," saying to himself that he was in a blind alley now, and that the only way out of it was to go back to his starting point, and begin all over again.

As he stepped on board the "Europa," however, Lady Honor's telegram was put into his hand, and then, hey presto, the sun broke through the clouds again, and life seemed worth living once more.

For he read his own wishes into that telegram, and grew triumphant over it.

Lois in a convent! That, of course, meant merely that she had temporarily taken up her abode in one of the numerous religious houses which receive lady-boarders, on the very natural supposition that it would not be possible for her to find a better hiding-place for herself.

That she should for a moment entertain the idea of making herself into a nun did not once enter his brain.

"I shall be hugely grateful to the mother-superior, or whatever they call her, if she has taken good care of my darling," he thought, with pleasant visions of the substantial form his gratitude would assume. "At the same time, I shall be uncommonly glad to get her back to the work-a-day world again—I don't want her to be growing wings before her time."

His gratitude to his cousin for her indefatigable energy, and her unswerving devotion to his interests, outweighed even his gratitude to the mother-superior who was supposed to have taken Lois under her wing. "How can she have found out the child's hiding-place, what can have set her thoughts travelling to Irish convents?" he wondered. Then presently his thoughts travelled to M. Van Zandt as a possible coadjutor, and a third person came in for a due share of his gratitude and goodwill.

But although the telegram, so far as Lois was concerned, evoked the most ecstatic visions of a bright future, it yet on other grounds puzzled him, and struck uncomfortable keynotes.

"Let nothing prevent your return—distrust any other telegram you may receive—M. Van Zandt will meet you at Queenstown, and tell you everything," it ran.

The "everything" that M. Van Zandt had to tell must be of an unusual character, if it could explain away the mysterious words which seemed to point to the likelihood of telegrams being sent to him with the view of preventing his return to England. The letters which he had received from his mother while in California, although brief, had not been disquieting, and had not led him to infer that anything unusual had been, or was now, taking place at the Castle.

He turned to the packet of letters which had been put into his hand, together with Lady Honor's telegram, thinking that possibly in them he might find a key to the mystery. This packet of letters consisted of a steady succession, which had been written by Mr. McGowan, in hopes that sooner or later they might find their way into Herrick's hands. They were sequels to the one in which the lawyer had conveyed the tidings of the appointment of Lord Southmoor as trustee to the Gaskell estate. They were variously dated six weeks, a month, ten days, and a week back. Herrick had left no orders with his New York agent to forward his letters after him to California, so there they had lain at New York awaiting his return thither.

He did not break the seal of these letters until he was on board the "Europa," and the disquietude caused by the latter portion of Lady Honor's telegram was beginning to throw its shadow over the bright visions evoked by its opening sentence.

"After all, Honor is only a girl, excitable, impetuous, and wilful, and possibly has formed very erroneous opinions on matters which are outside her experience. Here, no doubt, I shall find satisfactory solutions to things that have been a fine puzzle to her," he thought, as he arranged Mr. McGowan's letters according to their dates, preparatory to reading them in due order.

But "satisfactory solutions" seemed farther off than ever, when the last line of those letters was read.

Letter number one enlarged discontentedly upon the theme of the undesirability of Lord Southmoor's appointment as trustee to the estate, and hinted at dangers ahead.

Letter number two stated that the lawyer's worst fears had been realised, and that Lord Southmoor had inaugurated his trusteeship by consenting to the purchase of his own property, under conditions more advantageous to the seller than to the buyer.

CATHERINE LOUISA PIRKIS

Letter number three adverted, in passing, to Lady Joan's evident reluctance to give Mr. Gaskell's address in California, and then went on to relate Mr. McGowan's refusal to conduct the legal preliminaries connected with the purchase of the Southmoor property, for the twofold reason that he considered the matter was being "rushed through" in a most extraordinary fashion; and also that he could not conscientiously assist in the withdrawal of the large sum of money required for the purchase of the property, from its present satisfactory investments.

But it was letter number four which sent a chill to Herrick's heart, and filled his mind with the gravest apprehensions.

Mr. McGowan was not a man to beat about the bush. He said right out what he had to say in the most straightforward fashion. He began this letter asking if Mr. Gaskell knew anything of a man named Gallagher? Could he recall his name in any connection whatever? Had he any reason to suppose that his father or grandfather might have had dealings with him?

"He came to my office," the lawyer went on to say, "requesting that I would take up some trifling business he had on hand—the recovery of a small sum of money which had been owing to him for years. As a reference he gave the name of Lady Joan Gaskell. I soon discovered that his law business was merely a blind to get the entry to my office, in order to have the opportunity of putting questions to my clerks on matters connected with the Gaskell family. Naturally, the only information he could obtain from my clerks was information that he might have picked up in the village street; with this difference, however, information picked up in the village might have been nothing more than idle gossip; whereas, information picked up at my office would be reliable. In the circumstances, I thought it as well to make a few enquiries respecting the man, and commisioned my agent at Liverpool to find out all he could about him. My agent's report has just come to hand. In it he states that Thomas Gallagher is a duly qualified medical man, with something of a reputation for the treatment of the insane. Of late, however, from various causes, his patients appear to have fallen off, and he has undoubtedly been guilty of practices which will shortly bring him within the grip of the law. Evidence at the present moment is collecting which will prove beyond a doubt that he, in connection with another doctor, has been guilty of signing false certificates of lunacy, and thus incarcerating sane people in asylums. Relatives interested in the matter have paid him heavily for so doing, and one or two petty conspiracies of this sort will shortly be brought to light. My agent wondered that the man had not long ago bolted, and opined that he must have some highly remunerative business on hand thus to run so daring a risk of penal servitude."

So far, Herrick's curiosity respecting Gallagher's antecedents was but vaguely excited. It was, however, the concluding sentences of the lawyer's letter which sent the sudden chill to his heart, and brought back to his mind a a rush of painful memories.

"I think it my duty to tell you," Mr. McGowan concluded, "that Gallagher's enquiries, made of one of my junior clerks, have turned entirely upon two points, viz.: The will that your father made nearly thirty years ago, and the different position in which Lady Joan would have found herself had not old Mr. Gaskell's death preceded your father's. Pardon my bluntness in stating these facts, but I think it right that you should be fully informed on the matter."

Herrick, with something of a groan, dropped the lawyer's letter. For a moment the bright, dancing waves, and the dappled blue sky were blotted out by a picture of a darkened room, where his father lay stretched upon his deathbed, his mother clung in terror to his arm, and the frightened face of a nurse showed in the doorway.

And instead of the rush and plunge of the steamer, and dash of the ocean, there seemed to sound in his ears his mother's voice, saying, in an odd, strained tone:

"Let there be no mistake—write down the exact hour and minute at which old Mr. Gaskell died."

IX

H errick had a rough passage across the Atlantic. The "Europa," took the whole of fourteen days to make it, instead of the ten to which she was pledged by the advertisements of her owners.

During those fourteen days life came to a standstill for Lady Honor, and she had to pay the penalty for her neglected cold and severe drenching with the racking pains of rheumatic fever. Old Dr. Scott, hastily summoned, averred that in all his experience he had never before known rheumatic fever to approximate so closely to brain-fever, and he wondered not a little over the strangeness of the girl's delirious fancies.

Here was a young lady whose daily existence must have rippled on as smoothly as any woodland stream, talking incessantly of things which must have been altogether outside her experience; of a "serpent" which she prayed might be kept from approaching her; of one who was "dead, young, and broken-hearted," and of "Red Sisters"—whoever they might be—who she fancied were incessantly chanting that dead one's requiem.

The old doctor and nurses exchanged glances as the delirious girl tossed restlessly on her bed, and muttered over what seemed to them the wildest of delusions.

To tell the truth, a good deal of exchanging of glances and of whispered confidences was going on just then between the members of the Castle household. The gardeners, who cut the finest hot-house fruit, that never was eaten; the grooms, who grumbled that never an order was sent down to the stables now for carriage or saddle-horse; the housekeeper, who ordered dinners that were never graced by Lady Joan's presence; "my lady's" own maid, who had fine tales to tell of restless nights, and sleeping potions daily increasing in strength; every one, in short, more or less felt that "things" were not exactly what they ought to be, and assuredly not what they had been when a master had held the reins, and laid down the law for the household.

The more charitably-disposed among the servants opined that "My lady was killing herself with grief for the loss of her husband, poor dear!" The harder-hearted ones shook their heads, and muttered that there was something behind it all which they could not understand. "Those who live the longest see the most," they said, with an air of great wisdom; but all the same, they would be uncommonly glad when Mr. Herrick came home.

"Glad when Mr. Herrick came home." Dr. Scott had the same thought in his heart, but he kept it to himself, although heavy anxieties were pressing upon him at the moment. He knew that Lady Joan's health was rapidly giving way—it was impossible for a skilled eye to look her in the face and not know it—but he was much too frightened of her to dare to tell her so, and advise the calling in the aid of medical skill. More than once, in days gone by, her grand manner had nipped in the bud his kindly officiousness on matters connected with her health.

"She used to make me feel like a caned schoolboy, and I've no mind to repeat the experience," he reasoned, as he sat beside Lady Honor's bed, holding her feverish wrist; "but, for all that, I heartily wish someone were here to share responsibility with me. There's this young lady, too. She's in a most critical condition. Her father is some hundreds of miles away, and her aunt might just as well be with him, for all the attention she shows the girl. If she should succumb, all blame will rest on my shoulders."

Lady Honor, however, did not succumb; her constitution was far too robust to give way under the first serious illness she had ever had in her life. On the day before the "Europa" touched at Queenstown, a change set in for the better.

She awoke early in the morning, after a long and peaceful night, and opening wide her bright, brown eyes, said to the nurse, who sat beside her, in a perfectly natural tone:

"What is that noise I have heard, off and on, through the night? It seems just outside the door."

"It's the dog, my lady," answered the nurse, delighted to believe that "serpents" and "Red Sisters" were now to be things of the past, "and fine trouble he has given us all to keep him out of the room. He has lived there ever since your ladyship has been ill. He has brought his bones and his biscuits to eat on the door-mat, and has whined, and howled, and scratched the door nearly off its hinges."

"What, my dear old Argus," cried the girl, "oh, let him in at once. What on earth possessed you to keep him out of the room?"

Then, when the mastiff, with a glad bark, came bounding in, and thrusting his nose into Lady Honor's hand, looked up into her face with eager eyes, the girl's first remark made the nurse fear that her brains were leaving her once more. It was:

"Your eyes are as like his as eyes can be, Argie, dear. With you beside me, I wouldn't give a thank-you for his portrait."

CATHERINE LOUISA PIRKIS

Dr. Scott was right. Lady Joan might as well have been hundreds of miles away for all the attention she showed her niece during her illness. Possibly no unkindness was intended by her; the explanation of her seeming heartlessness lay in the fact that she herself was just then passing through a strange experience—an experience born of an over-weighted, disordered, and self-absorbed brain, a brain incapable for the time of receiving impressions from without, and consequently inclined to intensify and magnify those received from within.

On the day of her final interview with Gallagher, she had waited with a feverish eagerness for letter or telegram from him, announcing that he had performed that part of the compact for which he had been paid so heavy a fee. Neither came, however; and, as the day wore away, Lady Joan's feverish eagerness grew upon her. When night came and brought no news, she filled in the silence with all sorts of terrors. Gallagher had turned traitor, and had denounced her to the nearest police authorities, and the next thing would be—ah, she dared not think what the next thing would be. Thought became as much a dread to her as a positive physical ill might be to one already sorely tried with disease. Sleep—heavy dreamless sleep—was, she felt, her only chance of keeping her brains together; so, in view of the long silent hours steadily creeping nearer, she doubled her sleeping draught, and threw herself, dressed as she was, upon the bed.

The double dose of chloral, however, did not have the effect she anticipated; instead of being steeped in heavy animal-like unconsciousness, her brain seemed to be suddenly endowed with a marvellous vivacity and creative energy. As she lay in the dim light on her bed, with wide-open staring eyes, her sumptuous and luxurious surroundings seemed little by little to fade into the threadbare and impoverished elegance of her girlhood's room at Southmoor. Damask and brocade changed into dingy and faded embroideries; the polished marqueterie tables and chairs gave place to worm-eaten oak, cracked and damaged with the wear of successive generations; and, strangest sight of all, in front of the yellow, badly silvered glass, which had done its best to turn a lovely maiden of eighteen into a witch of forty, stood the maiden herself, slim, pale, thoughtful, with hands clasped together, head slightly thrown back, and eyes looking away into distance, with a look in them which seemed to say, "I'm waiting for what the years will bring to me."

Lady Joan raised herself on her elbow, and looked around her in the dimness.

"It is a vision," she murmured. "It will presently vanish."

Yes, it was a vision, and it did presently vanish, all, that is, except the maiden, the Joan of early days. She, instead of vanishing with the worm-eaten oak and faded embroideries, remained standing amid the shining marqueterie and brocades. Yet not altogether the maiden, with the light of expectancy shining out of thoughtful eyes; a statelier, graver woman, older by at least three decades, was the Joan who stood now in her long, black robes before the mirror.

Lady Joan felt her blood grow chilled as, supported on her elbow still, she watched this second presentment of her living self.

"That other was the Joan of the past; but who is this—me, yet not me?" she wondered.

As if in answer to her thought, the vision turned and faced her; then slowly, step by step, drew nearer to the bed, pausing only when within about a yard of it.

Lady Joan, although frozen with terror, as if under some spell, had no power to withdraw her gaze. With eyes which must have told their own tale of horror, she looked full in the face of the thing which seemed, yet was not, herself. Not herself, assuredly; its hair was the dark, rich brown, which had been hers in her husband's time; its eyes, too, were true and clear, and could give back look for look; its mouth was not stern, hard-set, and rigid, but a full-lipped mouth, which told of tenderness as well as of strength and self-control.

Lady Joan gazed and gazed till her eyes lost their seeing power. The room swam round, and she sank back trembling on her pillows, while her heart seemed to whisper to her heart, "You did well to gaze as you did; that was the Joan who might have been, but who never may be now."

Thus, with closed eyes, she lay, till morning brought the wintry sunlight peeping in at her window, and her maid knocking at her door.

But all the same, though her eyes were closed, she was conscious that the dark figure had not left her side, and that if her eyelids had lifted she would have been confronted once more with the Joan who might have been, but who never would be now.

The vision of this Joan, it seemed, was to be an abiding vision. Again and again during the days of Lady Honor's rheumatic fever did it make its appearance at intervals, growing less and less with every recurrence, until at length, to Lady Joan's fancy, it seemed as much a part of her bedroom and boudoir as did her pictures and her furniture. At first the putting out of a lamp had seemed to be the signal for its issuing forth from some dark corner: later on, let the lamp be high or let the lamp be low, there it would be, standing beside her bed, or in front of her mirror, or, if in her boudoir, seated at her writing-table, or standing looking out of one of the long French windows, while she herself lay prostrate upon the couch.

"If I live long enough, my brains will go," thought Lady Joan, as day by day the vision seemed to grow more and more real and living to her, until at last, side by side with it, her own personality seemed to dwindle.

All her daily occupations were laid on one side. Packets of unopened letters lay upon her writing-table. Letters from M. Van Zandt, asking for tidings of Lady Honor, to whom he had written and written in vain. Letters, too, from Lord Southmoor's lawyers, enclosing important papers for Lady Joan's signature, and telling her, in polite and circuitous language, that if she would only be good enough to give her attention to these necessary matters of business, the purchase of Southmoor could be completed in a few days.

Thus, by a strange fatality, Lady Joan, with her own hand, retarded the doing of the one thing for which she had been willing to lay crime upon her soul.

Sometimes she would pull herself together, as it were, seat herself at her writing-table, and take up that packet of unopened letters. Then her eyes would wander round the room expectantly. If she saw the shadowy vision standing at the window, or advancing towards her from a distant corner the letters would be laid down again, she would lean back in her chair, and with eyes that seemed spellbound and fascinated, she would watch the movements of the thing that was and yet was not herself, until it vanished. If, on the other hand, as she looked around her, the mysterious shape did not appear, the expectancy in her mind, the wonder, "Where is it? When will it come?" equally prevented concentration of thought on any other subject. After a time her frame of mind grew to be constantly expectant and wondering. If the shape were present, her thought was, "How near will it come this time? Will it touch my hand— my cheek? How long will it stay? What will it do next?" If, however, as she threw herself wearily on her bed, the dark form was nowhere to be seen, her thought would be, "I wonder if 'it' is seated at my writing-table in my boudoir downstairs, and what 'it' is doing with my papers?" Or if she reclined languidly on her couch in her boudoir, and the room seemed empty of the dark shape, her wonder would be, "What is 'it' doing in my room upstairs now, I wonder? Is 'it' seated in my easy-chair, or standing looking at itself in my mirror?"

Only on one occasion, and this was the last on which it appeared to her, did she ever see the shadowy form anywhere else than in her bedroom or her boudoir, and that was one morning as she was leaving her bedroom on the upper floor. To her fancy the stately figure stood awaiting her at the head of the stairs in the gallery, and, as she advanced, swept rapidly before her down the staircase. Lady Joan felt that wherever it led she must follow, though it might be into an open grave. The figure seemed to her to lead the way across the hall to the corridor leading off it, into which she knew only too well opened old Mr. Gaskell's suite of rooms. These rooms, by her orders, had, ever since the old gentleman's death, been kept locked from one end to the other. Yet to her fancy the dark shape paused for a moment at the door of the first of the suite of rooms, then disappeared, leaving the impression on her mind that it had passed in.

All tremulous and shivering, she sought to follow; but no, neither door nor handle would yield.

"My lady," said the housekeeper, who chanced to be coming along the corridor, "shall I fetch the keys? The doors of these rooms are all locked."

"Locked!" repeated Lady Joan, beating with her hands against the closed door; "who says they are locked? Someone has just passed in."

"The butler has the keys, my lady, shall I fetch him? You know, my lady, that you gave them to him yourself," remonstrated the housekeeper. Then the white, fixed look on Lady Joan's face startled and scared her. "My lady, pray come away," she pleaded, "you are not well enough to stand the opening of these rooms today."

"Locked! Locked, never to be opened!" murmured Lady Joan, leaning half-fainting against the oak panels.

After this the whisperings in the Castle household grew louder and more frequent, and one and all were agreed that it would be a day of rejoicing when Mr. Herrick came home and commenced his reign.

　　　　　　　　　　　CATHERINE LOUISA PIRKIS

X

Herrick's apprehensions, called into being by Mr. McGowan's letter, kept their claw upon him, like some evil bird of prey upon its victim, while the *Europa* plunged over the Atlantic waves, or wallowed helplessly in their troughs.

To tell the truth, he had but little chance of shaking off those apprehensions. The terrors we dare not face and fight are those that hold us longest in thrall; and assuredly Mr. McGowan's letter had awakened terrors that nothing short of the sternest necessity could bring a man to face.

This young man, who combined the higher qualities of the money-maker—those of clear insight, method, and grip—with the courage and capacity for rule supposed to be the special gifts of the gods to those of patrician birth, suddenly found himself in a dilemma that he was as powerless to meet or to avoid as any clod of earth in a ploughed field.

When the *Europa* sighted Queenstown, it was with a gigantic effort that he pulled himself together, and said, "This day, at least, shall be marked with a white stone in my calendar," cajoling himself into the belief that the "everything" which M. Van Zandt had to relate would be all of a piece with the glad thought in his heart, that before the day was over he would hold his darling in his arms again.

Beside this thought, naturally enough, the terrors which had haunted him throughout the voyage paled and grew misty, and he was fain to persuade himself that they owed their origin to a series of hideous misconceptions which a clear head—such, for example, as his would be when his Lois had been given back to him—would set straight in half an hour.

His feelings towards M. Van Zandt had increased in warmth as the days had gone by, until now, as he weighed the possible services her lover had rendered Honor in her search for Lois, he was prepared to hold out his hand to him as his cousin's suitor. With the marriage which he himself intended making before his eyes, he could not in reason pass a very harsh judgment upon Lady Honor's choice.

"It is utterly absurd," he thought, "for people to set the accidents of birth and rank above the higher moral and intellectual qualities. My mother must be made to see the matter in a right light."

It was characteristic that Lord Southmoor's paternal claims in this connection did not receive a second thought from him, he having long since decided that "my lord's" intellectual qualities fell little short of idiotcy.

Lady Honor's description of M. Van Zandt had not led Herrick to form an exaggerated estimate of his personal beauty, and when, as the "Europa" touched at Queenstown, a middle-aged man, poorly dressed, with stooping shoulders, and hair going from brown to grey, came on board, he was quite prepared to greet him as M. Van Zandt. He fancied he would have been able to identify him as Lady Honor's suitor, even if M. Van Zandt had not sent to him by the ship's steward, together with his card, a telegram from the young lady herself. This was addressed to M. Van Zandt, and ran simply thus:

"Do not be uneasy about me. I have been ill. I am now quite well, and beg of you on no account to leave your post till Herrick arrives."

Lady Honor had credited her lover with possessing "the truest eyes in the world." Herrick was quite ready to endorse her statement when he shook hands with the Belgian drawing-master.

They were, however, troubled eyes this morning, and as Herrick looked down into them from his superior height, it seemed to him that they were misty and dim, as a man's might be with tears kept back by a strong will.

"It's the glare of sunlight and sea together," thought Herrick. And then, all eagerness to get ashore, he at once signalled to one of the sailors to follow him with his luggage.

"To there," said M. Van Zandt, pointing to the written address on his card, and not daring to trust his lips to pronounce the very Irish designation, "Murtough's Hotel."

"Why, yes, for the luggage; but of course we can take a car at once for the—the convent," answered Herrick, not wishing to lengthen by five minutes the separation which he had already found so hard to endure.

M. Van Zandt looked at him sorrowfully.

"My friend, come with me—a quiet room" he said, in his broken English. And then even that failed him, and all he could find to say was, "Il faut, il faut!"

It was still harder for him to find words, ten minutes later, when he found himself alone with Herrick in that quiet room.

"After all, there is a silence more eloquent than words," he thought, "that will tell him best."

So Herrick had to say twice over, "M. Van Zandt, I am all attention." And yet never a word escaped M. Van Zandt's lips, only the sorrow and pity in his eyes seemed to deepen as he steadily looked the young man in the face.

Then Herrick took fright.

"If you have bad news to tell me, tell it at once, for Heaven's sake, and be done with it," he said, almost fiercely.

But still M. Van Zandt did not speak.

"Is she ill—tell me?" said Herrick, his fears increasing upon him.

Then M. Van Zandt laid his hand on his arm.

"My poor, poor friend," he said, gently.

Herrick's face changed.

"Is she—dead?" he stammered, hoarsely.

And now M. Van Zandt's silence told him the truth.

If a cycle can be lived through in the "tick of one moment," Herrick lived through that cycle then.

He looked white, stunned, dazed. Then he said, feebly, faintly, as if his voice had aged with his heart:

"Tell me all you have to tell; but tell it quickly, for Heaven's sake!"

M. Van Zandt, knowing what torture his imperfect English would inflict on his agonised listener, complied with Herrick's request by spreading Mdlle. Mélanie—"Aunt Mélanie"—Van Zandt's letter before him, and bidding him read it.

This letter was in effect the repetition in detail of the mournful story which M. Van Zandt had already communicated in outline to Lady Honor. It was a lengthy epistle; but throughout was written in simple unidiomatic French that a school-girl could have read with ease. Herrick, however, took long to read it, for his brain felt benumbed, and all but incapable of grasping the fact that the Sister Héloise, whose saintliness Mdlle. Van Zandt lauded enthusiastically, was the golden-haired darling he had held in his arms, vowing that nothing in life should wrench her from him.

The letter took up the narrative at the point where Sister Héloise had been brought to the convent by a priest, a certain Father Elliot, who, the writer said, appeared to take the deepest interest in the girl, concerning whom he gave minute instructions to the Mother Superior. On account of her delicacy of health, all sorts of indulgences were to be allowed to her, and her religious duties were in every possible way to be lightened. The girl, however, was no sooner within the convent walls than that which Mdlle. Van Zandt designated her saintliness of temperament declared itself. She outshone the nuns alike in her devotions and in her penances, rigorously excluding from her daily life everything that savoured of relaxation, even that lawfully allowed to the Sisters. Her deep sadness and great depression of spirit seemed to grow upon her as the days went by, and it soon became apparent to the Mother Superior that it would not be long before Sister Héloise would be called upon to reap the rewards of her sanctity in another world. Neither the Mother nor the nuns, however, anticipated the end to be so near as in reality it was, and the young girl's death had been a terrible shock to them all. Missing Sister Héloise from her accustomed place at five o'clock prayers one morning, a nun was sent to her cell in search of her, and there found her lying on her bed in a dying condition. They had hastily summoned the father confessor of the convent, a certain Father O'Halloran, who was pastor of a small church about a mile and a half distant. He had administered the last rites of the Church to the girl, and within an hour she had passed away. Neither to this priest, nor to any one else, had Sister Héloise expressed a wish of any sort, nor had she left any message to be communicated to her friends. Her whole soul had seemed to be absorbed in her vocation, and Father O'Halloran believed firmly that she had no wish or aspiration outside it. Two days after her death she had been buried in the convent graveyard, no friends having come forward to express a wish to the contrary. Mdlle. Van Zandt ended her letter with the pious hope that the friends of Sister Héloise, who were instituting the present inquiries respecting her, would rejoice that one so evidently designed to be a great saint had found her calling.

As authority for the facts she had stated, Mdlle. Van Zandt gave the name of Père Antoine, father confessor to the Sacramentines at Ghent, who, she said, was on terms of the closest intimacy with Father O'Halloran. In a postscript to her letter, she added that this Father O'Halloran had written to Père Antoine, saying that although the rules of her Order would prevent the mother-superior of the convent of Saint Alphonse from receiving visits of a secular character, yet if any friends or relatives of Sister Héloise would like to visit her grave, they need only mention his name, or that of Père Antoine, and they would at once be admitted by the porteress, a Sister of a less austere Order, to the convent cemetery.

Herrick read to the last syllable of the letter, the dazed, stricken look on his face deepening.

In good truth, a man in full health reading what purported to be the record of his own death and burial, could scarcely have found the narrative more difficult to realise than did this young man to give credence to the facts which identified the devout and sorrowful Sister Héloise with his loving, tremulous, child-like Lois.

He leaned back in his chair, covering his eyes with one hand. There rose up before him a picture of a stately avenue of beeches, of a great sea of green sward, marked with heavy blots of shadows cast by a blazing, cloudless sun, of a golden-haired girl with a bunch of field-flowers in her hand, of a young man whom he could scarcely think of as himself, so full was he of life, hope, and vigour, bending over her with words of passionate love upon his lips. Then suddenly, sharply, through the autumn stillness of the afternoon, there seemed to sound in his ears once more the tolling of a summoning church bell.

A great cry of agony arose to his lips. He stifled it. "Where was the use?" he asked himself, bitterly. As well might a child's ball tossed in the air cry out against the laws of gravitation which brought it to the ground, or the thistle-down rebel against the winds which carried it hither and thither at will. Life ended for him that day—that hour; that was all.

"My poor friend!" said M. Van Zandt. laying his hand on Herrick's shoulder.

The young man withdrew his hand from his eyes. They glowed and burned, but there was never a tear in them.

"Why pity me!" he said, in hard, dry tones. "Nothing in life can hurt me now."

M. Van Zandt's vocabulary was too limited to admit of his playing the part of comforter efficiently. All he could find to say—still with his hand on Herrick's shoulder—was: "You are so young, my friend—ah, so young!"

"Am I?" was the whole of Herrick's reply, spoken scornfully, defiantly; and then there fell a silence between them once more.

The voice and the dry, glowing eyes frightened M. Van Zandt. Here was a desperate man in a desperste mood, not a doubt. Better floods of tears, a storm of passionate declamation, than dry-eyed, stony grief like this.

"You will go see her grave in the cemetery?" he said, presently, of purpose emphasizing the cruel words.

A change passed over Herrick's face; the fire died out of his eyes.

"It is two hours to drive there; I have ordered voiture with two horse," went on M. Van Zandt.

Herrick rose impetuously to his feet.

"Leave me alone—for Heaven's sake leave me to myself for five minutes," he said, hoarsely.

M. Van Zandt rose immediately, and left the room.

XI

The short winter's day was drawing to a close when Herrick's and M. Van Zandt's two hours' drive across country came to an end at the foot of the range of hills on which stood the convent of the Red Sisters. It had been a long, dreary drive. M. Van Zandt prayed that, to the end of his life, he might never again be called upon to go through such another two hours of silence and gloom.

The instinct which makes a man veil his face before an overmastering sorrow was strong upon Herrick, and for the greater part of the way he had leaned forward with elbows on his knees, his head bowed on his hands.

M. Van Zandt, to break the dead monotony of the drive, had occasionally broken into voluble and vehement French. He was careful, however, that it should be French as provincial and idiomatic as he could make it. "Then," thought the kind-hearted man, "if he doesn't wish to answer, he need not wake up his brains to understand me."

And Herrick did not "wake up his brains" to understand idiomatic French or anything else. Creation, for the nonce, was a blank to him. What little of reasoning power was left to him was absorbed in the endeavour to realise that his golden-haired, blue-eyed darling lay, in a nun's veil and habit, in a convent grave.

"Thou hast beaten me with all Thy storms," was the cry wrung from David's heart when crushed by overwhelming sorrow. To Herrick's fancy not only had he been beaten with "all Thy storms," but creation had been taxed to furnish new and unknown tempests with which to buffet him; for surely never, since man had been man, had three short months of life held such a record of "mourning, lamentation, and woe."

Their road had lain in a westerly direction from Queenstown. During the last few miles of their drive hamlets had grown to be farther and farther apart, outlying farmhouses had ceased to break the monotony of the landscape. The road had steadily wound upwards, growing narrow and narrower with every quarter-mile they covered, until at length the curly-headed, ruddy-faced Irishman who drove their waggonette pulled up, and told them that they had best make the rest of their journey on foot, for the path was now little more than a sheep-walk, winding round the hills.

A great green, treeless stretch of country surrounded them on three sides, on the fourth the rocky hills bounded their horizon. Behind these the sun had just disappeared. The blue of the wintry sky was fading

CATHERINE LOUISA PIRKIS

rapidly now into the silvery grey of twilight. Shadows there were none, and every object far and near stood out boldly, vividly, in the cold clear light with which the whole landscape was, so to speak, saturated. Every brown, rushy tussock, which broke the greenness of the miles of bog lying right and left of the road they had just quitted, could have been counted and catalogued, as well also as every crag and turret of the steep, stark hills, which turned the dome of sky in front of them into a wall-supported ceiling.

Halfway up one of the steepest and stoniest of these hills the grey of the convent walls showed hard and crude against the tenderer grey-green of the weather-beaten hillside. Of the convent itself little was to be seen; a turret or gable, showing here and there above the wall at unequal distances, however, led one to conjecture that it must be a long, low-roofed building, or perhaps succession of buildings.

As they mounted higher they could catch the glint of a gilded cross, which possibly surmounted the convent chapel. Not a sound far or near, never so much as distant sheep-bell or flutter of bird, broke the stillness of the winter landscape. Few words passed between the two men; but every one of Herrick's weary, lagging footsteps seemed to say what, in reality, was the thought of his heart, "I am going to a grave—the grave of the girl I have loved better than life itself."

In very truth this was the one thought which, with every step he took, he was trying to beat into his brain: "I am going to stand beside a grave and say to myself, 'my darling lies there sleeping her last sleep.'"

The effort was futile. It would have been far easier for him to persuade himself that, bright-eyed and golden-haired as ever, in her white frock and big sun hat, she would presently emerge from those grey convent walls, and come forward to greet him with tender, loving words, as of yore.

With every upward step they took the silence around them seemed to intensify. There were no signs of human life anywhere, nor so much as a whisper of wind to set the light clouds overhead sailing across the silvery sky.

It was a twofold silence. On the right hand the restful stillness of the valley, on the left the enforced stillness of the convent. Here on one side was Nature bowing her head to a great physical law, the law which bids rest to follow labour, night to follow day, winter to follow spring—a law with which every blade of grass, every buzzing fly, or light-winged bird was thoroughly in accord. There on the other was a full tide of human life, of human love, hope, dread, stemmed at its flood and stricken into silence by an arbitrary, dogmatic fiat, to which no parallel could be found in the natural world.

The silence of the convent was, however, presently to be broken. As they stood immediately under the grey walls, and M. Van Zandt had lifted his hand to ring the bell which hung by a chain beside an iron-studded door, there came a sudden burst of soft music.

"It is the Benediction that they sing," said M. Van Zandt, and good Catholic that he was, he at once lifted his hat, went down on his knees in the gritty road, and began saying his prayers.

Not so Herrick, he was in no mood for either reverence or prayer. Benediction, was it? To him it sounded more like a wail, a cry wrung from human souls for the sweet things in life, which somehow they had let slip from their clasp: for the human hopes and loves which they had flung on one side ere they had tasted their fulness.

The soft voices of the Red Sisters rose and fell, and rose again. Herrick turned his back on good M. Van Zandt at his prayers, and went wandering along the narrow pathway.

Twilight was deepening rapidly now, the green all round was changing into blackish grey, the lustre in the sky was dying out. Herrick wandered along beside what seemed to him an interminable length of wall. The nuns' voices seemed to haunt and follow him step by step as he went. Word for word he could hear their solemn chant. The "O Salutaris Hostia" had ceased now, and in a soft minor key they were chanting their "Salve Regina." The melody was arrestive; he paused, leaning for a moment against the rough stone wall.

To stand still for a moment was to gather his mantle of sorrow around him. In that sweet, soft-voiced choir, not so very long ago, a softer, sweeter voice than any there had joined. Lois had wailed her heart out there as those others were wailing now, wailed over the grave which lay behind her—the grave of youth, hope, love—stretching out her hands to the grave which lay before her, as the best hiding-place for her broken heart and weary spirit.

Dimmer and darker grew the twilight; more slowly, more solemnly, rose and fell the voices of the Red Sisters. Herrick felt the numbness, the torpor, lifting from his brain, his marble-cold heart was yielding. He leaned his brow against the rough wall, and tears, such as he had never in his life shed before, forced themselves from beneath his smarting eyelids.

Presently the creaking of the convent gate, as it swung back heavily, and the sounds of footsteps in approach, made him look up. Was it

M. Van Zandt, and perhaps the porteress of the convent, coming to summon him to Sister Héloise's grave, he wondered. No, there was the pious M. Van Zandt kneeling still in the gritty road, and evidently rejoicing heart and soul in the service.

But these—who were they, approaching with slow, even tread under the shadow of the high wall? A tall, dark man of dignified carriage; a slight girl clad in the black dress, not of a nun but of a nursing sister.

Herrick shaded his eyes with his hands. "I cannot see—the twilight bewilders me—my eyes are misty," he thought as he made one step forward, then stood motionless, petrified, thinking that his brains were leaving him. The man and the girl drew nearer. It was easy to see that the man was a priest elderly, grave, dignified. But the girl! Herrick's heart seemed to stand still, his lips parted, but no sound would issue forth. For beneath the prim, neat bonnet, he had caught the gleam of golden hair and of deep blue eyes, and though the face was pale and changed and wan since last he had looked on it, there was no need to tell him that it was the face of Lois White.

XII

Those ancient hills, in the old days of rough chivalry and fierce fighting, must have frowned down on many a drama of passionate love-making and reckless blood-shedding, but they never threw their shadow athwart a more pathetic meeting and greeting than that of Herrick and Lois. For a moment they stood silent, looking each into the other's face, then Herrick seized the girl's hands passionately, and, looking down into her eyes, stammered—not the vehement words of greeting a man might be supposed to utter in the circumstances, but simply "Why? Why?" and then broke off, saying nothing at all. In good truth his heart was over-strung, his brain over-charged, and feeling of any sort was for the moment less a joy than a pain.

Lois also did not flush into the gladness such a meeting might naturally be supposed to evoke. She turned marble-white, her eyes grew troubled. She looked at the priest standing a yard or so apart.

"How shall I tell him? How is it possible?" she said, faintly.

Father Elliot's answer, given with a gravity which deepened into solemnity with its final words, told Herrick that he and pain were not yet to part company. It was:

"Not here, not now, but by-and-by, alone and in quiet, I will tell him the whole truth. Let him make his heart strong to hear it."

Herrick felt his brain grow dizzy with fore-bodings. Time to speak them was not to be given him. M. Van Zandt, his prayers ended now, came swooping down upon them with a roulade of questions in an odd commingling of French and English. The name Sister Héloise repeated very often, gave Father Elliot a clue to his meaning.

"This is Miss White," said the priest, by way of explanation. "She came over this afternoon with me from the children's hospital at Sandyford—where she is working—in order to lay her wreath upon the grave of Sister Héloise." Then he turned to Herrick. "Sister Héloise, Lucy Harwood that is, was a young girl in whom I took the deepest interest. Her vocation was the religious life, and it brought her the happiness she had sought for in vain in the world. Come, let us descend the hill; I will tell you her story as we go along."

Movement came as a relief to all. M. Van Zandt was in a perfect delirium of delight. Ten years seemed suddenly lifted off his shoulders. He broke into all sorts of odd, ecstastic expressions; and then, in his

CATHERINE LOUISA PIRKIS

queer mongrel dialect, reiterated again and again how delighted his Honor would be to hear the glad tidings. As for Father Elliot, his voice, his manner, showed that he was strangely disturbed. He had needed no introduction to Herrick. To look at him was to see a vision of the Joan of the days gone by: to conjure up a picture of a Joan with more warmth and colour of face, perhaps, than the real Joan had ever owned to, and with a truer, clearer light in her eyes: but all the same of a Joan who had won his heart, then crushed it and flung it from her.

Herrick did not hear the story of Sister Héloïse, for the very natural reason that side by side with Lois once more, he wished to hear no voice but hers. The two walked on ahead down the stony pathway, leaving the priest and M. Van Zandt to follow.

"Those who don't know how to keep deserve to lose," Herrick said, as he held her hand tightly in his own. "I never again trust you for five minutes out of my sight."

Then questions came in a rush to his lips: "What had scared her? Why had she fled? Where had she been? What had she been doing during the bitter months of separation?"

Lois's sad face, as she put on one side all his questions unanswered save the last two, seemed to reiterate the words of the priest: "Let him make his heart strong to hear the truth."

To the last two of his questions she replied that she had, on leaving Longridge, by Father Elliot's advice, taken refuge in a convent at Liverpool. There she had had a serious illness, brought on by anxiety and intensified by a severe cold she had caught. On her recovery she had found that active work of some sort was a necessity to her, and hearing of the need for helpers at the children's hospital at Sandyford, she had volunteered as nursing sister there. In the course of her duties at the hospital she had been thrown into the society of Father O'Halloran, the Father Confessor to the Red Sisters at Helstone Bridge. From him she had heard the pathetic story of Lucy Harwood from beginning to end, and, deeply interested in it, had requested Father Elliot to take her to the convent graveyard, in order that she might lay a wreath on Sister Héloïse's grave. Father Elliot had called upon her at the hospital, in order to see and to advise her before he started for Africa.

But here Lois broke off her story, turning her face sharply away from Herrick; and his next question brought only the vehement entreaty:

"I beg—I implore you, don't ask me to tell you more. Father Elliot will tell you everything."

Meantime Father Elliot was relating to M. Van Zandt Lucy Harwood's mournful history, her pathetic search for the ideal mother of her childhood's fancy, the sad effect it had had upon her health, her entrance into the convent of the Red Sisters, and finally her peaceful death-bed.

But the darker story of chicanery and crime so closely interwoven with Lucy's history was not told to M. Van Zandt, as he and the priest journeyed down the hill side. That was reserved for the quiet of a midnight hour, when Father Elliot and Herrick found themselves alone in a room in Father O'Halloran's cottage. Sandyford, where stood the children's hospital, was within easy distance of the Red Sisters' convent, and the waggonette which had brought Herrick and M. Van Zandt from Cork speedily conveyed the whole party thither. Father O'Halloran's house was within walking distance of the hospital, and the three gentlemen, after escorting Lois back to her temporary home repaired thither to receive a kindly welcome from the Father, and a hospitable invitation to pass the night under his roof.

That was to be a memorable night to Herrick.

"For Heaven's sake tell me as soon as possible what you have to tell!" he had found opportunity to say to Father Elliot, feeling much as a man might feel who, under sentence of death, longs to lay his head upon the block and be done with the torture of suspense.

It was not, however, until the kindly host and M. Van Zandt had withdrawn for the night, that Herrick's torture of suspense was to be ended.

Then Father Elliot went straight to the point at once.

"In two days' time I sail for Dahomey," he said as the door closed on Father O'Halloran and M. Van Zandt. "Into no ear but yours will the tale I have to tell ever be spoken. On your shoulders, my young friend, a terrible burden will be laid; may they be strengthened to bear it. After tomorrow I shall have neither part nor lot in the matter."

Then he had taken up the story of Lucy Harwood from the day of her entering into the service of Lady Joan.

A few days after this, quite accidentally, the fate of Lucy's mother had become known to him. When the poor lunatic mother, in search of her baby child, had escaped from Dr. Gallagher's house at Ballinacrae, she had wandered in the direction of Helston Bridge, begging bread and water at the cottages she passed. Eventually, late in the evening, in the midst of a heavy snow-storm, she had wandered up the hill to the convent gate, and there had sunk, famished and exhausted to the ground. In this condition she had been found on the following morning by the porteress, who had had her conveyed into the convent, and had administered restoratives to her. It was all in vain, however. Before night fell again the poor woman had passed away, and, as no one came forward to claim and identify the body, it had been buried in a quiet corner of the convent cemetery. The enquiries made by Gallagher and by old Mr. Harwood were not of an exhaustive nature. The woman's clothes were of the most ordinary kind, and the only means of identification left was a small locket, containing the photograph of her baby, Lucy. It was quite by chance that the whole sad story came to Father Elliot's ears. He had at once requested that the locket might be sent for his inspection; the likeness and the date at its back, which corresponded with the date of Lucy's birth, confirmed his suspicions that the secret of the mother's fate was solved at last.

Then rose the difficult question how to break the tidings to Lucy. While he debated it he received a visit from Ralph, who came to consult him respecting Lady Joan's munificent offer to provide for Lucy for life, on condition that she were placed under Dr. Gallagher's care. This offer was quickly followed by another equally bewildering to the Father, namely, an offer to pay any amount of money that might be required to facilitate Lois White's entrance into a convent. Father Elliot weighed both offers, sent to Lady Joan a message by Ralph, that he declined in any way to influence Miss White in her plans for her future, also that he strongly advised Ralph not to place his sister under the care of Dr. Gallagher, of whom he knew next to nothing. At the same time he added, that if Lady Joan chose to pay to the convent of Saint Alphonse, on behalf of Lucy, the sum which she had offered to pay on behalf of Miss White, it would be accepted.

It was at this point that Gallagher's plot had begun. Affairs at that moment were in a critical condition with him. He knew that a criminal prosecution was hanging over his head, and lacking means for his flight to another hemisphere, he was pressing Ralph for repayment of certain small sums of money which from time to time he had lent to the young farmer. Ralph took him into his confidence respecting Lady Joan and her bewildering offers of money, and the wily doctor at once seemed to see a mine of gold open at his feet. He represented to Ralph the danger of losing so munificent a patroness if her wishes were not complied with, induced him to inform Lady Joan that Father Elliot had accepted her offer for Miss White, and persuaded the young man to introduce him to Lady Joan as the doctor willing to take Lucy under his care. Gallagher had no intention of keeping up the fraud longer than was necessary to line his own pockets preparatory to his flight. Fate seemed to favour him. Ralph, to a certain extent in his power, did not dare to refuse to play the part of his tool, though the young man's better nature revolted against it, and eventually led him to repudiate it. Lady Joan and Father Elliot were equally deceived by the two men, and the identity of the two girls confused to the mind of the former.

It may be remarked in passing, that M. Van Zandt's mistake as to the identity of Sister Héloise with Lois White was none of Ralph's doing. It arose simply through Mdlle. Mélanie's enquiries being made for the novice under her religious, not her secular name—a mistake for which Lady Honor in part also was to be held responsible, by her misinterpretation of the conversation which she had overheard in the pine wood.

From a small beginning the plot had grown apace. Gallagher could very fairly gauge the time that must elapse before proceedings could be commenced against him, and employed every one of the precious hours left him in getting as strong a hold as possible over Lady Joan. Fortune favoured him in more ways than one. Herrick's wild goose chase in America, Lady Joan's refusal to have any direct personal intercourse with Father Elliot, the Father's sudden resolve to join the African Mission, to a certain extent left the ground clear for the plotter.

All this Father Elliot related clearly, fully, to Herrick, in calm, even voice. One thing, however, he left out of his narrative—the fact that Lady Joan's first messenger to him through Ralph had sent him praying to his superiors for permission to quit the place, and to court death among the cannibal blacks at Dahomey. "For thirty years I have prayed that the sight of her face may be spared to me," he had said, with clasped hands and face upturned to the wintry stars; "yet a little while, and the need for the prayer will be at an end."

But this was not a thing to tell to Lady Joan's son.

When the Father came to the story of Sister Héloise's death, his voice had vibrated and his eyes were shining. "The Mother Superior," he said, "told the poor child the story of her mother's fate, and led her to the quiet corner of the graveyard where she lay. Within a month from that day the child was lying in the same grave." He broke off for a moment, cleared his voice, and went on to tell how the tidings of his

CATHERINE LOUISA PIRKIS

sister's death had shaken Ralph's nerves, and sent him to tell to him the whole story of chicanery and wickedness.

"Not under the seal of confession," said the Father, "but frankly and openly, that I might make it known to the authorities. This I have already done, and the man, although he has managed to get away in an Australian steamer, will be met on his arrival at Melbourne and sent home again for his trial on other criminal charges. On other criminal charges," repeated the priest, slowly, now fixing his eyes full on the young man's face as he sat facing him, "for there will be no one to prosecute him on this matter."

"No one to prosecute!" repeated Herrick, astounded, and thinking that the priest could only be referring to his own approaching departure to Dahomey; "why I will prosecute him myself if you will not be here to do so. Such a scoundrel as that must not be allowed to escape."

He did not say, "my mother will prosecute him." To say truth, after the revelation of the double part Lady Joan had played towards him, he could not bring himself to mention her name. "My mother and I must to the end of our lives live apart," was the thought in his heart now. "I could forgive her even for hating Lois; but I cannot pardon the double dealing and subterfuge to which she has descended to keep us apart."

But his mother was to stand in another light to him before his midnight interview with Father Elliot came to an end.

"Though I remained in England, there would be no one to prosecute," repeated Father Elliot, with greater emphasis than before, and still with his eyes fixed on Herrick's face.

Herrick grew uneasy. After this bewildering story of crime could there yet remain anything else to tell? Back in a troop came the forebodings he had fought so hard to keep at bay.

"Fold your hands in prayer, my young friend," said the priest, solemnly, "bow your head. There are sorrows in life bitterer than death, more cruel than the grave."

Herrick was tongue-tied now. His lips would not even form to the words with which he had before hastened the priest's disclosures: "For heaven's sake say what you have to say quickly!"

The priest went on in a voice that sounded stern from the restraint he put upon it.

"After hearing Ralph's story of villainy, which was told to me at Cork, I came here to say good-bye to Miss White, to ask her for the last time if I could be of service to her, to beg her to think over her rigidly adhered-to wish that her place of abode should be kept secret from you.

Ralph's story had suggested to my mind possible reasons for her wish for a hiding-place. I had prayed that these possible reasons might not be the true ones. I found Miss White stronger in mind, stronger in body, than when I had last seen her, and willing, nay more, eager to give me her confidence. I have her permission to repeat to you what she has told to me, but I can only do so by referring to events that occurred at Longridge on the night of your father's death. Have I your permission to do this?"

"On the night of your father's death!" Once more the darkened room, the father stretched white and dying on the bed, the mother clinging to his arm, and the face of the frightened nurse showing in the doorway, rose up before Herrick's mind.

His voice was hoarse, and unlike his own, as he said: "Go on."

The priest went on:

"On the night of your father's death there was a storm threatening, and Miss White, with her mind full of anxieties on old Mr. Gaskell's behalf, found herself unable to sleep. About one o'clock or a little after, she came downstairs in her dressing gown, eager for news of both the sufferers. Taking it for granted that you would be sitting up, as you had told her you would, in your grandfather's dressing-room, she opened the door of that room and looked in. To her surprise she saw, not you but Lady Joan, standing immediately beneath the lamp, with a cup in one hand and a phial in the other. Acting on the spur of the moment, she quickly closed the door and retreated, not wishing to intrude on Lady Joan at her sick-room duties. She did not attach any importance to the matter until she heard that the old gentleman was dead, then, all in a flash—"

But here Herrick, with a low cry as of one in pain, had jumped to his feet, and had seized the priest by the arm.

"Say no more, for Heaven's sake say no more!" he cried.

And then he sank back in his chair and bowed his head on the table, realising to the full the priest's words that "there were sorrows bitterer than death, more cruel than the grave itself."

XIII

The pale light of the winter's dawn, as it flowed coldly, slowly through the latticed windows, lifted the shadows from two haggard faces which seemed to share one stricken, despairing look between them.

For a brief five minutes a terrible storm of passion had swept over Herrick. While it had lasted he had spoken words the like of which had never passed his lips before. He had bitterly cursed his own folly in not allowing Lois to watch beside his dying grandfather on that fatal night; his own bodily weariness, also, which had made his vigil such a lax one.

Then, with eyes opened at last to the full measure of his mother's sin, he had lifted up his voice, and, in language awful on a son's lips, had cursed her also; had vowed never again to cross the threshold of his home, or to look his mother in the face.

This five minutes of passion was terrible to witness. Father Elliot, with white face and knotted brows, stood leaning against the wall while it spent itself.

"I have lived to hear this!" he said under his breath. "Joan, Joan; this is worst of all!"

Herrick caught the words, faintly spoken though they were. They seemed, though, wherefore he could not have said, to quench his fierceness of spirit like the touch of a cool hand on a burning brow. Through the turmoil and chaos of his thoughts he seemed to catch an inkling of a love and of a sorrow which, for aught he knew to the contrary, might surpass his own.

Father Elliot saw that his passion had burned itself out, and that the time to speak had come. He laid his hand on Herrick's shoulder.

"A man," he said, "sometimes without a moment's notice, is called upon to face a terror worse than death. What are you going to do?"

"Do!" repeated Herrick. "I have already said what I will not do: cross the threshold of my home or ever again look my mother in the face."

"In other words, you mean to lay down your colours—turn your back on your duty."

Herrick stared at him blankly.

"What would you have me to do?" he presently asked.

Father Elliot made no reply. Slowly, backwards and forwards, he began to pace the room. "Grant me this one mercy—that I may never again in this life look upon this woman's face!"—had been his prayer for the past thirty years, and he had himself essayed to bring about an answer to this prayer, by begging his superiors to allow him to court death in wild Africa. Yet now, as he slowly paced the room, he was saying to himself: "It must be done. I must see her once again, it is imperative, though torture come of it."

Presently he stood in front of Herrick once more.

"This is what I would have you do," he said, in a strangely-solemn tone: "stay here for one day, so as to give me time to see and to speak with—with Lady Joan—for see her and speak to her I must before I start on my journey. Then, tomorrow, I would have you go back to your home, do your duty there—face the worst."

Herrick, awed into a sudden calmness by the look on the priest's face, as well as by the tone of his voice, answered:

"It shall be as you wish."

Father Elliot walked to the window and flung back the lattice. The keen, cold air of the morning poured into the room, bringing with it something of refreshment to the weary brains of the two men. Outside, the air seemed full of a lustrous vapour, from out which afar off the hills, like so many brown, gaunt giants were emerging. Between them and the lichen-covered palings of the cottage garden, the valley lay submerged in a sea of mist. Immediately outside the window a thorn-bush spread a delicate tracery of bare, brown branchlets. Perched high on one of these, a robin poured forth a full-throated song.

Herrick heard it in a vague, dreary sort of way, and found himself wondering vaguely that there should be left a song to creation after the tale of wickedness to which he had just been listening.

The priest heard it also, and said to himself:

"There will be no cheery robin's note to greet me in Africa. Better so. There is a time to sing and a time to cease from singing. The time to cease from singing has come to me now."

Presently he turned to Herrick, and said:

"You need rest, food, refreshment. There will be breakfast soon. Will you like to get some sleep first?"

Herrick shook his head.

"I have something to do before I can think of food or sleep, and the sooner it is done the better," he answered, wearily dragging himself to his feet.

That "something to be done" sent him to the children's hospital at Sandyford, and set him asking for Sister Lois.

She came down at once, equipped in cloak and bonnet, for she rightly surmised that he had words to speak to her that could be better spoken in the quiet of the country road than in any one of those big wards or dormitories, where doors seemed perpetually opening and shutting, people for ever walking in and out.

One look into Herrick's face told her that he knew the whole truth now, and that the part she would be called upon to play before any other would be that of comforter.

Side by side the two wandered along the road, between the rows of scattered cottages which made the whole of the village of Sandyford.

It was not until the last of these was past, and they had gained the open country, that Herrick broke the silence which, after their first greeting, had fallen between them.

Lois was totally unprepared for his words. In her great humility she could never have imagined them being spoken by Herrick to any living soul, least of all to her.

This was what he said, slowly, emphatically, in a voice that left no room for doubt but that it was spoken of deliberate intention:

"Lois, cases are reversed now between us with a vengeance. Be honest with me; don't hesitate to say if you shrink from bearing a name which has been dragged through the mire—nay, more, which will soon be shouted from end to end of the kingdom with contempt and anathema."

In her astonishment, Lois came to a standstill, facing him with parted lips and eyebrows arching.

His meaning was plain and easy to understand; but to her thinking his words were as incongruous to his lips as they would have been to those of a crowned king.

He did not misconstrue her silence; but his will was strong to make her speak out plainly.

"Don't be afraid to tell me—don't think that, if you throw me over, it will kill me. After last night I shall think that nothing short of shot or shell will send my soul out of my body; but if—"

There came a step behind them, then a touch upon Herrick's shoulder, and looking round they saw Father Elliot, bag in hand, equipped as for a journey.

"I am going to catch the coach for Cork, at the foot of the hills," he said. "If we do not meet again, good-bye to you both, my young friends."

Tears rushed to Lois's eyes. She felt that the good-bye so simply spoken was to be a good-bye for all time.

"Must it be!" she exclaimed. "Oh, why cannot you stay in England? Why will they send you so far away? It is too, too sad."

"Hush," he said, gravely. "It is my own choice. I am going of my own free will. Sad, do you say it is? Life is all sadness, my child, from the hour in which we struggle into it with tears, to the hour in which we struggle out of it with no tears left to shed."

He broke off for a moment, then turned to Herrick, saying:

"There is something I wish to speak to you about before I say good-bye. I have been talking to M. Van Zandt for the last half-hour; he seems a good man, and devoted to your cousin, Lady Honor. Are you inclined to favour the idea of a marriage between the two?"

"It will have my warmest support; you may consider the marriage as good as arranged," said Herrick. Then he checked himself, adding, bitterly: "That is, unless M. Van Zandt, when he knows the whole truth about—about us—wishes to withdraw from an alliance with our family."

"He is not likely to do that," answered Father Elliot; "he has surmised the truth for some time past, but his heart is too true to be shaken by it. Once more good-bye, my young friends. May the peace of God now and always rest upon you both."

Then he went on his road, with steps a little less firm, with shoulders perhaps a little more bent, than they were three months back, when he had parted with Ralph and Lucy on his way to Longridge.

His footsteps died away in the distance. Herrick and Lois stood watching him out of sight. Once he turned and waved his hand to them, and then a curve in the road hid him from view.

Then Herrick turned to Lois once more.

"Answer my question, Lois," he said, perhaps a trifle imperiously; "be honest with me. I have the blackest, the most terrible of sorrows to face now. If you shrink from the misery, the disgrace, that lies before me, say so at once and be done with it."

Lois did not immediately answer. Her eyes were swimming, her heart was beating fast.

Overhead the morning clouds parted, and a sudden gleam of sunshine sent the cloud-shadows chasing each other across the distant hills. A bird, with a startled cry, flew from out the roadside hedge.

In the stillness of the quiet road Lois's heart seemed to speak to her as with human voice.

"It is because of the childishness, the weakness, the want of courage you have shown, that he asks this question," it seemed to say. "Tell him, make him understand, that three months of sorrow have made a woman of you, and a brave, true-hearted woman, too, who will face, not flee from the worst that life can bring."

But Lois had no voice wherewith to tell him this. All she could find to say, brokenly, tremulously, were the sweet old words of the faithful Ruth, although with a special meaning which Ruth could never have put into them.

"Thy people shall be my people. Nought but death shall part thee and me now."

XIV

Longridge Castle stood a black, grim pile in the winter moonlight. A silence, as of death, seemed to environ it. Little more than three months back the blazing August sun had lighted up a very different scene—a scene of banqueting and health-drinking, of revelry and rejoicing. Now, if King Death himself, tired of his invisible sovereignty, had chosen to assemble his ghostly train, and, in bodily shape to hold his court, he could not have found a more suitable castle than this, where life seemed literally to have come to a stand-still. Not trees planted beside a dead-sea lake could have tossed their branches over a picture of greater stagnation than did the bare brown elms which formed the background to the Castle. Here was a stately house; a wide-stretching park; gardens and terraces planned, planted, and kept up to the last degree of perfection, yet as utterly destitute of the human impress which says, plainly as words could, "these things are mine, I love them," as was the lonely churchyard where John Gaskell and his father were so quietly sleeping their last sleep.

Within, the Castle presented a companion picture to that of its gloomy exterior. Here were rooms, corridors, staircases, palatial in their dimensions; palatial, too, in their decoration and furnishing; yet, with never a sound of young voices or light footsteps to waken an echo in them; no, nor so much as an appreciative eye to take note of the beauty of form and colour so lavishly displayed; for Lady Honor, although convalescent, was still a prisoner in her own room, and Lady Joan, alas, too late, was discovering that she had paid for these things of beauty not only with thirty of the best years of her life, but also with the very heart and soul which alone could rightly appraise them.

Since her final interview with Gallagher, Lady Joan had passed through every phase of a lingering suspense, ending at last in the positive conviction that Gallagher had turned traitor. Practical proof of his treachery, she felt now, might at any moment be given her in the shape of a summons to appear before some local bench of magistrates, charged with her dread crime. She found herself more than once wondering, in a vague, dreamy sort of way, which of the local justices who from time to time had dined at her table would append his signature to the warrant which arrested her. Before which of the two or three magistrates with whom she was on terms of intimacy would she be called upon to stand as a criminal?

Her nerves had not recovered their tone with the disappearance of the shadowy vision which was, yet was not, herself. She still found herself watching, waiting for it in those midnight hours when sleep shunned her, although she knew well enough in the inmost recesses of her heart that it had passed as irrevocably out of her life as had her youth, her hope, her innocence.

"Life is impossible to me now," she would say to herself when she lay down to rest at night, with the terror strong in her heart that with the morning would come arrest and disgrace.

Then when morning dawned and she aroused to find her fears not realised, she would say: "It is only deferred—before night falls I shall, without doubt, find myself in a felon's prison."

So the torture went on. With thoughts such as these in her brain, external things waned in importance. She transacted no business whatever, made no endeavour to carry even the purchase of Southmoor to its completion; gave no orders to her servants; made no enquiries respecting Lady Honor's health; simply remained shut in her room, eating next to nothing; sleeping not at all; waiting, only waiting for the end, which, with slow, certain, unfailing tread she knew was approaching.

The servants of the household read her conduct in only one light now—that of insanity. They were confident that "my lady's" heavy grief at her husband's death had turned her brain. They hailed with delight a telegram which Lady Honor received from M. Van Zandt, on the day after Herrick's arrival at Queenstown. It ran thus:

"H—has arrived safely. Good news will follow by letter."

Lady Honor did not keep her telegram to herself; but at once let the glad tidings that Herrick was on his way home, circulate through the household. She did more, she sent her maid to Lady Joan with the message that she had received a telegram from Queenstown, telling of Herrick's arrival there.

The telegram, however, she did not send to her aunt, thinking it better to defer doing so till she knew what was the good news referred to and how it might affect Lady Joan.

"If Aunt Jo wants to see my telegram she can easily come up and ask for it," she thought, "and then I shall find out a little how things are going with her."

But although the news of Herrick's speedy return did not send Lady Joan to her niece's room for fuller information, it had nevertheless a strange effect upon her.

"This is the beginning of the end," she said to herself, as she rose wearily from the bed on which she lay; "Herrick, most likely, has heard the truth by now. Before night my son—the boy I have held in my arms—will look me in the face; curse me, perhaps, or scorn me—perhaps pity me!"

She began slowly, backwards and forwards, to pace the room. Presently her slow steps came to a halt in front of her medicine cupboard.

The key was in the lock, for it held, not only drugs for occasional use, but the nightly opiate whose soothing influence her nerves of late had defied.

It held something else too—the phial of aconite tincture which had already done such deadly work.

Lady Joan took the phial in her hand. It was of coloured glass, and the daylight was fading fast now, so she went to the window and held it up to the light, that her eye might measure how much was left of it. What an easy solution to all her torture and misery that phial held! She had only to pour about a quarter of what was left into a wine-glass, lay her head down on her pillows once more, and then good-bye to the racket and turmoil of life, welcome the long, blissful sleep, which she was fain to persuade herself would know no awakening.

How thankful, also, Herrick would be to have his difficulties ended in this way; all responsibilities, so far as she was concerned, lifted from his shoulders; the plebeian name of Gaskell, for which he had such a huge reverence, kept unsullied. There would then, too, be no painful meeting between her and Herrick, no enforced listening on her part to bitter anathema or heart-broken pity from his lips.

She drew the stopper from the bottle, and then—slowly, drop by drop, poured its contents upon the ground.

"That would be what weak souls would do," she said aloud, answering her own thoughts, "the souls who quake and turn white when they hear the Decalogue read. What I have done I have done. I will not deny it. I will face any penalty the laws of man may impose. I take my stand upon the laws of Nature, which preceded even the making of the Decalogue—the laws which provide for the survival of the fittest in the struggle for the good things of life, the laws which send the winter frost to kill the old life, so that the young life may grow and flourish."

A sudden change seemed to pass over her; a sudden strength seemed given to her.

"Herrick may come tonight, and I will look him in the face," she thought. "He may curse me if he will; pity me he shall not."

At this dread crisis, herself, her own individuality, utterly absorbed her. Lois, she thought, lay broken-hearted in a convent grave, yet she had not a tear to give her. Herrick's heart might be broken, too, his whole future might be blighted, but she had not a pitying thought for him. One aim was before her now—to gather together her strength, to concentrate the whole of her being on meeting worthily—if the word may be used in such a connection—the crisis which she felt was at hand.

She dressed herself for the evening with a care and attention to details which she had not evinced for many a day past. It must have been an instinct, strange in the circumstances, which prompted her to discard her widow's cap and deep crape, and to sit down to dinner that night in black velvet and diamonds. She did another strange thing—gave orders that the drawing-rooms, which of late had been out of use, should be opened and lighted. Then when her lonely, yet withal ceremonious, meal had come to an end, instead of retiring, as her custom was when alone, to her own sitting room, she repaired to the larger rooms and seated herself there in lonely grandeur, as if waiting to receive distinguished guests.

"Those men who wait at my elbow," she had said to herself as she sat at dinner, "will no doubt tomorrow help to spread the gossip far and wide that 'my lady' has been charged with crime and taken to prison. Be it so. To night at any rate they shall see 'my lady' and her dignity keeping each other company."

She had a small time-piece placed facing her in the drawing-room. "Now," she thought, as she seated herself in a high-backed, capacious chair, which her stateliness seemed to transform into a throne, "I can count the minutes till Herrick comes. Who will dare to say that I shrink from torture?"

There were only two trains, she knew, by which Herrick could arrive at Wrexford that night. One would bring him to the Castle about half-past eight in the evening, the other not until ten or a little later.

It was twenty minutes past eight now. In ten minutes' time he might be in the house.

Less like a human being than some marble statue, she reclined, motionless, in her high-backed chair, with eyes never once lifting from the clock, till it had told, not ten, but twenty minutes, and there was no possibility of Herrick having caught that train.

Then she drew a long breath and rose from her chair. Those twenty minutes had been literally counted out by heart throbs; and now there remained to her yet another hour and a half before she could hope to end this torture by facing the worst.

She walked wearily to the window, drew back the curtain, and looked out. The moon was on the other side of the house; the terrace lay in blackness, broken only by the gleam of stone balusters and flower vases. Beyond, the garden, and farther on still the park, lay in yet denser darkness. To the right stretched the little pine-wood, in whose planting her husband had taken such keen delight.

It struck a key-note of thought that she did not often allow to vibrate in her brain; brought back in a rush memories of her early married life; of her husband's hearty, honest love; of his subsequent coldness and indifference, of his truth and loyalty to her from first to last, coldness and indifference notwithstanding.

She turned sharply away from the window. She had an hour and a half to count out by the clock before Herrick could by any possibility arrive. If she gave rein to such thoughts as these, the end of that hour and a half would find her strength gone and her dignity not to be commanded for the crisis at hand.

"His only fault was that he had a father," she said to herself, of purpose arousing a bitter recollection in order to put to flight the tenderer memories.

Then, lifting her eyes, they were greeted with something that accentuated the bitter recollection—the picture of old Mr. Gaskell's cottage home, which had been presented to him on his birthday, and which he had insisted on having hung in the drawing-room.

"John should have come between me and such things as that," she said to herself, still intent on keeping down with an iron hand what little of heart was left to her.

A bowl of chrysanthemums on a table beneath the picture caught her eye. The flowers were of a crude red, which clashed in tint with the old china bowl in which they had been placed, and neither harmonised nor contrasted with the silk hangings of the room, which formed a background to the bowl.

It set her teeth on edge, so to speak, pained her like a bit of false colouring in a beautiful picture.

She rang the bell at once, and had the flowers removed.

Then, as it were, stung into appreciation of the beautiful things around her by this bit of harsh colouring, she began slowly to make the round of the room, looking at, or trying to look at, the works of art

CATHERINE LOUISA PIRKIS

with which it abounded, not with the eyes of Lady Joan, the mistress of the mansion, John Gaskell's wife, the mother of Herrick—but with the eyes of Lady Joan, the connoisseur, the lover of art and beauty, of perfect form and glorious colour, for their own sake only. It was all in vain. There was not a table, a chair, a statuette, or bit of china but what was in itself an eye-delight, and contributed its quota of beauty to a beautiful whole; all the same, not a table, or chair, or statuette, or bit of china, but brought back with it a rush of memories of her early married life. This one John had bought at her request, that one John had asked her to choose. Those curtains had been woven at Gobelin, from a design which John had requested her to make; for that bit of sculpture John had sent to Florence, for a birthday present for her.

It was too much. "Thought must cease or my brains will go," she said to herself. And so, because no other way of making thought to cease occurred to her, she opened her piano and let her fingers wander over the keys.

Surely never before was music played under stranger conditions. There was no audience, unless the beautiful, voiceless things about her could be counted as such, no lofty aspiration or emotion within calling for expression; her only inspiration was a dread crisis drawing near and nearer with every note she touched!

Yet Lady Joan had never at her best played with a finer touch, never thrown more of meaning into the weird, wild melodies—of Rubinstein, Chopin, and some unknown Polish musician—which came springing up from under her firm light fingers.

And if one versed in the tragedies of life had chanced to enter the room as she played he might have said not only, "that stern-faced statuesque woman is a finished musician," but also, "that woman has something equivalent to a soul in her body, although she is doing her best to keep it down in chains of iron."

XV

Some distant clock struck ten. Lady Joan rose from the piano and wandered to the window once more.

The moon had risen high now; the shadow of the house had shrunk away almost to the walls. The terrace and garden were flooded with silver light. Beyond, the skeletons of the park trees showed black against an even spread of luminous sky.

Hark! Was that the sound of wheels? Lady Joan strained her ear to listen.

"It is at hand now," she thought. "Either Herrick, or one of those men whose business it is to enforce the keeping of the Ten Commandents, is within my own gates now. Be it so. Whoever comes, I am here to receive him. Let others, if they will, take their stand upon the Decalogue, I will take mine on the laws which sent the thunder and the lightning together with the Decalogue—ay, on the very laws which built Mount Sinai itself upon the dust and *débris* of thousands of living creatures pushed out of existence by others who had a better right to live."

Then, because she distrusted her own powers of hearing, she opened one of the long French windows, and stepped out on the terrace.

She was right; the wheels bringing her visitor were within her own gates now, and in another moment the lumbering Wrexford fly showed—a black, square, moving blot—as it emerged from the shadowy avenue into the moonlit carriage sweep. It suddenly pulled up. There came the sound of voices, someone alighted, and, no doubt attracted by the square of light on the terrace, which proclaimed an open doorway or window, turned his steps thither instead of making for the front-door of the house.

But, whoever he was, he was not Herrick. His carriage was that of an older man, though his steps were swift and firm as a boy's. Lady Joan narrowed her eyes in the effort to scan the features half hidden by the low-crowned hat which the man wore. Could it be one of those local Justices, who had broken bread with her, come to give her a word of warning before the emissaries of the law found her out? Was it—ah! who could it be?

The man was about a yard distant from her now. He paused, lifting his hat. The white moonlight fell full upon the stern, dark face of Vaughan Elliot.

Lady Joan gave a sharp, low cry.

Thirty years since these two had last looked each other in the face; and now they met with the black, impassable gulf of a great crime between them!

White, rigid, motionless, she stood gazing at him, This was Vaughan Elliot, and this was what thirty years had done for him: quenched the fire in his eye, but thrown into it, instead, depth and tenderness; turned his hair from black to grey, but given to him a brow on which thought sat throned. In a word, they had turned a handsome face into a noble one; had stamped on it the expression of a greatness of soul, which compensated a thousand times over for any lost graces of youth.

And Vaughan Elliot, on his part, stood gazing at the hard-featured, white-haired woman who fronted him.

"Can it be—is it possible?" he muttered. "Where has her soul gone? Can this be Joan?"

The words seemed wrung out of his very heart. Not Father Elliot, priest, preacher, and missionary, stood looking at her now, but the Vaughan Elliot of long ago, who had held her in his arms and had kissed her on the lips, thinking, poor fool, that those lips would be his own for ever.

He mastered himself with an effort.

"Joan," he said, speaking in the deep, rich tones she knew so well, "I have come tonight to see you, not for mere idle talk of the days gone by, but because necessity is laid on me to speak words to you which not another soul under heaven can speak."

Lady Joan's lips parted, but not a sound came forth. A strange light leapt into her eye. She shrank back into the shadows, which made a margin on one side to the moonlit terrace.

"You will think me abrupt, stern, harsh," he resumed, "but bitter words, as well as sweet ones, have at times to be spoken."

He broke off for a moment to master his voice, then went on once more in harder, drier tones.

"What I have to say is this: among all those whom you have wronged and made to suffer, I stand your heaviest creditor."

Lady Joan started and caught in her breath. She had been expecting to be charged with a crime of later date, not in this way to have the sins of her youth flung in her face.

"The time left me is so short—I can only stay here a few minutes— that I am not able to say what I have to say in polite, circuitous fashion," he went on. "The harsh things I have to say must be harshly said, or not at all. You may, perhaps, think I have no right to speak, either smoothly or harshly, to you. I maintain that I have such a right—the right of a man to speak out his mind to one who has robbed him, made him a bankrupt, and has not the slightest hope of ever paying back a farthing of all the thousands he has stolen."

Farther and farther into the shadows shrank Lady Joan. She stretched out her hands towards him as if she would deprecate his harsh speaking, but still not a word could she find to say.

He went on:

"Look at your debt to your husband! Heavy though it was, it does not equal mine. His life was not ruined for him as mine has been. A year or two of happiness—not thirty, mind you—you may have taken out of his life, nothing more. Also you may have spoilt your son's life for a year or two, but not for longer. He has already found for himself hopes and interests in life which your hand is powerless to touch."

Again he broke off, then resumed in a lower and more solemn tone:

"And that old man—that helpless, dying old man left to your care— you robbed merely of a few hours of a worn-out life. Yes, black and infamous as that crime was, I say it did not equal the sin you sinned against me when you broke faith with me."

Lady Joan was leaning, absolutely for support, against the wall now, her face whiter than the moonlight which glinted so sharply on her white hair.

"Ay, I say, count up your debts, make a list of your creditors," the priest went on, his voice ringing out passionately now, "and put Vaughan Elliot at the head of that list, the man whom you have robbed of thirty of his best years. Think of that! Thirty years of youth, hope, happiness, taken out of his life; thirty years of a starved, hungry heart, given him in their stead! This is the debt he charges you with. Now what have you to give him by way of payment? Nothing—absolutely nothing. Why, therefore, I say I am your heaviest creditor. And who in the wide world can gainsay it?"

His last words rang out fiercely, defiantly, in the stillness of the night.

Lady Joan was trembling from head to foot. Her outstretched hands fell helplessly to her side. Where was now the plea which before had come so glibly to her lips, that the laws of red-toothed, red-handed Nature justified her in her hard-heartedness and self-seeking?

A change came over Father Elliot's face. The sternness of his features relaxed. His next words came in a strangely vibrating tone.

CATHERINE LOUISA PIRKIS

"But why do I say this?" he said. "Why do I come now, when your whole soul must be torn with anguish for your sins, to flourish your debtors' account in your face? Is it to call down vengeance on your head? Is it that I may look up to Heaven and say, 'As this woman's sin is beyond reparation, so let it be beyond remission?' No. I come here tonight because, as I am your heaviest creditor, so on me is laid the heaviest obligation to remit your debt. I come to say, 'Joan, from the bottom of my heart, fully, freely, eternally, I forgive you. Take heart. There is hope for you. When you stand before the great Judgment Seat, and the scroll of your crimes is unrolled, you will not be without your plea, but will be able to bow your head and say, 'Lord, if this man against whom I have so greatly sinned can freely forgive me, wilt Thou not have mercy?'"

His voice gave way with the last word. He was evidently sorely shaken. As for Lady Joan, the wall could no longer support her trembling limbs. She had sunk on her knees to the ground, hiding her face in her hands.

There fell a moment of silence, then she heard his footsteps descending the terrace steps, then she heard them pause on the gravelled walk beneath.

If she had dared to withdraw her hands from her eyes, she might have seen his white, agonised face upturned for a moment to the clear, cold sky, then downcast to the whitened earth at his feet. But she did not so dare, and thus she looked upon his face no more, only heard his voice, in low, passionate, pleading tones exclaim:

"O earth, earth, Mother earth, how can you bear to see the children, whom you have brought into the world, and nurtured, and cherished, sinning, suffering, agonising, and not open wide your arms and take them back to your bosom once more!"

Then she heard his footsteps retreating slowly, wearily on the gravel; and then there came to her the sound of wheels. Presently these died away in the distance, and she knew that she was left alone in the moonlight once more.

Her hands fell from her face; she dragged herself to her feet. She dared not upturn her face as he had done to the lustrous sky; her eyes seemed fastened on the earth at her feet, bathed in the white light.

"O earth, Mother earth," she repeated drearily, in a far-away tone, "how can you bear to see your children sinning and agonising, and not open wide your arms and take them back to your bosom once more!"

Then, scarcely conscious of what she was doing, she slowly wandered down the terrace steps and along the path that Vaughan Elliot had followed. Were angels leading her? were fiends driving her? She did not know. She was only conscious of an irresistible longing to be moving; to be going somewhere, doing something; though where or what she did not know.

So on she went. Now down the avenue, grim with its underlying fantastic shadows; now across a great green field, on which a mist, saturated with moonlight, was lying like a silver lake; now through a side-gate—the very one by which Lois had left the scene of festivities three months back—into the high road, shut in with its black, leafless hedges. And ever as she went she kept muttering Vaughan Elliot's words: "O earth, Mother earth, how can you bear to see your children sinning and agonising, and not open wide your arms and take them back to your bosom once more!"

Was it a prayer? She did not know. If one had told her to go down on her knees and pray, she would have said: "I dare not so much as lift my eyes to Heaven." But all the same, as slowly, with down-cast eyes, she wandered along the road, her lips muttered Vaughan Elliot's words ceaselessly, imploringly, as if she were addressing some hidden deity.

She did not take the road leading to Saint Elizabeth's church, but turning in an opposite direction, wandered on towards the bleak treeless heath which Father Elliot had crossed on his way to Longridge.

Blacker, bleaker than ever it showed in the white moonlight. A soft wind was rising now; light, fleecy clouds were gathering on the horizon, and ever and anon went fleeting across the moon.

Lady Joan's feet were saturated with the dewy grass she had gone over, her velvet skirt clung round her like some damp shroud. Yet on and on she went, her head bowed, her eyes down-cast, her lips moving to the words which had so strange a ring of prayer in them.

She had the whole of the desolate heath to herself, there was never a sound of life far or near. The black gorse bushes clutched at her clinging skirts, and every now and then a big, half-hidden boulder stone made her stumble, yet on she went straight across the waste, pausing only when she reached the disused coal shaft, with its tottering rail and piled-up mounds of weed-grown rubbish on either side.

Here she sank down wearily on her knees, leaning her head, her arms on the tottering rail, and looking down into the shaft, which yawned black, like some bottomless pit, in the midst of the white moonlight.

And once more her lips muttered Vaughan Elliot's words, shortened now to a simple passionate entreaty, "O earth, earth, Mother earth, open wide your arms and take me back to your bosom once more."

CATHERINE LOUISA PIRKIS

The light, fleecy clouds swept over the moon, and for a moment darkness like a great curtain fell athwart the heath. When the moon shone out once more and the darkness lifted, a broken rail swayed to and fro over the mouth of the shaft, but there was no white-faced, forlorn woman kneeling there, with a prayer to Mother earth on her lips.

THE END

A Note About the Author

Catherine Louisa Pirkis (1839–1910) was a British author known for her detective fiction. Pirkis wrote fourteen novels and contributed to many magazines and journals, sometimes publishing under her initials, C.L Pirkis, to avoid gender discrimination. Later in her life, Pirkis transitioned away from her writing career to join her husband, Frederick Pirkis, in his fight for animals' rights. Together, the couple founded an activist organization to save animals from cruel conditions. Their organization continues their advocacy today, and now goes by the name "Dogs Trust."

A Note from the Publisher

Spanning many genres, from non-fiction essays to literature classics to children's books and lyric poetry, Mint Edition books showcase the master works of our time in a modern new package. The text is freshly typeset, is clean and easy to read, and features a new note about the author in each volume. Many books also include exclusive new introductory material. Every book boasts a striking new cover, which makes it as appropriate for collecting as it is for gift giving. Mint Edition books are only printed when a reader orders them, so natural resources are not wasted. We're proud that our books are never manufactured in excess and exist only in the exact quantity they need to be read and enjoyed. To learn more and view our library, go to minteditionbooks.com

bookfinity & MINT EDITIONS

Enjoy more of your favorite classics with Bookfinity,
a new search and discovery experience for readers.
With Bookfinity, you can discover more vintage
literature for your collection, find your Reader Type,
track books you've read or want to read,
and add reviews to your favorite books.
Visit www.bookfinity.com, and click on
Take the Quiz to get started.

Don't forget to follow us
@bookfinityofficial and @mint_editions

Printed by BoD™in Norderstedt, Germany

9 781513 132891